Veracity

Veracity

Mark Lavorato

First printed in 2007 by Rain Publishing Inc.
Second printing offered by CreateSpace

ISBN 13: 978-1-897381-21-2

Cover design and layout by Mark Lavorato

For Colin

Acknowledgements

There were a few people who helped me tremendously throughout the writing of this book. My thanks to Uschi, for her patience in watching the process grow from a consuming pastime to an unhealthy obsession. Larisa, for always being exactly the friend I need, exactly when I need it. And a special thanks to Deonne, for her careful reading, constructive criticism, and unwavering support.

I would also like to thank a man in Switzerland named Walter, who told me his tale of finding a decrepit crow and nursing it back to health, at a time in his life when it would become his only friend. Then let it go.

1

This is my dying day.

It is that one day that I had so carefully convinced myself would come later on, after the years had stretched out into decades, after my reflection had become grey-haired, hunched over, milky-eyed. And even though I'd always understood that my days were counted – in the same way everyone does – I realize now that I had completely misjudged the way they were being counted. I'd pictured my life as a kind of continuum, as a hilly landscape that I was free to dawdle through, to take my time in. I had assumed that my end was off in some remote distance, and had pictured myself strolling towards it, casually, watching my feet, hands in my pockets. The idea never crossed my mind that, instead, my death could be creeping towards me, skulking as fast and constant as the shadows of clouds crawling over hills. Yet it was. My life was an hourglass losing sand by the second; and it wasn't until the last grain was rolling down the funnel that I finally came to see it that way.

And now that this day is here, and there's no denying it, no running away, I find myself asking a natural question: What is the most fitting thing to do on the last day of your life? Or, rather, what is the most fitting thing to do if, like me, you're strapped to a tree with an unknown number of broken bones floating under your skin, and something trickling down your leg that could be anything from blood, to urine, to gobs of their saliva that they spit onto you just before they left? Seeing as you can't move, and the only option you really have is to retreat into your mind, what exactly should you spend your time thinking about? Death? Should you mull over the details of how they're going to do it, how slowly or quickly they'll drain the life from your veins, and what it's going to feel like when they do?

No. I think I'll have more than enough time to consider my death just the second before they kill me; or begin the slow, agonizing process of it – whichever they find more satisfying, I guess. But until then, I'm going to keep my mind from wandering in that direction. Why waste the last hours I have by giving them exactly what they want, when I could be doing the opposite?

Which is a good point; instead of being ridden with fear, maybe I could set out to lose myself in blissful memories, think back to the few times in my life when everything seemed to fall into place, when I felt that strange, numbing contentment that we all accidentally fumble upon every once in a while, and then spend the rest of our time groping around in the dark for again. I could dwell on every one of their details, thinking back to when I was a child, long before I'd known anything about The Goal, splashing in the green water of the island. Or, later in life, living on the terrace, sitting down between the trees after harvesting some of the fruit I'd grown and feeding pieces of it to the raven – or crow – or whatever kind of bird it was. I could try to bask in those memories, see if I could steal something from a past quietude to reassure myself now. Even if I doubt that would work.

Or maybe it would be more constructive to think of my blunders, to go through each and every one of the decisions I made, or, more often, didn't make, which led me here. I could recall the murky colour of the bubble of water that oozed out from between his lips and streamed down the side of his face, his eyes serene, staring unblinkingly at the sky. I could remember how open his mouth was, and, if I had opened mine and said something beforehand, how he wouldn't have died.

But I also know that if I focused on either of these two extremes – my greatest memories, or my thoughtless mistakes – in the end, I'd feel like I had accomplished nothing with this time. I know enough to understand that my life can only be weighed as a whole, and that weighing it in carefully chosen pieces wouldn't have the slightest thing to do with the truth.

Truth. I smirk to myself at just the mention of that word. Though, considering the relationship that I've had with it, I don't think I could come up with anything more fitting to do with this time than to recount the whole of my tale, as truthfully as I can; to trace the faltering line that squiggles along the ground from the sand of the island, to the soil at the trunk of this tree.

Yes, that's exactly what I'm going to do with this day.

Though, finding where to begin might prove a bit difficult. I know that Coming of Age, when Harek took me into the shelter, sat me down, and walked into the centre of the room to commence his speech, seems like the point when everything started. But if I think about it now, there were a few things that happened earlier on that were just as important as Coming of Age. And probably the most significant of these 'things' wasn't even of a specific nature; it was simply the atmosphere in which we were raised; the illogical rules, the Elders' stifled frustration, the carefully closed doors. The secrets.

2

If I think back as far as I can, I don't remember faces. There was always an Elder there, but as we could only spend a day with them before being handed over to another, and then another, one of them doesn't really stick out in my mind. Instead, my earliest memory is one of sensations. The sound of waves is everywhere, its low frothing noise never letting up, tirelessly rolling on. I can also hear the sound of the breeze blowing through the palms, but it's impossible to tell where their rustling begins and the churning of the waves ends, the sounds meld into each other and become the same. And just above this cohesive sighing, I can hear the distant moan of a wood flute; though, I don't know where it's coming from, as if it's being played from around a corner, behind a boulder, or hidden in some dark place beneath the trees. The air is sodden with moisture, and the colour of the sky hazy. My feet are bare, and there is sand perpetually stuck between my toes.

After this memory comes a cloud of learning. It, too, is indistinct; but maybe none of us can recall when our education begins, it's just suddenly there, everywhere, and in everything we do. We're being shown how to do things, guided through the steps of processes, people moving our hands to trace the lines on a page, helping our clumsy fingers tie a knot, squaring our shoulders to a slate with some symbols scratched onto it and leaning over us, the reverberations being felt on our backs as their voices drawl out the sound of a letter with slow, deliberate intonation.

And this primary learning, of course, gave way to secondary learning; and I think I loved most all of it. The Elders and I complimented each other perfectly. I was interested, curious, and they wanted to explain everything. Indeed, it seemed there was nothing that they couldn't do, no contraption they couldn't build, no function in nature they couldn't make clear, no animal they didn't know the name or habits of. As a resource they were almost limitless. Almost.

13

I remember, and at a very early age, being frustrated that they seemed so puzzled by one of the simplest concepts in life: boyhood. Whereas, at the time, for me, it was as easy to understand as walking. I knew that an integral part of being a boy was the act of destroying things – it was that simple. We ripped apart plants, squished insects, threw rocks at the ground to smash them in half, or better, in three, or in ten, or in hundreds of pieces. We rolled boulders down hills and into the water to see how large a splash we could make, or sometimes into trees, watching with wide eyes as the impact shook the branches, undulating out to the leaves, and then running down to inspect the damage, fingering the torn bark, fascinated. I understood that this was normal. Yet, for some reason, it never ceased to baffle them, and then enrage them, until they felt impelled to scold us for our 'random devastation', as they often called it. (Consequently, we grew to be quite secretive about our entertainment; and, generally speaking, the more fun it was, the more secretive we had to be.)

But in spite of keeping as many of our activities hidden from them as we could, they sometimes still managed to catch us doing things we shouldn't. Often this was in moments when our guard was down, when we were sure we had nothing to hide. For instance, three of us might be chatting in the forest – which was the largest number we were allowed to gather in without an Elder present – and one of them would pass by anyway, just to make sure we were behaving ourselves. At first, it would look like he or she was just going to saunter past, but then they would stop dead, looking at the ground at our feet, horrified. We would also look down and see that one of us, without even having noticed, had yanked out the arcing branch of a fern, or some other plant that had been within reach, and had systematically plucked every one of its leaves off, from one end to the other. And so there lay the proof, a scattering of pitiful green teeth on the ground between us, wilting in the heat. Our postures would slump. Great. We would look up at the Elder, who would point a rigid arm at the leaves, and we would follow his or her finger back down to the ground again and look at the leaves more intently this time, trying to adopt gestures that also

14

seemed appalled, but not really succeeding. Then a stern voice would ask: 'Why did you destroy this plant for no reason?' And we would look around at each other, because, frankly, it was a tricky question to answer; apparently, we'd done it for no reason. So the only response left was to gape up at them with sorry, if stupid expressions on our faces, and wait for them to reprimand us. Which they would. After shaking their heads they would scoot us into one of the community buildings where we would have to sit at one of the long wooden tables and think about what we'd done.

Though, truth be told, we wouldn't really think. Instead we would make faces at one another, smear earwax on our neighbour's arms, kick each other's shins until someone yelped, which was sometimes all that was needed to be dismissed. The Elder who had ushered us into the building would stand suddenly, exasperated, pointing at the door and telling us to leave at once, maybe demanding that we go to another Elder, who was sure be more strict or consequent, and explain to them what we'd done.

Whenever this happened, I would purposefully be the last one to leave as we scurried through the doorway, because I'd discovered, quite by accident, that if one turned around and peeked back inside once the Elder was alone and unaware that he or she was being watched, occasionally, there was a mysterious thing that took place.

I knew that adults behaved differently in front of children; I knew that there was a kind of drama where they acted a part that wasn't really who they were, but who they should be. Because, for some reason, children aren't supposed to know that adults are as flawed as they are, instead, they ought to see them as an ideal being that they should strive to become. Of course, children will never become this ideal being, but at least by the time they're adults, they should be disciplined in contorting their behaviour enough to play the role of it, obviously for the sake of other children – who will, incidentally, see through it all anyway. This was one of the strange enigmas of adulthood that I didn't really understand, but nonetheless recognized. Yet these Elders, whom I would lean in to watch, were away from the eyes of children.

There was no part to play, no role to pretend. And I think I started looking in on these private moments only because I wanted to find a clue. I was convinced that they somehow knew they had reprimanded us for nothing, that they must also recognize that the fern, which we'd unknowingly dissected, was merely a plant like the ones we ate, and that it had no real bearing on anything. I was sure that once they were alone, I would only catch them grinning, maybe shaking their heads at the folly of us boys, and merrily going on with whatever they were doing. But I was wrong. They would continue to stand, but would slouch over, appearing tired, covering their face with a hand, sometimes pinching the spot where their nose met their eyes as if trying to squeeze the sockets closer together, the fingers of their other hand clenching into a fist, which sometimes trembled. And they would stay like that for minutes.

These were the moments that started to make me wonder.

They weren't reacting this way because of a few shredded leaves on the ground. That much was impossible. There was something more, something around us that we weren't seeing – that we weren't allowed to see – and I wanted to know what it was. I decided to look for it; and the most obvious place to start was in my schooling.

Almost everything in our education revolved around the resources of the island; we learned how to make cloth from the fibres of trees, how to tend and harvest fruits and vegetables, woodcraft, fishing; and this all eventually progressed to studying different systems for getting water, using wind, and sailing. Then there were the things that we learned indoors: mathematics, reading, writing, problem solving, evolution; and it was there, usually in a corner of the Community Hall, where I started to venture a few devious questions, hoping to catch one of the Elders at an incautious moment. Of course, they saw me coming from a mile away.

I can remember the typical conversation perfectly. An Elder places a pile of books on the table, sits down across from me, slides a dusty volume off the stack, opens it to a page that has been clearly marked as the spot to open to, and tries to begin the lesson. He introduces the session as, 'the island's ecology', or 'the island's weather', or 'the island's geology', and my eyes light up. I happen to have an interesting question in the same vein, and the fragile moment seems to have finally come when it's appropriate to ask. "Where's the next island?" I would venture.

The Elder, regardless of who it was, would almost look nervous at first, but when he replied, his voice was clear and patient; he knew just what to say. "To be honest, Joshua, I don't think that's very pertinent to this lesson." Then he would slide the book under my nose and point at a picture, getting ready to talk.

"Oh. Sorry," I would say, not looking at the picture, "But... well – where is it anyway?"

He would stop, suddenly stiff, and lean back ever so slowly, his hands sliding along the table as his body moved away from me, the cloth of his shirt hissing along the surface. And once he was propped against the back of his chair, he would suck an enormous amount of air through his nose, his nostrils caving in, until his lungs were almost bursting with it. Then he would breathe it all out again, little by little, looking at me the whole time, making me shrink into my chair. "That isn't for little boys and girls to worry about. Okay?"

I would nod quickly. Okay.

After the lesson, I would think about what he'd said. What did he mean by, 'It isn't for us to worry about'? I wasn't worrying about it – I just wanted to know. It seemed like such a simple question to me, why wasn't there a simple answer? And with the answer that he did give me, was I to understand that when I was older I would worry about it? And if so, what was it? What could be out there or around us that was so scary that we were going to have to spend the latter part of our lives 'worrying' about it?

I don't think the Elders handled these questions very wisely, because by completely barring them from discussion, they weren't creating a wall, they were putting a hole in one. It only impelled me to ask more questions, watch more carefully, listen more fanatically; they, of all people, should have known how much carefully spoken words echo.

And once I started to look, the discrepancies were everywhere. There were books that we couldn't read, and of the books we could read, there were pages we couldn't see, buildings we couldn't enter, rooms that sometimes had many people inside but the doors were closed and locked, hushed voices behind them, the Elders' movements being projected as shafts of shadow stirring along the line of candlelight that fanned out from the doorsill.

Until eventually, I noticed that I wasn't the only one asking questions; there were others, just as curious as I. Though, soon after realizing this, a community announcement was made, which was intended to wipe such curiosity out before it could get out of hand. They asked that all of the children of the island – which were a definitive group, as we were all about the same age – respect the fact that some of our questions would not be answered, nor would we be allowed to hear certain conversations, or enter the Great Hall at any time. However, there was a right of passage that would be known, henceforth, as Coming of Age, at which point in time we would be told everything on an individual basis, and, rest assured, would come to understand exactly why it was so important that several things be kept undisclosed until we were old enough. We were told that instead of worrying about the serious duties of the Elders, we should concentrate on our education; that, and enjoying the blissful life of a child. Nothing more. Nothing less.

But a secret isn't sacred information, it's just information. The only difference between it and other information is that a person is expected to use a quiet voice to pass it on – and that's all – because it moves through a community just as readily, in fact, often even more so. By the evening after the announcement, there was a whispered rumour being passed from cupped ear to cupped ear. Apparently, what we were going to find out when we Came of Age was that something very bad had happened in the world, but that, somehow, we were going to fix it. We, the island, were going to make everything right again.

The children looked around at each other, nodding their heads, the hands that they'd used to help hear the whispers lowering sombrely to their laps. It suddenly all made sense. No wonder they didn't want to tell us, this was a taxing thing to think about. Hmm. Well. I guess they were right. We shouldn't worry. Instead, we should be playing. Come on, I figured out a way to make a slingshot. And they all ran into the forest in groups of three.

I remember that after that day, it was as if the children had moved back a step. They stopped asking difficult questions, stopped listening against the doors, stopped wondering; I think they actually believed that, for the time being, they knew enough.

Whereas I was stuck thinking about the different Elders I'd watched without their knowing, standing beside tables, their fists tight, eyes closed, lips pursed. Those people weren't thinking about saving the world, and they weren't thinking about fern leaves, either. No. There was something else.

3

There was another important event that took place in my childhood. And I consider it important, not because Harek used it against me when I Came of Age, but because I've always solemnly wished that it had never happened at all.

There is a line that every one of us consciously draws, which, I think, is our fumbling attempt to differentiate between right and wrong. Of course, there is no such thing as right and wrong, and if there were ever to be a physical line between the two, it would be immensely jagged, its boundaries hazy, the colours of both sides endlessly bleeding into each other. 'But,' we stop and say to ourselves, 'we have to start somewhere'. So we pick up a stick, put a contemplative finger to our lips, and squint at the bare soil in front of our feet. And here is the interesting part: because what is natural for a human being to do is lean over, scratch their own individual quavering line in the dirt, straighten up, nod with satisfaction at themselves, pause, and then look over their shoulder to see if anyone is watching and step over it.

We'd killed hermit crabs before, raising stones above our heads and pummelling them into the stiff sand, and we'd also taken the heads off of beetles with the tips of our fingernails, watching their arms twitch frenetically in the air for a few seconds afterward; but a part of us knew that what we did with the lizard was going too far.

I don't remember where I was walking to, but I remember stopping in my tracks and listening to the sound of their giggles for a few moments, there being something inside of them that was undoubtedly mischievous, luring. I turned and went to investigate; whatever it was sounded like fun.

As soon as I broke through the trees and saw the backs of Mikkel and Peik, I felt incredibly lucky. The three of us were probably the most promising and intelligent children on the island, so the Elder's often put us into the same group to learn or to do problem-solving projects. But as we were discouraged in having exclusive friendships with one or two people, outside of our schooling we didn't really get to enjoy each other's company very often. Had it been allowed, I think we would have spent a lot of time together, as the three of us were similar in quite a few ways.

Everyone liked Mikkel, and I think this was because he was equally amiable with everyone on the island. He was taller than most of the boys, and had blue eyes and dirty blonde hair, which was always a bit too long and constantly hung in front of his face. Peik was a bit shorter, had high cheekbones, brown eyes, and straight black hair. His skin was much darker than the rest of the children on the island (though it wasn't nearly as dark as one of the Elders, whose skin was almost black it was such a dark brown). I'm pretty sure that both of them were a little older than me.

They obviously weren't expecting anyone to come through the trees that day, and as soon as they heard my footsteps, they spun around and stood shoulder to shoulder, hiding what they were doing. They relaxed once they saw it was me, but I remember that there was something in their manner that was different than usual, that they remained a little tense, edgy, which only signified that the Elders would be genuinely infuriated if they found out what was going on.

"What do you guys have there?" I asked.

"A lizard," said Peik, trying to sound nonchalant, but I could tell that he was excited. He looked over at Mikkel, who held up a few pins that he'd quickly hidden in his hands when they'd turned around.

"And these," said Mikkel, almost proudly.

I smiled, not really understanding, and stepped forward while both of them parted and faced each other, their bodies opening up like a gate to reveal their prize. The two boys had stolen some pins, probably from one of our clothing classes, and had also managed to catch a lizard. They'd stuck one of the pins through the centre of its tail, fixing it to a stump. The lizard was bright green, its beady eyes black, and it seemed to be struggling half out of confusion and half out of pain.

"Cool," I muttered, as if to myself.

21

"We just caught it," said Peik. I nodded, and we all stood there looking down at it for a few seconds, silent, the lizard seeming to look back. Then, without taking his eyes off it, Peik reached over and found Mikkel's hand, took a pin from it, and crouched down to the stump. "Watch this," he said. He stuck the pin into one of the lizard's tiny feet, and it reacted by opening its mouth and, oddly enough, biting its own appendage above the pin. And to us, at that moment, absolutely nothing could be funnier in the world. We started giggling, hysterically, almost unable to control ourselves, leaning in on each other, pointing down at it, stamping our feet on the ground. Though I recall that we still had the presence of mind to keep our voices down, as not to be heard.

As soon as we'd recovered a bit, Mikkel and I each picked up a pin and crouched down to the lizard as well, smothering the stump in shadow, our heads almost touching in a circle. It was all so invigorating, intoxicating; it's hard to believe how formidable a tiny pin can make one feel, how powerful. This was because we could see, with the lizard's head jolting from side to side, that it was terrified, watching us all closing in around it. It had become desperate, trying to squirm free with every bit of energy that it had in its tiny body, wanting to find a nook to hide in, a branch to climb, even some open ground to scurry across or water to jump into – anything. But we weren't going to give it that chance.

I stuck my pin into one of its legs, Mikkel stuck his into the skin by its ribs, and Peik pinned another of its feet. Of course the lizard kept struggling, kept twisting in pain, biting at its own flesh; and we kept laughing, and then laughed harder, water coming to our eyes, our stomachs eventually becoming sore. It was great fun. At some point, we started competing to see who could be precise enough to pin the smallest appendage, and I remember that Peik won this game, managing to get one of its fingers just below the nail; and when he did so, the lizard held its head up to the canopy and opened its mouth wide, showing a tongue of dull pink. This led to shoving leaves and twigs into its mouth to see if it would bite down on them, and then giggling when it did. We brought our faces down to it as well, seeing how near its mouth we would dare to put our noses, jokingly nudging each other when we were almost close enough to touch it.

After a long while, the lizard became completely exhausted, its reactions subdued, sluggish; it had stopped squirming altogether, stopped responding. So we prodded it with our fingers, tried piercing parts of its body that we hadn't yet touched, but nothing happened, and it looked like our game was over. Peik, seeming bored, finally picked up a pin and drove it through its skull. It twitched a bit, and then stopped moving forever.

But the moments after he did this were by far the most poignant. The three of us stayed crouching around the stump, glancing at one another, the smiles that had adorned our faces the whole time slowly, slowly beginning to fade. We all looked down and watched Mikkel's hand reach out to run a slow finger along the lizard's back. When he was finished, he quickly put his arm back at his side and looked out at the trees. Peik, after seeing this, leaned in and began retrieving the pins from the dead creature's body, taking them out of its coarse skin almost gently.

There was no more laughing. We'd become quiet, sober. Because we knew – we knew that we'd gone too far, that we'd overstepped some kind of boundary, moved something that we couldn't put back in its rightful place. Yet that was all we knew. If we'd had the capacity to understand why we'd done it, what had driven us, I don't think we would have started in the first place.

As we stood to leave, Mikkel picked the lizard up by the tail and tossed it into a few bushes, out of sight, and we walked out from the forest and into the naked light of day. I don't remember what happened after that, if we ever talked about it again, or even mentioned it, but the details of what we did and how we did it, are still fresh in my mind. And they would need to be. Because what we did to the lizard that day was incredibly important in helping me understand The Goal later on in my life.

Years passed. I continued to try and find out what the 'real' secret was all about, and I made quite a few guesses at it, some of which I thought were fairly educated at the time, though now I know they weren't even close. I was even brave enough to openly confront Dana with a few of them, and he replied appropriately, never giving me anything more than what the whispers on the island had continuously repeated; they all knew what I was looking for, and were careful not to give it to me.

Then I had my Incision, which was just after puberty, and which was the same surgery that everyone had after they'd physically developed enough. And after that, it's all just a blur of learning and more learning. I think the only other really important event that happened before I Came of Age was discovering Kara.

We'd grown up together and I'd known her all of my life, but we were so strictly forbidden to spend time or develop any kind of deeper friendship with the opposite sex, that I never really had the opportunity to find out how her mind worked. Then, one day, I had to do some pair work with her, and we'd been asked to discuss something or other – I can't remember what – and suddenly, listening to the things that she was saying, I couldn't believe that I hadn't found a way to seek out her company before. She was fascinating, engaging, wise, and I couldn't seem to hear enough from her that afternoon – which, of course, was a mistake. I even knew it as it was happening: we were looking at each other too intently, were too engrossed in the conversation, too interested. And from the ever-watchful corners of the room, the Elders saw the threat brewing, and quickly intervened.

We were pulled aside and given a long talk about exclusive relationships on the island, and we were cautioned of the inherent dangers that existed in them. And though they didn't specify what those dangers were, we were repeatedly told that they were critical, and that if we didn't respect the guidelines that had already clearly been set out for us, we could potentially threaten our whole way of life, in fact, they added with grave voices, our very existence.

But it wasn't only a firm warning, after that afternoon we were banned from each other. They made sure that we didn't sit together, work together, do chores together, learn together, or even walk together from building to building. They would watch out of the corners of their eyes as we ate in the Community Hall, waiting to see if we would risk a glance at one another, always suspicious that there might be something between us that they weren't seeing – a secret. And there was.

We'd been raised on secrets, and the Elders had taught us everything that one needed to know about keeping them, about living around them, through them. We found ways to meet, usually feigning a walk with some random person of the same sex, and then, once out in the forest, separating and meeting at a specific spot. It would only be for fifteen minutes, or maybe a half hour at most, but this turned out to be a blessing in a way, because it shaped our conversations and the way we talked. We had to think about things carefully, weighing out what we were going to say well before it came out of our mouths, and as soon as we met each other, we would have to get right to the point, our words intense, hands flinging in the air to help describe our thoughts, beliefs, theories, our bodies always leaning in close; though very careful not to get too close.

We were always cautious not to touch each other, both of us being privately convinced of some unspeakable and extreme consequence looming overhead. But I like to think that it was on both our minds – because I know that it was on mine. All too often my eyes would sink to various parts of her body, and I would find my thoughts suddenly racing into a very different direction from our conversation, and I would almost have to physically stop myself, shake my head, snap out of it. Because, given the circumstances, not only were these ideas wrong, they were also impossible. No, instead, we would have to settle for words; and, happily, her words were unusually fierce.

She experienced the world in a way that I had a hard time even imagining, she seemed to see a vibrant life and colour in things, heard voices, felt tremors. When I was in front of my peers, or even in front of the Elders, I always felt intelligent, but sitting in front of Kara, I felt stupid, slow. There were times when I couldn't keep up with her chains of thought, my eyes growing glazed, wishing I had more time to think her words through before I'd have to respond. And, unfortunately, I would often be given that time. We were caught out in the forest once or twice, and for a few months afterwards, we would be watched far too carefully to risk meeting again. But we, in turn, would patiently watch the Elders out of the furthest corners of our eyes, waiting for them to lower their guard, waiting for another chance; and in the meantime, saving our words, processing the ones we'd exchanged, and memorizing our responses for later. Sometimes, frustrated at having to wait months before seeing her again, I would lie awake at night trying to imagine what the Elders could possibly see that was so dangerous and reckless in intimacy, wondering how anything terrible could come out of something that, already before it had developed into much, felt so natural, so satisfying. It's interesting to think now that, as much as it eluded me then – lying in the dark, shaking my head at how ridiculous I thought they all were – later, I would come to understand their reasoning perfectly.

4

It happened much later than I thought it would, and it was interesting that once it arrived, the aura of secrecy and mystery that had always surrounded Coming of Age didn't disappear. I'd expected there to be some kind of formal announcement, but that wasn't the case. Instead, a young man or woman would just suddenly be gone, and when we asked about them, we were told, albeit guardedly, coldly, that they were Coming of Age and would only return to the community once they were ready. We noted that this usually took anywhere from a few days to a week. Of course, we'd all expected to find out what it was all about through the whispers, but when people returned, they were different, and seemed to have forgotten the secret understanding between us all that secrets weren't really secrets in the first place. Yet this wasn't the only change. Once people returned, they were reticent, quiet, seemed older; and likewise, the Elders had instantly come to regard them differently, always looking at them with long, understanding glances, giving them a sorrowful smirk whenever they passed.

Though, thankfully, this change in their demeanour didn't really last. Usually within a few days after their education had moved into the Great Hall, the young men and women who had Come of Age started to seem a bit more contented again, confident, even buoyant, and in turn, the Elders stopped favouring them, or at least stopped being so gentle around them. However, things were a little different with Mikkel.

The time between his disappearing from the community and returning to it was longer than most of the others. And when he did return, he wasn't well – he didn't even look healthy. Mikkel, who was normally one of the most social people on the island, became completely withdrawn. He would sit alone at the table for long periods of time after we'd eaten, his arms crossed over his chest, posture sagging, staring at the empty plate in front of him; and the Elders never stopped paying intent and specific attention to him, the women rubbing his back for a few

27

moments as they passed, the men smiling tenderly in his direction, whispering to themselves, nodding their heads. It was only after a month or so that something seemed to click in him, and he began reverting to his likeable, social self, slowly getting back into conversations and seeming a bit happier.

At about this time, I thought I'd noticed him looking at me more often than usual, smiling with a warm grin whenever our eyes met, and generally watching me out of the corner of his eye. Which struck me as odd. And as a rule, Mikkel didn't do things that were odd. I hoped to myself that he was genuinely 'okay'. Then, after meeting him in the forest one afternoon, I realized he was as far from it as he could possibly get.

I thought at the time that it was quite accidental that we should happen across each other when and where we did, but looking back, he'd probably been waiting for the opportunity for quite a while. I was walking along one of the trails that linked two parts of the community together when he threw a rock into the bushes beside me. I turned to look at him. This was one of the things that we'd learned as children: if you wanted to do something secretly, the last thing to do was make suspicious noises to indicate it – as it was the hushed 'psst' sounds, or whispers of 'hey', that the Elders had trained their ears for. If you really wanted to keep something secret, you didn't make a sound at all; and apparently Mikkel really wanted to keep this secret. He nodded his head towards the trees and underbrush away from the trail, and we both looked over our shoulders before walking into them, watching where we were stepping, careful not to break any twigs. When we were far enough into the trees, he came closer and we crouched down, out of sight.

"What's up?" I whispered. I was surprised that he wanted to say something to me alone. I respected Mikkel, thought the world of him really; like everyone did.

"Listen – I think you're going to Come of Age soon," he muttered. He looked a little nervous.

I raised my eyebrows. I'd never seen him nervous before, which wasn't exactly reassuring. "Really? How do you know?"

"Because they don't have to concentrate on me anymore. They think I'm alright, which only means they'll move onto the next one of us."

"So, how do you know it's me?"

"No," Mikkel shook his head, seeming more frustrated than I thought he had reason to be, "you don't understand. Not the next one of them, the next one of us."

"I… You're right. I don't understand."

"Yeah, I know. And you wouldn't – I'm not explaining myself very well here. But… I haven't had time to… I mean – I wanted to find something that…" Mikkel looked down at the ground and held his breath, seemingly as a means of calming himself. Then he looked up at me, his chest still expanded, and let the air out before he began to speak, his voice suddenly cool again. "Look. I wanted to ask you something. Would you promise me two things?"

"Of course," I said, wanting nothing more than to please him.

"First, I want to meet with you to talk. There're a few things I've been thinking about that… I wanted to pass by you, get your views on." He paused for a moment, reflecting, and then he lowered his voice to a whisper, "And, I want you to swear that you won't tell anyone we're going to meet. Do you swear?" he asked quickly, grabbing hold of my shoulder. "Do you?"

"Uh, yeah… yeah, sure. I swear."

"Good," he nodded, slowly, seriously. And then, as if remembering something, he gave me an uneasy smile, which soon melted away, "We should go."

"Okay," I agreed, and poked my head just above the underbrush to see if the coast was clear, but Mikkel grabbed onto my arm once more.

"No. You should walk the other way – meet up with the trail going to the Community Hall. I'll go this way." He stood and started creeping through the foliage, not waiting for a response, focusing on his feet, carefully weighting each step so as not to make the slightest crackle.

"Sure," I whispered to his back, probably a little too late. He didn't turn around.

That night, I recounted the strange conversation, rolling it over in my mind, looking for meaning, hoping to understand even the smallest piece of it. It was so exasperating! There always seemed to be facts around me that were just under the surface. Nothing was given to you. You always had to dig for it, steal it, hide it, shove it into your pocket when no one was looking. I just wanted to know, if only for a few seconds, what it felt like to be on the other side of the secrets, to know what was really going on around me and why. I earnestly hoped that Mikkel was right in saying that I would Come of Age soon. I was sick of being in the dark. Who really cared if I would have a month of sitting at the table and looking grave after eating my meals? At least I would know what there was to be grave about. And I told myself that I was undoubtedly ready for it, whatever 'it' happened to be.

And Mikkel was right when he said they would move onto me next. As it turned out, Harek would take me into the shelter the very next day.

5

I was meant to spend my last class of the afternoon in one of the thatched huts, furthest from the clutter of the other community buildings. I had been taught there before and so didn't really think anything of it. It was supposed to be an individual class as well, so I was walking along the trail alone when I came through the trees and could see the hut for the first time. Harek was waiting for me outside, his hands clasped together, his arms forming a patient "V" out in front of him. I suddenly understood what was about to happen, and smiled.

Harek was a large man who had a white, well-trimmed beard and unsettlingly bright green eyes. I'd always thought his eyes suited him perfectly, that they somehow matched the intensity he had in him, a fervency that, I believe, never really abated. Because he acted in only one of two ways: either he was disinterested in what was going on, completely lost in thought, his eyes jotting around as if tracing random thoughts bouncing off the inner recesses of his skull; or he was bursting with fiery animation right in the middle of things, his voice and presence demanding everyone's full attention. I liked him, mostly. Though like everyone else, I felt a tinge of fear with him as well. I guess I admired him in that peculiar way that one can admire a volcano while standing on the rim of its crater, an invisible and fascinating force murmuring below one's feet. And I think I liked him because of this strange volatility, because he always seemed either on the verge of settling into a long silence, or blowing up – but nothing in between. It kept things interesting.

He watched me as I approached, waiting to speak until I was standing right in front of him. "And? Do you think you're ready for this?"

I nodded, blistering with confidence, "Absolutely."

The corners of his mouth pulled up into a smirk, "Then follow me."

We walked the whole way without speaking. I'd assumed that we would go to the mystical Great Hall, where we would look through some of the forbidden books that resided there, so I started to become quite interested in where we were going when we turned at a fork in the trail and began to climb up a regular hill. Of course, as children, we had explored in this area before, but only found a kind of prickly vegetation that became either too dense to continue, or too painful. After walking for quite some distance, Harek stopped and turned to his left, facing one of these impenetrable bushes. He reached out and carefully picked it up, pivoting it slightly as one would a door, revealing a vague trail on the other side of it. He stepped aside to let me pass, and then closed the bush-like door behind us. The trail continued, walled with thick vegetation, until finally, it opened up into a tiny clearing high on the slope of a rise. I could see that there was something manmade that we'd come to visit, as there was a vaulted archway leading into the hillside, and a rectangular piece of grass missing from the hill itself, further away from us, which could only have been a kind of opening from the building underground. The archway had the same incredibly thick walls as the Great Hall, and a single metal door that barred the entrance. (As a rule, the architecture on the island belonged to only one of two schools: rustic and wooden, created directly from the raw materials around us, or fortified bastions made of thick concrete; this new building, obviously, being one of the latter.) I also noticed that there was a small panel of metallic buttons on the wall beside the door, which, as far as I would ever know, didn't have any function at all.

"What is this place?" I asked.

"I don't think it would make a lot of sense to you right now, but we can explain it later if you'd like." Harek looked at me and could see that the answer he'd given wasn't quite enough, and, though they usually didn't care if we were left in the dark, he seemed to suddenly sympathize. "Well, I can tell you it's something our ancestors made. How's that?" He looked up at the thick concrete, which had several different colours of moss clinging to its side. "Something to protect themselves from themselves," he added, as if to himself.

"What?"

"As I said, I can explain later if you'd like. But for now, let us go inside." He leaned in and started yanking on the door to open it, which, to my surprise, was as thick as my chest was wide, and from the looks of it, also incredibly heavy. As I passed through the doorway, I ran my hand along the volume of the metal, amazed, and then looked inside. It was a simple cemented corridor that was dimly lit with electrical lighting, a thing that was extremely rare on the island. Harek shut the massive door behind us, and after the darkness had echoed with a deep crash, we continued down the corridor, which eventually opened up into a large empty room. There was a single bench that lined the walls, and which almost continued around the entire perimeter, being interrupted only twice by other metal doors.

"Please, have a seat," he opened up his palm to point at the bench. I sat down, smoothing the creases in my pants more than I needed to, and watched him walk into the centre of the room. I seemed to be feeling a million things at once; I was nervous, afraid, excited, mesmerized. I couldn't believe that, finally, I was there, I was going to be included into the ring of secrecy. This was it. Everything I'd been waiting for.

"Do you know what Coming of Age is all about, Joshua?"

"Uh…" This caught me a little off guard. For some reason, I hadn't expected to be very involved. I thought it would be about listening, not speaking. I looked at the bench beside me, wondering what to say.

"Let me rephrase that question. Have you ever heard any rumours about it, made any guesses with the others?"

"Um… no, not really."

Harek cleared his throat, swallowed. He seemed to mark me on the bench with his line of sight, lowering his head slightly, as if he were aiming one of the slingshots we'd made as children. And indeed, it felt like his words were being fired at me; they were sharp, loud, quick. "Wrong. That is completely false. And not only is it wrong, it is the absolute worst answer that you could have possibly given me. And I will tell you why: we are going to be honest with each other, Joshua. We are going to be so honest with each other that there will not be a single secret between us. I will tell you things that are of the harshest, truest nature imaginable, and you will agree to do the same, or we cannot even begin the process that we are about to set forth. Do you understand that? Do you?"

My voice was small. "Yes."

"Good. Then let me ask you again. Have you ever heard rumours of what Coming of Age is all about?"

"Yes."

"And what were those rumours?"

"Um… that something went wrong in the world, and that we're going to fix it."

"And do you believe that?" he asked, watching my mouth open, reading my hesitation. "Remember, complete honesty."

"Not really, no."

Harek grinned, relaxed a bit. This, apparently, was the right answer. "I didn't think so," he said, sounding almost relieved. He put his hands behind his back and began to walk in slow, distracted circles around the room. "And, in fact, you were right not to believe. It was a complete lie. And we have told that lie to almost everyone that has Come of Age so far, and we will continue to do so. But not with you. You, Joshua, are among a tiny, tiny group of the most talented individuals on the island, and we have singled you out as someone who might have the skills and tenacity to take the truth, to hold it in your hands, but most importantly, to do what you should with it." He had been looking down at the ground while speaking, only raising his eyes to give me sidelong glances every now and then, but he turned to face me at this point, squaring his shoulders with mine before he spoke. "So then – let us start with that truth.

"First off, I should tell you a little something about what is beyond our island, as you were always sneakily asking about it as a child. I think it's probably obvious to you that there are other islands as well, some being a little smaller, but most of them larger, a few of them being enormous landmasses, which would take a great many years to travel across by foot. There are places where the terrain itself stretches out across the horizon, as does the sea from our vantage point. There are mountains so high that ice clings to their tops, barren deserts that stretch out for unthinkable distances without a drop of water, and basins of jungles so large that they act as a very lung for the earth.

"And the first truth that I want you to try and fathom is that, of all the land that wraps around the globe, of all the liveable spaces in the entire world – except for a few handfuls of people like ourselves – we are alone. There is no one else."

I shifted on the bench. The room seemed to have become uncomfortably small, stuffy. He was moving a little fast for me. I already had questions – many actually. But this was clearly not the time to ask them. I focused all of my attention on him, telling myself that I had to concentrate on keeping up. Nothing else.

"Yes, as you've probably guessed, there were people at one point, and those people were scattered everywhere, living in almost every imaginable place. But they are all gone now," he stopped for a second, "which... is another story in itself.

"But," he continued, suddenly walking toward me and sitting down on the bench. Once he was seated, he shuffled closer and leaned forward, his elbows on his knees, cupping his hands as if they were holding something small and important. As he paused before speaking, both of us looked into the shadows under his fingers at that nameless thing that he might be holding, and seemed about to explain. "But first, I have a quick history lesson to give you.

"See, about 30,000 years ago, in the middle of one of those large landmasses that I just mentioned, there lived a people called the Neanderthals. These 'people' lived a fairly unobtrusive existence, hunting, gathering fruits and other edibles, burying their dead, playing flutes made of bone, and building small religious monuments. But they weren't the only 'people' to be walking the earth at this time – there were others – a scattering of species that all belonged to the hominid class.

"I know, as we've had many classes together on the subject, that you have an excellent grasp of how the system of evolution works. The mutation of a species emerges which happens to be more fit in dealing with environmental changes that have happened, or are about to take place, and so is the one that survives and procreates, gradually weeding out its competitors. The most 'fit' form survives, and the others perish. It is a simple, efficient, magnificent system.

"The system, however, is based on the presence of mutations, on the fact that something goes wrong inside of every millionth cell. Usually, this 'thing that goes wrong', either dies out, or slightly improves the species. But let us just imagine for a moment what might happen if something went extremely, exceptionally wrong in one of those mutations. What if, by random chance, every, say, ten-millionth new species, a creature spawned from the system that could find a way to jump out of the system itself? Can you imagine the repercussions?

"If, inside the system, a plant were to mutate and sprout an abnormally large leaf, it would suddenly convert more energy, grow better than its competitors and pass this trait onto its progeny, improving the overall state and function of the bionetwork that it's in. But if the plant were to find a way to jump outside of the system, to supersede evolution by growing legs and systematically plucking every one of its competitors from the ground, what would be improved then? This, of course, would no longer be 'natural selection'; it would be 'artificial selection', being done by the one species arrogantly choosing itself, making the obviously bias choice for evolution. A catastrophe. Because once something is outside of that magnificent system, once it has taken arrogant control over it, there simply cannot be the same constant incremental improvement as there was inside of it – in fact, quite the contrary. Let's put it into an example of humans (for ease of understanding). Imagine there is a boat with various kinds of people on it. Let's say, a religious pacifist, a scientist, a doctor, and a murderer. And on this boat, there are only enough food rations for one of them to survive the journey. Let me ask you, who survives? Who lives to create a new society once they reach land, to pass their beliefs onto the next generation? Is it the kindest, most giving person? Is it the most moral, the most humane, the one with the highest sense of life, or of responsibility? Do you think the 'fittest' to survive that boat journey, would be the 'best' person, or the 'worst'?

Veracity

"So, to continue with the earth's history, as you've probably guessed from my speech, one of those rare depraved species did emerge, and subsequently, the world saw its first ever weapons, and within a fragment of time, the Neanderthals, of which I mentioned before, became extinct, along with every single other remaining hominid species that existed. They were all hunted down and systematically slaughtered by this new vile strain of being; a species that, for the first time in nature, seemed to realize the possibility of abusing its own power. And it certainly didn't stop at massacring its competitors, it moved on, decimating a staggering amount of other plant and animal life as well, adopting a disastrous conduct of excess, oppression, and destruction, even against its own kind."

Harek stood and walked to the centre of the room, "So then," he stopped and put both of his hands behind his back, "as you've probably guessed, that species of which I speak, the hominid that hunted down and killed the others of its class, the murderer that made it to shore and created its sickened world there," he turned to look at me, his eyebrows raised slightly, sympathetically, "is, of course, us."

Looking back, I think my reaction was to be expected. I just chuckled, shook my head. He had to be joking. In fact, I was sure he was joking, and seemed to be waiting for him to smile, to say something that would release the air of expectation. But he didn't. He only stared at me, gently nodding, until my smile began to fade into an expression that must have resembled concern, unease. Though maybe panic.

"Are you trying to say we're monsters?" I shook my head with slow distracted movements. "I hardly think… I mean – are you serious? We're not monsters. We're not. I'm sorry." But I suddenly didn't feel as sure as I'd sounded.

"I, too, am sorry," he said, continuing to nod. "But I am sorry that we are monsters. I'm sorry that it's all we've ever been. And most of all, I'm sorry that it's all we'll ever be." Having said this quietly, decisively, he turned to circle the room as he'd done before, and continued to talk. I watched him suspiciously.

"You wouldn't believe the things that we've done to each other and to the world around us. In fact, there is nothing we haven't destroyed, no amount of pain that we haven't inflicted upon the earth, the creatures on it, or our 'fellow man', no atrocity that we haven't carried out. We've boiled children, dismembered men, burned women, repeatedly raped, mutated, tortured, and then caringly healed the people we'd done this to, to be tortured again. We have studied ways of stimulating the body's nerves in order to make people feel more pain. We have…"

"Stop," I interrupted. "You're wrong. I mean – maybe someone else did that, but not me, not you. We haven't done those things."

Harek, who'd been speaking almost serenely while doling through his list of butchery, snapped his head in my direction as soon as I'd interjected, his eyes awake, wild. "Haven't we! Can you be so sure of yourself? Am I to believe that I'm standing in a room with the very first exception to the rule, of which, I might add, we have consistently and unfailingly laid down behind us for thousands upon thousands of years? Am I to believe that?"

"Well," I muttered, "I guess so, because I don't do those things. And I wouldn't." I was sure that Harek was going to be furious with this, but instead his body relaxed, and to my surprise, he began to laugh, throwing his head back and turning his body around once in a fit of hilarity. I didn't join him.

"So then! You believe that you are an exception, that you simply cannot have the same evil inside of you that somehow drove those 'other' people in history to commit such acts, hmm? Is that about right?" I didn't move. "Well then, you should know something: precisely because you think that you're an exception to the rule, that you are something above the rest, that you alone are better, proves to me, without a shadow of doubt, that you are exactly the same as everyone else. You can join the ranks – because you are only one among the innumerable, the countless 'exceptions' throughout history. Everyone holds that they are above evil. Not a single one of us wants to believe in the cruelty that we are capable of, which, incidentally, has been one of the greatest vehicles for executing it."

Veracity

There was a feeling like that of a storm in the centre of my stomach, churning and growing in intensity. I wanted to vomit, scream; or maybe just run, slip out of this place and away from everything he was saying, away from his booming voice, bouncing off the walls in the cramped space. But I couldn't move. I'd become small on the bench, my shoulders crawling up beside my neck; and I felt myself becoming even smaller as he took a few steps forward, his presence looming over me, his words resonating off of my rib cage.

"Tell me then, you who are above evil, how easily can you pass this test: As men are the weaker sex, the darkest of our innate traits come out in us; and men that haven't yet learned to keep their violent appetites within the rules of their culture, that haven't yet learned how to suppress what they naturally are in order to conform to societal norms, are called boys. And in keeping with that rule, every single boy who has ever walked the earth, with, I believe, no exception, has at some point in time been obsessed with his power; discovered it and abused it, exactly as their ancestors had done. The merciless pulling off of spiders' legs, the exploitation of another's vulnerability, the torture and killing of helpless animals, birds, fish; every single boy has abused the power that he somehow discovered he possesses – every one of them. Are you saying you're an exception to that? Can you honestly look me in the eye and tell me that you've never done any of those things?"

"Well... I haven't," I said, obviously lying.

"You're obviously lying."

Damn him. My eyes sunk slow and heavy to the floor, and I shifted uncomfortably on the bench, my gestures verifying every ounce of his accusation.

"I really expected more honesty from you. I can only hope that the seconds we've wasted on falsehoods will stop here – that you will join me with some sincerity, as I have chosen to do with you."

He was right. He was so right about everything. It was almost as if the lizard were right in front of me, as if it were that day in the forest, and I was a boy again, crouching down beside it, watching it squirm with pain, listening to our laughter. This was the line we crossed. Of all the other animals in the world that had the capacity to do what we did, we were the only ones that actually followed through with it, and then convinced ourselves that it was okay. I felt repulsive, stupid.

But wait. What was Harek staring down at me for? He said that every boy did the same thing, and that there were no exceptions. So what right did he have to stand over me and make me feel so vile, so guilty, when he must have done something similar?

"Okay, so I did do some of that as a boy. What did you do?" I pressed, still looking at the floor, hoping this was a question I was allowed to ask.

And it was, because he answered me, lowering his voice, ashamed. "We used to find birds' nests and toss them on the beach, and then sit to watch the fledglings get picked apart by scavengers."

"See," I said, looking up, "you did it, too." I don't really know what I meant to say with that. Maybe I just wanted to put us both in the same position; to have him sitting beside me in a way, shrunken on the bench as well, feeling as defeated, as disgraceful as I was.

"Yes, of course I did such things. As I said, every one of us has — but that is clearly no excuse. Just because billions of us have done it, doesn't make it right, it only perfectly illustrates that we are innately wrong. Evil isn't something that is inside of us, Joshua — it is us. It's not the result of an individual, or a culture, or an epoch; it wasn't the Barbarians, or the Visigoths, the Vandals, Mongols, Moors, Chinese, the Crusaders, the Inquisition, the KGB, the Nazis…"

"Harek," I interrupted, again, "I've never heard of any of those people." His green eyes flared like fire.

"Because their names don't matter! Because it wasn't 'them', it was us! Can't you see that? We all have the same genetic makeup, the same inclinations, the same fear, the same malevolence! It is a product of our blood. This blood!" Harek, who was already standing too close, stepped closer, and held his forearm in front of my face to squeeze it, his thumb pressing along the blue vein under his skin. "This very blood running through my body! Through your body!"

He'd become incensed, unpredictable, and he realized, as I was pushing my back against the wall in an attempt to wriggle away from him, that he was scaring me. And with this realization, his eyes began to relax, his pupils slowly contracting, and he straightened up, turned, and walked back to the centre of the room again. He rolled his shoulders a few times and cleared his throat, composing himself a bit before speaking. When he did, his voice was quieter, calmer, but still hadn't lost its severe edge.

"I'm not going to ask you what you did, because I already know, in the same way that every one of us knows about the harm we've inflicted firsthand. But just stop to imagine for a moment: we are only two people – two people that don't really have any kind of governing authority over others, who don't have access to a lot of power – yet we have still found a way to abuse the little bit of power that we have. What about others? What about the scores of people who had more resources, more influence, who had the chance (and used their chance) to trigger suffering on the most extreme scales?

"Think about it. Have all of those horrible things that you and I did, that mankind did, just disappeared into thin air after we did them? I'll tell you the answer: they didn't. Every one of our deliberate wrongs, every last bit of pain, every shred of damage that our kind has cumulatively caused, has all incurred an enormous debt – and it is a debt that we must pay."

Harek turned to face me, nodding. "I know why you denied what you did when I first asked you. It was because you already wished that you hadn't done it. You wished you were perfect – or maybe just better. But the fact is, you aren't. And this alone is probably the hardest thing for a human being to admit. Yes, we might be able to look at our species as a whole and laugh at its absurdity, and we can certainly look at other cultures across the water and point out their faults, errors, and shortcomings, and we can even do this when we talk about our neighbours in the community, even our closest companions, but when it comes to looking at ourselves, things get a bit trickier.

Most often, the nearer we come to our own hypocrisy, to our own petty meanness and cruel tendencies, the further from the truth of them we get.

"Yet, that said, this doesn't always have to be the case. I believe – no, I know – that we have it in us to admit to ourselves exactly what we are. And this duty alone, this one incredibly taxing responsibility, happens to be the only possible salvation of the future. It is the most critical, most vital step that anyone can ever take.

"And this is one of the reasons why I believe you show such potential, one of the reasons we've selected you. You've proven to have some analytical talent, the capacity to offer insight into yourself and the world around you. You seem to be able to question yourself, doubt yourself, which, strangely enough, is exactly what we need you to do.

"As it turns out, your Coming of Age isn't about a careful lie, as it was with almost all of the others; it is about truth. But more importantly, it is about finding out if you have what it takes to grasp that truth – because it is always a concept that is extremely intricate, challenging, and often enough, even dangerous. And this struggle to hold onto the coldest, hardest, and most difficult truth, to ask yourself, and then re-ask yourself, and then re-ask yourself again if what you see in front of you is really there, and not just what you would like to see there, this constant and gruelling dedication to truth has a name. It's called veracity. And it isn't an ideology or a religion, it's a path. And the only reason that you are here today is because we honestly believe that you have it in you to stop and consciously choose that path – and then, to walk with us along it."

He stopped as if he was waiting for a response of some kind, but I didn't have one; in fact, I didn't feel like I had much of anything. I felt spent, worn, like I'd been ripped apart and thrown onto the ground, stepped on, spat on, left for dead. The very last thing I wanted to do was say anything, so I gave Harek a look that I hoped would indicate my wish to forfeit any active dialogue from this point on. He seemed to understand, and continued.

"However, before any of this can even begin to take place, you need to have some time to reflect on what we've said, to think about it, because one of the most natural reactions that a person has to difficult news is to initially suppress it in their minds, to blind themselves from it. It's called denial, and before we can move on any further, you will have to get through this stage; which, we believe, is something best done on your own (at least initially)."

He walked to one of the other metal doors in the room and began to tug on it. It had the same ridiculous width as the one at the entrance, and opened to another corridor, which seemed to be lit with natural light. I realized that this might have something to do with the rectangular depression I'd seen missing from the hill. "We have a room for you to stay in while you do this. It has food in it and opens up into a garden." I raised my eyebrows. Did he say a garden? "Well, not really a garden… it was designed to be a kind of laboratory to test the air outside of this shelter (again, for reasons you wouldn't really understand right now), and we've just let things grow wild inside of that space. There are also a few writing materials for you to organize or express your thoughts, if you find that helps you in any way."

I could already see the small bed from where I was sitting, and I stood and began walking toward it, my steps vacant, clumsy. I passed by Harek without looking at him and continued toward the bed, and maybe it was seeing how dejected I was walking, which made him stop me once more.

"I know that this must all seem so incredibly depressing, but you should bear in mind that we haven't brought you to this place to sadden you; there's obviously a greater intention here. And believe me, you will soon see that there is nothing to be miserable about at all. In fact, quite the contrary."

"What do you mean?" I asked.

"Well, as I said, we won't get into it now, but… but what if I told you there was a way to restore what we've ruined? What if I told you that we've figured out a way to mend the damage we've caused?" Harek broke off and grinned at the floor for a moment. "There was a time in my life when a man asked me that very same question; and then he wanted to know if I might be interested in learning more." He looked up again, "Are you interested in learning more?" I nodded drunkenly, and Harek smiled at this. "I'm happy to hear that. Because so was I."

We looked at each other in silence for a few seconds. "Well then... someone else will come to see you early tomorrow morning." He reached out and started to heave the door in an effort to close it, and looked at me just as it began to move. "I'm sorry for the noise this will make, but there's no other way to close it." He gave a feeble grin as the metal swung between us and crashed into its frame.

I collapsed onto the bed, somehow exhausted.

So this was the great secret that I'd been searching for all of my life? This was what I had longed for, the covert glances of my childhood decoded? That we were a 'thing' in nature that went horribly and catastrophically wrong? Monsters?

No. This was all impossible, unthinkable.

Though, didn't that ring of denial, that 'stage' I was supposed to be in?

But if... I could rise above it...

I stopped to think about what monsters were for a moment. When I was a child, I used to look out into the shadows of the underbrush, the lantern light cutting out a cavern of perceived safety, the darkness pressing against its fringes. I was always afraid that some horrible creature might come along and break that sacred border, risk walking boldly into the light, only with the intent of hurting me. Later, I had convinced myself that such a creature was a figment of my imagination, that there was no such thing as monsters. But suddenly, I was forced to ask an intimidating question about that rationale: Could I picture a man walking into that same light? Could I picture him carrying a weapon and approaching me? Could I picture him coming for no other reason than to harm? And if so, wasn't I a man just like him?

As the night fell, I kept looking into the garden, feeling as afraid as I had been as a boy. I could almost see them, a handful of nondescript men, stepping out of the shadows, closing in around me, raising their clubs and sticks, their knives and spears – their pins that they'd stolen from clothing class.

Who knew? Maybe we had wrecked everything. Maybe what had gone horribly wrong in the world was even because of us. And what if he was right? What then?

But before I found sleep, something incredibly important had occurred to me: if Harek were right about our being monsters, then he might also be right about there being a way to repair things. And if so, then there was still hope.

Yes. I thought about it over and over again. Because if he were right about there being a possibility to mend things, then, of course I wanted to help. Of course I wanted to walk along this 'path' that could make things better. 'In fact', I thought, rolling over in bed and squinting into the darkness, having suddenly forgotten about the men I'd envisioned coming out of the shadows beside me, 'I wanted to learn everything there was to know about that path, and exactly how we proposed to fix things. Everything.'

6

I woke to the grating calls of a monkey. I shot up from bed; eyes wide open, listening to its sounds recede into the distance, crashing through the branches near the shelter. My hand was on my chest, and I looked down at it for a moment, feeling my pulse thump under my fingers. I could certainly think of better ways to wake up. "Stupid monkey," I mumbled, relaxing a bit and squinting at the morning light for the first time. After a few seconds of shaking my head, I flumped back down onto the sheets.

It had been a long night. Let alone was it a new place that I wasn't used to, I couldn't find a way to stop my mind from thinking. A continual stream of questions had kept me awake, rolling through my head restless hour after restless hour, and all of them having to pass by me unanswered. They were difficult questions. Such as, if we ourselves were some kind of fatal flaw, how could we possibly feign to 'fix' anything? And if truth was the path that we were supposed to walk, how could we ever know that we actually had it, that we were walking in the right direction? After all, what was truth in the first place?

Once, after Kara had asked the Elders to teach her everything there was to know about our senses, we had talked about this very thing, and she blew my mind with some of her ideas. She had concluded, leaning in to tell me – as careful as always, of course – that our perception was, at best, completely incomplete. She'd learned about the narrow spectrum of light that we see, the limited range of sound we hear, the enormity of smells that we are oblivious to; she pointed out the minute hairs of insects that feel an entire world of air currents that our sense of touch is unaware of, and told me of fish that could taste things in the water that were fathoms away. And this was only the information that our senses were too crude to pick up. There was much more information out there that our bodies didn't even have the capacity to detect: magnetic fields, cosmic rays, countless types of waves, chemical reactions. If, while sitting in a room, we could only take in a miniscule percentage of the possible stimulus inside it, how could we ever say we understood the room for what it really was? Truth, she held, was unperceivable. And for the most part, I agreed with her – or at least I'd nodded at her when she'd said it (looking as stunned as always I'm sure). How could we profess to hold the truth in our hands while it was pulsing inside of our fingers in more ways than we could ever know?

Yet, everything that Harek had said sounded so accurate, so substantiated. I knew that what he meant by the 'truth' was really 'as close as we could get to the truth', and I imagined that he had it, and that I would eventually be given access to the books in the Great Hall, and that, after reading them and splaying the evidence before me, I, too, would have it. But, I decided in the end, I would need to do that before I would accept that we were monsters; I wasn't going to be so easily won. I would need proof, something more than a well-rehearsed speech to throw away my faith in what we are.

I got out of bed and stretched beside it, looking into the tangle of bushes and vines inside the garden, which had a rectangular path around it that had been cleared for walking. Then, I looked down the corridor and noticed that the door was ajar.

At that same moment, there was a muffled rustling, as of clothing in movement, which was coming from a recess in the courtyard that I hadn't noticed before. I stepped forward to see who it was.

"Did you solve your problem with the monkey?" asked Dana, who was sitting at a small table, apparently waiting for me to stick my head around the corner.

"What?"

"I heard you mumble 'stupid monkey' a few minutes ago."

"Oh, yeah. Solved." I rubbed the sleep from my eyes.

"Good. Then come, have a seat with me," he said, eyeing the only other chair at the table. Both of his hands were wrapped around a cup of steaming liquid, which smelled of pepper leaf tea, and one of his legs was casually draped over the other. He

47

brought the cup to his mouth and sent a few swirls of steam eddying into the air before sipping from it.

Dana was a thin man, whose movements were always slow, his gestures methodical, deliberate. He had long curly hair that was aging and stranded in rusted colours, ranging from brown to grey. His beard, which shared the same varying colour, was longer and much more unkempt than Harek's. As the light material for our clothes was produced from the fibres of certain plants on the island, the cloth was naturally beige, but Dana took to privately dying his shirts with a kind of berry, which produced a pale maroon colour. I once speculated that this might be a way of separating himself from the rest of the Elders, though, really, it might also just have been his taste.

I walked over and sat on the other side of the wooden table, both of us angling toward the courtyard where a few small songbirds, hidden from view, were singing away. I was happy to have the chance to speak with him. Out of all the Elders, I held him in the highest regard, hung on his words, and pondered them carefully. For my part, we seemed to get along quite well together, or at least seemed to feel at ease in each other's company.

"I've come by to see how you're coping with things, and also to begin answering some of the questions that I'm sure have begun to spring up." He said this last sentence while turning his head in my direction, opening his eyes as the last words were spoken. This was one of his peculiarities. Often when speaking with him, he would look away for quite some time, and would keep his eyes closed when turning back to face you, and then open them when he imagined they would be aiming at your face. It was a touch odd.

"Well," I mumbled, picking a tiny dead leaf off the table between us and throwing it to the ground, "I think I'm doing alright. We're not the greatest creatures, but there's something we can do about it, right?"

Dana looked at me as if I'd just spat onto the table between us. He lowered his eyebrows, focusing on my face. "Is that what you got out of the conversation with Harek yesterday?"

I shifted in my seat. "Well, yeah – basically."

It took him a few uncomfortable seconds to react to this. He was dumbfounded, almost lost for words. His mouth formed several different vowels before he finally decided on what to say. "Harek… told you about denial, didn't he?"

My voice was soft, "Yes." I knew what was meant by it.

"Because I can't imagine him ever saying the words: 'we're not the greatest creatures, but there's something we can do about it', as that's completely inaccurate. Firstly, there is nothing we can do about what we are. And secondly, what we are is the darkest, most evil animal the fossil record has ever seen, and we had hoped you were on your way to at least understanding a little bit of that."

"Oh," I said. I put my hands on the table and started fiddling with them. This wasn't easy. Because I might be able to admit to the fact that we had it in us to do some appalling things, but to blanket everyone with a description such as 'atrocious' or 'vile' seemed a little simplistic to me. As far as I was concerned, there were a few people on the island who I would have a hard time stamping with such words, and I wondered what Dana would have to say about that. Could he really point at Thalia or Mitra and sincerely brand them with the description of 'vile'? "But… I mean – there must be some piece of us that isn't so horrible."

"Possibly, yes. But as a whole, at the most basic, fundamental layer, which is obviously where it matters most, we are essentially that: horrible."

I tapped a fingernail on the table before speaking. "But how can you know that for certain?"

Dana grinned, "How I know what we are isn't nearly as interesting as how you don't. I haven't pulled my ideas from the air, haven't rehearsed them from a book; I've formed them from observing our every action, and I would suggest that you begin to do the same.

"The easiest place to start is to think of children, as they are acting almost directly from that dark, fundamental layer that I'm speaking of. I know that you don't have a lot of experience with younger children, and that we don't have any on the island to draw examples from, but try and think about Anu or Siri as far back as you can remember. As soon as they'd learned how to talk they were exhibiting their innate behaviour: hitting each other, stealing and hoarding things to themselves, deriding one another. There has often been a misconception that we are born pure, but that notion couldn't be more mistaken. Babies aren't born innocent only to be later corrupted by society; they are born corrupt, and if they aren't effectively deprogrammed, then it is they who spread their malignancy throughout society."

"Did you say 'deprogrammed'?"

"Yes. Deprogrammed. Adults don't 'teach' children to be non-violent, caring, kind individuals; in fact, in a person's formative years, there isn't any 'teaching' that's done at all – it's only constant dissuasion, deterring, and discouragement that keep children from doing what they naturally want to do. Though of course, this must also be done while encouraging them to do the opposite, all with the aim of eventually coercing them to act in a way that isn't nearly as inborn. In its most basic sense, the raising of a child is but an attempt to rewire a rogue brain. It's a conscious unshaping, which is done in the hopes that the child might come to act as far away from their instinctive tendencies as possible.

"So, as to your question, is there a piece of us that isn't so horrible? Well, let's take a look. Let's imagine that there is a well-mannered, compassionate individual standing inside of this courtyard with us. And as they are such, we can only assume that the deprogramming stage of his or her life had gone over flawlessly. I ask you, is this a 'good' person? Does it really matter if they say please and thank you when they should, that they share, treat others respectfully, stifle their violent thoughts? Is the essence of a being measured by its shell, by how well they balance on the wobbly pillar that juts out of the mountain of things that they've 'unlearned', or is the essence of a being measured by its core, by what's beneath it when it falls?"

"By its core."

"Of course it is. In fact, the image of someone standing with one leg on a pillar is perfect, because I like to think of anything that we do or make (societies and cultures for example), as a kind of construction, as building blocks. And of course, the only way to find out what a structure is really made of is to grab hold of the bottom of it and shake, and see how it holds out when it has to fall back on its most rudimentary foundation. What do you think history has continually shown us, what do you think happens when we shake the wobbly pillar of the commended lady or gentleman that we imagined? Where do they land when it collapses? I'll tell you: suddenly, they find themselves remembering everything that they'd been raised to forget; they become precisely what they always were, yet had been striving their entire lives not to be.

"And as I said, we can be certain of this because it has been woven into every page of history that has ever been written. The dates change, as do the traditions and costumes, but the story has always been the same. The moment there was some kind of pressure, whether a group of people overpopulated an area, or was excessive for far too long and allowed their food stores to become depleted, or another group of their very own species marched across some of the imaginary borders that they created to separate one ideology from another, greed, fear, or arrogance bringing them there with weapons in hand, whenever things became difficult and something shook the very structure of what we are composed of, we have consistently crumbled to the ground into an ugly heap, and masses upon masses of people have suffered and died in unspeakable ways.

"And because we are outside of the system of evolution, things could never improve; even though it would seem reasonable that, as the centuries progressed, humanity might learn from its past mistakes, or at the very least from the banal repetition of them, in reality we never did. Instead, every passing age found new ways to create even more destruction, more suffering, more pain. And this can only be explained by the fact that what we are underneath of our 'not so horrible' shell, the very essence of our being, the foundation that all of the greatest societies have unsteadily balanced upon and have eventually collapsed into, is truthfully and irreversibly hideous." Dana finished, and, closing his eyes first, he turned his head to look back into the garden.

With each sentence that he spoke, I continued to wilt in my chair, until finally, I was sitting with my head bowed, looking like a child who had just been reprimanded. I was beginning to get a feeling as to what Coming of Age was all about. I wasn't there to make my mind up about anything, wasn't going to spend any time discussing things. Someone else had already done the thinking for me, and I was expected to ingest it. That was all.

Before that day, I'd always considered Dana to be a calm man. He was opinionated, yes, but always gentle. Yet suddenly, and just like Harek the day before, he was managing to come across as cold, almost confrontational, lashing out at my every thought as if they'd offended him in the deepest way. It occurred to me that they might be doing this intentionally, hoping to set a precedent of some kind, creating an environment where I'd be forced to choose my words with the greatest of caution. If so, they'd already succeeded. I was afraid to open my mouth.

Yet I had to, because there was something that wasn't making sense. I was sure that I'd come close to directly quoting Harek when I said there was something we could do to right the wrongs of our species. But if Dana was correct, and we were 'truthfully and irreversibly hideous', what kind of solution lay in sight? It obviously wasn't a new government or system; from what he'd said, they all ended in the same way. So what did Harek mean by 'a way to restore what we've ruined', 'a way to mend the damage we've caused'? The truth was, I was already sick of hearing how dead-ended we were – I wanted to hear how we planned to move forward in spite of it. I pressed him further. "Dana, maybe Harek wasn't supposed to tell me, and maybe I can't remember his exact words, but I'm positive he mentioned there was a way for us to fix things. Was I wrong about that?"

He took in a deep breath and eyed the ground in front of his feet, "No. You weren't." After raising a hand to his face and grooming his beard for a few seconds, he continued, "And to be honest with you, that is the sole reason I've been asked to see you this morning: to tell you the story of what happened to the world, and where we, the island, fit into it all."

I promptly sat up straight and folded my hands together on the table, trying not to look as impatient as I was. Seeing this, he turned just enough to look at me. "But before you get too excited, you should know that it's not going to be an easy story for you to hear. Because after hearing it, the way that you see your world – our life here, the island, and all of us on it – will never be the same again."

I remember that my face numbed with this last sentence, that there was something in its tone that made a liquid weight settle into the bottom of my stomach. I realized, at the last possible second, after having swum too close to the centre of the whirlpool to return to safety, that I'd completely underestimated the depth and magnitude of what I was about to be drawn into. Yet there was no turning back, no way to swim against the currents. The only thing I could do was listen, be pulled under.

I watched Dana face the garden again, hesitating for only a moment before he began.

7

"This story began with one man. He was a charismatic man – well spoken, compelling – but most importantly he was standing behind some fascinating ideas. Basically, just as Harek told you yesterday, he'd determined that humanity was nature's one fatal flaw, that we were the most deviant mutation, the greatest cancer, the final parasite. He recognized that we had found a way to shirk the governing systems of nature, and as a result were undoing everything in our wake, and would only shamelessly continue to do so.

"Of course, such an idea wasn't exactly novel – every culture that has ever lived has had its tiny population of truth-seekers – but what makes this story different is that this man finally had a clear and realistic plan to do something about it. He proposed a simple remedy: end our destructive reign altogether; rid the world of our species and give nature the chance to heal, to renew itself, to create something better.

"Yet, how does one go about such a thing, especially considering that the very stem of our brain, the nucleus from which all our actions are based, is solely responsible for keeping our species alive at all cost? Well, he knew that there were two ways a person could override this powerful, intrinsic urge: either through complete desperation, or through the highest form of intellectual reasoning and belief. Obviously, he focused on the latter. Because if there is one thing that sets us apart from the common parasite, it is that we have the capacity to be self-aware; and if that awareness is exceptional, if our self-understanding is thorough enough, we can overrule even our deepest instincts.

"And so that man set out to look for people who might possess such a high level of understanding – and he found them. Everywhere. Quickly and quietly he gained support among the scientific and academically elite, and received funding from a few wealthy individuals, who, he'd discovered, happened to be radical idealists behind closed doors. He then set up a system of almost complete anonymity, so that if one person were caught, or even wavered, the whole organization would continue to function. And perhaps because each person's identity was so veiled, people felt more comfortable to offer whatever service they could, and soon the anonymous messages, which were being secretly relayed through tight social rings, were flowing.

"Within a short period of time this man's organization, which never once adopted a name, had become a silent, compact union, consisting of only the most crucial and strategic members at its centre, and which then fanned out into a grid of resources all over the world; regular men and women who were employed in every facet of intelligent society, including research, communications, and military.

"That organization formed a three phase plan called 'The Goal'. The first phase was clearly the most significant. As strange as this may sound to you right now, traditionally, an enormous amount of time, energy, and money has been put into developing more effective ways to kill each other. And as such, there were laboratories all over the world that were busy cultivating diseases to be used as weapons. Some of the scientists in those laboratories appeared to be working for their governments, but were really working for the society. Collectively, they developed five separate strains of an exceptional virus – five to account for possible individuals or pockets of population that might prove naturally immune to one of the forms, as sometimes happens in nature – it was a virus that slowly affected the nervous system and ended in paralysis and death. These infectious agents were amazingly hardy, but also had a long incubation period, making them virtually impossible to detect for about five years. Yet during that time the person carrying the disease seemed healthy and continued travelling around, unknowingly spreading it on a global scale.

"As you might be able to imagine, the first phase... well, it worked – to say the least. Suddenly, almost overnight, it was discovered that there was a global pandemic of a terminal disease. Panic set in. First, everyone scattered to find a cure, but they quickly realized that it was too late – which was when things became unbearably ugly. Different groups of people, organized into skin colour, languages, and thoughts on God, began blaming one another, pointing fingers, and eventually even dropping some very potent weapons in a few places. They did what every human culture throughout history did when faced with the need to hold together: they fell apart.

"The second phase involved secret secluded shelters that were built by the military of several different countries to withstand huge environmental changes, which might be brought on by those same potent weapons that I just mentioned. Obviously, it was the rich and powerful that had the connections and resources to make it to these safe havens, but they also had at least one society member among them. That society member then poisoned the elite, secured the shelter from the inside, and admitted other members, who, incidentally, had been living nearby and in quarantine for years.

"Once everyone was safe inside, they hunkered down to watch and wait. They could monitor what was happening in the world from instruments deep inside the bunkers, which communicated with devices that circle the earth (in fact, some of the moving stars that we see crossing the sky at night are those very instruments). They carefully recorded both the movement and concentration of people as the population diminished throughout the decades.

"After many, many years, there were only a few tiny pockets of survivors left outside the shelters, which had either created strongholds and had managed to keep the viral contamination out, or had outlived any of the potential carriers. It was at the end of the second phase that groups of specially trained soldiers (who had obviously been sterilized before setting out) were dispatched from the shelters around the world to destroy these last clusters of people. Once they'd succeeded, they fanned out to spend the rest of their lives to search for, and then wipe out, any smaller groups that the instruments in the sky might have missed.

"Which brings us to the third and last phase of The Goal. The third phase involves another group of specially trained young men that will be sent out from the shelters. These expeditions will be acting as a kind of sweep, a last check for undetected pockets of human life. And if any of these expeditions should find people, they will have been trained to infiltrate the group, and then to chemically sterilize them. In this last phase, violence should never enter into the equation, as there are too few people, and too much land to cover, than to risk any loss of life to the expedition members."

Dana stopped for a moment and scratched the back of his head, then, in that odd way of his, turned to face me with his eyes closed, opening them just as he began to speak. "As I'm sure you've been able to pick up along the way, our island is one of those safe havens. And you, and all of the younger people on the island, were born and have been raised as a pool of individuals with varying talents, so that we might select the best suited of you to run or support one of the third phase expeditions." He paused, clearing his throat.

"So, that should give you a pretty good idea of how it all fits together; who we are, why we're alive. Obviously, we are all members of that amazingly far-sighted and responsible society that I've been talking about – and you, Joshua, are among the last generation of our vile race."

He stopped talking and raised his eyebrows, as if waiting for a response, as if this were the perfect time for me to share any thoughts or reflections I might have; as if a person, after hearing such a story, would be capable of having a calm and articulate discourse on anything. I could only stare at him, wide-eyed, noticing that the birds had either flown away or fallen silent, as there was no sound whatsoever in the courtyard except my breathing; quick, shallow breaths, drying my throat. I swallowed to try and wet it. Which didn't work.

I don't know if there are words that exist which could describe what I was feeling at that moment. But it's occurred to me since it was probably an emotion in and of itself; something that could only be described as 'the feeling people get when they find out the only reason they're alive is to assist in the eradication of their own species'. I couldn't move a muscle – something slow and tingling had crawled across my neck and down my back, and seemed to be paralysing me, cinching me uncomfortably to my chair. I focused on every tiny movement that Dana made, the expanding of his chest, the blinking of his slow eyelids, the delicate flaring of one of his nostrils.

In only a few minutes, it had become vividly clear to me that he – along with every single one of the other Elders for that matter – was a mad, crazing lunatic. I didn't even feel safe enough to shift my eyes; though at the same time, I was straining to take in the detail of my periphery, looking for a way out, running through the possibilities. I thought about the courtyard, the walls around us that were too high to climb; then the door that was left ajar, but would only lead into the other chamber where the entrance was almost certainly barred. And it all became clear to me right then: they brought me to a fortress on purpose. They knew how I was going to react. They were probably even expecting me to try and run – or fight. Come to think of it, maybe he had a knife under his shirt, and was just waiting for me to lash out.

I eyed the folds of his knuckles, swallowed again, felt the saliva scratch down my oesophagus.

After a few moments, Dana leaned over the table toward me, and, unable to stop myself, I leaned back, keeping the same amount of space between us. He snickered at this. "Joshua. Relax. You should really see yourself right now; you're deathly pale – your hands are trembling. Come on. I mean – ask yourself: What are you afraid of? Do you really think that anybody on this island would hurt you? Do you think that the same people who have cared for you all of their lives, who have nurtured you from birth, would ever allow any harm to come to you, let alone inflict that harm?" He shook his head, "And if it's the future that you're fearing, ask yourself this: Could you picture any of those same people forcing you to do something that you didn't believe in? I mean – true, we might have some philosophies that you weren't aware of, but we're still the same people you've known all your life. So do us the service of keeping that in mind before you judge, all right?"

I nodded, and he leaned back into his chair again, reflecting for a bit before continuing. "Though, to be perfectly honest, I might be a bit to blame for your reaction here. Maybe I was moving through the story a little fast, maybe I should have given you a bit more time to keep pace, to ask questions." His voice was calm, reassuring. "And really, if I were to think about it more objectively, we're almost asking the impossible here, we're asking for you, in the span of only a few minutes, to keep pace with an idea that took years to develop. I guess that would be enough to confuse or frighten anyone.

"But I want you to bear in mind one thing. We didn't tell you the whole story because we thought you'd agree with us; in fact, we were almost certain you wouldn't. I think every Elder can admit that, at a glance, the concept of The Goal can appear fanatical, even deranged; and indeed, if that's what you're thinking, that's perfectly fine. The only thing that we wanted to accomplish this morning was to provide you with a completely transparent view of the big picture. That's all.

"And now that it's done, the next step should come fairly natural. We need you to doubt. We want you to question, in the deepest way, the ethics and rationale of everything inside the story I just told you. Because the last thing we want you to do is unthinkingly nod and adopt our beliefs. No. We want you to probe them instead, scrutinize them, rip them apart and piece them back together, only to see if you happen to come to the same conclusions we have. If you don't, then you're welcome to continue living a sheltered existence here on the island (albeit under much stricter supervision of course, as – and I think you can appreciate this – we've trusted you with a few extremely volatile facts here). However, if you do find that you come to the same conclusions we have, then we would train you to set off across the ocean with a select few from our community, where you would be asked to wander around a landscape that is gloriously healing from our wounds, and make sure that it is uninhabited, unmolested, and pristine. And then, once you were finished there, to continue onto other lands, exploring, discovering, and adventuring for the rest of your days." He watched me for a few seconds, as if allowing time for these last words to sink in.

"So then – you'll need to begin asking yourself a few questions. And, in order to find answers to those questions, you'll have to do a bit of research. Consequently, you will be one of the few people who have unrestricted access to the volumes of information in the Great Hall, and I would encourage you to use that privilege as much as possible. However, that said, having such an enormous breadth of data at your fingertips, it would be easy to get lost or sidetracked while delving into open-ended questions. For this reason, you'll need someone to help you formulate a process, someone to bounce ideas off, and to dig up relevant information in the Great Hall for you. I will be that person, supplying you with whatever you need – history books, war chronicles, atlases, or other reference material – and will meet with you every day to discuss your thoughts, and help you move forward through your own process.

"But to get your mind shifting a bit, I want to pose an interesting question. Do you remember that charismatic man that I spoke of earlier? Well, he died long ago. Yet you and I are still breathing. Think of that for a moment. We are some of the last people alive on earth. Why is that? Are we better? Are we more worthy? Was our life granted to us because of some exceptional thing that we did for the universe? Do you think we 'deserve' to be here, Joshua?" he asked.

I squirmed in my chair, realizing that I was expected to answer. When I spoke, my voice was almost a whisper. "I... can't really say. I mean – I have a hard time imagining that anyone deserves anything, really."

Dana's face lit up with a warm smile. "I couldn't agree more. We don't deserve this life, neither of us has earned the right to be here. No. No, we stole it. And I understand that this is a hard fact to face; but a fact it is – we are living on stolen time, time that was taken from countless others. And as odd as it may be, The Goal hasn't taken either of our lives; instead, it has given them to us. So then, doesn't it fall logically that, in some curious way, we are also indebted to it? And if so, what is The Goal really asking from us? Is it something unreasonable to give in exchange for our very lives?"

I felt my forehead contorting with thought, and, as if content to see my mind at work, Dana lowered his eyes and tipped his teacup to peer inside. Then, in his slow and deliberate way, he lifted it to his mouth and swallowed what was left.

"Okay. I'm going to leave you for a bit and come back later this afternoon. I'll bring a few different books from the Great Hall for you to start paging through, which will hopefully spark an idea of where you'd like to start." He stood up and gently replaced the chair to the exact spot where he must have found it, and disappeared around the corner. I listened to him walk down the corridor, and almost jumped out of my seat with the sudden metal clang of the door slamming shut, which was followed by the subtle sounds of his testing the latch to make sure it was locked. A few moments later, I heard him clearing his throat as he walked down the trail away from the shelter. After that, I was alone.

I looked around the courtyard, knowing that I was expected to start thinking about things, but the truth was I didn't, I couldn't. My mind was a complete tangled clutter of everything I'd ever thought or felt in my life. Nothing, not even the slightest segment of my existence, was what I thought it had been. Memories, stories, sensations, lessons, explanations, everything leapt into my head at once, and I was suddenly forced to judge them with the greatest of scepticism. Which of them was a lie, which of them truth, and which of them fell somewhere into that grey area between? Was this what they had meant by veracity? Was this what I would have to do for the rest of my life, wade through the dense muck of a reality that was constantly reinventing itself, scouring the horizon for the only high ground that wasn't an apparition? I hoped not – because if that were the case, I was already lost.

My head dropped onto my arms, and I felt my eyes rolling around in the confusion of their sockets. Where was I going to begin? I knew that I would have to take every one of my notions, every belief, the very structure of everything I thought was true, and rebuild it all again board-by-board, nail-by-nail. What a daunting task, overwhelming even – especially as it seemed likely they wouldn't let me leave until I was finished.

I sat there until my eyes eventually slowed, and gave way to a blank stare that brimmed with tears. It didn't take me long to figure out that, even if I didn't want it, even if I was convinced the Elders were mistaken, I would still have to accept a little guidance from them. It was really the only chance I had.

8

"That's an interesting book to put into the selection."

I lifted my head from the pillow at the sound of Harek's voice wafting over the walls from outside the shelter. There was something curious in his tone, the words colder than they should have been, cutting almost. Another voice, which I would learn was Dana's, gave a muffled reply. I stood up from the bed, which was where I'd been laying for most of the afternoon, and walked out under the sky of the courtyard, hoping to hear something more. But I couldn't. And the reason for this wasn't only that the men had stepped closer to one another and lowered their voices, it was mostly because of the birds.

It's funny how appreciative of silence one can be while eavesdropping on a conversation that is towing the fine margin of earshot. I hadn't even noticed the birds before that, but they suddenly had all of my attention, chirping away inside one of the garden's trees. I would manage to catch one of the men's words, maybe two, and would strain my neck into the air, ear cocked to the clouds, hoping to catch the sense of what was being said, but the birds' racket seemed to be drowning out everything important.

Finally, clicking my tongue, I walked as close as I could to the tree and threw up my arms, hoping to scare them away. But instead of flying they became instantly and solemnly quiet, which, I thought, suited me just as well. Before turning around, I squatted to look through the thick leaves and saw a few of them hunched over, reverent, still – it seemed like it worked. So I turned my attention back to the conversation outside the walls, jotting around the courtyard to find the spot that had the best acoustics, and eventually found that standing on top of the table was as good as I could get. But the moment I stopped moving, the songbirds started up again, first twittering hesitantly, and then quickly gaining confidence, their volume swelling with each second.

"...Actually, I think you're being a bit..." I caught one of them saying, before his voice was obliterated by the chorus. I looked over at the tree and shook my head. Then stepped off the table, picked up a rock, and pitched it into the leaves as hard as I could. An explosion of tiny wings burst into the air and spiralled out of the courtyard. I watched them until they'd completely disappeared from view, as if they might deviously manoeuvre back into the garden again if I wasn't careful. But they were gone for good. I stepped back onto the table and twisted my neck to the sky to listen. I could tell right away that this conversation was going to be worth every effort I'd expended.

"...Well, no. I guess what I'm asking is, don't you think this might confuse things more than clarify them? I mean – he has enough on his plate as it is, without our introducing imaginative tidbits from obsolete cultures," said Harek.

"Hmm. Yes. Well, to be perfectly honest, I would have a hard time calling anything in this book a mere 'imaginative tidbit'," retorted Dana, doing a horrible job of masking his irritation.

A stiff pause followed before Harek said anything, and when he did, all of the melody in his voice had become flat. "Look. You've painted a few pictures in your time – some of them I even liked – but I'm really wondering if introducing this as a topic would be part of our collective mandate, or your personal one. I mean – what do you really see this book serving?"

Dana cleared his throat. "Okay, I'll give you my reasoning. I was wondering what might happen if, while simply walking among the ruins, they stumble upon a striking piece of art or architecture. If we just pretend that humanity has never done anything exceptional, how do you think they're going to react to such objects? Do you think they'll doubt the essence of the person that made it, or do you think they might doubt their education, which, in its complete one-sidedness, made no mention of such things? Now, just think of it, if that were to happen – and I think we can both agree that it's a very real possibility – it would throw a lot of other things into question as well, wouldn't it? And to me, it's obvious that such precarious questioning should be done under our close supervision, instead of in a place where we have no contact, and never will again. If there are any weak points in our outlook, Harek, I want to nip them in the bud right now, not wait around crossing our fingers, hoping they never surface. To me, bringing this book in is an attempt to be proactive, not – I assure you – out of a desire to complicate things."

There was a thoughtful hesitation. "Mm hmm. I see..." Harek finally murmured, and then broke off for a few seconds, sounding as if he were shuffling the soil at his feet with his sandals. "I really wish you'd brought this up in the last assembly. Then at least we could have some kind of consensus on it. It's just that... I'm not sure this is the kind of thing we should all be throwing our own individual twists into. Which is – let's be honest – exactly what you're doing."

"Yes, you're right; and I do realize that. And on account of it, if you don't agree with my idea of being proactive, I'd be happy to leave this book outside on the ground, and we can all talk about it during the next assembly at length, and..."

"No, no... no," Harek interrupted. I could picture him holding his hand up for a moment, his head turned to the side, "I... I think it's fine. Just make sure that it's done in a way that steers clear of idealizing any of the artists in there. I mean – most of them were tyrants, perverts, and criminals who just happened to paint in what little time they were sober. Make sure he knows that."

"Of course, of course," Dana reassured.

I could hear the awkward trundling of two sets of feet.

"Well... then – a good day to you."

"Good day."

Dana's footsteps entered through the open door of the shelter, while Harek's began walking away.

Thinking about it now, I don't really know why Harek was at the shelter that afternoon, though it's safe to assume that he was busy doing something, somewhere in one of the more secretive parts of the building that I was never allowed to see. I remember once, while working in the shelter's laboratory a few months after that day, I was left alone for a couple of minutes and snuck a quick look behind one of the many doors. It gave way to an impossibly long corridor, which burrowed deeper into the hillside until it diminished into blackness. I shut the door soundlessly, my hand pressing against its surface for a few seconds afterwards, as if it were about to burst open again. I understood then that I was living – and would always be living – strictly on a need-to-know basis, and if there was anything to do about this fact, it was learn to accept it. That was just the way it was.

I heard Dana unlatching the metal door to the corridor and fighting to open it. I scurried off the table to sit in one of the chairs, trying as hard as I could to look as if I'd been relaxing there the whole time. He came around the corner with a stack of books in his arms and smiled, then walked over to the table. As he reached out to put the pile down in front of me, his movements suddenly stopped, and he frowned with intense concentration at a few pieces of dirt on the tabletop. He gave me a glance. In response, the edges of my mouth rose into a suspicious grin. At that same moment, Harek stepped onto a twig somewhere along the trail, and the distant, yet clear snapping of it was enough to tell Dana everything.

He relaxed, smirked. "I see. So – did you manage to hear the whole discussion, or just part of it?" I was relieved that the tone of his voice wasn't an angry one; if anything, he sounded amused.

"Uh... only some of it. I think. I gathered that it was about a book of some kind?"

"Hmm..." his smirk grew, "I doubt very much that that's all you gathered." He finally set the books on the table and sat down. "I won't make the mistake of underestimating you, Joshua. You're a clever young man; and I know that because you were a clever child, always taking in more than we wanted you to, focusing in on exactly the things we were trying to avoid – continuously. And maybe it's even because of that that I wanted to get this out of the way, that I wanted to show you the one thing that you might consider a glitch in the machinery, a discrepancy. Because I have a feeling that, with you, if we don't deal with this at the outset, we'll be dealing with it every day afterwards.

"So then," he said, leaning forward and sliding the top book off the pile to reveal the one beneath. The book in question was titled An Illustrated History of Art, and had a man who'd been carved from white stone on the cover, staring serenely off to one side. I looked at it for a few seconds, searching for some deep implication, something that was dangerous, that would cunningly undermine everything that the Elders believed. But no matter how I looked at it, it was still just a naked man carved from stone. If there really was a profound controversy here, it eluded me. I slumped my shoulders before looking up at Dana. As strange as it was, he seemed a little disappointed with my disappointment. He looked down at the cover more intently than he had before, as if encouraging me to look again. "Go on," he entreated, suddenly waving his hand between us, gesturing for me to examine it more carefully, "take a look inside."

"Oh, sorry." I pulled the book toward me and opened it, releasing a surge of sweet, musty smells into the air. The book fell open with a painting on either page, both of which were by a man named Francisco de Goya. One of the paintings was a scattering of men that were either lying down and bleeding, or lined up against a wall looking like they were about to bleed; the other painting depicted two people buried in a field up to their knees, apparently clubbing each other to death, which was even more confusing. Let alone couldn't I imagine how any of this would go even slightly against the Elders' beliefs, I was having an even harder time thinking of ways I might 'idealize' the people who created them.

"You... didn't exactly pick the happiest paintings in the book," Dana began, almost sounding a touch offended, "but, really, they bring up the point I wanted to make just as well. Which is that art, in its many forms, has existed wherever humans have existed. You can think of it as a kind of voice, a tap into the bloodstream of a culture. It's been used in countless different ways throughout history (the paintings in front of you were a kind of protest, for example), but it's always come from the same sliver of the societal spectrum. It is almost always the voice of the liberals, the freethinkers, the tolerant.

"So, as I'm sure you can imagine, there are monuments, sculptures, music, poetry, literature, and paintings that are strewn about ruined buildings all over the world, and there will also be countless references to them when we start going through our species' history together. For that reason, I wanted you to know that art, and the hoards of references to it, are real. But more importantly, I wanted you to understand that, though some of the things created might be impressive, and their role might come across as important, at the end of the day, they were completely worthless.

"You see, there is this incredibly frustrating process that has occurred repetitively throughout history. It looks like this: A society forms, usually in the disastrous wake of another society that has just crumbled, and things begin anew. At first, the society seems to function quite well, even flourish, but soon corruption, the lust for power, and patent greed begin to choke out the 'weak'. As gaps begin to form between the people who are reaping the rewards, and the people who are just plain reaping, a quiet struggle arises. But, to no avail – the privileged ranks only continue to prosper while conditions worsen for everyone else. The tension begins to mount, and the social strain cumulates. Hoping to stop things from falling apart, the society decides they need a new leader. And of course, all of the would-be-leaders instinctively know that to come into power in even slightly strained conditions, it's to their advantage to exploit people's fear and greed, rather than their kindness and philanthropy. So, obviously, the wrong people gain control. (Though even if they weren't the wrong people, they quickly poison themselves with their own corruption, and become the wrong people anyway.) Then, the only thing left to do is make a few horrible decisions based on the same fear and greed that got them into power, and poof: war, disease, famine, genocide, or other calamities ensue, resulting in the society collapsing in on its own filth. The people who manage to crawl out of the ashes afterwards are the lucky ones that get to start the cycle all over again. And then again. And again. In fact, if one were to repeat this process continuously and span it over about 10,000 years, you would have a rough overview of the history of civilization.

"So then, there are some remarkable things that have been created out there; and those things were usually expressing the artists' take on where their society was inside of the cycle I just explained. So, accordingly, you'll find art representing all of the different stages: art from the flourishing periods of cultures, art remonstrating the disparity that starts to surface, and art monitoring the spiralling decay of it all. And as I said, it's always been the voice of that tiny population of liberals, people who wanted to communicate their insight to the masses. And what they were communicating was often warmly embraced, provided, of course, it didn't challenge the masses standing in any way. But when it did, at that exact moment when their perceptive message became crucial, when the demand for tolerance was needed, or a call to the fair-minded shifting of wealth, or the changing of corrupt systems before the society reached a critical point, at that precise instant, the impact that artists thought they'd had would vanish into thin air. Unfortunately, this is the way it is with human beings; the moment that truth is most needed is the moment that it's least wanted – the millisecond that it is essential to see, hear, and speak out, we become blind, deaf, and dumb.

"And so my fear is that you might see a building, a sculpture, painting, poem, something from one of those small windows of time when a culture was flourishing, and take this to mean that we had the potential to be enlightened, to be something better than we actually are. Obviously, my advice to you is: don't. Don't be misled. Tomorrow we'll begin to study our history, and as we delve into the mistakes of the world that once was, you may see some interesting or beautiful things, and that's perfectly fine. But if you find yourself secretly thinking of them as extraordinary or remarkable, I want you to bear in mind two things. One, that it certainly wasn't reflective of the masses, and two, if it was, it didn't last long.

"Because you must recognize that if anyone is in danger of mistaking some of the things we've done as 'progressive', it is people like you and me, people who were raised in an isolated environment, far removed from any kind of external difficulty or social strain, and by loving and supportive people. And I'm sure we wouldn't be the first, either. I'm sure that there were many times throughout history when people have been tempted to look around themselves and think of their world as one that was moving in the right direction. But I assure you, these people were unquestionably among the tiny percentage of the privileged ranks, and were happily (if ignorantly) wallowing in the wealth that stemmed from the oppression of others. It's a simple rule: the only human beings that have ever looked at their race and believed they were surrounded with promise, were seeing it that way simply because they could afford to."

Dana reached forward and moved the stack of books to the side so that the table between our bodies was clear except for the book of art. He sat up, interlocked his fingers, and placed them gently on the wood in front of him. "Flip it to another page," he insisted. I pinched a clump of the glossy sheets and turned to another section of the book. This time it opened to a painting of people sitting in sun-dappled shade, smiling, eating, drinking, chatting, a lake lined with trees and grass sprawling out behind them. Dana shifted in his seat, took in a deep breath. Within only a few seconds, he seemed to have become anxious, his lips a thin line, his jaw clenched tight. When he spoke, his voice was stifled, shaking. "So... if you're ever tempted to see hope, Joshua, you must believe, you must know that there is none. None. Can you understand that? None. The only answer that exists is complete regeneration, complete renewal – an all-encompassing rebirth. That's it. That is the only choice we have." He looked out into the garden, blinking quick blinks. "Now close that book." I nodded and quickly hinged it shut, sliding it away to the side.

We sat in silence for quite a while after that – me watching Dana, Dana watching the trees. It was strange. I didn't know what had upset him; in fact, I didn't know what any of these bizarre nuances and inferences meant, I only knew that they were suddenly trickling out of everything. They were in the pauses in the Elders' speeches, the selection of words in the dialogue between themselves, in the cold silences that followed, in the constricted saliva of their gritting teeth. It was obvious that, again, there were more things at play around me than what I was seeing, and that I couldn't really do anything about it. And not that I wanted to. If there were conflicts between the Elders, or even inside of them, it wasn't my concern. I certainly didn't need more levels of complexity to deal with, more things to try and figure out – I could barely keep up with what I was expected to.

Because there could be no mistake, this wasn't education, wasn't a simple imparting of knowledge from one person to another. No. No, it was a frantic dissection; it was the picking apart of mad concepts in search of something reasonable inside of them, and it was proving to be more work than I'd ever imagined. Nothing was cut and dried. Nothing could be gently taken from the table and put into my pocket to forget about. There was always more to consider, more to weigh, more to doubt. I bit my lip and tried to sum up Dana's main points while they were still fresh in my mind. He'd basically said: if you find something compelling, know that it didn't work; if you think you can spot a glimmer of hope amid the detritus, know that it's false; and if you ever wonder about there being a different solution for humanity, know that there isn't.

Great. Where should I have begun with this? How was I supposed to strip off the layers of these ideas without even knowing where they came from, or what the world looked like when they were formed? How could I ever expect to pluck out what was true, if anything, if everything?

But the answer was easy: I couldn't. It was hard enough scrutinizing my own beliefs, let alone breaking down someone else's.

I wanted something simple. I wanted something I could ingest without having it move around inside of me later. I looked over at the spines of the books and read some of the titles. Except for the art book, violence seemed an integral part of every one of them, which, I imagined, was probably the reason they'd picked them. Though, I didn't really mind; at least it would be interesting reading – and at least I wouldn't have to pause and question the basis of every single word that was inside them. Everyone knew that books only contained facts. And facts were exactly what I wanted.

"I notice you skimming the titles," Dana interjected, looking as if he'd just woken up. "They seem interesting, don't they? And they are – you'll see. I didn't only bring them in to help spark ideas of where you'd like to start, I also thought you should see some of the topics that we'll definitely be covering – just to get your mind moving in that general direction. Of course, for your Coming of Age we'll only touch on the surface of it all, but then we'll move into it in much more depth during the training."

"Training?" I asked.

"Yes. There's a reason that you are one of the few people we've chosen to tell about The Goal, and that is that we think you might potentially have the skills to lead one of the third phase expeditions. So the plan is to train everyone in that tiny group to do just that, and, during the course of the training, see which of you is best suited to take on the challenge. The same goes for the crew. After Coming of Age, whether people are told the truth or not, everyone's training starts to focus on specialized skills that might benefit a life-long expedition. That way, we'll be able to pick out a first-rate support team as well.

"But," Dana shook his head at himself, "we might be getting a bit ahead of ourselves here. So, let's stick to the task at hand." He stood up and sprawled the books out across the table in front of me, exposing their covers for the first time. Some of them had pictures of hairy men walking in small groups, hunched over, spears in hand, while others depicted costumed soldiers with metal shielding plastered all over their bodies, massive knives dangling from their hips. "We'll begin teaching you about the history of our kind; what we've done to each other, how, where, when. That way, at least you'll have a string of information to actually ask questions about and form your own process with. Does that sound like a reasonable way to continue?"

"Uh… sure."

"Brilliant," he said, nodding slowly and looking across the splay of books. "So, what I'd like you to do this evening is…" he bent over and hovered his pointer finger above a few of the titles before letting it drop onto one. It was called The Evolution of Weapons – The Neolithic Period, "…flip through this. Why not start at the very beginning.

"So then – tomorrow we'll go through some of the main points together, and discuss things along the way. Sound good?"

"Sure."

"Good." He turned to leave, but then stalled in mid-stride, "Actually, something interesting that you might want to look for in that book tonight: The oldest mummified human ever found lived during that era. And when his remains were discovered (almost perfectly preserved in ice), archaeologists from around the globe gathered to learn what they could about our earliest behaviour. Guess what they found?"

"What?"

"An arrowhead in his back." He grinned before turning away, "I'll see you tomorrow."

9

I'd always thought of the Elders as people who had set limits for themselves and then, in some kind of superhuman way, managed to keep inside them. And because they'd always acted with this amazing degree of restraint and self-control, I was somehow sure that I'd never see them step anywhere close to their limits, never see them press up against one of the boundaries that they'd firmly engraved in the stone of their conduct. But I was wrong.

They would begin by asking a vague question, sitting with their hands gently folded in their laps, an encouraging grin dressing their faces. They would casually invite my opinion into the conversation, coaxing it out into the open. After all, they would assure me, this was simply an open discussion where any point of view was welcome, where there were no right or wrong answers; I was free to say whatever I wanted, whatever I believed. So please, they would whisper, raising their eyebrows expectantly, go ahead — tell us what you think. And then they would grow silent, transfer their weight from one side of the chair to the other, refolding their hands in their laps. Waiting.

After speaking my mind the first couple of times, I soon found out that, in fact, there were right and wrong answers, and the Elders certainly made me want to learn which was which, and quickly. Because it was when I gave them the wrong answers that I discovered how close they were to their limits. Their reactions seemed to fall just scarcely on this side of control, as if the skin of their patience had become taut, as if it were quavering with pressure beneath the surface and right on the verge of rupturing.

I would say what I thought, and they would exchange a sharp glance before letting their eyes drop to the ground in front of them, their expressions disappointed, burdensome. Then one of them would wipe his forehead, slowly pull his weight forward, his fingers gripping the arms of the chair, and stand up. While he walked over to select the relevant book, which he would then use to make his point in the clearest, most concise, and irrefutable way, he was either biting one of his lips, or tapping a stiff finger on his chin. When he found the right volume, he would slide it into the middle of the table, creak open the cover, glide a slow and heavy finger down the table of contents, and, once he'd found what he was looking for, raise his eyes to meet mine. Yes, he might sympathize, he could see how I was able to come up with an idea like that, but what the medieval period consistently taught us, unfortunately, is quite the contrary. He would start to flip to the chapter he wanted, his hand tossing the sheets onto one side of the book with aggressive, jerking movements, his eyes focused wildly on the increasing page numbers. And once he reached the chapter, he would run a rigid palm along the crease, slowly rotate the book until it was oriented for me to read, slide it under my nose, and then lean in until I could feel his breath on my face. But, he would say softly, maybe we haven't read enough about the medieval customs for you to have known that. Let's take another look, shall we?

And so it continued, endlessly, day after day after day. They drew on examples, cases, models, paradigms, and historical references that proved, beyond any shadow of doubt, the complete malevolence of the human condition. And if I thought I could see an inconsistency somewhere, they had seen it months before, and would point it out before I even had the chance to, brusquely explaining how it wasn't an inconsistency at all, and then backing that claim up at length. They had thought of every angle, every hole, every weakness, and were completely prepared to patch them over with better arguments, impenetrable reasoning, and – to be honest with myself – entirely superior intellect. They were organized, resourceful, deliberate, and systematic. I was outmatched in every way.

I started to feel deadened, torn down, worn out. I would sit for hours at a time, listening to their every dismal word, feeling fetid, ashamed of my race, ashamed of the history I'd never even known existed. And the worst part of it was that I couldn't shut them out, couldn't even retreat into my own mind, as the image of the people in my thoughts, even the core of my memories, weren't reliable anymore. The fibre of my past, present, and future had become too gauzy to hide behind; there were no folds to escape into, no familiar ground to run across; nothing was the same. And really, if I thought about it, nor was I – my role in life had completely changed. And this was a strange realization to come to: I could only exist as someone else after this was finished, couldn't live as the same person ever again. Because the purpose of my existence, the sense of my being had twisted into a completely new shape without my say, and it was obvious that I couldn't bend it back. What was I going to do? Who was I going to be? But mostly, did I really have a choice in the matter?

I spent a haunted and sleepless night thinking this over, tossing in bed, a handful of hair in my fist. In the end, as far as I could figure out, there were only two options: either contort myself to fit into their mould as far as my beliefs would allow, or dismiss them as lunatics and live the rest of my life with them, further constrained, and having to drift aimlessly through an empty reality. Not exactly a hard decision.

And like Dana said, was it really so horrible, were they really asking so much – wander around new places that were rejuvenating themselves, live from the landscapes that I'd only seen pictured in books, traverse hills, mountains, forests, rocky shorelines, all while deepening lifelong friendships? The Elders seemed pretty doubtful that any of these expeditions would ever come across people, so it wasn't as if we would have any blood on our hands. And even if we did find somebody there wouldn't be any blood, it was simply a matter of slipping them something in their food and moving on. It seemed clean, unassuming, easy.

Once, the thought crossed my mind that I wouldn't even have to follow through with what the Elders instructed me to do. But that idea quickly faded away. I knew all too well that they would see the slightest inkling of doubt from miles away. In fact, it was the only thing they were looking for. If I promised one thing while intending another, I'd be caught – plain and simple. And I knew it. They would sense a concealed plan as vividly as they'd seen what we'd done to a lizard in our childhood. Because it wasn't a matter of knowing specifics, it was only a matter of sensing a flicker of hesitation at the right moment; and they'd probably already planned that moment – a barrage of quick and exposing questions up their sleeve, being saved until I was so exhausted, my guard lowered into a drained apathy, that I would tell them anything. No. If I had a plan to circumvent them, they had a plan to see through it like water.

So the solution was easy: if the only way for me to get off the island was to be the leader of the expedition, and the only way to be selected as that leader was to believe in The Goal, then I would have to choose to believe in it, and trust that what the Elders were doing was right. And as crazy as that rationale sounds to me now, it really was that simple. And maybe it's always this simple – for all of us. We select our beliefs from the world around us, stitch them together into a tapestry of common threads, carefully ignore the contradictions, and then boldly stand behind them, ready to be led.

The next day, they commented that my attitude appeared to have changed overnight, that I was more attentive, eager, more interested in what was being discussed. They were ecstatic (or at least as ecstatic as the Elders ever got about anything), and I caught them exchanging a few encouraging grins throughout the day. Of course, I'd prepared myself for an internal battle before the day began, thinking that I would be straining to agree with them on every issue, that I would have to compromise my deepest philosophies at every turn, but I found that this wasn't the case. Their points were concrete, well founded, well thought out. In fact, the most challenging thing about them was their truth, or rather, how much that truth grated against my instincts.

Sometimes, as a matter of making a strong point even stronger, we would stop to pick apart some of humanity's ugliness; and to do this, we would use ourselves as an example, maybe recalling times that we'd abused what little leverage we had over our 'loved ones', and inflicted a bit of 'socially acceptable' damage, savouring the taste of our petty cruelty afterwards, smirking to ourselves with our backs turned. I would shake my head, amazed at the reality of it. They were right. We all really did these things – which sparked an obvious question: if we did this to each other everyday, motiveless, and living under ideal conditions, what kinds of things would we (the very people around us, the very people we thought of as mild and benign) do to each other if the vice of our culture were tightened a bit? And of course, if I happened to wonder these things aloud, the Elders would have an explicit answer ready for me. Well, they would say, reaching across for another book of graphic pictures – pictures of emaciated corpses piled so high they needed giant shovelling machines just to move them – let us show you what happens.

Slowly, gradually, over the course of the days that passed, I started to understand, in a very odd way, what they were trying to do. In the biggest possible picture, this wasn't really a horrific act; true, it was extreme and controversial, but it was also the most logical way to counter our wrongs, our conduct, our very nature. It was about accepting a responsibility that reached out so far beyond what was seen as realistic or attainable, that it dipped into a region that appeared fanatical. Yet anyone could admit that the incentive behind it all, the drive that fuelled these people to take action, was something to be admired. They were only doing what they thought was right. And really, once I figured this out, the rest was easy.

I suddenly wanted to learn from them. I wanted to learn about our fumbling mistakes, our cyclic tragedies, our foibles, blunders, the enterprises that always ended in catastrophe. And after that, I wanted to learn about the third phase, about the area our island's expedition would be searching through, about who had lived there, what kind of damage they'd caused, who their traditional scapegoat was. I wanted to become an involved pupil again, to absorb their knowledge like a sponge, to finger their wisdom like a greedy child. I wanted them to teach me about the world.

The Elders saw these changes taking place in me, and accordingly, their questions became more tame, their answers less sharp. They were slowly reverting into their gentle selves again, letting their kindness resurface. And for the first time in my life, I noticed their mannerisms becoming less formal; they seemed at ease, calmed, as if they were happy to have another person they could speak openly in front of. Every day that passed found us talking to each other more like friends: for my part, feeling comfortable asking things that were really on my mind, and for their part, answering my questions with a kind of relaxed candidness, a complete and serene honesty. It was wonderful. Finally, I felt like I was almost part of their circle. Almost.

I discovered that there were still issues that made them stiffen a bit, made them clear their throat and think very carefully about their wording before they spoke. And, understandably, these were usually the issues that had details or implications that were hard for me to accept as well.

"Harek," I began one day, putting down my fork during our midday meal at the shelter, "I was wondering about something." Harek, who had already finished eating and was peeling some fruit for dessert, looked up and gestured for me to continue. "It's just that, we're always speaking about men when we talk about the phases of The Goal. What about women? What role do they play? I mean – why is it they're never even mentioned as an option for going on the expedition?"

He sat up a bit, put the fruit and knife onto his plate for later, and then proceeded to lick his fingers for a long, thoughtful while before speaking. "Women aren't as well-suited to deal with… different aspects of The Goal on the 'front lines', so to speak. Their role will be to help in the training here on the island instead."

I cocked my head. As far as I could remember, the Elders had always taught us that the sexes were completely equal. What did he mean exactly by 'well-suited'? I needed a little clarification on that. "I'm sorry, I didn't quite understand. Do you mean that women couldn't do something that might be needed, or shouldn't, or wouldn't, or…?"

"Okay. I can see you're not going to leave me alone with this," he said, sounding a little terse. He moved his chair back enough so he could lean forward and talk with his hands, "It has to do with the very organization of our brains. See, as you well know, we have two hemispheres in our brain. Very, very simplistically speaking, one is responsible for logical thought, strategy, and spatial tasks, and the other for language, emotion, and the expression thereof. As any one task could involve things from both sides of the brain, there is an organ devoted solely to the communication between the two hemispheres. That organ is called the corpus callosum, and if one were to compare it between the sexes, they would find that it's much more developed in women than it is in men. What this means is that women make decisions that are more holistic, automatically taking into consideration things like the value of life and the potential of suffering, blended with technical stratagems, which may or may not be compromised by the input of the emotional hemisphere. Whereas a male, who has the limitation of thinking patterns that are more localized in the brain, would find it easier to separate his emotions from a possible outcome to his actions. For example, if you asked both a male and a female soldier to go and kill everyone in a house, in order to gain a tactical position for an army, the woman soldier, seeing the action in both a logical and emotional way, would, most probably, be more reluctant to do it. Whereas a man on the other hand, would be more inclined to plod into the house and act on his orders, separating the cause from the effect.

"Now, there was, and there may still be, situations that arise which might need... that sort of definitive action inside of... questionable circumstances." Harek's eyes, which had been focused on the fruit in his plate for this last sentence, drifted up to meet mine, his hands frozen in the air between us, his expression tentative. I could see he was hoping with all of his might that I wouldn't ask him to expand any more than I had. "Does that make any sense?"

"Yeah... I think so," I answered. His body relaxed, relieved.

What he meant by 'questionable circumstances' was that, were the situation to arise, I would be expected to do 'whatever it took' to ensure that The Goal succeeded, including all of the things that women would have a harder time doing than men. Like killing people. Or maybe inflicting pain on someone in order to find out where others were hidden. Who knew?

I watched Harek eat the rest of his fruit, and thought this over. Things were getting a bit trickier to agree with. But even more intimidating than that, it was becoming increasingly clear that, if I were going to be the leader of this expedition, I wouldn't only need to agree with these things, I would have to be as fanatical as the Elders about them. I would have to train my eyes to see the track of a person as a direct link to the long, drawn out destruction of the planet, and then I would have to hunt that person down, barely able to sleep, until I was sure they were sterile. The Goal would necessitate my feeling this strongly about it, that much was clear. Yet, the fact remained that I doubted I had it in me to be fanatical about anything, to be entirely consumed by a belief, to have it eat away at me, night after seething night. How does anyone feel that strongly about something? I wasn't sure. But I was sure that, whatever those people had, I did not.

And this was the strangest part of it all: I saw it coming from the beginning. I understood perfectly well that I wasn't the right person to lead one of these expeditions, that I didn't have what it might take. Yet I still tried as hard as I could to be the one that was chosen, to be the 'winner'; still churned over everything that they said in my mind until it settled obediently into place, until it stopped squirming inside of my conscience. And it's funny to think that I did this all without ever considering any problems that might come up in the future, were I to become this 'unfit leader'. I convinced myself somehow that getting off the island would be the hardest part, and that the rest would all fall smoothly into place.

The discussions in the shelter continued, and over the days I saw their reactions – as restrained as they were – become more and more satisfied with my responses. They could see the seed of conviction germinating under my skin, the delicate tendrils of its budding root system fanning out into my blood, taking hold, until finally, they started talking about letting me back into the community again, where I would begin my training.

On my last evening of Coming of Age, Dana came in to give me a lecture, which was 'of the gravest and most critical importance'. He emphasized, with an overstrung urgency, that under no circumstances would I ever be justified in talking about The Goal inside the community; to anyone; ever. It was essential to understand that only behind sealed and soundproofed doors was it ever safe to talk openly about anything that had been said during my stay. He underlined the fact that only those elite few, who – it was hoped – could override their instinctual impulses for a greater cause, were to be trusted with the information that was shared. I was surprised to find out that, apparently, there were even some Elders whose knowledge about the different phases and what went on in them was limited. And because of this, if even unsupported gossip of The Goal were to leak out into the general community, the consequences would be disastrous. There would almost certainly be a rebellion; in fact, he said, lowering his voice to a solemn murmur, in many respects, when I left the shelter, I would be carrying with me nothing less that the responsibility of the entire island's well-being, the very welfare of every person that I was close to. Did I understand this, he asked (and to help accentuate the word 'understand', he pounded his fist on the table with each syllable: UN-DER-STAND?).

Yes, I promised, of course I understood. Of course.

Early the next day, they let me go.

10

When I was released, I was told that after the midday meal I was scheduled for a normal afternoon of chores and schooling, but that my morning was free.

Free. It was a strange sensation standing on the other side of the shelter's door again, listening to a few of the Elders' footsteps recede into one of the hidden branches of the building behind me. There I was, left alone, completely unrestricted. It was almost hard to fathom – I had time at my very own disposal to do, think, and say whatever I wanted, wherever I wanted. It's interesting, I don't think we ever weigh out our freedom until it's suppressed, never question it until someone questions it for us. I smiled, drew a long breath into my lungs, my arms hanging limp at my sides, face pointed at the sky, and just stood there for a moment, feeling blessed. After that, I walked down the path from the shelter and linked up with the main trail system, and then headed toward the peninsula. On my way, I met Siri, the youngest girl on the island.

"Oh. You're back," she said, matter-of-factly. The moment she'd stopped, she starting playing with the end of her hair.

"Yup."

"Huh." She looked over her shoulder, then back at me, "Well. See you later." And she shuffled by, continuing on her way.

I watched her walk down the trail, recounting the few words we'd exchanged, and was completely struck by them. Normally, I wouldn't have noticed, but as it were, I was seeing the world through fresh eyes. She hadn't asked me a single thing; not where I'd been or how I was – nothing. And whereas I would have taken this for granted before, even seen it as normal, suddenly, it perfectly represented the depth of the plot I was entwined in. This was all part of the method, the precise management of the lie. Siri was young enough to be missing one of her front teeth, but already old enough to know that questions shouldn't be asked unless they're prompted. I looked around, feeling as if the walls of my world were unpeeling, as if I were uncovering the apex of a monolith realization, from which the naked air fell away from me on every side. I carried on down the trail with the need to sit and think.

The peninsula was one of my favourite places on the island. As I stepped out from under the shade of the palms and into the open sunshine along the water, crustaceans scattered into hiding and a seabird, its wings sleek and pointed, sprung off the rocks and flew away. Waves crashed onto the basalt, and then subsided, tiny air bubbles clinging to the surface for a few seconds before disappearing into the shining black skin of the rock.

I soon found a warm boulder to sit on, and tried to slow my mind down so that I could take on one thing at a time. But this was proving difficult. It all seemed to be opening up in front of me at once, one thing leading to the next, a domino effect of implications chattering into the distance. I'd never really sat down to objectively probe some of the things that we did on the island, some of our customs, our practices. And maybe it was this way in every culture; maybe no one stopped to question their own traditions, always working on the grand assumption that their ways were the 'right' ways, that they represented a kind of gauge, an accuracy of which to judge the misguidedness of others. But meeting Siri on the trail had sparked me to re-evaluate a few things – like our Incision.

Never once in my life did I stop to think about the function of such an operation. It was just something that everyone went through, no questions asked. Yet if I'd taken even a minute to look at it in a different light, the answer would have been obvious. And of course we would have to be sterile! It would defeat the purpose if we were sent out to wander the world in search of people to sterilize while being fertile ourselves. But it wasn't that which was disturbing; it was the control of it, the complete manipulation of everything sexual in our lives. We'd been carefully kept from all sorts of knowledge – and as a result, I didn't know a single thing about human offspring. What did a pregnant woman look like? How long was she pregnant for? And what about the relationship between her and her mate? Was there even one? Did that happen with people? I couldn't know. I'd certainly never seen anything like it on the island, which, I realized, was also on purpose. It suddenly all fell into place: There were no babies because, once they had enough children to supply a reasonably diverse 'pool' of which to choose from for the expedition, all of the Elders were sterilized. And the Elders that did have children could never be a parent, as we had seen taking place in the animal world, only because they were afraid of dangerously tight bonds forming. Instead, we were raised by a collective group of people, any of which could be our actual parents, but whom exactly, we could never know. Though, the thought also crossed my mind that, maybe it was so strictly controlled that the parents were sent away, banished because of what they might do. Or maybe it was the children who were moved, shipped from one safe haven to another, a swap between islands and continents that would ensure that ties wouldn't be too close.

And all of this, every last detail, had to be planned, carried out, and then the lie or misguiding truths constantly upheld and maintained. What devious manipulation! And it struck me that this was exactly what the Elders had meant in saying that we couldn't trust ourselves to make decisions, couldn't put any faith in our instincts. They were excusing their actions, absolving themselves from meddling with our nature, from detaching every one of us from our biological impulses. Yet, as unfair as all of this seemed to me at first, I was already trained enough to wonder if the Elders were, in fact, justified in some way in going about it the way they had.

I was already getting a handle on how their minds worked. Their reasoning would have been something like this: as they could prove that our nature was completely malevolent and distrustful, that it was essentially amiss, then whatever was contrary to that nature, would stand a very good chance of being 'on track'. (Was this also starting to make some kind of bizarre sense to me as well?) Could we, in a way, be certain that we were walking the best path with our species because it was the very path that appeared to us as counterintuitive? Couldn't we use our nature as a type of inverted guide? Why not? I mean – it wasn't as if this was a foreign concept, considering the fact that we apply the same logic to our lives on a small scale every day. After all, that was morality perfectly defined in a nutshell: the act of restraining ourselves from doing what we're naturally inclined to do, because, if there is one thing that we've learned from our impulsive blunders, it is that when we do exactly what we are impelled to do, it ends up being detrimental to our world. They had only taken this idea, which we all subscribe to, and pushed it one bold step further.

So, in many respects, yes, the more I thought of it, the more I saw they were sensible in keeping so many things from us. If they had given us the details, we would have only gotten absorbed in them, lost sight as to why they were kept from us in the first place, and then we would have lashed out because we wanted more. In fact, if I looked at it in a certain way, the most remarkable thing wasn't the depth of which we were kept in the dark, but rather the degree of which I was so maddened by it. What was there to be angry about, really? We all know how accomplished we are at quarantining ourselves from the whole story in order to avoid grief, so why should we be so offended when others do the same thing for us? And this was true; they weren't only being cautious with information for the island's safety (or, for that matter, the world's) it was also simply being done for our own good. And it was important for me to finally understand this.

I flinched a bit as a small stone bounced onto the slab of rock in front of me and landed in the water. When I turned around to see who'd thrown it, I was surprised to see Kara standing in the shade, already hunkering down into the underbrush to avoid being seen.

Within the younger generation, the code of conduct to be adhered to when someone threw a rock and crouched down into the bushes, was to check if the coast was clear and, without hesitation, walk over to crouch with them, quickly exchanging some clandestine information before heading off again. But hesitate I did. I wasn't sure how I felt about speaking with Kara at that given moment. It had been a while since we were able to sneak off and have one of our conversations, and I hadn't exactly had the will or energy to rehearse a clever follow-up to it. And whereas before, such rehearsal seemed useful to me, I knew that now, it was essential. I would need to weigh out and filter every last word before letting it pass through my lips, because, rest assured, as I spoke, she would be trying to pierce through the veil that shrouded what wasn't being said, listening for patterns in the things that were avoided, and then slyly chasing after them. So, as I stood up and walked into the trees (as casually as I could, in case someone was watching) it was nervousness that I felt more than anything else.

I was attracted to Kara. She had these intense eyes that were always fixed on the person she was talking to, and they'd lowered with me as I crouched down into the shrubs, surveying my movements. Her hair was dark brown, almost black, and was just long enough to hang lazily beside her neck, the very ends of it waving out in different directions. Her skin looked to be incredibly smooth to me, and I'd always wanted so badly to reach out and touch it, which, considering what I'd just been thinking about, would probably only have led to something disastrous.

"I just bumped into Siri," Kara began. "She told me that you were out, and that you were walking toward the peninsula. So I thought I'd come and see – you know – how you are."

"Oh."

She smiled with a bit of impatience, probably knowing that we would only have a fifteen-minute window to speak with each other and wanting to get right to the point of things, which, in all fairness, was the nature of all of our dialogues. "So…" she leaned in, unable to wait any longer, "tell me – how are you?" Of course, what she really meant by this was: Tell me about where you went, what happened, what Coming of Age is all about – tell me what the big secret is.

But I couldn't. I really, truly couldn't. I was just beginning to appreciate the long list of deep-seated reasons why I should keep quiet. In fact, I realized, looking over both of my shoulders, it was crazy to even be sitting with her without having prepared for it first. I wasn't ready for this. She intimidated me.

I tried to squirm out of it as best I could. "To be really honest with you, I've been told explicitly not to talk with anyone except the Elders about quite a few things. So… I mean – I'm sorry for not being able to say anything, but… it has to do with the safety of the island."

"What?" She pulled her head back, as if in disgust, "Wait, wait, wait. You go away for about a week and you come back sounding exactly like them? Is that how it works? No. I don't get it. So I'm afraid you'll have to explain yourself a bit. Why? Why can't you talk about it with me?"

"Safety."

"Oh…" she nodded her head mockingly, "of course – safety. So… if you were to utter just a few honest words, what random, 'dangerous' thing might happen? Would the waves rise up and drag us both out to sea?"

"Come on."

"No? Hmm." She made herself look as if she were playing a guessing game, squinting at the leaves above us, a contemplative finger tapping on her lips. Then her eyes lit up with a probable answer, her finger pointing into the air, "Ah ha! Or maybe…" she paused, leaning in again, her expression growing serious, "maybe the people of the island would rise up, and drag everyone who knew the secret out to sea. What do you think?"

I wanted to give some quick-witted retort to this, but nothing came out – just a bit of anxious breath. This was exactly the reason I didn't want to talk to Kara; she was a little too sharp. The Elders and I had gone over exactly what I was to say to people who were wondering about specifics, but none of those fixed phrases would have worked with her. She would have only asked a few quick questions to get around them, questions that sounded like they were just on the fringe of safe enough to answer, and then plucked out the few clues and hints that were worth keeping, and sketched the gaps in between. (It occurred to me at that point that Kara would probably make a great Elder one day.) In the end, I decided to just keep my mouth shut until she spoke again, which took a few discomfiting moments.

"Okay, okay – don't worry about it," she said, dismissively, and looked away. "I mean – if you really can't talk about it, I'll have to respect that." I watched her suspiciously. "But… there is one thing that I want you to tell me; and I'm sure you'd be allowed to, because everyone that Comes of Age says the same thing word for word. I guess I just want to know if what they say is really true – the rumours I mean." She gestured out toward the horizon, "Were there really a lot of people out there once?"

I thought this over carefully. She was right that I was allowed to say it, and I couldn't see the harm in letting her know that it was actually a fact, as the pretence for the expedition would involve everyone knowing it anyway. "Yeah. There were people out there. There were cultures and communities all over the world. But they're gone now."

For some reason, Kara acted like I'd thrown a weight onto her back with this. It seemed that, even though she'd heard the story re-circulated countless times, she'd always taken it as a kind of impossibility. But it wasn't; and that fact seemed to be settling onto her for the first time. "How…? I mean – what happened to them all?"

I scratched my chin. Things were getting a bit more delicate. I'd been afraid that the answering of one question was only going to lead to the asking of another. I wondered what the best way to go about this was. If I told her anything, it would have to be evasive, yet conclusive, it would have to be something she couldn't really follow up on with a series of new and awkward questions. I worded and reworded a few wily statements in my head, but realized that, in the end, she would see through it all anyway. No, if I was going to give her an answer – and I wanted to give her an answer – there would have to be some element of truth to it. So, I finally decided to offer a very blanketed and vague piece of truth that she'd probably already come up with on her own. What could be dangerous in that?

I sighed before I began. "Well, as I'm sure you've witnessed yourself, we're beings with a fairly self-destructive nature. I guess it was only a matter of time before something happened on a global scale. And it did."

She turned to face the waves, shaking her head. "Wow," she said, and fell into a thoughtful silence, scanning the blue of the water, the crashing waves, the foam that those waves shot into the air, the few bubbles that bounced onto the dry rock, the dark circles of moisture they left behind. Her expression was constantly changing, her face lighting up with a painful grin for a moment, then an anxious glare, a distracted frown.

After a while, she started speaking out at the ocean, quietly. "You know… sometimes, if I really listen hard, it's like there're voices out there, under the waves. Not normal voices; more like a low moan, a murmur. Anyway, I was just thinking that, maybe that's where they come from; from all those people that died, from all the horrible and beautiful things they did to each other. Because that's what it sounds like. There's this deep sadness in it, a kind of relentless suffering, but also something that seems to say: Everything's okay. Everything's – I don't know – healing."

I sat there, dumbfounded. This was Kara; this was her world, a reality where, no matter how hard I tried to keep up, I always felt left behind, deficient.

"Can you hear anything in them?" she asked, turning to me and catching me gawking at her.

"Uh… no. I can't."

But I didn't need to hear them to recognize the wisdom in what she'd said. Without knowing a single thing about The Goal, she'd both explained, and justified it in a few brief sentences better than the Elders had done in a over a week of drawn out discussions. She was exactly right. There had been an enormous amount of suffering, of unnecessary pain, yet now, finally, it had stopped, and the earth was recovering from it, slowly mending what we'd destroyed.

Something unexpected happened that day. It was true that I hated the way the Elders had gone about things, the way we were all being funnelled toward a decided end. It was true that the lie they'd constructed and maintained was unfair to us, oppressive, even cruel. But none of that – absolutely none of it – meant that they were mistaken about our species. All of their rules, secrets, strategies, and actions weren't a measure of how misled they were, it was a measure of how desperate they were, of how far they'd been driven to do what was right with a creature that was wrong. It all clicked into place. After listening to Kara, if there were any doubts in my mind, if there was any part of me that was still wavering, still holding off, waiting to make a definitive choice, it was suddenly gone. Something inside of me caved in looking at those waves, trying to hear the same voices that she was hearing, ones that spoke of the great consequence of our collective actions, yet also of the chance to start things anew.

Yes. I had finally been pushed over the edge. I believed. I'd become a believer.

Which, incidentally, was exactly what Mikkel thought I would be – and was busily preparing himself to deal with.

11

The manner in which the Elders talked about the expedition, the way it was unquestionable, imminent, and the way it was taken for granted that everything would go wonderfully, all helped to engrain the idea of becoming the leader in my mind. But as much as I wanted to be chosen, I never really thought of it as an exceptional opportunity, rather, it was just a better alternative than staying on the island under ever-stricter control. However, when they brought me into the disclosed wing of the Great Hall and showed me some of the things that I'd be delving into throughout my training, that all changed. Every map that they unrolled across the table, every sea chart they held up against a wall, every atlas they rotated to face me, all began to open my eyes to something I hadn't seen before: the magnificence of adventure itself.

It struck me, except for our island, I'd never visited, known, traversed, explored, or touched any of the vast globe of possibilities that existed. But the expedition would do this. We would be seeing the unseen! There would be something to learn with every mile travelled, in the same way that we'd learned as children – touching things for the first time, turning them over in our hands, fascinated – there would be a new lesson under every leaf and around every corner, something fresh to our senses, some event we'd never before experienced. And as soon as I realized this, something else deep inside of me amended itself, and the thought of setting sail out across the ocean had become something unbelievably intoxicating.

I would put my hands down on either side of the atlases and lean overtop of them, arms straight, eyes scanning the terrain like a hungry frigate bird. There were waves of sand that must have spread out like the limitless ocean, forests that belted across the belly of the largest landmasses, freshwater lakes that one could sail in for days without seeing a shore, jungles, grasslands, tundra, and strangest of all, ice, endless sheets of ice that were kilometres thick, swathing whole continents! And mountains, folds and ripples of the earth's crust that had been heaved into the air so high that the temperatures plummeted, and something called snow (which, incidentally, looked exactly the same as ice on the maps, so I'm not sure why they insisted on calling it something different) stuck to the peaks like saliva to teeth.

And this was only the land. One of the first things that I'd realized while being lectured and taught about the different periods of our atrocious history was that, besides the sameness of the violence, oppression, cruelty, etc., the various cultures of the world had been quite distinct from one another. They spoke different languages, ate different foods, believed in different gods, and built different styled dwellings; and this would be yet another thing the expedition would learn about, simply by walking through and inspecting the ruins. I would flop into the chair behind me, my mind teeming with new questions, and the enticing thought of answering every one of them in our travels; and in the meantime, I decided to set out and gather as much groundwork as I possibly could.

I was a model student, and seemed to become more devoted with every new thing that they taught me. As time passed, and my opinions began to match theirs more acceptably, more naturally, new doors opened for me, as we were finally free to move away from the slow ideological subjects, and into topics that I was more enthusiastic about.

Though, admittedly, the Elders hadn't really set out to spark my imagination, nor had they intended on spending any great amount of time teaching me about the landscapes in different corners of the world, or about the cultures that once existed there, which, of course, was what I was most curious about. No. What the training was intended to do was solidify my understanding of the maleficence of our species, and then begin building the skills and knowledgebase that I would need to run the expedition should I be chosen. The interesting things were only a spin-off from the requisites, and they tried to make sure I wasn't too distracted by them.

They gave me a lot of information to go through, study, and then discuss, and after I was caught once, pouring over maps and encyclopaedias instead of reading the material they'd given me, they took their role of 'keeping my interests focused' quite seriously. They would often walk in to check that I was learning the right material, and sometimes even sit down with me and ask me to summarize what I'd just read. But I didn't find this frustrating; because they weren't really keeping me from my interests, they were only forcing me to be more creative in researching them. And I soon discovered that I could pick up obscure, and often even forbidden facts from almost anything they gave me. I spent a lot of my time reading between the lines of the history books, uncovering all sorts of answers to outstanding questions. For instance, I'd learned from reading about kings and queens that, in fact, men and women did have long-lasting relationships and often even lived together, that our gestation period was nine months, and that our offspring seemed to be decidedly adept at killing one another off to vie for 'crowns' and 'thrones'.

But among this swamp of both revealing and interesting information, sometimes I was given material to study, which, regardless of how hard I looked, didn't seem to have anything hidden beneath the surface. When this happened, it was just a matter of bowing my head, reading it, and memorizing points to talk about later. Of all the Elders, Chalmon – who was a stocky man with a pale complexion and strange, pitted features on his cheeks – was the one who seemed most determined to give me these boring topics to study. Sometimes he would come to visit me while I was wading through volumes of his tedious selections, and ask me about what I was reading as if he were genuinely interested, the tone of his voice rising enthusiastically at the end of every sentence. I would reply in the dreariest monotone I could muster, but he never seemed to get the hint. However, little did I know that, one day, it would be his dull subject matter that would lead me to stumble upon the most dangerous thing that existed in the disclosed wing; and it certainly wasn't censored facts or volatile information that was buried inside one of his books, but rather a tiny wafer of metal that I discovered, and only because the book was so boring.

Veracity

I was on the third or fourth day of suffering through chemical theory – which, I was assured, would be an essential basis for learning how to create sterilization mixtures later on – when I'd finally had enough. I slid my chair back (as silently as I could, so as not to trigger any of the Elders to come and check on what I was doing), and folded my arms across my chest, sprawling my legs out lazily in front of me. I was nauseated with chemistry, and began to look around the room for something to distract me, anything, maybe another book, which would have to be thin enough to hide under the one in front of me, should the need arise. I scanned the few shelves of books on my right. Nothing. But as I moved my inspection from one side of the room to the other, something caught my eye. It was on the floor in front of my feet, directly underneath the table, and I was sitting at just the right angle for the light, which was coming from a window opposite me, to reveal it as plain as day. It was a handprint.

Odd. Why exactly would there be a handprint directly underneath of a large table in the disclosed wing of the Great Hall, one might ask? I couldn't begin to guess. I tried to remember a time that I'd ever seen an Elder crawling along the ground, let alone on a library floor, but couldn't bring one to mind. I squinted at it again and could see that it wasn't a negative imprint, but a positive one, meaning: it wasn't a handprint missing out of a film of dust, but a handprint of natural oils left behind on a spotless floor. And this lead me to wonder just how moist a hand would have to be to leave such an accurate profile behind. I ventured to guess quite moist, as if the person who was crawling under the table were nervous. I smiled. Finally, something interesting.

First, I listened for any movement in the next room. None. Then, I memorized where the handprint was on the floor, stepped out of my chair, walked around to the side of the table, and knelt down. I put my hand exactly on top of the print, ducked under the table, and there it was, right in front of my face.

A lip of wood followed the perimeter of the table and was grooved deeply enough to hide small objects on, and, realizing

95

this, the person who'd left behind the handprint, had also left behind a tiny piece of metal. I reached out and plucked it from its place. It was incredibly thin, rectangular, tapered on both sides, and had a strange geometric shape missing from its centre. It looked like it was sharp, and to test if it really was, I ran my thumb against one of its edges. A fine line of skin parted into a bloodless gap. I held it for only a moment more before putting it back in exactly the place I'd found it, and returned to my seat.

Thinking of it now, it's a wonder that such a wafer of an object could, in terms of action to reaction – to overreaction – nudge every one of us in a specific direction, begin us all plodding toward that horrible day. It was, after all, just one tiny piece of sharp metal. But, as it turned out, that was enough.

It was clear to me why this blade was hidden in that part of the library, and also why the person who hid it was nervous when they did so – they had a lot to be nervous about: they were smuggling forbidden information out of the Great Hall. But exactly what information they were smuggling, or to whom, or for what purpose, I couldn't know. And so I was quick to brush it off as just another one of the mysterious things that the Elders were involved in, yet another particular that I would never learn more about. Instead, what was much more pressing in my mind was the egocentric question: what could I do with this blade? What information was worth trying to smuggle to people in my life? I perused the titles of the books for all of three seconds before it occurred to me. Kara.

I thought about some of the paintings that I'd seen in the book of art. Granted, to me, most of them only looked like blotchy illustrations that weren't as good as photos, but I remembered that they did something to Dana. He was moved by them, saw some kind of message or significance buried inside those smears of mottled colours. And it occurred to me that maybe he was right, maybe he could see something that I couldn't, something vague and indistinct that was hidden inside the pictures, like illicit information was hidden between the lines of history books. If that were the case, then I really wanted to show some of the paintings to Kara, and maybe find out what they meant. Because if anybody could see life in something where others couldn't, it was her.

I remember meeting her in the forest once, after scuttling away from the people we'd 'gone for a walk' with. We'd crouched into the underbrush as we usually did, and I had leaned in and begun my well-thought-out speech – but soon stopped, my words trailing off into a senseless mumble. She wasn't paying attention. In fact, she wasn't even looking at me. She was staring at a massive leaf that was arching between us, fixated on it, mesmerized by it. I asked her what she was looking at, and she smiled and said she was looking at the sky, which of course only confused me. And then I leaned in closer and noticed all of the plump globules of water resting on the leaf. I focused, leaning in even closer, until, exactly as she'd said, I could see the sky reflected inside every one of the beads of water, tiny clouds passing by, a net of miniature leaves framing them. But that wasn't enough. She urged me to look even closer; and once I did, inside of the largest droplet, I could make out the bulbous shapes of both our heads, which were, in turn, busy looking inside the drop at the clouds and trees that meshed the sky above us. Then I distinctly saw the bottom part of the lump that was my head smile. Needless to say, I knew it would be worth smuggling a couple of paintings from the art book to her.

I waited until after Chalmon came to check on me, which he usually did every half hour or so. Once I'd heard him walk back into the other room and settle down to his work again, I snuck out of the chair and took the art book down from the shelf. I chose the two pictures I wanted before I took the blade from under the table, and then I cut them out, running the thin metal edge right along the crease. The loudest part of the whole thing was folding the pages, my body tight with concentration as I was doing it, every movement slow and calculated, ears perked for sounds from the other room. But eventually, I'd folded them small enough to shove down the front of my pants. I was safe. I returned the art book, sat down, and became suddenly riveted with chemical theory, a smug grin on my face for the rest of the afternoon.

I didn't feel guilty. If anything, I felt delightfully mischievous. I mean – what was there to feel bad about? It wasn't as if cutting a few pages out of a book was going to kill anyone.

12

Mikkel and I were the first two people inside that 'select group' who did their training in the disclosed wing. But as much as I was looking forward to spending more time with him, we didn't really get to see a lot of each other. First, he was given a separate room to study in, and second, because he was a bit ahead of me in the subject matter, we couldn't have classes together (as the Elders wouldn't have been able to lead productive discussions between us). So the only time we really had a chance to speak was when one of us was getting a book from the other's respective corner of the library, where we would exchange a few brief words in passing. After a while, this small talk became quite a habit between us, and I wonder now if Mikkel had made a conscious point of this; so that, when the moment he'd been waiting for finally presented itself, the Elders wouldn't be leaning out of their chairs in the other rooms and straining to listen to our every word, that they would have long since disregarded our mumblings as routine chat, as trivial niceties.

"Hey," he greeted, sauntering into the room that day. He walked over to one of the bookshelves and ran his finger along the spines, searching for a title.

"Hey," I answered, and returned to my reading. I was studying the history of torture, and there were graphic pictures that sucked my attention away from everything else around me, including the text of the book for that matter. I distractedly heard Mikkel pull a book from the shelf and then begin to walk back out of the room. But he didn't. Instead, he stopped at the table I was sitting at and looked down at me, silent, waiting until I looked up.

"Don't – uh… don't we have our exercise hour at the same time today?" he asked.

I shrugged my shoulders, "Don't know."

Mikkel glanced out of the open doorway, cocked his head to listen for a second, and then turned his attention back to me, his expression having grown serious. "Yeah, I think we do. Actually, I'm sure we do."

"Oh."

He moved closer, lowering his voice a bit, though careful to keep the same tone that he'd just been using, "But – I'm going to cut out in the middle of it, and go to the vantage point." Then he winked, straightened up, and walked out.

I sunk back into my chair, staring forward, suddenly leaden. I hadn't forgotten about our little plan to meet in secret, but I think a part of me was hoping that Mikkel had. After I'd Come of Age and understood exactly what had been weighing on his mind for that month, as he sat there after the evening meal, staring down at his empty plate, listless, I thought a lot about what he'd said during our mysterious conversation in the forest. Though I hadn't mulled over his words nearly as much as I had his voice. There was an unsettling urgency in it, something frantic, reckless, and I'd recognized it even then. But as much as I wasn't exactly overjoyed with the prospect of talking to him in private, I also didn't have much of a choice in the matter. A promise, after all, was a promise.

He had done his research. That day I was told to spend my exercise hour hiking to the top of a massive rise in the forest, and then to check back in with an Elder who was waiting for me at one of the garden plots below. A blunt ridge connected my hill with the vantage point, and, provided I moved quickly, and Mikkel's route was about the same distance as mine, we would have enough time to chat and return without raising the slightest bit of suspicion. I arrived first, and sat down to take in the panorama while I waited.

I was told that the vantage point served as a lookout for the island at one time, giving the people that once lived there fair warning when their fellow man was en route to rape, plunder, and slay. It was quite high and we kept the trees cut back, so the view was spectacular. Kara told me that she thought she'd once observed the curvature of the earth from there; like the edges of a map, she'd explained, curling over with an immeasurable weight into the distance. But that particular day it was hazy, and

I doubted I could see a few nautical miles, let alone the ocean arcing away into the universe.

I heard Mikkel's thudding footsteps coming over the rise just before he came into sight. "Hey," he greeted in his usual way, panting to catch his breath. He walked over and sat down beside me, looking out at the view until he'd recovered a bit. However, once he did, neither of us said anything, and there was a bit of an uncomfortable silence while he looked for a tactful way to begin. In the end, he didn't really find one. "So... you uh... you probably know why I asked you to come here, no?"

"Um... not really, no." But, listening to the way he'd asked that question, I did. I knew exactly why. Mikkel wanted to talk to me about The Goal, about how crazy it all sounded to him, how he wasn't convinced it was the right thing, and how he had some outstanding questions that maybe – just maybe – I could help in answering. And I could only sit there, my stomach rising into my throat, hoping that I was wrong, watching his mouth as it formed the beginning of his next sentence, wishing with all of my being that he wouldn't say those forbidden words, whispering in my mind, 'Don't say The Goal; don't say The Goal; don't say The Goal...'

"It's about The Goal, Joshua."

I sighed, deflated. "Mikkel, you know perfectly well that we're not supposed to talk about this alone. If they caught us, do you know what kind of trouble we'd be in?"

"Why?"

I straightened up, "What do you mean 'why'?"

"I mean: why would we be in such serious trouble? Why do you think it's so 'dangerous' for us to talk about things without strict supervision? What do you think they're afraid of?"

I shook my head at him, "Wow. I don't think you were listening too well when you Came of Age. What they're afraid of is our acting on the primitive part of our brains, of our fear taking over the higher processes of our intellect. I mean – we're reading the same books so this shouldn't be new to you, but, wherever you find a few fear-ridden people throughout history, you also find a pile of dead and mutilated at their side. The

Elders, understandably, would like to avoid that from happening on our island."

Mikkel's nod was exaggerative, "Thank you. That was a perfectly verbatim answer." And then he lowered his voice, "But I don't need you to regurgitate the bullshit you've heard – I need you to think.

"I mean – let's just take a step back here and look at what we're proposing to do." He was squeezing his thumb and his pointer finger together, bobbing them in the air between us to help make his point. "We're talking about killing ourselves, Joshua. That's what we're doing – we're killing ourselves. Do you understand that?"

"Of course I do. And... while instinctually that might seem a little crazy, you know as well as I do that – in terms of bearing a profound responsibility and owning what we are, what we've done – it's the only thing that really makes sense."

"Makes sense?" He looked around, as if to see if anyone else had heard what just came out of my mouth. "Makes sense? ...Okay," he paused for a second to compose himself, "let me run a few things by you, and you can tell me if they 'make sense'.

"You're right, we've been shown, over and over again, that we are horrible creatures. And maybe we are – if those history books are right, then we really did continuously kill each other in the masses for thousands of years. Terrible, I agree. So, what do we do about it? To prevent these horrific genocides from ever being committed again, we come up with the great idea to commit the most comprehensive genocide imaginable? Because we've historically set out to annihilate one another, we've decided to 'fix' the problem by annihilating the annihilators? That doesn't sound absurd to you? And this contradiction goes on and on! I mean – out of a desire to stop all of the needless suffering in the world they created a long, drawn out, debilitating disease and unleashed it onto billions – I can't even understand that number – billions of people? Is that the perfect cure for our lack of compassion: inflicting the most pain and suffering that human history has ever seen? Does that really 'make sense' to you?"

Veracity

"No – yeah... I mean – in a way, it does. I know it sounds hypocritical, but everything that human beings do is hypocritical, which, to me, only supports the idea of The Goal. The only way to finally rid the world of that endless hypocrisy that you're pointing out is to pull it from its roots. And the sole way of doing that is by getting rid of ourselves. It's the only option."

"Is it? You sound so sure of yourself, but really, how can you be? First of all, have you ever let yourself explore any different options; and secondly, even if you have, what about the other options that might exist outside of the ones you thought of? Because – let's be honest– you and I have no idea what we're dealing with here. Do we know what the world looked like before? Do we know what people were doing to each other between those awful events in the history books? No. We can't. We don't know anything firsthand. Think of it, we're standing firm behind a solution to a problem that we've never even seen." Mikkel broke off to look at the ground in front of us for a moment, and chortled before continuing,

"It's interesting – right now I'm studying these waves of people who crusaded into other lands, not to slaughter, but to force their beliefs onto other cultures. Obviously whenever this happened there was violence and strife, and countless people died, but that's not the point. The point is that these people who were crusading were acting on what they saw as their moral obligation; to them, everything they did was ethically sound, it was perfectly rationalized – just like the Elders. Only now, the history books don't exactly view what those people did as 'prudent'. No, now that we look back at it, we can see how deluded it was. The Elders said these exploits stemmed from 'pompous arrogance'. But if you think about it, aren't we doing exactly the same thing: forcing the world to live with our belief system and the consequences of it? Isn't it the same kind of 'pompous arrogance' to decide for all of humanity that they don't deserve to live?"

"Hmm. I'm not sure. Isn't it pompous arrogance to assume that we do deserve to live, that we automatically take precedence over all of the nature that we exploit and obliterate around us? I

103

mean – how can we intrinsically hold the right to live, if we don't intrinsically hold the responsibility that goes with that right?" I had to hold back a clever smirk that was pulling at the edges of my mouth. I was quite happy with my response, even if I hadn't thought of it myself. Dana and I had had a similar discussion only a few days before that, and I was citing him almost word for word. But still, I thought it was a legitimate point. Whereas Mikkel, on the other hand, didn't seem too impressed by it.

He had turned to look out at the sea, shaking his head, and then plucked a few blades of grass from his side and threw them into the air in front of us, both of us watching the twirling needles until they'd settled onto the ground. "You know – I don't remember you being so opinionated, but that's what you've become. And the funny thing is, they're not even your opinions. I mean – look at you; you are one perfectly programmed student."

This insult made me sink back a bit. Let alone was it coming from Mikkel, he'd also used a word that I'd heard before – one that troubled me. "Wait. What do you mean by that?"

"By what – 'programmed'?"

"Yeah."

"Well, basically, it means exactly what it sounds like. A while ago, they had me studying psychological phenomena, wanting to show me how easily the masses could be moved to act out with violence (moved to do anything really), and I came across it in one of the books. They were working with me closely at the time, and I only had about a minute to skim a section that I wasn't assigned, but that was enough. The section was about exactly that: programming people.

"Simply put, if you want to change someone's beliefs, especially if those beliefs are against the opinions a person has already formed – or against their logic, or nature – then there's only one way to do it; you have to isolate them for a period of time, away from any kind of outside influences. Then, once the person is inside this 'mental vacuum', they're simply shown over and over again that the failure to comply with the new way of thinking results in negative consequences (like being ostracized for the rest of their days), while the changing of their thoughts to match the new belief system, results in positive outcomes (like the chance for a life of freedom and a grand adventure). Any of that sound familiar to you?" he asked, dryly.

"Yeah… but… no… wait, it's not the same. We're being asked to question. That's the difference."

"Are we really though? I mean − I know that's what they say, but do you honestly feel like you're encouraged, or even allowed to express your qualms about The Goal?"

It took me a few seconds of hesitation to answer this, "No. I guess not."

"See?"

"But… I always thought that that was because we needed some guiding. I mean − we're dealing with something here that the very structure of our body is trying to steer us away from, something that our minds would do anything to keep us from seeing, all out of the fear that it's true."

"Yeah, but… couldn't it also be that our minds and bodies sense that it's a bad idea simply because − well − it's a bad idea?"

I didn't respond. I needed time to think about these things. True, he had some good points, but this, more than anything else, was only frustrating to me. After I'd already painstakingly worked it all out, after I was sure that I'd set everything in its rightful place, suddenly, it felt like I was being asked to dive deep into my mind again, to scrape at the quiet seabed there, to disturb the sediment, cloud the water. He was complicating things.

After watching me for a few seconds, my eyes searching the sky above the water, Mikkel cut in, "Trust me, I know what you're thinking. You're wondering what's true and what isn't − all of it; the things I just said, the Elders, yourself. I know because sometimes my head is a complete mess as well. Everything gets jumbled; the things that I used to think and believe get mixed up with the things that were drilled into me, and sometimes I can't tell them apart anymore." He looked down at the ground and picked a twig out of the grass, holding it in front of him and staring at it. "Which is exactly why I wish I'd known about the possibility of programming people before I went into the shelter. Maybe it would have kept all those complicated issues in perspective, or at the very least, maybe I'd feel more convinced that the views I have are actually mine."

I wanted to say something to respond to this, but didn't really have anything to offer. And this was fine, because Mikkel had looked away, and was quickly getting lost in his own thoughts, which led me to do the same. For the most part, I was having a hard time imagining how a person could infiltrate someone else's ideas and re-wire them. And the more I tried to think of ways that it might be possible, the more it didn't seem all that realistic to me. I mean – yes, I understood that one's influences could be controlled, but I also knew that exactly how those influences were interpreted, couldn't be. Because when we do this interpreting, when we sort through the skewed information around us, keeping only what we think is accurate and discarding the rest, no one is there to see what we throw away, no one hovers beside us, sieving through our ideological trash heap, frantically shoving the scraps back into our heads while we're not looking. We are alone at night when we stare into the space above our beds, contemplating the events of our day. And if you think about it this way, in many respects, we are our greatest influence; because as much as people might try and shape us, we always have the last say as to how that moulding fits.

Whereas Mikkel seemed to think that the Elders could have complete control over our minds, that everything they'd revealed about the truth of humanity was really some kind of clever scheme designed to mislead us. He'd said 'if the history books were right – if. Did he really think that the endless supply of texts and photos (some of which were so tattered and old that they had to have been written before The Goal was ever conceived of) were all conjured up from nothing? If so, how could he rationalize that? Because even if he managed to ignore the supposed 'forgeries' of our education, what about the examples that we drew from the world around us, or from our very selves, how did he suppose the Elders manufactured those?

I shook my head. Yes, the more I thought of it, the more I was becoming annoyed with this conversation. What exactly did he expect to come out of it; did he think I was going to overturn

106

my entire belief structure to match his, which, at best, was an exceptionally lazy one?

I'm afraid that, when I finally spoke, I didn't do a great job of hiding the impatience in my voice, "Mikkel, this is all good and well, but... really, whether our beliefs are ours, theirs, or something in between, I can't say it really matters much anymore. I mean – the ball's been rolling for a long, long time now. There's not really much we can do about it."

As if in response to this, he leaned in to squint at the stick in his hand, seeming to imply that the few colourful dots of fungi on it were more worthwhile than my pathetic attitude. "Yeah. I could see how you might think that – sort of. But it's not quite right. Because there is something we can do."

"Like what?" I sniggered.

He turned toward me at that point, and I'll never forget the expression on his face when he did. He was biting the nervous flesh on the inside of his cheeks, looking me over, weighing out whether or not he could continue, whether or not he was going to allow, what had until that point been a forbidden conversation, to fumble over a dangerous line that couldn't easily be re-crossed. And for whatever reason, after the few pensive seconds it took, he decided he could. "Well – I'll tell you what we can do."

He shifted his weight to get more comfortable, casting a quick glance at the spot where the trail entered the clearing before he began. "Okay. Let's start with what we know: we know that we're competing to be the leader of the expedition, and that, after that leader's chosen, another five to maybe eight of us will be selected as the crew. We know that the leader will probably either be you, Peik, or myself, as we're the only ones that would really have the right skills for it. That means that – almost guaranteed – one of us three will have access to the boat before it leaves, authority over the crew, and the trust of the Elders. We can also assume that the ship they'll give us will be the largest sailboat on the island, because it's the only one that's really seaworthy anymore; which means that once we leave, no one will be able to come after us. Ever.

"Now, they haven't actually said it, but it sounds like the two of us who aren't chosen as the leader, will have to stay behind. Not the greatest of prospects, is it? So, the three of us would have quite an incentive to work together in order to get what each of us individually wants, which is obviously to go on the expedition as well."

"So… all of this is to say that you think we should find a way to smuggle the two of us, which aren't chosen to lead the expedition, onto the ship?"

"Um… not really. I just wanted to point out that the two who aren't chosen would automatically have the incentive to secretly get on board. What I'm trying to say is that, if the three of us agree to do something like that, then we might as well smuggle two other people onto the ship as well. Two people who have the potential to change the future of everything."

"I… don't really follow." But the truth was that I didn't really want to. I'd risked a lot to come and meet with him, sneaking through the trees, looking over my shoulder as I veered off of my exercise route – and for what? To listen to him natter about mind control, 'changing' the future, and herding an entire line up of people onto a ship while the Elders supposedly had their backs turned. It was a bit ridiculous. And was only becoming more so.

"I can't believe you haven't pieced together the potential here," he said, almost sounding offended. "Okay… you have already figured out that our Incision is actually a sterilization operation, right?" I nodded. "Good. And I also imagine that you've picked up – from the way the Elders talk about what the expedition will come across – that there probably isn't anyone left in the world, let alone people who'll be able to bear children. So, from what we know, there isn't anyone, anywhere, who has the possibility of carrying on our species, except – if you think about it – two. The only children on the island who haven't had their Incision yet."

I was squinting. "Anu and Siri?"

"Exactly. Anu and Siri. If all three of us agreed to work together, I'm convinced we could figure out a way to get them on board."

I leaned away from him, speechless, my eyes busily searching his face. It was almost impossible to believe what had come out of his mouth, and I wondered if he had even begun to grasp the implications of the words he'd chosen. Though, I have to admit, that seemed unlikely. "So... let's get this straight, Mikkel. What you're proposing to do here is exactly – exactly – the opposite of what everyone on this island is alive to do. You understand that that's what you're talking about, don't you?"

He nodded slowly, "Yes. I understand that that's what I'm talking about. I understand that I'm talking about saving our race, about ending this insanity of killing ourselves. I'm talking about giving us a future again, Joshua."

"And... you don't think there would be some serious repercussions to that; you don't think, after generations of preparation for this, that they just might have some kind of contingency plan for something along those lines? I mean – think of it: soldiers were trained on this island. You've seen the weapons in the books! Wouldn't it make perfect sense if they had some of those buried somewhere in the shelter?" As I said this, already, images of what might happen were flashing through my mind. I could see the commotion, the scrambling of bodies in and out of buildings as they realized there was a critical breach of some kind, the screams, the waves of people fanning out toward us, the swinging of metal through the air, the hollow thudding sound that weapons might make as they slashed through our rib cages. I could picture our hands uselessly cupping open wounds, trying to stop the deluge of blood streaming from them, our eyes wide open, fingers soaking red.

Gee. Seemed like a great idea.

As soon as I started speaking, everything in Mikkel's mannerisms changed, his eyes dropping to the ground, his posture becoming a disappointed slouch. And when I stopped, he tossed away the stick he'd been holding with an aggressive throw, and then settled back, leaning onto one of his elbows. "Yeah. You're probably right," he'd suddenly agreed, adjusting his weight, getting comfortable, as if knowing that I'd have a lot more to say. And I did.

Mark Lavorato

"Of course I'm right! And think of it: those would just be the immediate consequences. What if this 'seamless plan' that we would supposedly invent actually worked? What if a few of us managed to survive the drama of getting off the island, and could sail the two children to a mainland; what then? I mean – let's just imagine for a second that the Elders are even partly right about what they say? Could you honestly go to sleep at night knowing that we were single-handedly responsible for the second coming of a species that would proudly bring the abuse of power back into the world – and greed, and suffering, and oppression? Think about how far those upshots would be felt, how many centuries you would expose to war and genocide, how many other species would become extinct, how much more of the earth would be irreparably ruined. You really want all that on your head?"

"No," Mikkel answered, shaking his head at himself, his voice shrinking even more. "I know. I mean – you're right. You're absolutely right." He was relaxed, all of his frustrated energy having drained away. "And the crazy thing is: I even know where these ideas of mine come from. It's my brain stem, my survival instincts trying to override what I know is true. It's exactly what they say we should look out for: my mind over-rationalizing things, allowing me see what I want to see – all that stuff." He lifted a hand against the sun and looked out at the ocean. I joined him, and after concentrating for a few seconds, realized we could hear the waves murmuring against the shore far below. "Yeah," he concluded, after a thoughtful pause, "it's a stupid idea – the whole thing."

"Yeah, it is," I agreed, trying not to sound too harsh. Because the truth was, I could see where such an idea could come from, how appealing the thought must have been to him at first glance; the three of us meeting in secret, organizing ourselves, skirting behind buildings to listen for where the two children would be the day we left, all of us, drunk with the illusion that we were going to change the future of the world, do something 'good' to mend what 'bad' people had wrecked. But the reality was obviously something very different, and to me, the mere thought of us huddled in the shade of the trees, serious whispers

110

hissing under the leaves like snakes, was enough to make my stomach turn. We weren't children anymore. We knew better now.

After a while, he broke the silence with a voice as gentle as water. "You know – if you uh… if you ever told anyone about this conversation, I think it's safe to say that I'd be hung out to dry."

I rolled my eyes at him, "Come on – give me some credit here. It's not as if I'm about to run off and 'report you'. I mean – I think it's almost natural for ideas like this to come up once in a while. But we both know they're just that: ideas. So… don't worry. I won't repeat a word of it to anyone. Promise."

"Good. And – I mean – I think you're right: it is natural. It's exactly like the Elders say; we're waging a lifelong battle against our deepest nature here, having to fight our every thought before we win it over. So it only makes sense that if we get tired and lower our guard, even if it's for a couple seconds, sometimes, our nature is bound to get the best of us, which is when everything gets mixed up in our heads. Like it was for me a few minutes ago. And like it probably is for all of us from time to time."

I had to stop chewing my bottom lip to speak, "Yeah. Probably."

We left soon after that, saying an awkward goodbye, and then turning to descend in opposite directions, meandering through the trees, our paces slowed by encumbering thoughts. For my part, I could only hope that this would be the end of it, that this whole weighty discussion would turn out to be one of those things in our lives, which seems so pivotal and important when it first surfaces, but that then somehow manages to sink into our past without ever having much of a rippling effect on the world around us.

But, of course, it wasn't one of those things. And, in fact, everyone on the island would be impacted by it before the month was through. All of us, bouncing on the surface of our reality, shocked by the magnitude of the waves that a single battered corpse can make, rolling in the swells among us.

13

At any given time, there was a lot happening on the island. People were fishing, picking fruit, growing vegetables, gathering shellfish, building and maintaining huts, and making clothing; and amid all of these chores, the Elders also had to find time to teach things and allot the younger people with time to be taught. So, for the sake of efficiency, we all had a schedule that was organized, structured, and synchronized with everyone else's, and we kept on this schedule by flipping the hourglasses that were waiting at every important site, the very moment we arrived. Every day there was a total of exactly one and a half hours – a half hour in the morning, afternoon, and evening – which were free of assigned responsibilities or meal times. These were given to us as a means of dealing with unforeseen things that had come up, to reorganize ourselves, to rest, or to simply chat with other people (provided, of course, that they were of the same sex, not the same people we'd gathered with the day before, and in groups of three or less). As might be expected, there was a lot of frenzied activity during these breaks, and the braid of trails connecting the different sites on the island were swarming with people moving in every direction.

Obviously, if one were interested in doing something secretive, this would not be the best time to do it. In fact, it would be the absolute, categorically worst time to do it. Which, I guess, shows the state of mind he was in better than anything; that and the fact that he sent – of all people – Niels to spread the word.

Niels was one of those unfortunate children, and then one of those adolescents, and finally one of those younger men, who permanently looked suspicious. Even if he was doing something that couldn't have a clandestine nature to it, like pulling in a fishing net or tying a knot, he still managed to look like a thief; his gawky neck kinking around, hunched over, busy eyes darting from side to side. He was dark, lanky, and constantly fidgeting, often balancing on the balls of his feet as if he were just about to break into a sprint to save his life. When we were younger, we avoided him as much as we could, and not because he was a bad guy, but because wherever he was, so were the Elders – always investigating the area around him, wondering if he'd actually done something as conniving as his manner suggested. The interesting thing was that he was never really mischievous (though this might only have been due to the fact that he didn't stand a chance of getting away with anything had the inclination ever struck him.)

That afternoon, he was walking toward me on one of the busy trails and had stopped the person in front of me, mumbled something in his ear, and then quickly moved on. I was the next one he came to. "Hey," he whispered, grabbing onto my elbow and looking up and down the trail as if to check that the coast was clear. Incidentally, it wasn't, but he didn't seem to mind, "Peik wants to talk. He's in the clearing." He let go of my arm and continued gangling down the trail, stopping every young man he saw along the way. By the time he'd disappeared around the corner, I'd seen him telling four different people in plain view. Not good.

Peik had left the community to Come of Age only about a week and a half before that, and, as he wasn't in the dining hall at breakfast, I imagined he'd been released only hours, if not minutes before. So the obvious question was: Why would a person who had just been drilled at length, and made to understand the absolute importance of abiding by all the rules, set out to break them the very first second he could? Of course, every answer I could come up with to this question was only a variation of the same worst-case scenario. Which is to say that I understood perfectly well that some kind of disastrous event was probably beginning to unravel before us. But that didn't mean that I ran off to tell the Elders about it, nor did I try and seek out any way of preventing it from happening. No. Not me. Instead, I went to watch. Because, let's be honest, preaching to Mikkel about consequences was one thing, but we all know that practicing it is quite another (especially when the consequences don't really involve us).

As I walked into the clearing, my pace slowed as if I'd hit a pocket of air that was so thick I had to wade through it like mud. My mind – actually, every one of our minds – was trained to see the entire scene as simply 'wrong'. Peik was squatting down on the top of a fallen tree, his arms wrapped around his knees, presumably waiting for a few more people before he began, while a scattering of young men were peppered across the grass in front of him. There wasn't an Elder in sight, and I could see that I wasn't the only one to be put on edge by this. People were visually anxious, arms crossing over their chests, feet thumping impatiently, heads twitching to look over their shoulders at the sound of every new person that appeared from between the leaves. We were as jittery as scavengers low on the food chain, which just happened to be the first to stumble across a prized piece of carrion, white-rimmed retinas scanning the shadows around us, knowing that something bigger was bound to emerge soon.

Niels finally came into view with Mikkel, who was walking somewhat cautiously behind him. Mikkel and I had been quite aloof, if not cold with one another, in the time that followed our meeting at the vantage point. In fact, for a couple of weeks prior to that day in the clearing, we'd ceased really acknowledging each other unless we absolutely had to. But this was different. Things were not what they should've been, and he sought me out in the crowd to exchange a worried glance.

As usual, it was also Mikkel's presence that signified the beginning of things, and Peik finally stood up to speak, which prompted all of our eyes to rise with him, following his shape into the air above the log, the whispers instantly fading into silence.

But before he even began, we could see that something was wrong. He didn't look so well. His shoulders were tweaking erratically, as if he were trying to shake a number of unseen insects off his back, his face pallid, chest rising and falling with quick little breaths, beads of sweat clotted onto his forehead. He was petrified; as anyone would be really, standing in front of a throng of expectant faces, all the while trying to summon up the courage to do the stupidest thing in your life.

"Thanks for getting everyone, Niels," he said, speaking under his breath. Niels nodded and smiled, his eyes flitting in every direction, his quirky mannerisms finally matching the situation.

"Okay," Peik began, addressing us in a much louder voice than he needed to. "As you probably all figured out, I've... just Come of Age. And uh... I wanted to... speak to everyone... uh – because..." he paused to swallow and draw in a long, worrying breath, "because... it's time everyone knew the truth about the island."

My mouth dropped wide open. Instantly, everyone broke into mutters of amazement, their eyebrows raised, heads spinning to look at one another. Mikkel's posture had stiffened into a rigid stick, a look of appalled disbelief on his face.

The crowd recovered from its restlessness as quickly as it could, people shushing each other, becoming quiet, waiting for him to continue, already hanging on the claims he was about to utter. I remember noticing a few complacent grins dragging across people's faces as they realized that this was going to be well worth coming for.

"But..." he carried on, "you have to know that... what I'm going to tell you... isn't easy to hear. And that is... that..." He stopped as if to think about the right words to use, the tension quickly escalating around him, people leaning in, ready, waiting. Meanwhile, Peik had fixed his eyes on the ground a ways beneath him, thinking, straining, looking for a quick sentence that would express what he'd learned over the course of several days (because, realistically, that was probably all he would have time for). But concise words seemed to be hard to come by in his mind, and, finally, unable to find them, he shook his head at himself, let his arms drape at his sides, and decided to summarize everything as quickly and crudely as he could – and unwisely deeming it best to start from the last line, and work backwards from it. "The Elders... the Elders want to kill everyone in the world."

Silence. People stood blinking for a second or two, before an invisible hand seemed to reach out to everyone at exactly the same time and push their faces back in puzzlement.

"What?"

"Huh?"

"What did he say?"

"What the hell?"

Everyone began mumbling among themselves, shaking heads, clicking their tongues disappointedly, even giggling; a wave of letdown gestures and expressions, people realizing that they'd just taken a huge risk to listen to the ramblings of someone who was obviously mentally unbalanced, who, it seemed, 'couldn't take' Coming of Age, and so had cracked. It all hardly seemed worth their effort anymore.

For my part, I could only let out a sigh of relief. It was incredibly lucky, for all of us, that Peik had been too flustered to choose the right words; and I could easily imagine why he'd fallen apart at the last second. He'd been through a lot. Let alone had he mustered up the energy to resist every one of the Elders' arguments in his mind, he'd also managed to fool them into believing that he hadn't resisted them at all; and actually succeeded, because, as sceptical as they were, they'd felt confident enough to release him. Which could only mean that, at that exact moment, while he stood up in front of us all, after having been through the long, taxing ordeal of convincingly being two people at once under the most intense scrutiny, he probably didn't have a lot of wit left to draw from. I almost felt sorry for him.

"No! Listen!" he called out in an effort to redeem himself, his voice obnoxiously loud. The group of young men, some of which were already turning to leave, decided to give him their attention again; albeit reluctantly, hands on their hips, heads slanted to the side in disappointment – or pity. "I know that this sounds crazy. Okay? I know that. But just listen for a second. I... I have something. I have proof." He reached into his back pocket and brought something out from behind his back, carefully, neurotically, fingers cradled delicately around it, his face knotted with concentration, eyes focusing on his hands as they moved through the air, until he held it out in front of us. It was a rectangle of folded pages (which had evidently been sat on for quite a while). He smiled slightly, satisfied that we were all beholding the glory of this flattened, discoloured, wad of text, and then he proceeded to unfold them with meticulous care, handling them as if they were just about to disintegrate into a million illegible pieces, or burst into sudden flame. If Peik's psychological status was dubious before this little ritual, after it, there was no question whatsoever: he was most definitely 'not well'.

But at that point, a strange thing started happening to me. As he held out the sheets of paper, obscure references and details in the back of my mind started to pull together, amassing themselves into something coherent. I looked at the edges of the glossy pages, which had obviously been taken from a book. They were cleanly cut.

"See: brainwashing. Do you know what they do when we Come of Age? They program us – well... some of us anyway. And... and then... everyone else... they just tell lies to."

I turned to look at Mikkel. It was him. It was his blade that I'd used, his blade that he somehow found, then stole, then hid, all so he could leak information to Peik, sell the poor sap on his romantic notions of saving the world. This was what he meant when he mumbled something about 'wishing he'd heard of programming before going into the shelter'. In fact, had I not pounced on the stupidity of his ideas, he probably would have told me all about how he was busy 'informing' Peik – and that he was being very careful about it. Because it was clear that he'd understood the risks involved, which was why he'd found an anonymous way of handing the information over, so that, if Peik snapped, or decided to tell someone about the strange sheets of paper that probably appeared under his pillow one day, Mikkel would still be safe. I could see it all perfectly. I could suddenly understand every detail of the sequence of events that had led us all to that pathetic scene in the forest.

I glared into the side of Mikkel's face, trying to relay the fact that I'd made the connection, but more than that, trying to convey that I considered everything that he'd done to be incredibly, incredibly reckless. But he wasn't looking at me. He was busy watching Peik, stunned, horrified. I saw him mouth a silent curse; a specific one that had been introduced into our vocabulary when one of the Elders dropped a massive log onto his hand, rendering two of his fingers forever useless. It was a curse that seemed to be reserved for the most dismal instances alone, and his lips articulated it perfectly; "Fuck."

I nodded. I couldn't have put it better myself.

Because what were we going to do now? How was this going to end? Once the Elders had the papers, they would know that someone was conspiring, and then search obsessively until they'd found him or her – or them. And that was right: I was involved here. The very fact that I hadn't told the Elders about my encounter at the vantage point with Mikkel made me a kind of conspirator. I'd promised not to tell. And helping to hide a conspiracy makes you just as much a part of it. Great.

Yet really, what could we do? How could we stop Peik from speaking? He obviously wasn't in a state to listen to reason – no; he was through with listening. And forcing him to stop, jumping up onto the log and ushering him off, would only do one of two things: through the eyes of the Elders, it would make the person look like a collaborator, one of the paper cutters trying to protect himself; or through the eyes of the crowd, it might look like part of the wild conspiracy Peik was talking about, an attempt to try and silence him, and maybe even lend some credit to the things he was saying, which, thankfully, were still being seen as madcap ravings. No, there was nothing Mikkel or I could do; though, even if we could, I don't think we would have. Peik was quickly spiralling downwards, and was going to meet with some very serious consequences in the very near future. I couldn't begin to guess what they were going to do with him: maybe imprison him in the shelter and try and talk some sense into him again, or maybe even drop him off on the nearest island to live the rest of his days, alone, and ranting of injustices to the trees. Either way, he wasn't exactly a person you wanted to be siding with, or even getting near. I understand now that humans follow the rules of all group animals, and whether it was conscious or subconscious, we all recognized Peik for exactly what he was: a limping, sickly creature inside the sprawling herd. He was choice prey, the very first one that intense hunting eyes would fall upon. None of us would risk stepping forward to protect him; instead, it seemed natural enough to back away, knowing that his stalking fate was creeping ever closer, and wanting to be at a safe distance when it pounced. (Though, still close enough to witness of course – which was, after all, why I'd gone there in the first place, wasn't it?)

"Soon... soon there will be a voyage," he continued. He was looking through the faces, his head sweeping back and forth, "and that voyage is only meant to make sure..."

And then he stopped – froze actually – suddenly gawping at the trees behind us. We all turned around at the same time, tracing his line of sight; and once we found what he was looking at, I'm sure that every one of us stopped breathing.

It was Chalmon; standing silently on the edge of the clearing, his hands clasped gently behind his back. He didn't look too happy. "Gentlemen!" he bellowed, his voice so loud that a few people took a step back. He brought a fist up to his mouth and cleared his throat before continuing in a softer tone, "I was just told to gather everyone as quickly as I could, but... obviously couldn't find any of you." He was taking the time to eye each one of us individually, as if marking our names onto a slate for later reference. "The reason I was asked to find you was to let you know about an emergency community meeting, which is being held right now. It will address some very serious issues that affect the entire island, so, needless to say, your attendance is necessary." He was so livid his voice was shaking. "So then – in light of that – I will give you one minute to be seated inside the Community Hall. Commencing now."

At first, no one moved. We only exchanged a few frantic glances, suspended in the thick air of panic like the dull herd animals we are, waiting for the first twitching signal of flight. Which came. Somebody shifted their weight forward and took a step, and that was enough. All at once, everyone bounced to their toes and began racing to the Community Hall as fast as they could, a stream of bobbing heads and flailing hair breaking through the leaves and thin branches, thumping into the distance.

I wasn't one of them. For some reason – and I don't think I'll ever really understand why – I thought I was different, thought I was an exception to the rules. After all, I knew the truth. In my mind, I was practically an Elder, so why shouldn't I stay behind? But this line of reasoning was, of course, wrong.

I stood alone between Chalmon and Peik, who had remained exactly where they were, their eyes fixed on one another. Peik was shifting his weight from his right leg to his left, the transfer increasing in speed, a kind of desperation building in his gestures, until finally, he stopped, crumpled the pieces of paper into a ball, flung them onto the grass, spat disgustedly in Chalmon's general direction, spun around, and jumped off the tree. He crashed into a bush and, untangling himself in an instant, began racing into the forest in the opposite direction of the Community Hall. I could see his hands flinging into the air to help him leap over logs, his head ducking and swerving through the branches. He looked like he was running for his life.

Chalmon watched Peik until he'd disappeared from view, then turned to face me, his hands still cupped into the small of his back. I'll never forget the sound of his voice when he spoke, the eerie, seething calm of it, "There are only forty-five seconds of that minute remaining, Joshua."

I ran. I ran as fast as my legs would take me, out of the clearing, down the trail, and straight into the Community Hall.

14

What I found when I burst through the door, wasn't an orderly meeting that involved everyone on the island, nor, for that matter, any kind of organization in the least. The only people there were the group from the clearing, scattering throughout the room in chaotic groups, gathering, then quickly dispersing again, looking around for an Elder to obey (as if this might help to lessen the disobedience we'd just demonstrated). There were whispers and rumours passing through the crowd, people theorizing what was going to happen. We all understood that a stern punishment would be dealt out, but couldn't guess if it would all fall on Peik, or if everyone would have to share it. At one point, we could hear a horn of some kind being blown in the distance, but no one was brave enough to step outside to see where it was coming from or what it meant. No, we were too busy inside, having suddenly become the epitome of compliance, the very embodiment of devoted respect for rules.

After quite some time, Dana came into the room and commanded us to sit down. He told us that we would have to wait a while, and that he could only hope, in light of our complete disregard of policy, that we had the self-possession to remain absolutely silent while we waited. He asked if we could be trusted with that one small responsibility. We nodded. But just in case, Thalia was asked to stay in the hall to make sure.

Time crept by. We watched the door for what seemed like an eternity, waiting for it to open. Then waited more. And as we passed the hours in that horrible, clothes-rustling silence, I had a clear view of the table Mikkel was sitting at, and we'd exchanged a few mutually understanding looks. He knew that he'd placed both Peik and I in an awkward predicament, and I knew that he didn't feel great about it. He hadn't meant for things to turn out this way; and he certainly hadn't meant for Peik to become so unstable that he would recklessly bring the whole thing out into the open. Yet that's exactly what happened. And now someone was going to be in serious trouble because of it. (I have to admit

121

that there was also a juvenile part of me that wanted to wag a finger in a classic I-told-you-so taunt. This was the very reason I was so afraid of – even entertaining – dangerous ideas: it's because they have the tendency to take on a life of their own. And I just hoped that, finally, Mikkel was beginning to understand that.)

Eventually, we heard the trampling of footsteps approaching the other side of the door, and everyone in the room perked up. It was Harek that opened it. He walked to front of the hall and stood there, waiting patiently while every last one of the remaining people on the island streamed in behind him. They found themselves a seat, legs stepping over benches mechanically, their expressions dazed, vacant. Once everyone had settled into place, and the quiet had spread throughout the room, we all faced the front of the hall, waiting for Harek to speak. But he didn't, even though he had our full and undivided attention. He waited a while, swallowing hard, thinking harder, and by the time he actually began, every neck in the community was stretched high, craning around the head in front of them to see better.

His words were slow, plaintive, "For those of you who have not yet Come of Age, I want to tell you that it is an incredibly difficult and taxing philosophical process. As you have no doubt guessed, there are serious issues that are dealt with during that time, issues that every one of us will have to bear at some point, which concern our very world, both here, and beyond the island. So I think we can all appreciate that people might feel an immense amount of mental, and even social pressure to comprehend things that are – well – extremely difficult to comprehend, to be honest. And... I imagine that it was for that reason, and through no fault of his own, that Peik reacted in the way that he did. Regrettably, it seems he simply could not cope with the mental burden that was handed over to him. Peik – as some of you had the misfortune of witnessing today – somehow... spiralled into a state of insanity and delusion, which we were not aware of this morning when we congratulated him on his completion of Coming of Age, and welcomed him back into the community."

Veracity

People looked at one another, some with expressions of concern, others with sympathy. Some of the women Elders had stepped closer to one another and were touching each other's backs or arms, their thumbs like soothing pendulums, stroking from side to side. "And... I regret very, very much to say that..." Harek's voice had become higher for a moment, and he swallowed hard to keep it from breaking again, "...that our tragic news does not stop there.

"We... gathered to search for Peik, and finally found him in the very last place we thought to look: the north shore." There were a few gasps throughout the room, a few looks of sombre comprehension. The north shore was the most hazardous place on the island, with a battered and steep shoreline and every kind of dangerous current that was known: undertows, riptides, and rotating flows that whirled around the many hidden shoals and coral channels. "I... simply cannot imagine what his state of mind was, the desperation that he must have felt, or the purpose he thought it would serve, when he set off swimming from there, away from the island, and into the open ocean."

There was a breathless silence. No one moved, not even to bring a hand up to their face or shake their heads. Nothing. This news didn't seem to be real to any of us; it was as if Harek were talking about another person, someone we hadn't just seen and listened to, somebody we didn't even know. Yes, that was it – he must mean someone else, he must be implying something else. Surely Peik, with his olive skin and boyish eyes, wasn't suddenly dead. He couldn't be; we refused the idea of it, regardless of how obvious it was.

"Sadly..." Harek continued, his voice having become hesitant, as if he were afraid of breaking the stunned spell we were all under, "sadly, our beloved Peik is gone." Everyone started shifting in their seats, shuffling their feet beneath the benches, a few people bowing their heads. "We spotted his body being swept out to sea. It was... badly battered." There were a few defeated sighs, some whimpering sounds beginning to spread. "We watched him sink – powerless to do anything about it," Harek finished, suddenly pressing a hand over both of his eyes, his chin trembling.

Finally, people began to cry. Thalia leaned forward into her hands and started weeping uncontrollably, while others let fat tears stream down their faces. However, some people, like myself, were only dumbstruck, and didn't seem to do anything at all, except look around at the walls, at the ceiling, at the floor, at everyone else who was busy grieving. And there are times that I wonder if there were others in that group of 'unaffected people' who felt a tinge of guilt for their response to the news. I know I did.

Almost everything in the way that I reacted to Peik's death was surprising to me, because – to be completely honest with myself – I really didn't feel much. Not that day, or even afterwards. And I've wondered if this was because Peik and I never really had a 'connection', because we were never bound by some shared awareness or common interest of any kind. If it had been Dana, or Mikkel, or Kara, I like to think that I would have reacted differently, that I would have been one of the people sobbing into their hands, instead of one of the people wishing they were sobbing and staring at the walls instead. That day, to try and explain my cold response to his death, I theorized that some other day it was all going to suddenly hit me, that I would unexpectedly be crippled with an intense remorse; that ultimately, the true and inconsolable feelings that I was repressing inside of myself would surface. But they never did.

The sounds of the entire community grieving continued for quite some time, until Chalmon walked to the front of the hall and stood before Harek, who was leaning against the back wall with an empty stare. He swallowed hard, his Adam's apple rising and falling, before he addressed us, "I am so sorry for us all.

"Though – as much as I doubt it helps to think of this right now – we should keep in mind that the energy inside Peik, the energy that created him from chaos, is something that will exist forever, carrying on eternally in different and varying forms. Although we will never see him again, what he was made of will never die." He broke off and turned around to look at Harek, who then nodded and straightened up.

124

"So," Chalmon said, turning back around, "We would like to move this all outside into the fresh air, and spend the rest of the day in each other's company, supporting one another in whatever way we need to be supported.

"I think it's safe to say that the next little while is going to be a difficult time for our island, and that we will need to pull together as a community more than ever." He moved to the door and opened it as quietly as he could.

"But before you go," he called out, holding a hand up as a gesture to stop people from standing just yet, "we wanted to have a quick meeting with everyone who has access to the disclosed wing of the Great Hall. It'll only be a few minutes. Everyone else: Please," he held his arm out to the open door, "Please find someone to comfort, and be comforted by."

The respective people stood and walked out, moaning and sniffling, a few arms draping over shoulders, a few people leaning on one another. Once they'd all filed through the door, Chalmon closed it as gently as he'd opened it, a tender expression on his face, leaning against the wood for a few seconds, staring down at his feet. But when he turned around, that expression was gone.

As soon as he'd mentioned the disclosed wing, Mikkel and I, the youngest people remaining in the room, had straightened up. We knew what this would be about, who they would be trying to find; just like we knew that they would be using every tool they could conceive of to do it. I'm sure that we both understood that we would have to stay unshakably calm throughout the entire ordeal, as they would be looking for the slightest nervous twitch, the smallest movement of uneasy tension. To prepare myself for this, I folded my hands patiently in my lap, and began, for some reason, to count backwards silently.

Ninety-nine, ninety-eight, ninety-seven, ninety-six...

Harek stepped forward and pulled the pieces of paper that Peik had thrown to the ground out of his pocket, and then held them up high in the air with the same ceremonious importance as that of our unbalanced friend. No one in the room (about a third of which being women) seemed to have been told what the

125

crumpled pages were all about. Seeing this, Mikkel and I did our best to look baffled as well, even though Chalmon knew perfectly well that we'd seen them earlier.

"What these are," began Harek, infuriated, speaking through a thin space between his lips, "are three pages of encyclopaedia text, which were cut out and pilfered from the disclosed wing of the Great Hall." He lowered the evidence and took a couple of steps forward, his eyebrows sinking as low as his voice, "Understand this: I will not think of that poor boy's death as a suicide – nor will I think of it as some kind of flustered and irrational escape attempt. Because it wasn't – make no mistake. It was murder."

Harek gave the pages in his hand an aggressive flick, holding them out to the side so everyone could see them again, "The person who put these foolish, quixotic ideas into his head, the person who slipped him these pages in order to deliberately mislead him... that person is the one who led him to his grave. Does everyone understand that? That person killed one of our children." He was looking at different faces throughout the room, his chin quivering again; though he seemed determined not to let his voice break this time; it was deep and controlled.

"I can't think of anything more threatening to the life of our island than some spineless man or woman, skulking around among us, putting dangerous ideas into people's heads, and then watching the gruesome results from the sidelines. What vile, disgusting cowardice! What pathetically empty idealism one of you has!" he spat out, mostly eyeing the women, though pausing at a few of the men as well, Dana in particular.

Seventy-three, seventy-two, seventy-one...

"What would we do with such a person if we knew who they were – how would we deal with them? What do you think a fair punishment would be for attempting to undermine our very existence, and taking the life of a loved one along the way?"

Fifty-six, fifty-five... fifty...

I paused. Harek didn't have to say it aloud; we all knew what he meant, we knew what would happen to that person if they were caught.

Which was something I had to stop thinking about.

126

Fifty-four, fifty-three, fifty-two... fifty-one...

But I couldn't stop thinking about it. One flickering image kept pulsing into my mind. It was a picture of Mikkel, somewhere at the bottom of the cliffs on the north shore, his body draped over the stones, limbs sprawled out in unnatural angles, a few threads of blood branching out along the dark rock, clawing their way to the thirsty water like lightening to ground.

And I should never have allowed it to enter my mind. I should have just kept counting instead. Because stopping to let this picture slip through, stopping to imagine Mikkel twirling through the air as the ground rose to meet him, the detail of the rock increasing with each millisecond, was just enough to make me shift in my seat. And that, in turn, was enough to make Harek's attention dart toward me with all of the focus of a bird of prey. Finally, he'd uncovered a lead.

He strode over to the table I was sitting at and stopped right in front of me, every eye in the room following him, already weighing my mannerisms, ready to measure the pauses between my words, and wondering if I was the one.

But – and this is the strangest thing about that whole loaded moment – I didn't really panic. In fact, I can't say I remember even being worried. I was just... detached, calm. I knew what had to be done. I was going to be asked a direct question, which, in turn, I would have to answer with a lie. And I would have to do this convincingly; my voice would have to be spoken in a tone that everyone would believe, unconditionally. Or Mikkel would die.

My ears were ringing. But my answer was ready.

"Joshua, I don't suppose you would have any idea who might have removed these papers and given them to Peik, would you?" he asked, jerking the papers in his hand again. I could see Mikkel in my periphery, being very careful not to shift uneasily in his seat.

"No, I don't," I said, my voice plain, the words not spoken too quickly or slowly.

Harek relaxed, believing it. At the same time, everyone else's shoulders in the room perceptibly loosened, some people even beginning to look around for the next person to be grilled – one down, everyone else to go. But, as it turned out, Harek had very different ideas for this interrogation; namely to end it.

As he stood in front of me, I watched his expression distort into something appalled, saddened, as if he wanted to apologize for the state he'd let himself digress into – that he'd let us all digress into. He shook his head and returned to the front of the hall where he stood with his side to us, his eyes lowered to the ground. "No," he began, his voice tired, "I shouldn't have started us looking for blood. We all know that 'an eye for an eye' isn't any way to balance things – it only enforces the imbalance in us all that caused the incident in the first place. No. I will not have our island ripped apart by a witch-hunt. This will end here. Whoever it is, they will live the rest of their days with the blood of an innocent boy on their hands, which is punishment enough – though a punishment well-deserved." He looked down at the pieces of paper and gave them a sad, ironic smirk, as if they were covered with the repetitive scribblings of a single tactless joke. Then he ripped them in half, and in half again, and again, his motions sluggish, exhausted. He folded the pieces tight into his palm and put them in his pocket.

"Besides – how could we even be sure that it was somebody in this room? As vigilant as we are about the security of the disclosed wing… anything's possible.

"No. What we need to do is be there for our community." He turned to face us, his arms dangling limply at his sides, "One of our children died today. Now the rest of them will need us more than ever. Come," he gestured toward the door, and then turned and walked out, his feet slow and dragging. We all stood and followed.

As we filed through the doorway, people took advantage of the uncommon closeness of our bodies to pass on a gesture of consolation, touching one another on the shoulders, some people patting others' backs. At one point, I was pressed up against the door for a moment, unable to move as everyone squished against my other side, which was when, among all the knots of limbs and torsos, I felt someone squeeze my arm incredibly tightly, and then tap it twice before letting go. I knew that it was Mikkel, and I knew that, given the circumstances, he was thanking me in the loudest way he could.

It wasn't until I stepped out into the fresh air, and could finally begin to let my guard down (as the atmosphere of suspicion receded) that I realized, of all things, I was proud of what I'd done. After all, Harek was right; Mikkel would have Peik's death on his head for the rest of his life, and as far as I was concerned, that was more than enough 'justice' for one day. He didn't deserve more.

After we'd fanned out into the forest, Dana pulled me to the side and asked, as it seemed I wasn't having too many problems coping with things, if I might be able to 'support' Anu. Of course, he was really asking me to be on damage control, hoping that I might prevent him from running around as wildly as he usually did, distressing everyone at such a sensitive time. I agreed and pulled Anu as far to the side as I could, and, feeling as if I should at least see if he wanted to talk about things, I asked him if he knew what was going on. He looked at me deadpan and told me that Peik went into the sea. I nodded and asked if he knew that Peik would never come back, at which point he looked me up and down as if I were stupid – of course he wasn't coming back, he went into the sea. Then he looked around for something to destroy and found it almost instantly; a line of large ants moving across a piece of exposed soil right in front of us. He quickly set out to squash them all, lunging forward and thumping his sandals flat on the earth, a hand on his knee to help with the pressure.

Generally speaking, I didn't much enjoy Anu's company.

"Would you stop that please?" I asked, trying to keep my volume down.

"Why?" he shot back at me, his voice as loud as normal.

"Because," I whispered, bending closer to him, "it's disturbing."

He looked at me slantwise for a moment, suspicious; then turned defiantly and continued quashing the life from the line of insects. I sighed, and in the end, just let him – at least he wasn't running wild through the mourning community.

I looked out at the tiny clusters of people spread throughout the trees, and tried to listen above the stamping of earth behind me. I could hear people crying, mumbling, consoling one another – talking. And I had to admit: I thought there was something strange in the sound of the murmurs; or maybe it was just in the air, around us, in the very back of everyone's mind. Something had changed above and beyond the fact that one of our lifelong companions had died, and it wasn't distinct, it was remote and nameless; it was the type of thing that I'd probably never be able to put my finger on, yet somehow still knew was there.

This made me think back to what Peik had said to everyone. True, it was only a few sentences that he managed to get out, and thankfully those sentences were openly rejected as delusional and paranoid, but that didn't change the fact that every word of them was true. It was a bit unnerving – because, if you think about it, there are no words that can ever really be ignored. No. They're still there; regardless of how much we'd refused them at the time, they are still buried in our minds, resting in one of the derelict acres of our memory. And in many respects, those words that we dismiss are like seeds, biding dormant, waiting, quavering with life beneath the surface, until the moment comes when the conditions are just right, and then, suddenly – they make perfect sense.

15

Understandably, quite a few things changed on the island after Peik's death. Just as Harek promised, there was never a formal attempt to find out who'd stolen the infamous pieces of paper, but that didn't mean that precautions weren't taken to prevent the mysterious smuggler from doing any more damage. For one, they developed a new system of going into the disclosed wing, which allowed everyone to monitor one another more closely. Instead of certain people being in there at different times, it was decided that it would be safer to unlock it for a few hours every couple of days, and have everyone who had access to be in there at once; the more wary eyes the better, I guess. They also became even stricter about keeping track of where people were and who they were with, especially Mikkel and I – and not because they were suspicious of us, but because we would be the obvious targets of that 'malignant individual' among us, just as Peik had been. But, as far as I was concerned, of all these things, the biggest change that was made was in something that wasn't done.

From what was explained to me, the Elders had wanted to train all of the most promising young men on the island, and then choose the leader from within that pool. But – and this was contrary to Mikkel's theory – besides the three of us who'd already been selected, I thought there were a couple of other young men on the island who had the potential to run the expedition as well. However, after Peik died, they must have decided not to risk giving anyone the truth again. Because knowing that the paper cutter was still at large, and was probably just as willing to throw the wrench of his or her conflicting beliefs into the works, the last thing they wanted to do was give them an opportunity to throw it. After all, there was the potential for a much larger scale disaster to unfold – an undermining conspiracy, for example, a revolt. Which meant that this great talented 'pool' they'd planned on forming, would have to remain a measly two people: Mikkel and myself. And of those two people, it was quickly becoming clear which one of us was going to be chosen.

Frankly speaking, we all knew that Mikkel was the better choice. People naturally followed him, listened to him, and wanted to please him. He was intelligent, socially skilled, rational, and as we'd all witnessed throughout the countless sailing lessons in our lives, could orchestrate a large crew in difficult conditions with the greatest of proficiency. The only problem was that, like so many other things that had changed after Peik's death, something inside of Mikkel had as well.

It wasn't anything obvious, but it was there, and I'm sure the Elders had quickly noticed it. It wasn't in his words or his walk, or in the way he behaved with people, but rather how he acted when he thought no one was watching, the look on his face when you came around the corner and met him on the trail, watching the ground in front of him with a desolate stare. He seemed dampened by something. And of course, I knew exactly what that 'something' was: guilt. Mikkel had simply come to the grim understanding that he was partially responsible for someone else's death.

The Elders probably recalled how he'd seemed this way after Coming of Age as well, and might have seen it as a potential pattern – and obviously not a favourable one. Because if this was how Mikkel acted in the face of adversity (a thing that was bound to come up on a life-long journey, time and time again) it meant that, were he the leader, there might be periods of time when his lagging melancholy might leave the expedition directionless. A possibility that didn't inspire a lot of confidence, I'm sure. So, in the end, they probably decided to wait and see how long it would take for him to revert back to his normal self, as if to time it, as if to weigh out how long the crew might have to fend for themselves without clear guidance. And once they recognized that he wasn't really coming around, the decision was probably all but made.

Suddenly, I became the focus of all their energy. The intensity of my education increased, the topics shifted and became more detailed, and the amount of time that I spent studying and talking with the Elders took up almost all of my waking hours. It was exciting to know that I'd been bumped up to their first choice, and there were times during those promising weeks, as I shuffled from one building to the next, that I would find myself looking out at the sea through the trees, the shining surface moving along with me between the branches, and just let my mind wander as to what we were going to find out there – mountains, plains, forests, relics, ruins, ice – and invariably, I'd have a smug little smile on my face by the time I'd opened the door to the next building. I was getting closer every day, was almost within reach, and I could feel it. Until finally, after spending so much time imagining what the opportunity would look like in the palm of my hand, one day, I opened my fingers to find that it was actually there.

So, yes, when they announced that I'd been chosen as the leader of the expedition it wasn't really a shock, but one of the details that came along with it, I must say, was. Apparently, not only would Mikkel be joining the expedition, he was also going to be second in command! And the reason they cited for this was as logical as could be (and I felt stupid for not having seen it myself): if I were the only one who actually knew what the purpose of the journey was, and I were to get killed, become injured, or even fall seriously ill, then that purpose would become void. So, as was now plain to see, they had always planned on having at least two of us on the ship that knew the truth, hence providing the option of handing over the hidden responsibilities, were that need to arise. The Elders were sly – I'll give them that. Because they knew perfectly well if we were under the impression that only one of us would be going, we'd compete more fiercely, nudge our elbows in front of the other person more ruthlessly, and provide them with the perfect arena to find out who was most bought in, who had the most conviction. And thinking of it that way, I guess it wasn't really Mikkel or I who'd won this little skirmish, it was them. Again.

And I have to admit that, of all the things I could have felt when I heard that Mikkel would be coming, mostly, I was disappointed. Because I had set out to beat him, to be better than him, to believe in things more deeply and honestly than he had. I mean – if both of us had always been guaranteed a place on the ship, it certainly wasn't worth all the effort I'd put in. Come to think of it, I could see that I'd put in too much – really, I would've been happier as second in command, to be able to have a say without having all the responsibility, to be able to go along without having to break up any of the potential squabbles of the crew. Yet I also knew that what was done was done. It wasn't as if I could ask Mikkel to trade places with me, even if I'd thought of doing it behind the Elders' backs once we left the island; simply because, ideologically, I didn't really think he could be trusted as captain.

Which was the strangest part of it all: Mikkel, that rogue paper cutter that we were being so vigilantly protected against, that one person whose ethics and intentions were the most questionable of the entire island, was also the one who was going to have a level of authority in the very thing he could do the most damage with. It was a bit worrying, to say the least. And Mikkel must have sensed this hesitation on my part, because he made a point to pull me aside one day when no one else was around, to try and alleviate that very fear.

"Joshua," he began, putting his hands in his pockets, "I hope you realize that things that might have been said in the past don't really stand anymore. You know that, right?"

"What do you mean?" I asked, knowing exactly what he meant.

"I mean – you remember when we talked, and I was a bit confused? Well, I just want you to understand that that's all under the bridge now. I mean – I know why those ideas struck me back then, but I also know that they were wrong."

"Oh. Yeah. Well – don't worry about it." I said, trying to be nonchalant. But really, I was interested to hear more – something a bit more convincing maybe. "Though, uh – I'm interested to know – why did those ideas strike you... back then?"

He seemed hesitant once I asked this, but cordial nonetheless. "Well... I think that, mostly, it was because what we're doing is not only going against our nature or our instincts, but also against the very purpose of life. I think all of my confusion stemmed from that. But – I mean – that's over now.

Everything's straight in my head; and I can't wait to be on the expedition. It's great that we actually both get the chance to go, no?"

I held a hand out between us, "But wait – what do you mean by 'going against the very purpose of life'?"

He looked down at the ground, pushing his hands deeper into his pockets, "No, it's just that... Okay. The one thing that all life has in common is that it wants to reproduce, spread out, and be as successful as possible. Think of trees, insects, animals; I mean – all of nature is exploitative and devious. Everything alive is as thoughtless to the world around it as it is to its own species, because its purpose is to be greedy and corrupt, to thrive as best it can as an individual, which only helps the big picture of things. Population explosions, the hostile taking over of territory, the callous weeding out of the weak; there isn't a day that goes by that we don't see them all taking place in the forest, on the beach, in the ocean. And, it just struck me back then that maybe our 'abject nature' was really just... nature, and so didn't necessitate being destroyed."

"Hmm." I cleared my throat, "That's... an interesting idea, I guess."

"Not really. It was an interesting idea. But not anymore."

"Right."

He took a hand out of his pocket and scratched the back of his head, then twisted to look behind him for a second. "Well... we should really be getting the boat ready for sailing class like we're supposed to. I just wanted to let you know that things were straight in my head, and that you've got nothing to worry about in terms of my 'philosophies', so to speak."

"Oh. Well, thanks."

For the next week or so, I thought a lot about this conversation that we'd had, but for some reason, couldn't really get a handle on it, or, more specifically, on a way to prove or disprove it. Until finally, probably because I was becoming frustrated, I decided to bring it up with Dana and see what he had to say (though obviously made it sound like it was a question of my own). "Do you think that there's a purpose or meaning to the life that's in the world?" I posed, rather out of the blue.

135

He was sitting across from me, flipping through a book, and getting ready to quiz me on plant varieties that we would find in the lands we were travelling through, which had active chemical agents that I would need to use. When I'd asked the question, he looked up at me as if he'd been waiting for this theme to come up for a while, or had at least been prepared for it. "No, I don't," he muttered, flatly. "But you should know that that's a very human question to ask, and hence dangerous."

"Why? I mean – why is it so 'human' and so 'dangerous'?"

"Well, it's human because we as a species are forever straining to decipher some hidden message buried within, always trying to attribute reasons and significance to the things that happen, and to what we see around us. We love to give things this 'meaning' you're talking about. But the truth is, there isn't one that we can know of – not to life, not to anything.

"In fact, when we find ourselves asking what something 'means', we should just replace it with the question we are really asking, which is: what do we want it to mean? See – the very fact that you asked that question, tells me that you're already inclined toward an answer, already bending in one direction or another. Because, let's face it: we see what we look for, hear what we listen for, and sense what we want to feel, and the asking of something's meaning is only the sound of our struggling minds trying to create an appealing answer."

"So... that's it? Everything around us is empty? And the question is dangerous because it's always fruitless?"

"No, I'm not saying that. I'm saying that it's dangerous because it's impossible for us to know if the answer that we create fits reality, but that regardless, we fit it anyway – with whatever substance we want or need to contain. We bend this supposed 'will' of the world around us to suit our own means, and, most often, to support ideas that, otherwise, we would never be able to find support for. We shove a meaning into something when we want it to rationalize our dirty work, or at the very least, to make it appear cleaner. And even if we don't do it for that reason, even if we do it while innocently trying to subjugate the universe, to make it all seem orderly and planned, it is still just as absurd. Because the real truth of the matter is that life is far too complex to be contained by the petty human notion of meaning. Life – that unending, undying, throbbing tangle of complexity – will never be summed up or affected by the silly little labels we pin onto it, will never take notice of the tiny selfish proposals we've had the audacity to stick onto its innermost atoms. It's greater than anything we could possibly ever pretend to be. Period."

I nodded slowly. That's what I'd thought. Mikkel wasn't really on top of things; he just had the illusion that he was. And this was the problem with weighing anything that he said too heavily. Because Mikkel was clever enough to take things apart in a cognitive way, but not clever enough to realize that his fear was shaping how he splayed the dissection across the table for examination. Though, this didn't mean that he was going to be a problem on the expedition, didn't mean that he was going to inhibit it in any way. It just meant that he sometimes had a tendency to mislead himself, and that, knowing this, I would have to be careful not to recklessly follow him. And, really, being the leader put me in the perfect position to do exactly that. Yes, I rationalized, it was beginning to seem like the roles we'd been given would fit together perfectly. (Somehow, no matter how questionable things were shaping up to be around me, I was becoming increasingly confident that none of it would be a problem, that this expedition of ours was going to run smoothly from the very second we embarked.)

"Now," Dana said, looking down at his book and snapping me from my thoughts, "getting back to what we were doing. Can you describe to me the vegetative characteristics of Atropa belladonna, please?"

I interlocked my fingers on the table in front of me, "Yes. It has dull green leaves, violet or greenish flowers in the axils of the forking branches, shiny black berries, and a large tapering root."

"Excellent. And can you give me a detailed description of where you would find it growing?"

And I could, because after I'd been chosen, this was what a lot of my training was centred on, locating and keying the correct plants to make sterilization mixtures. The reason we had to spend so much time on it was because I would be using different vegetation from what was found on the island, and so had to know how to identify plants that would be foreign to me, and how to isolate their active ingredients. For months I worked in a lab inside the shelter with vegetation close to what we would supposedly find on this mainland that we would be exploring; boiling leaves and roots down to create tinctures, and sometimes adding them to others, to either intensify, or further separate a toxin inside of them. And generally speaking, that was what we were always trying to do: isolate a toxin; and usually a fairly potent one at that (as was made clear by all the precautions we had to take in the lab). And seeing how careful our safety measures had to be, led me to ask whether or not there would be any side effects to these sterilization mixtures; at which point I was met with a roomful of nodding heads. Of course there would be, they'd responded, as if it were a stupid question. They were quick to add that it was essential to understand the implications to that little detail as well. Which was that we'd have to flee from anyone I ever administered the mixtures to, the moment I found a way to slip it into a food source that was sure to be eaten by everyone in their group at the same time; because, rest assured, every one of them would be able to tell that they'd been given something, and would probably lash out because of it. Which also meant that we'd have to avoid them at all cost afterwards; though, they pointed out, that would be easy enough to do, provided we just continue on in the grid-like search pattern that had been routed for us on the maps.

To be honest, exactly how the sterilization mixtures worked on the different sexual systems of men and women didn't really make a lot of sense to me. The Elders had pulled out a few of the most advanced chemistry textbooks, along with a few physiological diagrams to try and explain it to me once, but, and maybe because they knew how much I hated chemical theory, they decided to spare me the finer points. All I really had to know was that, apparently, the concoctions I was being trained to make had a specific kind of toxicity that would render sperm inactive, and cause the cell walls of women's eggs to weaken and collapse, leaving anyone who ingested it to be permanently

138

sterile. They never did mention what the side effects would have been, but I can imagine they were significant, only because, if they weren't, we probably would have used a similar kind of chemical sterilization on the island, instead of having operations, which must have always had a risk of infection to them.

But all of this training on how to make the mixtures didn't mean that the Elders expected me to start concocting them the moment we reached the mainland. No, instead, they'd already made a substantial amount of them for me to take along. In fact, considering how low the probability of finding anyone alive was, there was probably enough to last decades, if not our lifetime. These pre-made mixtures were kept in curious looking vials that would be stored in sturdy cases inside the captain's quarters, along with the lab equipment to make new ones when the time came. The cases themselves seemed to be designed exactly for this, as everything fit inside of them like a puzzle, carefully cut foam securing the different apparatuses, and tiny alcoves clutching the many vials of murky orange and green liquid. No space was wasted, and not one piece of glass was in danger of breaking.

But all of this focus on the mixtures in my training would have been useless if I couldn't get close enough to people to plant it in their food. So, for quite some time, we also focused on the difficulties we would come up against in infiltrating a community that was probably unnerved. And then, to try and put the theories that came out of the brainstorming into actual practice, they had me running after a group of monkeys in the forest for a few days, experimenting with different behaviours to try and become accepted, and analyzing what seemed to work and what didn't. This all emphasized how unobtrusive we would have to be in order to enter a group of people, and that the prospect of being truly accepted by them wasn't all that realistic, or, in fact, even important. Rather, if we just concentrated on gaining sufficient trust as to have them lower their guard a bit, and take their eyes off us long enough for me to get near their food, that would suffice.

But to do this, I would obviously have to be able to converse with them, and so we also spent a fair bit of time doing adaptive communication exercises. Because it was impossible to predict what language people might speak, or how dialects of languages that were spoken might have evolved, they focused on teaching me how to communicate without language, and how to direct people to unknowingly teach you theirs. Most of this focused on moving from the naming of concrete nouns, to the isolation of useful structures. And just as it was with sailing and gardening, quite a few of the women were involved in these lessons, some of them surprising me by suddenly speaking in a completely different tongue, giving me a perfect chance to practice what I'd learned.

Needless to say, I dove into all of these new topics with the greatest of energy – maybe even a bit exaggeratedly. I think there was a part of me that wanted to prove to the Elders that they'd chosen the right person for the job; and I think that, mostly, I succeeded. Every day saw their confidence in my abilities growing, and I know this because, for the first time in my life, they weren't afraid of letting me know when my progress impressed them. And it often did. I would do wonderfully, they sometimes assured, roughing up the back of my hair as they passed, or after closing their book at the end of a long lesson and then grinning at me with nothing short of pride in their expression. And, to tell the truth, I absorbed their encouragements, soaked them up until I believed their every word. I can almost picture myself now, caught in some private moment after one of my long days of training, staring at the ocean, smirking, hands on my hips, nodding with confidence. Yes. I would do wonderfully.

16

It was completely different from how I'd imagined it. Nobody, either on the ship or lining the shore, was saying a word. No hollers of farewell, no cupping of mouths to shout out last-second goodbyes. Nothing. Instead, we just looked at each other, as if dazed, watching the span of water between us grow, and the details of facial expressions, and then of figures, and finally of land features, as they blurred with the distance. Every once in awhile someone would wave, an arm lifting from the throng of bodies like the flash of a tail in a group of animals, and this would, in turn, evoke a quick gesture of reply from the opposite line-up, but the arms would soon sink back out of sight again. While we worked to man the sails, the crew only paid attention to whatever they were doing for the absolute minimum amount of time required, their heads twisting back toward the island the moment it was safe to; all of them so intent on watching this scene of people stupidly watching each other. I think it's safe to say that this 'big day' that we'd all been anticipating was, to say the least, a little anticlimactic, especially considering the hectic nature of the preparations; and for myself, considering the build up of all the bizarre moments that led up to that morning.

At first, there had been a lot of confusion as to whether or not the expedition should set off when it was originally intended to. They'd spent a lot of time trying to decide whether it was better to leave during the month that had the smallest risk of storms, or the month that had the most favourable currents and winds for our destination. Eventually, it was decided that we would set sail in the month that fell between the two, which everyone seemed content with; until, that is, a few unexpected problems came up with the ship, delaying us by a few weeks. And as our target date drifted by, the pressing question was raised: should we wait an entire year for that ideal window of time to appear again, or set sail as soon as we could? Or, to put it another way, could we risk giving the paper cutter an extra twelve months to study our weaknesses, to patiently watch and wait for our guard to drop? Their eyes probably skirted around the room with this thought, followed by a prompt clearing of throats and straightening up, the room grumbling with a sudden decision – the expedition would leave as soon as possible. Which is what gave those last weeks the urgency they had.

Suddenly, on top of getting everything organized for a lifelong voyage, the people who had assumed we would wait another year, now had very little time to say their goodbyes, make amends, or hand down pieces of advice that they'd always wanted to hand down. And though there had been ample opportunity during our training to do this, everyone chose to wait until the last second; myself included, I guess. As a result, what could have been tender or thought-provoking moments were pressed into a few rushed minutes of frenzied words.

Like Mitra, our sailing instructor, taking me out alone on one of the smaller boats and doling out technical advice as to what to do in a few rare circumstances, most of which, she was sure to add, she'd never actually experienced, but had at least read about. She paced around me while I was rigging the sails, explaining things, speaking faster than I'd ever heard her speak before, blinking like mad, touching me on the shoulders every time she passed, even if there was enough space for her to walk by without coming near me. Of course, knowing what I know now, I should have been hanging on her every word (and if I could go back in time, I would have certainly probed her brain with many a specific question), but, as it was, I spent the hours just waiting for the uncomfortable ordeal to be over with, calculating how long it would take to get into the harbour while nodding in her general direction whenever she paused.

Then there was Harek, calling me into a room after the midday meal, constantly grooming his beard, standing in front of me while I sat down, reiterating all of the different aspects of my responsibilities that we'd already been through ad nauseam. As he spoke, a twitching smile would light up his face for a few brief seconds, and then disappear, his expression always either too happy or too neutral, neither of them seeming to fit what was being said.

And poor Chalmon, who was probably the most ill at ease of them all, plying his hands together, bobbing his head up and down as he spoke, and talking in circles about nothing. Then, as we walked back out through the doorway together, both of us mystified as to what he'd actually wanted to say, he took the opportunity to pat me on the back with a stiff hand and quickly walk away.

Though, I have to admit that, with Dana, things were a bit different, if only because he didn't set out to give me some advice that I'd never asked for. Instead, he just wanted to hear a few honest words from me; and not expecting this in the least, it seemed it was my turn to feel a little discomfited. We went for a walk one afternoon, and midway through it broke off from the trail and headed toward a fallen tree, where he'd gestured for me to take a seat. I was so convinced that I knew what was going to happen, so sure that I was about to be witness to yet another painstaking ritual of closure, that I prompted him to begin once we sat down, as if to get it over with as soon as possible. "So – do you have a few wise words you'd like to pass on?"

He seemed a bit taken aback by this, if not a little regretful that, in fact, he didn't. "Uh… not really, no. I guess I just wanted to pull you aside before you left and find out if there was anything you were nervous about," he shrugged his shoulders. "Maybe see if you needed some last-minute reassurance of some kind. That's all."

"Oh," I said, feeling guilty about the intonation I'd used to start things off. It was a rare thing to have an Elder really, sincerely asking you what you were thinking. And the question of whether I was privately intimidated by something was enough to throw me off kilter a bit, because, well, there was something that I was worrying about before I fell asleep some nights. Actually, every night. "Um, yeah – I mean – once in a while, I guess… I wonder if the crew is going to act differently toward me once we're away from the island."

"Hmm," he murmured, pausing for all of one second to consider the likelihood of this happening, "Well… if you mean that you're wondering if they'll test your authority – believe me: they will. And don't be offended when they do; it's only natural.

143

Just make sure that, when it happens, you stay confident and self-assured, and if anything, be more assertive than you think you should be. Loosening people's reins later on is always an option, whereas tightening them isn't. Though, I think that only makes sense, no?"

I squirmed a bit on the log, "Yeah, of course – I mean – I'm sure I'll do fine when the time comes. I just – you know…" I trailed off, growing more uncomfortable with the topic by the second. We were talking about a weakness of mine here, and one that I didn't like admitting to myself, let alone to others – and most of all to Dana. I bent over and removed one of my sandals, brushing off the sole of my foot and fanning my toes out to get the sand out from between them. Dana watched this little nervous display with a grin, and then focused his attention on the peculiarity of my toes.

Unlike anyone else on the island, the two smallest toes of my right foot were joined together, a sheath of skin and flesh wrapping around them until about midway, where they finally stuck out individually at the end. It was something that everyone had always known about me, but Dana seemed to be looking at them as if he were seeing them for the first time. I joined him, both of us stopping to stare down the length of my leg, and it felt comically appropriate to wiggle them a bit, as if to add some life to the display.

"Actually, your toes bring to mind something that I've never really thought to mention. Do you remember my telling you about some of the potent weapons that were dropped in a few places, near the end of the first phase?" He waited until I'd nodded before continuing, "Well, as you know, mutations, like your toes, happen all the time, but the effect of these weapons is that they drastically increase their likelihood. Now, if you continue to cycle through the route that we've marked out for you on the maps, you won't come anywhere close to the places where those weapons were dropped, but that doesn't necessarily mean you won't see animals that have migrated from them, or maybe even just through them. Which means that if you ever come across creatures that don't seem to make any evolutionary sense, you know why – it's the result of those weapons. (Though, come to think of it, it might also just be the effect that transporting plants and animals between ecosystems for hundreds of years has had on the earth.) Regardless, there's the possibility of seeing some very strange flora or fauna out there, which, as I'm sure you can imagine, will only help evolution in the long run."

I must say that I was a little lost at the disconnectedness of this tangent. It certainly had very little to do with the crew acting differently toward me once we left the island, and I wasn't sure if he'd brought it up to save me from the awkwardness of the subject, or out of genuine interest. "So, Dana – I'm sorry – what are you trying to say with this?"

"Nothing really." As was his habit, he turned to look at me with his eyes closed, opening them once they were pointed at my face, "I guess I'm just pointing out that you'll have some interesting things to look out for," he concluded, grinning at the ambiguity of his words.

"Right," I said, and then looked down at my toes. "Right."

After that, the goodbyes again returned to being clumsy and graceless for the people who had dragged me into a corner to say them. But at least (for the most part anyway) they seemed to pass by fairly quickly, until there was finally no one left to say goodbye to. And of course, looking back at all of these fumbling exchanges, it's obvious that Kara's is the one that stands out the most; and not only because it was the most stressful, but because, considering how disastrous things could have unfolded that day, it was probably one of the luckiest moments of my life.

Most of that potential for disaster had to do with the pieces of paper that I'd cut out of the art book to give her, which had only proven to be a burden that became heavier with time. Needless to say, having stolen them was already enough to land me in serious trouble, but when Peik had held out his wad of pages, and then cracked and sprinted into the sea, they had suddenly become the sole evidence that was needed to confirm the identity of the paper cutter. And even if it wasn't me, that's exactly what I would have become. Because let's face it: if I were caught with a couple of inconsequential paintings, it would have been doubtful that someone else had gone through the

145

considerable trouble it would have taken to smuggle them to me. Their rationale would have been straightforward: the kind of person who would cut something trivial out of the library could only be the kind of person who was so used to cutting other things out (i.e. disclosed material) that they'd started pilfering things simply out of interest. They would strip me of my position, ban me from the expedition, and probably punish me for Peik's death; none of which I wanted to take a chance with. So, it was clear that I had to get rid of them. However, knowing this was one thing, whereas finding a way to actually do it was quite another. After Peik's death, Mikkel and I had to be accounted for at all times, with Elders even being assigned to sleep near our rooms (and they were incredibly light sleepers, too, sitting up in their beds when we stepped outside to urinate, alert to where we were standing, waiting for us to go back to sleep), and other Elders to escort us from one site of the island to another throughout the day – not exactly an atmosphere conducive to the disposing of illicit papers. The idea did cross my mind to just leave them where they were (which was jammed between two boards under my bed), but I knew that if anyone ever discovered them after we were gone, they would note that they were paintings, which would only have led people to suspect Dana of everything, and I felt like I owed him a little more than to leave him with a brutal onus like that. But as much as I mulled this over, the only way I could think of getting rid of them was to shove them down my pants and walk around with them, waiting for a safe opportunity to bury them somewhere, which, during the last few days of preparation, is what I started doing. And this looked like it was going to work out fine, because as the errands that had to be done before disembarking were growing in number and urgency, everyone was finally too busy to be waddling beside Mikkel and I at every hour, and as I was doing just as much as everyone else, I often found myself running around on errands as well, and knew that a time was bound to come along when I would find myself alone and unwatched. Which is exactly what happened that day.

I was helping with the organization of the expedition's food, gathering things to compensate for what we were falling

146

short on, when I realized that I was the only person on one of the trails. I stopped and, after spinning around, saw a few bushes that I would be able to hide behind while burying the pieces of paper. Wonderful. I craned my neck in every direction, listening for people coming from either side before stepping off the path – but, unfortunately, after a few seconds, I could hear that there was. Frustrated, I slapped my leg and started walking in the direction of the sounds, trying to keep myself from looking either annoyed or suspicious. But as luck would have it, of all the people that could have come into view on that particular afternoon, it happened to be Kara. And she was alone.

It had been so long since we'd met to talk that neither of us really knew what to do at first. We'd stopped in our tracks, frozen, and then, seeming to snap out of abstraction at the same time, started mouthing silent words, both of us pointing at different groups of shrubs where we could scamper to and take cover. Finally, smiling, she shook her head and just started walking into the underbrush toward one of them, and soon sunk out of sight behind it. I followed, trying to remember what we'd talked about last, and, getting a little annoyed at myself that I couldn't, stooped down next to her.

From the outset, things were strange between us that day. There was a nervousness in her movements, and one that was very different from what I'd seen in other people who were saying goodbye. It was guarded in the same way, but beneath it there was this jittery energy, something intense, anxious. For myself, as was usually the case when I was with her, I was struck dumb at first, and though I concentrated on looking her in the face, I couldn't stop my eyes from dropping to the smooth hollows of her neck, or to her chest, or then to her waist, where I stopped; because she was sitting at an odd enough angle that a sliver of skin could be seen between the bottom of her shirt and the waistline of her pants. Soft skin in creamy shadows, which did nothing but make my imagination slide away, helplessly away, onto a warm and smooth landscape where I know I shouldn't have been.

I shot my eyes back up at her face, my scalp warming with embarrassment. In the short silence that followed, I also became incredibly self-conscious as to how much I was swallowing, sure that I looked as if I were sucking saliva into my mouth just to drink it down. It was time to try and save myself. "I – um…" I began, but my whisper quickly fell away. I wasn't really sure what I was supposed to say, or for that matter, seeing as I couldn't remember what we'd discussed the time before, even what the general topic was that I was supposed to be saying something about. But when I scanned my mind for something else of substance to blurt out, I remembered the paintings. "Oh!" I said aloud, "I – uh… I have something for you!" And then, in a rather ill-advised impulse, I slammed my back onto the ground and shoved my hand down the front of my pants to fish around for the pieces of paper.

She was, to say the least, a little shocked. Until that point, she had seemed unusually passive, sitting fairly still, an amused little smile on her face, but as soon as I started digging around inside my pants, she'd sat up a bit, her eyebrows working between expressions of disgusted curiosity and aversion, her hands placed on the ground on either side of her, as if she wasn't quite sure of whether she should move away from me or not. Understandably, she relaxed when she saw the pieces of paper, smiling with a bit of relief, and then adjusted her legs to kneel down, positioning herself to better inspect the pages.

"I've been meaning to show these to you for quite a while," I whispered as I unfolded them, "but… well, didn't really have a chance." I flattened them as best I could and rotated them until they were oriented for her to see. "I guess… I wanted to find out if there was something in them – you know? Like some kind of code, or message or something. And I thought that, if there was anything to see, you'd be the one to see it."

I had always been right in thinking Kara would be affected by the paintings. As soon I put them in front of her, her mouth had fallen open a bit, and she leaned in closer to look at them, her eyes busy, her hand sometimes reaching out to run a few fingers along the glossy surface, as if she'd wanted to feel its texture, her focus seeming to pause at every individual colour, licking her lips like she could taste them. She studied the two paintings for longer than I'd ever expected her to, and as the minutes passed, we could hear the muffled sounds of two people pass by us along the trail.

When she was finally finished, she straightened up, still kneeling, and slid her hands from the ground, over her knees, and onto the top of her thighs. I watched her fingers move over the cloth of her pants until they settled there, and then I shuffled a bit closer. "So," I said, speaking as quietly as I could, just above a whisper, "what – uh... what are they about?"

"Well," she began, searching the leaves around us. Then she reached forward and, quite unexpectedly, placed her hand on my arm. Her thumb swept back and forth along my skin. I swallowed. "To tell you the truth," she ventured to say aloud, "I think they're about how we're worse than we think we are;" and then her face lit up with a curious smirk, "and better."

Even if I'd had hours to think her words through, they wouldn't have meant anything to me then, if only because I wasn't ready to hear them. Though, that isn't why I didn't think about them that day; I didn't think about them because I was concentrating on the warmth of her hand, on the smooth sweeping motion of her thumb, on the pulse that was beating ever louder in my throat, on the fact that both of us had stopped breathing. However, there was an even greater reason why her words evaded me; which was that, before I had a chance to ask her to expand, or even before I could begin to let my imagination run wild with what was going to happen next, another voice entered our conversation.

"Kara?" the voice called out, an accusatory tone ringing between the letters.

Everything stopped. Our mouths dropped open. I saw the pupils of her eyes dilate, the black of them ballooning out toward the edges of her irises. Her hand flung off my skin, her arms shooting out to her sides, fingertips sinking into the soil as if getting ready to launch herself out from the leaves and run. Whereas I had the opposite reaction, in that my body had instantly become useless. I was petrified, and slumped over, settling silently onto the ground, my head to the side. In my mind, I repeated the voice that had called out, and recognized it as Mitra's. It had sounded ridiculously clear, which meant that

149

she was probably standing on the section of trail that passed closest to the vegetation we were huddled in. It would take her five – maybe ten – seconds to get to us. I looked at the pieces of paper in front of my face. It was useless to try and hide them. It was useless to try and hide myself. There was nothing to do but lie there and watch Kara as the ugly mess unfolded.

But Kara had composed herself in an instant, and was busy staring forward, thinking. "Yeah?" she called out in reply, just before the pause would have become a suspicious length. But she didn't wait for Mitra to say anything before moving onto the next task that she'd somehow organized inside her head within the few seconds that had passed. She rocked forward onto her feet, being careful to keep her head low and out of sight as she did so, and turned to the side. Then she proceeded to untie her pants, and tucked her thumbs into the hem at the waist, ready to pull them down.

"What are you doing?" Mitra pressed.

"Well – if you must know – I'm taking a pee," she said, poking her head above the bush and flinging her hair to look behind her. At that point, she slid her pants down her legs with the most fluid motion she could, making sure that her head didn't drop a subtle inch out of Mitra's sight as she did so. For my part, even being as terrified as I was, I still had the presence of mind to take in every smooth detail of her thigh that I could.

"And talking?" asked Mitra.

"Singing, actually. But apparently not very well," Kara replied jokingly. It was amazing how calm she was, how shamelessly truthful she sounded.

"Oh." All at once, Mitra's voice had lost its sceptical edge, "Sorry."

Kara pulled up her pants as she stood up, looking down at the strings as she tied them, and then walked out from behind the shrubs and toward the trail.

"Are you going back to the gardens?" Mitra asked, her tone completely back to normal.

"Mm-hmm."

"Good. So am I."

Veracity

The dampened sounds of their walking on the bare soil began to recede, and I could hear snippets of their conversation as they walked away, talk of who would be doing what chores and when. I listened to their voices until they faded, until the whispering sounds that the trees were making drowned them out. When I was sure I was alone, I started to breathe again, the air cooling the inside of my mouth, my tongue, my throat.

At first, it was all I could do to just stare at the cleanly cut edges of the papers, watching as they shifted with a bit of breeze, one of the folds in the middle acting as a fulcrum, and the lazy weight on either side of it trying to decide which end was heavier. After a few minutes of staring forward like that, completely stunned, I lifted my head off the ground, tiny balls of dirt falling from my hair. I'm sure that the reason I was so dazed wasn't only to do with what had happened, it also had to do with the countless underlying urges and possibilities that had just been rendered null and void because of what had happened. I brought a slow arm up to my face until I could look at the spot where Kara had touched it, at the semicircle she had run her thumb across, at the tiny hairs there that were pointing in different directions. It was obvious that we would never touch each other again, never see each other again – ever; except maybe to wave goodbye as the ship set sail. I flopped my hand onto the ground in front of my face.

There are few words that could describe how frustrated, how furious I let myself become. My hand flexed. And then I watched my fingernails claw into the soil, the tendons bulging straight, digits sinking beneath the surface, digging their way deeper. I remember the shadows of the leaves darkening behind my hand, a ringing in my ears, and then my head clearing, just before it became very, very busy. The truth is, I don't even like to think of what went through my mind at that point – or at least not of the bleeding details.

They were images mostly, cold, flashing pictures in bluish-grey hues that told the vicious story of how Kara could come with us on the expedition. Sequences of running to get Mikkel, of finding out how he'd once planned on smuggling people onto the ship. I pictured nodding at him, smiling a cutting

151

smile. Then both of us bursting into the kitchen area. Throwing the men and women aside to get to the drawer of knives. Spinning around and sweeping a blade through the air. The walls spattering with dark dots. People backing away, showing their palms, staring at the floor, at the twitching, gurgling evidence of just how serious we were. The slamming open of the door again. The wild rushing to the ship. The crew scurrying to raise the sails. Kara and the children huddled below. The knives in our hands, thrashing through the air, through skin, through muscle tissue. The hollers of the Elders, the frightened, desperate hollers, commanding us to stop. Our blaring deafness to those commands. Mikkel and I, shoulder to shoulder, gripping the handles of our blades.

And then I stopped. I remember feeling the earth squishing between my fingers then, lying on my side behind the bushes, the pieces of paper still teetering semi-balanced in the slight movement of the air. I pulled my hand out of the soil and held it in front of my face, feeling that pressure under my fingernails that tells how stuffed full of dirt they are. I recall that I was breathing quickly, but was also calming down.

Because I had suddenly come to understand something that I'd discussed and analyzed so many times, yet had never really grasped: This was exactly why the Elders had so strictly forbidden Kara and I from seeing each other. It was because of the great potential that such relationships had to stir dangerous things inside us, things that were volatile and desperate, that could, and probably would be used to rationalize and carry out all sorts of troubling exploits. Like the ideas that had just flickered across my mind of killing people who were close to me, ideas that had seemed, not only justifiable, but almost glorious in some way, almost valiant. And the scariest part of all was knowing that, were Mikkel to have come by while my fingers were in the dirt, while I was grinding my teeth at the 'injustice' of not getting exactly what I wanted, I would have almost certainly stood up and let myself get swept away by it all. I would have become numb, blinded, and most likely ended up with blood splattered across my face. After months of tedious discussions, I was finally becoming aware of just how short the walk is between what we are, and what we can be. We only need a catalyst, something to nudge us forward onto the slippery slope, and the rest falls tragically into place. And the Elders, knowing this, were wise enough to guard us from it, to cautiously keep us from the devices of our weaknesses. They knew perfectly well that Kara was a likely vulnerability of mine, that she represented a place where I was prone to falter. And the more I recognized it as well, the more I understood that I had to get as far away from her as I possibly could.

I looked at the paintings again and shook my head. I had risked everything, and were it not for a bit of stupid luck and someone else's quick thinking, I would have lost it all. And how incredibly self-defeating that would've been. How ridiculous. I sat up and stared at the earth that I'd gouged out with my hand, and knew exactly what to do. I bent over and started digging a deep hole in the ground, ripping through roots and lifting out rocks, cupping handfuls of dark soil and piling them beside me. But when I was finished, I found that it wasn't enough just to throw the pages inside. No. I wanted to do more, wanted to make sure that I would never find myself down this stupid, frightening road again. I poked my head above the bushes to see if the coast was clear, and then ripped the paintings in half. And then again, and again, until they were tiny squares of colour, rimmed with a slender frame of white fibres, every one of them completely indecipherable. I sprinkled them into the ground and buried them, shoving the earth and stones back into the hole, until I was patting it down dense, pushing it with all of the weight of my body, my arms straight, hands stacked on top of one another. When I was satisfied, I sat back, cleaned my fingernails, and after listening for a long while to make sure no one was coming along the trail, I slipped out from the bushes, and walked away feeling completely relieved.

After that, it was only a collection of scattered moments as the last preparations were made, the rolling of food barrels up ramps, the inspirational talks to the crew, the final checking of equipment, until the raising of the mainsail in the sunlight that morning. And then we were off, there, on the ship, watching everyone on the island watching us, as we drifted away forever.

We stared at the shore until the people became indistinguishable from the foliage, until the waving of hands could have been the slight motion of branches on distant trees. Only then did the crew's attention to the stern of the ship begin to wane. And as soon as I noticed this happening, I ordered the raising of a jib sail on the foremast as an addition to the main, in hopes of keeping their minds occupied on something other than what we were leaving behind. Which worked, I think.

Hours passed, and things were running smoothly. The sun had crept up until it was directly overhead; our shadows slinking beneath our feet, and the winds were in our favour and even slowly picking up.

I was standing at the helm in the early afternoon when Niels' shout interrupted the quiet. "Joshua!" he hollered. I had my back to him at the time, and at the sound of my name, I was unsure of whether or not I should answer.

Just before we left (and I doubt it was a coincidence that it happened shortly after Dana and I had our little talk), the Elders had given the crew a long speech about the importance of maintaining the respect for rank on the ship. The crew were commanded to refer to me from that moment hence as 'captain', which was, I guess, Dana's way of pre-empting the questioning of my authority. Though, it wasn't really anything new for us. Throughout every sailing exercise we'd ever had in our lives, there had always been a clearly defined captain who was referred to as such, but I think this was viewed as an adolescent novelty more than anything else. We certainly didn't treat that person with more or less respect, it only indicated who would have to make the final decisions, maintain course, and divvy out orders. Among the younger people of the island, headings had never really held any meaning, and when I thought about the way Niels had called out my name instead of my title that first afternoon, it hardly seemed like a deliberate undermining of my command. Instead, given the fact that it was the very beginning of a lifelong journey, and that everyone was sure to have more than a few things weighing on their minds besides petty labels, it seemed like a fairly reasonable slip. And one that I decided to let slide.

"What?" I shouted over my shoulder.

"It's – uh," his voice lowered a bit, "it's gone."

I turned around. "What's gone?"

"The – um… the island." He was looking down at the deck, well aware of how childish he seemed. Though, whether it was childish or not, we all turned to squint at our wake as it fanned out behind us, looking for the vague outline of a mound in the distance, pressing out of the haze like an apparition. But he was right; there was nothing.

"Huh," I muttered. And then, very slowly, everyone on deck pivoted around to face me, their expressions expectant and uneasy for some reason. "Well," I cleared my throat, "thanks Niels," and then turned around to face the helm again, feeling everyone's eyes on my back. I listened to what was going on behind me until they returned to whatever they were doing, which didn't take long.

Meanwhile, Mikkel was in front of me, organizing some ropes. I could see that a playful grin had spread across his face after hearing Niels' grand proclamation, and with the universal inquiring gesture, I shot my chin out at him and raised my eyebrows. "What is it?" I asked.

Seeming a little surprised that I'd addressed him at first, he shrugged his shoulders and threaded one of the ends of the rope through a pulley. "Nothing really," he finally responded, and then paused for a moment to stare off into space, his grin broadening into the strangest smile, "I'm just happy."

"Huh," I acknowledged, looking down at the helm for a second, trying to understand. "Why?"

"'Cause…" he mumbled, giving me a sidelong glance, his eyes half-closed, "we're on our own now."

17

There is a strange excitement out at sea; and it isn't rooted in anything mysterious or ethereal, but rather inside a fact that everyone who has ever seen a map of the world can plainly see, and that is that the earth is mostly blue. Which, if you think about it, means that the moment you can become self-sufficient in a boat is also the moment every imaginable limit is lifted from you. You can go absolutely anywhere. And I think that once a person truly understands this, that the same water that they stare into when they lean over the rail of a ship is also stretching out to wrap around the entire globe, simultaneously lapping against every shore and spit of land that exists at that one sacred elevation called sea level, then, inevitably, their mind opens up like the sky.

But in the first few days of the expedition, that energy, which was normally so charged with promise, had become something very different, something muted, even gloomy, and I'm positive that I wasn't the only one to feel it. We were as quiet as we had been when we pulled away from the island. And maybe this was only due to the fact that the uncomfortable reality of our situation was slowly settling in; that situation being that we were boys fond of calling ourselves men, who had just left our home, never to return. Which, regardless of age or experience, is a sobering fact to face. And though the Elders had reminded us of it countless times, I don't think its certainty had ever really sunk in until those first few days, when the glaring solitude finally asserted itself from every possible angle.

Though, I venture to guess that it wasn't only loss that we felt, but also a tinge of disappointment. I remember noticing it for myself, organizing some ropes and thinking about Kara (or, rather, about how smooth her skin might have felt – and how I really shouldn't have allowed such a thought to come into my mind in the first place), and I happened to look over at Toivo, who had his hands in his pockets and was busy scratching at his crotch. He noticed me staring at him, and attempting to maintain some kind of grace, snorted a gob of phlegm into his mouth and turned to spit it into the water. I remember thinking, 'Well then. This is my new family. These are the closest relationships I'll have in the remaining span of my life, the people I'm going to grow old with. How very splendid.'

But in spite of the general miserableness of the first few days, slowly, slowly our spirits began to gather vitality, and I recall that when the first few jokes were made, the laughter was forced, but also eager, welcomed. Until finally, each on his own terms and to a different degree, we came to grips with the reality of our endeavour, and soon the crew was socializing and intermingling as we would have done on the island – or, almost as we would have done on the island.

There was one clear difference; when we'd done it there, we were living safely inside the roles that we'd already established for ourselves, whereas after the first few conversations without the Elders present, it became very clear that these roles were about to change. And almost immediately, everyone in the crew began that age-old rivalry that exists within groups, people asserting themselves with various tactics – some of them delicate, some crude – all in the hopes of finding a favourable niche to fit into, which, for some reason, would turn out to be different from the ones they'd always filled. Most often, this posturing was done while sailing, as people ran about from task to chore along the deck, while other times it was done below, as they huddled in the shade of their quarters, their bodies shocked by the unrelenting sun and heat of the multiple days at sea – something we hadn't really experienced before.

When the Elders first explained how the crew would be chosen for the expedition, they gave me the impression that I would be handpicking them myself. Like Mikkel predicted, they'd calculated the optimum number for the ship to be about eight. So, with this number in mind, I began making my selection, only to find that I wasn't going to be nearly as free to decide as I'd been led to think. The Elders were quick to council, intervene, and often even completely veto my suggestions. They told me that they simply had a better handle on individuals' characters and that I could trust them in 'helping' me to find people who would be compatible with one another. After all, they'd said, the last thing they wanted was to have me worrying about personality issues. So, it was decided, we would all create guidelines together, and they would help me follow those guidelines, one step at a time. I'm happy to say that we at least agreed on what we should look for: talented, hard working sailors with some endurance, who could be easily led, and who would, ideally, each add to the overall faculty of the crew. However, I'm not very happy to say that this 'selection process' that the candidates all went through, wasn't quite as regimented as the people they'd expected to come out the other end of it. And it began, like most things on the island, with a lie.

When first approaching the young men to find out whether or not they would be interested in going on the expedition, a very careful and elaborate story was concocted; and one that quickly leaked out into the community (as it was intended to), where it was enhanced and idealized into the noblest endeavour imaginable.

The story went like this: The Elders, as was already clear, were scientists, but what we'd never learned about them, and which was directly related to that strange 'secret' that we were raised under, was that they were scientists whose sole interest was examining the remaining people alive in the world, whose lives had been spared from the global disaster that had somehow befallen the earth. For the sake of critical research, an expedition would be sent out to try and locate any remaining pockets of people, and then to perform experiments on them, in hopes of finding out if they had become contaminated by the strange and dangerous sickness that had almost annihilated our kind, but most importantly, to gather information about this disease, and to see if the cure that the Elders were experimenting with, had any effect. Periodically, maybe once every few years, the expedition would return to the boat so that I could report back the findings via a technological device reserved only for the passing of this information, hence preserving our precious findings for the benefit of future generations.

I was in the room sometimes when the story was told, and could see their faces light up. How deliciously tempting it all was. Though most people had already been told a less specific variation of this tale when they Came of Age, they acted like they were hearing it for the first time, and would settle back into their chairs as if pushed by the sudden weight of it, the answers to so many of their unasked questions all falling into place. So this was what the Elders had been keeping from them. And understandably so, we'd all been living under the shadow of a daunting responsibility, one that would have been far too serious to be worrying about as a child. Just think of it: a very select few young men on the island were going to be charged with nothing less than the assurance of the future of our race. 'Wow, what a noble pursuit,' a voice in their minds probably cajoled, 'a crusade to save the world'. And ironically, blinded either by the truth or from it, that's exactly what everyone believed it was.

The story was clever – I'll give the Elders that. It would buy the crew into scouring the landscape for signs of survivors, and then, if they ever found the slightest indication of them, to track those people down with the greatest of focus. They had the foresight to allude to our experimenting with a possible cure, which would provide an answer for the presence of the peculiar chemicals on the ship, and the reason for me bringing them along on our travels. The story also accounted for my being determined to put some of those chemicals inside people's food without their knowing it (after all, it was just an experimental cure). It even had a loophole that would explain why we might have to make a sudden dash away from a group of people, and to then avoid them at all cost from then on in; which was that I could possibly discover (conveniently right after slipping them a good dosage of sterilization mixture, no doubt) that they were all, in fact, contaminated with that slowly infectious and horrible disease that we were trying to cure. We were in grave danger, I would say to them one day, leading them away, fleeing over the hills, away from the people who would probably be staggering around, clutching their stomachs after their evening meal. As far as I can tell, the only hole in the story, which, as I now know would come back to haunt me in the worst imaginable way, was the 'technological device' that would be left on the ship to 'communicate' our findings, which of course didn't exist. But I

159

also know that the Elders had to include it in the tale – because how else would the crew rationalize our gathering all of this information if it was just going to die with us, and never be passed on? I'm sure the Elders also thought that returning to the ship or base camp to stage a 'purpose' of the expedition to the crew, wouldn't necessarily be a complete waste of time, but that it would give me an opportunity to make more sterilization mixtures with the extra lab equipment there, should we not come across other such equipment along the way.

Predictably, everyone that was offered a placement jumped at the chance. And in the end, this promising crew of mine – of which, within the first three days, had already become voraciously bent on developing a pecking order among themselves – consisted of eight young men of 'varying beneficial capacities'. Which really only meant that they were all bringing something – even if it was something we didn't want, or something we needed but didn't like, or even just themselves, which, I would learn, often wasn't enough. (Though, maybe I'm being a bit unfair here, and I should just admit to myself that these judgments I'm making had little to do with people's capabilities, and more to do with whether I liked them or not.)

Toivo, unfortunately, was one of those people I didn't really like. He was dark and muscular, and could be (at very selective times, mind you) a hard worker. He was also one of those people that had the misfortune of appearing confused in almost any situation; even when asking him a trivial question, like how he was doing, he would still squint at you as if you were the incomprehensible sun, his mouth open, the corners of his eyes hard at work. It took me a long while to get used to this while growing up, and being around him on the ship, I realized that I'd somehow forgotten how to deal with it.

"Toivo, could you rig up some fishing lines? I think we should troll for a bit and catch a few meals," I said, as I was passing by him on one of the first days; but stopped, as it seemed that not a single word had been absorbed in the slightest way.

"Huh?" he mumbled. I would describe his expression as looking puzzled, but that would imply that it seemed he was attempting to understand, and this wasn't so – he was just blank.

160

"Fish. We have to fish, Toivo." But he didn't move, a strand of hair flapping into one of his eyes, causing it to narrow a bit more than the other. "Toivo?"

"Huh."

I waited a moment. Still nothing. "Did you hear me?"

"Yeah," he said, as if this were perfectly obvious to the rest of the world; almost sympathetically, like he might feel sorry for the person that couldn't take in such a simple fact.

"Oh...well, could you rig the lines then?" At this point, I too was squinting with Toivo.

"Yeah," he said in the same way. Of course he would rig the lines. Hadn't I just asked him that? His tone seemed to suggest that perhaps I was a little slow.

And for the first while, this was how most of my conversations went with him. But – and this was the strangest part – he wasn't really an idiot. He was actually one of the people who got things done; sometimes even complicated things, and sometimes even things that required analytical thinking. In fact, if there were a long enough silence in a discussion of how to solve a problem, he was occasionally the one who would throw in the most viable solution. So eventually, I just got used to his requisite moment of staring into the air in front of him for a few seconds before plodding away to do the job. But when the vying for unofficial rank began on the ship, I was sure that this frustrating peculiarity of his would push him to the wayside. However, strangely enough, it didn't; and maybe this was only because of his size – that or the fact that he rarely said anything to offend, if anything at all. And it was lucky for him that he was accepted, because I happen to think that belonging was one of his priorities.

Then there was Aimil, who, frankly, was a little simple. He, for one, fit seamlessly into the Elders' guidelines. He was a great worker, and would happily jump up and do anything that was asked of him without questioning it in the least. True, he couldn't really offer a lot in terms of problem solving or abstract thinking, but what he lacked in this he made up for in his manner. He was calm and even-tempered, and when we were children, was venerated for his ability to befriend interesting

161

little creatures. (I can still picture him picking insects off of trees, and then crouching down to the ground and waiting an eternity to feed the things that eventually crawled out from under the leaves; which, after plucking the insect from between his fingers, would just spin around and dash back into invisibility. But in the realm of boyhood this was a notable achievement.) His hair was red, and he had an assortment of freckles that coloured his face with a murky brown spray that stood out against the bright white of his skin. His expression never really changed, which was a bit unfortunate in his case, as it was a fairly ridiculous one; his eyebrows raised as if he were constantly and overly interested, his upper lip drooping a little over the bottom one. Like Toivo, he was quiet, but instead of seeming slow and somewhat resistant, he came across as complacent, giving you the feeling that he would always be satisfied with whatever was decided, which, somehow, was comforting. And also like Toivo, I was always half expecting him to slip into the unhappy role of being someone to pick on; and, realistically speaking, I think one of them would have, had Solmund not already effectively filled that niche.

Solmund was, without doubt, the most intelligent person on the boat; he was probably the most intelligent young adult on the island come to think of it. At an early age, it was discovered that he had a remarkable comprehension of mathematics, physics, and generally all things technical. I'm sure that he was one of the first people to be chosen to go on the expedition, and that that conclusion had been drawn years before, when his gift was first recognized. I believe this because he had a very specific education.

Like the rest of us, he was first taught about natural principals, but then went on to learn about more theoretical physics and their specific applications, and by the end of his education, he was studying from books that always had the title 'engineering' on their covers. And I understand that there was good reason for the Elders to see him as an invaluable tool, as no one could foresee what we might have to build during our lifelong quest: a bridge, a raft, another boat, a fortification, maybe even a weapon. But regardless, we would almost certainly

162

have to construct some kind of hauling system to take the boat out of the water and onto land, where it would serve as our base camp; though if it turned out to be less work, Solmund could also instruct us on repairing a hauling system that already existed (one of the many reasons we planned on disembarking in a ruined port).

He was the only person on the island to have had an entire section of the Great Hall reserved for his education alone; a few interesting instruments scattered around the tables, and sometimes even large sheets of paper to draw diagrams (though of course, most of the time he just used a slate and a piece of the greyish stone from the east shore to write with, like the rest of us). His assignments were always intriguing to me. They would ask him to design something, a bridge for instance, and then he would meddle there for days, scribbling obscure formulas and drawing lines with concentrated precision, an Elder ogling over his mathematics, until finally, there was an orderly diagram of a bridge unifying the edges of some make-believe chasm. And by and large, people reacted to his finished product in the same way: they would look at what he'd done and then disappear around a corner for a short while, only to return with someone else, which was when they would both lean over to look at the sketches for a few thoughtful minutes, eventually straightening up with their hands in their pockets, and nod at each other. Meanwhile, Solmund would be huddled in the corner, pretending not to notice what was happening, trying to hide that skittish head of his under bony shoulders, which were always hunched a little high.

He was small, stunted, and awkward, and when he spoke to people, he could only look them in the face for a few seconds before dropping his eyes and speaking to their feet or the ground beside them instead. I found there was something strange about his eyes, too; though it might have just been that his sight was horrible, which he would never admit to, but was something I'd grown increasingly convinced of. When he read or drew his immaculate diagrams, he held his face directly above what he was working on, and during sailing classes or on the boat, when someone pointed into the horizon at a breaching whale or a distant bird, he wouldn't even raise his head to the endeavour. And a part of me actually hoped his sight was bad, because at least that would explain his habit of looking at people with his nose all shrivelled up, his face squishing into an expression of complete disdain (a quirk of his that didn't do much to help his social standing).

On the ship, we'd taken to lowering the sails and heaving to every few days, in order to swim in the ocean and keep clean. But Solmund wouldn't swim with us; and I couldn't ever remember him swimming back on the island, either. I only remember him standing in the water with some of his clothes on, splashes bouncing off his knees, looking as if he were sneering at the people in the distance. I had assumed that the reason he chose not to swim on the boat was that he wanted to avoid stripping down naked in front of us, which had quickly become the custom. And as we'd all been witness to the juvenile mentality of some of the crew, he might have been justified in avoiding it, because, really, he probably would have been ridiculed, whether he stripped down or not.

This fact that people badgered Solmund, and that he did nothing to prevent it, or rather, almost seemed to go out of his way to provoke it, was a problem that I spent a lot of time thinking about after the battle of snide remarks began. But unfortunately the only conclusion I ever came to was the miserable one that I wasn't really cut out to deal with these things in the first place, which did nothing but make the situation seem even more hopeless. So much so that once – though only once – after Solmund had received a particularly scathing barrage of insults from some of the crew, I even swallowed my pride enough to ask for Mikkel's advice.

He came to take the helm for the night and I lingered around on the deck after handing it over to him, thinking of ways to bring up the issue, stopping to look at the sky as the blue paled, then darkened. When I saw the first few stars being sifted out, I realized how long it was taking me, and quickly convinced myself that there was really nothing disgraceful in asking a bit of counsel every now and then. The second this seemed to make sense to me, I walked up behind Mikkel and spoke over his shoulder. "So – uh… what do you think we should do about the crew teasing Solmund?" I asked, not bothering with any kind of lead up to the question.

He twisted his neck around to look me up and down for a few seconds, "You mean, what should you do about it?" he corrected.

"Uh… yeah, I guess."

He drew in a long breath, turning to face the bow again, and tilted his head at the foremast. After a long while, he shrugged his shoulders, "To be honest, I don't really know."

I nodded my head, and then waited for him to continue, waited for him to expand on what he thought we should do, or what might work. But he didn't; he just stood there with his back to me. And as the silence only grew more awkward, the air between us becoming stiff, I decided it was time to leave. "Well… thanks anyway," I muttered. He barely nodded in reply, and after leaning over to check our bearing on the compass, made a small adjustment to the helm, seeming to forget that I was ever standing behind him in the first place.

But the truth was that Mikkel did know what I should do. He knew all about what to say to people and when, how to quietly discourage them from acting in one way, and how to encourage them to act in another. He probably had a slough of words in his head that would have guided me in the right direction, and I'm sure that those words would have come so natural to him that they wouldn't even have felt like advice. Yet he decided to keep them to himself. And by consciously making that choice, he was implicitly communicating something, warning me that he sure as hell didn't think he was on the ship to stick his neck out whenever my shortcomings obliged him to, that he saw the expedition as 'my game', and that he would be content, if not amused, to be a spectator from the safety of the wayside. Without so many words, Mikkel was letting me know that he was only going to do his job – nothing more – and was going to leave me to do mine.

Of course, this wasn't the most reassuring message I could have received, but I'm happy to have had some forewarning. Because, as a matter of fact, he was right, I had always intended on lumping a few thorny situations onto his shoulders, or at least the ones that had to do with people. And knowing that that wasn't an option anymore meant that I was going to have to become incredibly attentive to the petty one-ups and defeats that were taking place between the crew; though, more specifically, I would have to watch over Knut's little antics as vigilantly as I could, because if there were going to be any problems, they would almost certainly begin with him.

To my credit, I was against Knut's coming on the expedition from the very beginning. It was Chalmon, who had taught all of us advanced navigation, and whose star pupil was Knut, that had adamantly insisted on the fact that 'every ocean vessel should have the most skilled navigator it could possibly get its hands on,' which was a rationale that sounded so valid everyone backed the suggestion within seconds. But what the Elders didn't know was that we'd all learned a few things about this 'expert navigator' of ours while growing up. Things we weren't so quick to forget.

It wasn't only the fact that Knut could be a bit of a bully – as every child can be vicious in his or her own way – it was the disturbing event that happened after someone showed up at the scene in response to the crying that they'd heard. What made Knut unique was that, though he could turn a person into a snivelling heap of flesh just as efficiently as anyone else, he could somehow manage to look convincingly guiltless about it afterwards. He would stay quiet, standing casually, never overacting, never overreacting. If the Elder who'd come to investigate asked him a question, he would always have a persuasive answer ready, as if he'd been calmly thinking it through the entire time he was standing there in the spotlight. And even if they doubted he was telling the truth, even if all of the facts and the fingers in the group were pointing at Knut, they would still choose to be lenient when reprimanding him, just in the case that he really was as innocent as he seemed. And this phenomena never ceased to amaze me, because the act of manipulating and misleading is something that we all do to some fumbling degree, but to actually be able to consistently pull it off, to so naturally succeed in deceiving the majority of the

166

people around you into believing that you hadn't deceived them in the first place, was just plain creepy. I knew that in order for a person to do that, they had to have an intimidating level of detachedness to them. And once I realized this, I made a specific point to keep myself at a guarded distance from Knut, which meant that the idea of being shoulder to shoulder with him for the rest of my life wasn't exactly the most enticing of options.

It was Dana who finally persuaded me to listen to the rest of the Elders, pointing out that we were simply 'not going to be in a situation where we could afford to make navigational errors.' And he was right of course, but I was still reluctant; and I'm sure that my reluctance – after everyone turned to look Knut over, his blonde, boyish hair neatly drawn to the side, a gentle, reassuring grin on his face – seemed completely unfounded. What was more, I didn't have a shred of evidence to back up my argument that he shouldn't come; it had been years since he'd made anyone cry with his opportunistic jabs, but this was probably only because he knew what he could and couldn't get away with on the island, and I had an unsettling feeling that things were going to change once we were in a setting that was removed from it. Yet how was I supposed to explain to a group of learned old men that I had a 'bad feeling' about him? I could already see the flaring white of the bottom of their eyes as the entire room rolled them at me. 'A feeling', they would grumble, shaking their heads and picking some lint from their pants, extending their arms out to the sides and dropping the feathery debris on the floor.

True, I don't know what intuition is or where it comes from, but I do know that the more mystical and otherworldly we make it, the easier we allow our logic to rule it out, which, I've come to the conclusion, is dumb. Because there are times that I wonder if intuition might just be the sum of all those subtle and subconscious facts that we receive about things beforehand, a tallied list of significant information that we've derived from details that seemed insignificant at the time we took them in. The fluttering of an eye at a certain question, the miniscule pause at a moment when there shouldn't have been one, the flicker of an expression on a person's face before they have time to model something more appropriate, or the odd trailing off of a phrase, a word, or even the intonation of a letter. Maybe, in the end, there is no such thing as intuition. Maybe that 'feeling' that we get is really only cumulative fact that has been collected from sources that are just too obscure to reference. And if that were the case, it would make ignoring those 'feelings' quite stupid, wouldn't it?

But ignore them I did. Finally, albeit half-heartedly, I accepted that Knut would join the expedition as another one of our 'valuable' members. We were away from the island for all of two days before the bullying of Solmund began, and I've silently cursed that I ever let the Elders persuade me since.

Of course, he hadn't been a problem for me directly for a long while – years actually. I had established myself as a confident individual at the beginning of our adolescence, which seemed to be enough to keep him at bay. But in the back of my mind I knew that, if he ever actually wanted to, he had it in him to be a stubborn obstacle for anyone. And after he started bullying Solmund, and I started reproaching him for it, there had been some tense moments between us, usually while he lingered around Solmund for a few worrying seconds before backing down, a knowing little smirk on his face, eyeing me with very carefully weighed hostility. I wasn't sure what was going through his mind, but I certainly was hoping to myself that he wasn't preparing to challenge me in some way, that he wasn't weighing me out, meticulously watching my hesitations, listening for signs that would suggest just how much Mikkel was prepared to back me – or not. Though, now I know that that's exactly what he was doing, but for the time being, it would remain an unfounded concern, a paranoid suspicion; or it would until the incident with the knives at least.

18

The same perfect weather that we were lucky enough to have the day we embarked stayed with us for quite a few days afterwards, the skies always clear, a light wind at our backs, and the sailcloth taut and bulging, pulling us forward with effortless speed. In fact, our lives were made so easy that I couldn't help but become somewhat lax about how many people we kept on deck, as the vast majority of time the crew just sat around in the sun becoming dehydrated and nitpicking at one another (which was proving a little annoying to listen to, no matter how much I knew I should). So, considering the fact that two, or even one person alone was enough to operate the ship under such conditions, it made sense to send people away when they came up for their shift. But at first, instead of giving them free time, I thought it best to assign them some kind of cleaning job, or the tedious work of maintaining and repairing sections of rope (neither of which was really necessary yet), which, not surprisingly, wasn't met with the greatest of enthusiasm. And when I eventually admitted to myself that there was good reason for their reluctance, that I was forcing people to do things that we all knew were pointless, I decided that maybe I should just leave them alone and let them enjoy the easy seas in whatever way they wanted to; and this usually meant disappearing below deck where they would become surprisingly quiet. Of course, I understood that giving them time to be idle wasn't the greatest idea either, but some amount of boredom was unavoidable, and if I set a precedent of keeping them entertained every waking moment, I would only regret it later on. So, when the skies began to sheet over with high clouds late one afternoon, and it looked as if our bout of good weather was going to be slowly winding down, I found myself nodding at the stratum, welcoming whatever system was moving in, relieved that people would finally be busy again. Unfortunately, the potential damage that might have stemmed from their idleness had already been done – and I would find out all about it that same afternoon.

169

Mikkel and I were talking near the helm when it happened – or at least I was talking to Mikkel; he seemed a little more absorbed in the wood flute that was being played nearby than in our conversation. "So – yeah, I would definitely take a detour to see them," I was saying, continuing my rambling speech about mountains, "I mean – they're the most striking thing on the maps, and even more impressive in the pictures. (Personally, they've always looked like giant, pointed clouds to me – don't you think they look a bit like clouds?)"

"Uh... yeah, I guess," he said. He looked over at Onni who was sitting near the rail, and had just finished playing one of his melancholic tunes on the flute he brought along. He put the instrument in his lap and turned away from us to look out at the ocean. "Nice," Mikkel praised, speaking to the back of Onni's head.

"Thanks," he replied, without turning around, his voice muffled, "it's new." What he meant by this was that he had just composed the song on the spot, without ever having practiced it before, which was a feat that never ceased to amaze me.

Onni was my idea. He was the last of our crew to be picked, and I remember that when I brought up his name to the Elders, they were a bit puzzled. He certainly wasn't a hard worker, nor was he a great sailor, and as we rotated the chore of cooking, we soon found out that he wasn't exactly gifted in the culinary arts, either. In fact, there wasn't much at all that Onni could contribute, except his music and who he was, which, as far as I was concerned, was already a lot more than others had to offer. He had always been the most musical person on the island, and throughout the span of our lives, was constantly there in the background, tapping at his legs, humming, pattering his fingernails on a shell he'd picked up, or plucking at a string that he was stepping on with a sandal and pulling tight with the other hand, his head cocked to the side to listen to the flexing twangs. Sometimes, on the ship, he would stand at the rail and drum at it in a way that would stop the entire crew, all of us, pausing to turn our heads and listen as if we were – to use Kara's words of how she'd once described the way people twisted around to hear him, forgetting what was in their hands, suddenly still and captive – 'like the faces of flowers to the sun'.

In order to get him on the crew, I made up stories about his sailing heroism that Mitra certainly couldn't back, but for some reason did; probably because she liked him as much as me. And though I'm sure the Elders saw through this little fabrication of ours, they let him come anyway – most likely for the same reason.

He was one of those people that everyone, no matter who they were, was drawn to. His hair was long, straight and black, his body delicate, his features sharp; but it was his mannerisms that set him apart. I would describe them as dreamy or distant, but that would insinuate a kind of absentmindedness, and this wasn't the case. He was definitely there – because when he spoke, which wasn't very often, he would say the most insightful things, muttering his take on the situation with a matter-of-factness that sometimes stunned, but never really injured. His world, I think, was an unvarnished one, and he seemed to look at people in that same light, eyeing you from the periphery, giving you the feeling that he was seeing you for exactly what you were – though not in a judgmental way – it was more with a kind of graceful forgiveness than anything else. Which, in the end, was probably exactly why people were drawn to him.

But getting back to the knives. That afternoon, while Onni paused between songs and was busy looking out at the sea, and Mikkel, sick of hearing about mountains, had walked over to lean on the rail beside him, there was a window of time when all three of us fell into silence. And it was in that pause that I started to become aware of a faint knocking sound, which was coming from the lower deck every half minute or so. The sound was just above the swish and clatter of the sailing, but the more I listened, the more it became apparent; until it dawned on me that it had been in the background for quite some time. What was more, I was pretty sure that I'd heard it other times I was standing at the helm as well, thudding just beneath the din of the ship. But what had probably brought it to my conscious attention for the first time was that the sounds were now accompanied by muted jeers and hollers. And the moment I recognized them for what they were, I straightened up to listen even more intently, memories of a not-too-distant mischief flooding my mind.

"Hey guys? What are they doing down there? I mean – that thumping sound – what is it?" I asked.

Onni turned around and wrapped both his hands over the flute on his lap, as if it were a bar that he would have to hold onto before he spoke. He waited until our eyes met, and even then, paused for a few seconds. "Knives," he finally said, deadpan.

I squinted at him, then at Mikkel, who'd also turned around, waiting for one of them to offer some kind of elaboration. They blinked. So I looked down at the deck, trying to work it out myself: There were two kinds of knives on the ship, the filleting knives in the kitchen, and the diving knives, which were intended to help us in scavenging for food along the coast once we'd arrived on land. The Elders had foreseen that it might take some time to either locate food, or cultivate it, so it seemed logical to have the tools to get them from the sea, where we already had plenty of experience providing for ourselves. But as far as I knew, the diving knives were still secured in one of the storage compartments, and I couldn't really think of any way that the delicate blade of a filleting knives could be responsible for making a sharp thudding sound followed by taunts and laughter, which, incidentally, seemed to be getting louder with every second. I looked up at Onni again, "Sorry – could you... could you expand a bit on what exactly you meant by 'knives'?"

"Sure," he mumbled, using the same tone, almost managing to sound bored, "They're throwing them."

I leaned forward, "They're what?" But I could see that neither of them was going to give me any more information. Instead, they just slowly nodded their heads up and down, their expressions caught somewhere between amusement and sympathy. I shook my head and began following the sounds to their source.

I descended into the lower deck and passed through the gangway, ducking my head at all the appropriate places. As I got closer, I saw Solmund standing with his arms crossed, slouching over as usual, succeeding in making himself look even smaller than he was; he was busy watching the spectacle in the room from the safety of the open door. When he saw me, he froze, and as I approached, he shuffled back, making room for me to enter. I stepped into the doorway.

Everyone, besides the three of us who'd been on the upper deck, was crammed inside. They were backed up against the walls or sitting on the berths, making a space in the centre of the room for the person who was throwing the knives, which, at that moment, happened to be Toivo.

I soon had the entire room's uneasy attention and spoke as slowly as I could, hoping to emphasize just how furious I was, "What in the hell are you guys doing?"

Looking back, I actually think that Knut had encouraged everyone to be louder that afternoon, that he'd intended to be heard, because he was prepared for me in every possible way, as if he'd rehearsed exactly what he was going to say and do before I'd ever stepped foot into the room. Very, very coolly, he sauntered over to Toivo, who was looking as confused as ever, and lifted the knife from his open hand. Toivo quickly scuttled to the side and placed his back against the wall like the others, happy to be away from the focal point of the action. "Well, Joshua, as you can see…" Knut said, pausing in front of me without the least bit of intimidation, and manipulating the knife until the blade was held with the tips of his fingers. He suddenly spun around and flung the knife across the room. The handle of the blade was brightly coloured, moulded out of the unnatural material called plastic, which made for an interesting sight as it twirled end over end through the air. It stuck into the wood with a thud, very close to a red circle that had somehow been drawn there – though with what, I don't know (maybe some of the dried berries from the kitchen). To be dead honest, I was actually impressed by this demonstration, though obviously couldn't show it. Knut turned to face me again, resting his weight on one of his hips and crossing his arms in a relaxed, almost playful stance. "We're throwing knives."

I heard Mikkel and Onni crowd into the doorway behind me. They must have followed me when I left them; and understandably so.

173

I looked around the room, sizing things up as quickly as I could. The crew had sharpened two of the diving knives, probably using the whetstone from the kitchen, and had filed the dull ends until they were pointy enough to stick into the walls. And it was obvious that they'd spent a lot of time on this project, as they had to have first found the knives, then stolen the whetstone to sharpen them, figured out a way to make the red mark, and then, as was evident from Knut's performance, spent many an hour getting better at throwing them. From what I could tell, this might even have been some kind of organized competition.

I shook my head before speaking, "What's amazing to me is that you've all deliberately done this behind my back – which only shows me that you understood I would disapprove of it."

Knut didn't flinch. He was quite ready for that sentence to come out of my mouth. "You would? Why? I mean – what is there to disapprove of?" he asked, turning his back on me and walking to retrieve the knife from the pitted wall. After he had pulled it free, he held it again by its tip, ready to throw, and walked toward me until he was standing uncomfortably close, his body leaning forward, but with a warm grin on his face. "I honestly can't see much of a problem. It's just a bit of fun."

"Fun? No. Let's be clear about this Knut: it's violence. Period." My words were quick, the pronunciation abrupt. "And what every one of us has been taught – all our lives – is that violence only breeds more violence. Which is why I will not have it on the ship. Is that understood?"

Knut shook his head slowly, pityingly, "Man, Joshua – you've gotta lighten up. I mean – we're not on the island anymore, so why pretend we are?" He looked down at the fluorescent green handle, which was wobbling in the air between us, "We're just throwing knives against a wall, which, if you think about it, is as violent as cleaning a trail, or chopping some fruit from a tree, and much less violent than, say, fishing, which we did all the time on the island, and do all the time here." He paused for a moment, then chuckled to himself, "I mean – it's not like we're throwing them at Solmund or something." The room broke into nervous laughter, and Knut took the opportunity to eye a few members of his supportive audience before continuing. "Besides, we'll probably have to hunt when we get to land, or at least until we can figure out how and what to grow, which means that honing a little hand-eye coordination now will come in pretty handy later on, no?" He nodded condescendingly, as if to answer for me, and then threw a hand in the air, "But hey – if you're really dead set on keeping things the same on this boat as they were on the island, then fine – but keep in mind that friendly competition was never forbidden there, so it shouldn't be here, either. Right?" He raised his eyebrows and tilted his head a bit, "Come on – what do you say?", and then paused for a second before sticking out his lower lip and speaking in a shrunken, mocking voice, "Please...?" The room erupted into stifled giggles.

Maybe that was the moment that Dana had warned me about. Maybe this was one of those decisive points that come up in every one of our individual histories, which, provided we act in the right way, have the power to change our future for the better. Yet, even looking back at it now, I still don't know what that 'right way' would have looked like. How could I have taken control of the situation? Seize their shiny toys and hide them, right after hearing a plea that had sounded both reasonable and unanimous? Punch Knut in the face after asserting my decree of non-violence, and then shove him into a room and lock him there until he agreed that throwing knives was a bad idea? Or maybe I should have just snatched the blade from his hand, hurtled it against the wall, and won the competition. Every option that came to mind was either absurd or senseless. And the more I turned it over in my head, looking for the best way out, the more I came back to the easiest and most appealing option: to simply walk away. Let them have their little game and hope that this was as far as it would go. It wasn't the best move, or the smartest, but it was the only thing I could come up with at the time; or to be more honest with myself, it was probably the only thing I was brave enough to do.

I edged past Knut, who didn't really move out of my way, and stood between him and the target, and then slowly panned through the room, pausing to look each one of them in the eye, just like an Elder would have done in the same situation.

There was Toivo, still looking as confused as ever. I imagined that he was one of the people who was most easily swayed by Knut, and could picture him sneaking around and gathering material when no one was looking, hiding in his quarters to grind one of the knives across the whetstone, stopping every time someone walked down the gangway to look over his shoulder at the closed door, hoping that if it opened, it wasn't me who poked my head in.

Then there was Aimil, his expression exactly the same as it always was, looking as if you'd just asked him a question that he didn't know the answer to, but was waiting for someone to tell him. He visually stood out from the others in the room, with his red hair and pale skin, and the rest of the crew with their tanned arms that were just a bit lighter than the wood of the walls.

Niels, with his eyes skirting restlessly around the room, folding and refolding his arms, shifted his weight from one leg to the other. Part of me wondered if he were any good at throwing knives, because, somehow, I imagined he would be.

Knut, incapable of wiping that smirk off his face, beaming with confidence, knowing that he'd outwitted me, that he'd won this little skirmish of power, that rehearsing words that might come up in a confrontation beforehand had paid off for him, again. There was something about the way his hair was neatly drawn to the side that suddenly struck me as maddening, and I wanted to reach out and ruffle it, or maybe find him asleep one day and cut it into jagged lines.

Onni, who was lightly tapping the side of his leg, looking at me with his lips pressed into a kind of encouraging grin, seeming like the only one in the room that might have a bit of sympathy for the awkward position I was in.

Solmund, still watching from the gangway, looked afraid, probably already wishing that he hadn't come on the expedition at all, wondering why he hadn't just stayed on the island, bridging the gaps of the Elders' imaginary voids for the rest of his days.

Mikkel, casual as always, standing beside him, watching the situation unravel through the doorway, careful to have positioned himself on neutral ground in every way possible. He still had that slight look of pity in his expression, as if he wanted to shake his head at me, but under the circumstances, couldn't.

And that was my crew, standing in the room, waiting for my reaction after having purposefully done something inappropriate, waiting to see how much I was going to mirror the Elders in my response, how much I would dare act like one of the people that I had personally rolled my eyes at many a time, often while standing next to some of the people who were now looking at me. Yes, this was a test, just as Dana had predicted. But somehow, I don't really think their incentive was what he'd imagined it to be; I didn't get the feeling they were testing me to find out where their limits were, it was more just a matter of seeing if I would fail. And I did.

"Alright," I sighed, "you guys can have your stupid little game. But I want you to know how disappointed I am that you did this secretly, that you all intentionally did this behind my back. There are better ways to go about these things – and I expected more from you." The room was quiet, except for the sounds of Onni's hand tapping at his thigh, which he'd bowed his head to look down at when I began speaking. But he was the only one who had looked away; everyone else seemed to be watching me square in the eye, looking as if they were struggling to keep a grin from splitting their faces in half. And after I'd walked out of the room and down the gangway, I'm sure every one of them had done exactly that, because as I was climbing the stairs to the upper deck, I could hear a muffled explosion of giggles in my wake – which was probably even a response to someone jumping into the middle of the room and mocking me with some fine juvenile display that I can only guess at.

I went back to the helm and corrected our course. And while I stood there, I continued to hear the now familiar thudding sounds, each one followed by an ever-increasing hilarity, which had to have been exaggerated, overemphasized for my benefit alone. They were rubbing it in my face. And to me, at the time, each one of those dampened clunks against the wood seemed to be communicating something more than just 'we won,' it also seemed to be whispering, 'and more easily than we ever thought we would.'

No, I can't say I was very happy with the way things had gone, but I also knew that the bitter taste of this small, petty defeat would pass, and that what I had to concentrate on was making sure that when something like this happened again, I was prepared for it, that I had a kind of plan of action in the back of my mind, ready, like Knut. I convinced myself that I wouldn't make the same mistake twice, that I would learn from my errors and stand my ground from that point on. And as long as I did that, I was sure the crew and I would find a way to fumble forward, and not regress any further than we had. Yes, I finally said to myself, nodding at the greying skies again and thinking of everyone bustling around in the wind, things were only going to get better.

And the slow reeling clouds pressed down on the water, tightening the gap, quietly shutting the horizon's eye, and seeming to wink at my self-encouragements in the strangest way. The sky was bowing its head, filling its lungs, holding its breath.

19

The layers of grey clouds, some of them marbled with dark folds, kept slating in above us; and as the sky filled, and the ceiling crouched ever lower, like a slow sinking blanket coming down over our heads, the winds began to build. But none of us were too worried. We all thought we'd seen similar skies to this on the island, where the streaking sheets would usually dissipate without ever spitting a drop of rain. We weren't even bothered to watch how fast or in what way the system was developing – we knew it was coming, and that seemed to be enough. Though, Mikkel did notice something a little strange, and mentioned it to me, calm as always. He'd noted that specific layers of the clouds were moving over us in one direction, while the bulk of the others were moving in the opposite, but that the interesting part was, of all these varying cloud directions, none of them corresponded with the main direction of the wind we were sailing with. Odd. Finally, a tiny virus of worry seeded itself in the pit of my stomach, and I made a point to watch the clouds more closely than I had been. I had to hold onto the rail when I did this, as the waves had been building throughout the days prior to that as well. Yet, for all my scrutinizing, I still couldn't find any real reason for concern, and wouldn't, until after the midday meal, when we caught sight of the swells.

"Hey Solmund – what are you drawing there?" Knut's tone, as it always was with Solmund, was acerbic, mocking.

"Nothing," came the defensive reply, like clockwork. He pressed the slate that he'd been drawing on against his chest.

Knut approached him and leaned over to speak into his face, while Toivo stopped and stood behind them both, smiling. "Is it a girl Solmund? Is that what you were doing in the library all that time – were you drawing girls?" He reached into Solmund's arms and started to pry the slate from his grip, "Come on – let's see who it is."

Mikkel disarmed the situation in a second, before I even had time to react to it. He was passing in front of Knut, and simply shot a quick look at him, letting him know that he wasn't impressed with what he was hearing, that he thought he was being childish and pathetic, and that seemed to be all that was needed. Because Knut quickly straightened up, a little embarrassed, "Okay, okay... forget it," he said, waving a dismissive hand through the air, "Just hope it's not one of us you're drawing," he joked over his shoulder, hoping to get a reaction from Toivo. But Toivo only pretended he didn't hear, probably wanting to avoid a similar glare from Mikkel. And that was that.

We all watched Knut as he walked away from Solmund, after being openly snubbed. He seemed to be busy looking for something on the deck, and when he didn't find it, he started looking at different people sitting around, and when that didn't seem to work, he finally lifted his head to scan the ocean. I'm sure what he was looking for was simply something to deflect our eyes off his back, to draw people's attention away from the bit of humiliation he'd just suffered. Though, in the same token, when his gaze finally fell on the seas to starboard, his reaction seemed sincere enough. "Holy shit," he mumbled. Everyone followed his line of sight out to sea – and there they were.

The swells were remote, secluded in a shaft of brighter light where the clouds must have thinned, or a few layers had parted for a brief minute or two. On the sea, a shimmering surface like this usually signifies the presence of stronger winds, but this was something very different. There were shapes in the water, lines being drawn fathoms away by the curling of waves. At that same moment, the tiny seed of worry that had been planted in my stomach suddenly sprouted roots and exploded with foliage, wrapping its fingers around my intestines. Because it was obvious – at least to me – that the only thing that could have created such isolated, capping rollers, would have been a severe storm of some kind, where the waves, like the influxes of fugitives in the history books, had fled from some hub of violence, and were becoming weaker with every mile travelled. Only they didn't look very weak to me, which, considering the implications, it was a little more than a tad unsettling.

Veracity

"They've been there for a while," Onni said, in his straightforward way, and to no one in particular. He was sitting against one of the rails at the time and to my great irritation, reached up to the metal tubing and started tapping away on it with a frantic rhythm that seemed to correspond perfectly with the feeling in my stomach.

Reflexively, stupidly, I started stammering out orders, "Okay – everyone listen up. Aimil, I want you and Niels to rig the lines for fishing. Keep everything you catch – even garbage fish. Toivo, go with Solmund to double check that everything is secured properly and get the storm sail out and ready for rigging. Knut, I want you to take an accurate reading of where we are, and keep taking one every half hour."

"What do you mean? It's best to do it at night, no?" Knut retorted.

"I don't care when it's best. Take a reading now and continue into the night. And Onni... stop tapping the rail." But he didn't.

I called Mikkel into the cabin, where we closed the door and sat across from each other. I'm afraid that, when I spoke, I sounded ridiculous, even to myself. "It's a storm. No? Do you think it's a storm? I think it's a storm."

"Umm... What I think is that you should calm down a bit," he replied, speaking much slower than he needed to. "I think you're getting everyone worked up here over nothing. And – well – it's your job to stay composed, don't you think?" I tilted my head at him, trying to communicate that that wasn't what I wanted to hear. In reply he rolled his eyes and tried again, "Okay... let's say, just for the sake of it, that we do get some choppy weather. This ship can take it – easily. The reason we have the schooner in the first place is because it was the best ship on the island. I mean – at worst, whatever this system is, it might give us some interesting conditions to sail in. But in terms of thinking we're in any real danger – and passing that onto the crew – I don't think is all that warranted." He paused for a moment, then, as an afterthought added, "And it's a little embarrassing."

181

"Oh." I said, feeling stupid. What was embarrassing exactly? Me as a person, revealing that I was afraid, or me as a leader, being afraid like a person. Is a leader's job really to avoid illuminating the fact that they are just a human being with all the typical weaknesses and inhibitions, who gets hungry and thirsty, who bleeds and drowns like everyone else? It seemed so. Which only meant that the more I learned about being a leader, the less I thought I could ever be one.

"I hope you're right," I said. Then, standing and turning from him, I spoke to the wall. "Now could you go and check that all of the hatches and doors are sealed."

He sighed at my back and left without a word, clearly unimpressed with my reaction to the situation. And I admit, I might have been a little melodramatic, reacting like I did to a couple of extra waves that hadn't even reached the boat yet; but there was a gravity to our situation that no one seemed to understand. The only thing that could have been strong enough to cause those waves to form was a major sea squall or a massive convection system, or maybe even an abnormally early tropical storm, which, considering the month we left in, was possible. Yet regardless of which one of these it was, any of them would require us to find a sheltered harbour. I looked at the map. There wasn't land for days, maybe even a week. The closest tangible earth, which was not our intended destination, was a tiny peninsula that stuck out like a sharp tooth into the sea, and which was probably four, maybe five days away. Nothing was around us, only endless ocean. We were entirely defenceless and exposed. I could still hear the urgency of Onni's rhythm, thumping the hollow metal, and I found myself chewing the skin on the knuckle of my thumb, listening to the beat reverberating along the rail to either side of him, wrapping around us, closing in.

In the first hour, I caught some quick looks between the crew, looks that were intended to scoff at my nervous reaction. But as the hours passed, the clever glances that were being exchanged altogether ceased, and were replaced, one by one, with an eagerness to take orders. And I'm sure this was because, after the swells had encircled the boat and had started tossing us high above the seascape one moment, and plunging us down into dark caves the next, every one of us knew we were in trouble. They were much larger than we'd supposed, and the ship flailed between the troughs and crests like the flimsy hair of seaweed. The winds had also increased, and together with the blackening sky, only added to the overall drama of getting things done on deck. Our balance was easily lost, it being impossible to anticipate the random motions of the ship, and our hands were always reaching out to snatch at the rails or the rigging, often grabbing hold of them just before we stumbled, though sometimes not, and a few of us even fell, quickly jumping back to our feet again, a little self-conscious, humbled.

The looks, if we found the time to exchange them, were edgy, worried, and after breaking eye contact, the two people who'd met eyes would invariably gape at the water, as if making sure that the conditions hadn't worsened in the split second they weren't watching them. And sometimes it seemed they had. Every minute that passed saw the ocean filling its heaving chest with a newer and more ardent energy; flexing its enormous muscles beneath us, around us. The boat seemed to be shrinking.

The sky continued to stoop ever lower, obscuring hints of brightness, making it difficult to tell where the evening ended and the night began. We finally received the first showers of thick rain, which started and stopped intermittently, until finally, it didn't stop at all. The wind, becoming increasingly sporadic in its speed and direction, mercilessly pounded the steel drops against our faces.

We had all grown up with rain, but there is something very different about it on a ship. On the island, most of the precipitation systems were isolated convection storms, so when it rained, the only thing we had to do was wait, choose a good tree or the doorway of one of the buildings, and stand there for the few minutes that it took for the storm to pass. So we were never really in the rain, never a part of it; and we certainly weren't equipped with any of those strange 'oil-skin' coats that the explorers in some of the history books had, which might have allowed us to be a little more effective when we had to be in it. But as it stood, we only had our usual thin clothing, which

183

when wet, clung to us like the hindering skin of a snake before it's shed, sucking the warmth from our bodies, and encumbering our every unpleasant movement.

But I think that we were doing the best we could with what we had, running back and forth around the foremast, trying to keep up with the changing winds. I'd heard tales of being swept by a weather system until a boat was days off course, so I was content with the fact that the ship seemed to be responding well to the storm sail we'd raised and reefed, which of course had very little surface area, but helped maintain the balance and consistency of the ship.

I split the crew into shifts with the idea that, while one half of the crew tried to maintain some kind of course, the other half could be out of the rain, resting, keeping warm, and hopefully even managing to nourish themselves for the long night ahead. And knowing that the worst was yet to come, I ate with the first shift.

Onni, Knut, Niels and I sat around the table, which was designed to stay level by swivelling on a weighted ballast. This little contraption had always amused me, but it had suddenly become unnerving; while the rest of the room sloped in all other directions, it stayed constant, gauging what was happening to the ship a little too accurately for comfort. A lantern hung above us, swinging back and forth and projecting our pulsating images onto the walls. We didn't speak very much.

"Joshua, do you think... I mean – the boat will hold up, won't it?" asked Niels, his eyes seeming to be paradoxically calmed by the general mayhem.

"I... honestly don't know," I replied, realizing this was the wrong answer. I quickly amended it, "Well, actually, most probably, it'll stay intact."

Knut rolled his eyes at me, and Onni let a tranquil little grin spread across his face; and I wonder now what he was seeing in the situation that I wasn't. At that moment, the boat shifted violently to one side, complaining of its own weight with a deep groan, and all of the attention in the room shifted between the sounds and me; I think they were hoping, even for the sake of empty encouragement, that I might revise my comment and speak a little more convincingly for the dependability of the ship. But I looked down at my food instead.

We sat there without speaking for quite some time, wobbling back and forth in the nauseous shadows, stuffing food into our weakening stomachs, until we felt a shudder that was very different from the rest, which was followed by the sound of water running over the deck above us, everyone stopping to look up at the roof as if we might see it streaming across the ceiling. When the sound receded, it was replaced with a constant and distressing dripping noise that could have been falling from anywhere, everywhere. The first wave had breached the deck.

Shouting to the others to recheck all the hatches, I ran up the stairs to see if everything was okay, hoping that no one had been washed overboard. I was already thinking about what to do if they had been – what to throw, where to get it, where the safest place would be to haul them in from – but when I opened the hatch and poked my head above, I stopped thinking about what to do. The waves had become massive, wild, and they were roiling around the boat like some crazed creature searching for an unknown thing, chasing it, pursuing it obsessively. It was clear that any rescue attempt from that moment on was going to be useless. If anyone went into the water, they weren't coming out.

I stumbled toward Mikkel. He was wide-eyed, gripping the helm as tightly as he could, and I wasn't sure if he was actually trying to steer the boat, or if he'd just found it a good thing to hold onto. His face flashed white for one blinding instant. Lightning.

"Is everyone okay?" I yelled through the wind, which seemed to have increased tenfold. Mikkel didn't look like he'd heard what I said, but nodded nonetheless; as if the flailing bodies of the crew being flung into the ocean were the least of his worries. He was fixed on the sea directly in front of us, and his expression was stiff, afraid. I turned to see what he was looking at and broke into exactly the same stare.

It was a wall – a barrier that sprawled across the horizon, teetering over top of us, trembling with black electricity. I remember every detail perfectly; the flickering blue light, the sheets of rain spiralling to the sea, the surface of the water fanning out in strange patterns that the downpour was grating into it. And there was nowhere to go. It would pass straight over our heads. I remember realizing, albeit numbly, that the conditions that we were seeing in front of us were nothing compared to the violence that must be directly behind that barrier, the centre of the storm; that abstract place that we couldn't see into, but would nevertheless find out about.

"We're in trouble, Mikkel!" I hollered at the storm.

"I know!" he yelled, sounding a little impatient at having to respond to the obvious.

I paused to consider a plan of action, or at the very least, to come up with something to say that wasn't so evident. I turned to speak, but held my breath for a few seconds more, thinking slowly.

"Uh... go and eat as fast as you can!" I screamed. This was clearly not an epiphany, but was all I had to offer. He first shook his head, and then shrugged his shoulders before limping off and gathering the other three that hadn't eaten yet. They all filed into the hatchway, and right after they disappeared, the other three who had been in the lower deck with me, filed out.

I'd grabbed onto the helm as soon as Mikkel let go, but within only a few minutes, it had become noticeably harder to keep it from spinning on its own. The ship wanted desperately to follow the whims of the sea, but I found that it was still, luckily, somewhat feasible to keep it from doing so.

There was nothing for us to do but watch that barrier creep closer, shivering in the frigid skin of our useless clothes, running back and forth to secure lines and rigging that were being knocked loose by the wind, and by the waves that were breaking over the deck with increasing severity; waves that reached their heavy white hands over the rail, and slapped us in the face with their shocking cold. Whenever this happened, our eyes would shoot open, mouths gaping, standing rigid as the stun of the cold water ran over our bodies, trickling to our feet and thieving every bit of warmth that we'd managed to regain since the last wave. And the amazing thing was that, despite having several waves crash over us, the surprise that they brought never really lessened, it was the same unbearable shock every single time.

But despite the endless shivering, the flinching of the water, the tossing of the boat in all directions, and the constant imbalance, our storm sail was still keeping the ship steady, and we were managing to carve through the hilly landscape relatively well. And because of this, the raised sail was, if not necessary, then undoubtedly an advantage; it was clearly helping us, not hindering us, and I honestly wouldn't have lowered it for anything in the world. So, given the circumstances, I think it was impossible to have prevented what happened – after all, the very last thing on my mind was a gust front.

Sometimes, inside the heart of a storm, the cold air that is being circulated throughout accumulates as one mass, and if that mass becomes too much for the updrafts to support any longer, the whole thing plunges to the surface, and once it hits, it sends out a frontal wave of dense and turbulent air in every direction – like a furious prophecy of things to come.

The wind was changing direction by the minute, the sail flapping at either edge, our telltales (the small bands of flailing material that are used to indicate the direction of the air current) had already wrapped around themselves several times, obscuring any accurate reading, so I had no idea where to steer the boat, and had resolved to simply follow the path of least resistance, veering from port to starboard, regardless of the wind, only watching the black sea, and shying away from the most intimidating swells as best I could. Unfortunately, we happened to be directly facing the storm when the gust front hit.

All of a sudden, the sail whipped full in the opposite direction. The ship shuddered, everyone tumbled forward, and above the waves and the wind, we could hear a horrible ripping sound over our heads and the distinct noise of metal wire cutting the air. I slid onto the deck, though still near the helm, and was covering my head with my arms, convinced that rigging of some kind would be crashing on top of me any second; but nothing came.

When I finally picked myself up off the ground and looked around me, I could see that the whole crew was on the upper

187

deck. I imagine they felt the jolt and heard the sounds, and so had come to assess the damage. They were all looking at something, and I followed their eyes to see that the storm sail was now flapping in the wind. It had almost ripped completely free of its rigging, only being attached at the foot.

Now we were really in trouble; and every one of them decisively understood that, looking around, desperate for someone to lead them, to save them, to do something. Instinctively, they looked to Mikkel. And seeing everyone's pleading faces pointing at him, finally, he decided to take control.

20

Mikkel turned and ran back to the hatch, kneeling beside it and gesturing for everyone to climb down into the lower deck to regroup. Thinking about it now, he might have already decided that we should just retreat to the safest place and hope for the best, but at the time, his intentions were unclear. The only thing that was clear was that he was in charge – and that none of us, including myself, were going to question that for a second. Obeying the order, I began staggering toward the hatch as quickly as I could, and as I moved over the flashing white floor, I noticed that there were streaks and smudges of blood running along the surface beneath me. At first, I actually thought they might belong to me, spurting from some wet and painless wound that I had yet to discover – until I slid down the stairs to meet everyone in the lantern lit darkness and saw Aimil standing there, his face oozing red. He must have been slashed with some of the rigging that had blown when the gust front hit, a diagonal slit cleaving his pale skin from forehead to jaw. Water ran down from his hair through the wound, thinning the colour and consistency of the blood as it dripped off his chin in thin, easy drops. Yet all things considered, I don't think the cut could have been a luckier one, as it had passed right between his eyes, but had somehow managed to leave both of them undamaged. And, being Aimil, he didn't really seem too bothered by it, looking as complacent as ever, an apologetic expression almost pushing through the seeping mess of his face, as if he were sorry for the inconvenience of his bleeding.

Once we realized he was well enough to function, we turned our attention back to Mikkel; there were more pressing things to worry about. The ship was now being tossed about as if it were a leaf bouncing along the surface of a swollen river. As soon as the storm sail was destroyed, we'd completely committed ourselves to the impulses of the ocean, and everyone could feel the difference, the ship suddenly swaying dramatically from side to side, running loose in the slopes of the waves.

We couldn't talk at first, trying to steady ourselves as a mass of bodies, first pushing, then pulling one another, but always ending up pressed against one of the walls of the gangway. Finally, some of us started to grab hold of the stairs, and one by one, we all caught onto the idea.

But just as we were beginning to feel steady and were waiting for Mikkel to speak, someone asked Niels what was wrong, which of course made everyone look his way. He was staring up through the hatch with nothing less than abject horror. "Oh no!" he exclaimed, giving us no information whatsoever. "No, no, NO!" he screamed, his voice escalating into hysterics. He looked back at us, seeming surprised that we were all standing in front of him. And then, almost as if he'd remembered that he had to get something vitally important from one of the cabins, he let go of the stairs, fumbled through the gangway, jumped into his quarters, and slammed the door behind him, sealing himself in.

"Huh," grunted Mikkel, and then contorted his body to look up through the hatch. We all joined him, still scrabbling with each other's unpredictable sways. A bluish green aura was lighting the top of the mainmast, and when we all saw it, everyone let out either a gasp of alarm, or of awe – nothing in between. It seemed that, somehow, this light had translated into an omen of certain death to Niels.

But I knew better. "It's St. Elmo's Fire," I called out. "I've read about it before. Sailors used to think that…"

"Will it kill us?" asked Knut, sharply, bringing the attention of the crew back to the lower deck.

"No. It's caused by the…"

"Then enough!" he screamed. "Who gives a shit what it's caused by? What are we going to do with the ship!"

He was right; this wasn't the time to give out scientific tidbits. And now that I think of it, maybe the reason I spoke so quickly afterwards was only a reaction to my feeling a little stupid at having tried, an attempt to regain some credibility. "Well, it would probably be best to have some kind of sail raised, no? We can feel that it's…"

"Then let's go!" Knut hollered in frustration, and started climbing out of the hatch as fast as he could. This was all, of course, too impetuous, too rash. We hadn't discussed the pros or cons of anything; in fact, we hadn't even discussed how we were going to do it, or who, or with what sail, what rigging, or if anyone had even seen that there was enough rigging left; we were only filled with the urgency to do something. (Though isn't this always the case – the more deliberate and careful a situation requires us to be, the more reckless and impulsive we become?) And accordingly, we all followed him, myself included – everyone filing up the stairs thoughtlessly, caught up in the insistence of the wind and the voices, of the pelting rain.

But none of us made it very far. There was a rumbling sound that wasn't thunder, and the ship quavered, jarring to port. A wave had broken over the deck again, and every one of us was positioned right below the open hatch. Myself, along with a few others, stopped to listen to the noise get louder, and then, very suddenly, it was much louder. I braced myself, closed my eyes. I even remember there being the tiniest moment of stillness, just before the water hit us. And then everything was white, and I was struck with the dull weight of falling bodies, pushing me down the narrow stairs to the floor where the water continued to wash us through the gangway. We passed Niels' door, gasping for air and holding our blind hands out to try and dampen the impact of whatever we might hit while rushing through the ship's interior. When I finally slowed enough, I shot my face above the surface, spitting salty foam out into the air, and shook my head to clear my eyes. I was furious. What complete idiots we were to have left the hatch open!

I looked through the gangway, and for some reason, was expecting the water to magically drain away. It didn't. Instead, it swished through the corridor, curling off the wood paneling, sloshing from side to side. The lantern hanging from the ceiling was still lit, and flickered long shadows of the crew everywhere, as they struggled to get to their feet, leaning on the walls, their hands squeaking against the surface, hair hanging in their faces. They looked exhausted, but not deterred. And as soon as they were standing, they all started making their way to the stairs again, their movements mechanical, instinctive, worried only about getting the task of raising a sail done.

I watched them climbing the stairs again, and for the first time I began to think about the reality of what we were proposing to do. In truth, I wasn't thinking of the danger to the boat's structural integrity, only of the crew's safety. If another wave broke over the ship while we were on deck, which seemed rather likely, there was no telling how many people we would lose. "Wait! What about the storm anchor? Maybe a sail isn't... uh..." I shouted through the gangway. And some of them might even have heard me, but no one stopped. They had a job to do, and were determined to do it. Aimil was the last person that I saw climb through the hatch, and I sat there alone for a moment after he'd disappeared, watching the lightning, which seemed to be climaxing, flashing against the stairs, against the dots of rain that were falling through the open square. The thunder had become indistinguishable from the sound of the waves; they had dissolved into each other, into one low, deafening rumble.

I got to my feet, sloshed through the gangway, and climbed the stairs into the cold air. Then I slammed and sealed the safety of the hull behind me, and turned to see what we were doing, only to find that I wasn't the only one who was unsure. There was complete and utter chaos. Everyone seemed to have a separate and urgent assignment, but not one of them looked as if they knew what that was. They were scattering and collecting like a group of confused animals fleeing from predators that were closing in on every side, flashes of light freezing them in still frames of confusion, of panic.

There appeared to be several captains. Mikkel was screaming something at the top of his lungs that couldn't be heard. He had a torn cable in one hand – the rigging from the foremast – and the other hand was holding tight to the foremast itself. As far as I could tell, he might have been trying to figure out a way to raise a sail with what little rigging was left. Onni was standing beside him, stunned, uselessly clutching the remnants of the storm sail with one hand as well, as it flapped soaking wet in the wind. There was also a small group scattering and collecting around the mainmast: Knut, Solmund and the sorry blood-smeared face of Aimil, his shirt already having formed a bib of red.

My plan was obvious: it was to get everyone to abandon the previous plan – as fast as possible. None of us should have been there in the first place, least of all to raise a sail. I screamed at them, and then screamed again. Nothing. No one heard a thing. I would have to get their attention physically. So I started making my way toward them along the rails, hand over hand, the swaying of the boat so severe that the gunwales were teetering ever closer to the surface of the water. I waited for a tiny lull in the waves before rushing from the rail to the mainmast, and grabbed onto it with the rest of them. I hollered something that wasn't a word and pointed at the closed hatch that we'd all come from. This, to me, meant that they should seek shelter below deck immediately, but to them, probably only meant the appearance of yet another captain. In answer to my pointing arm, they all gawked up at the height of the mainmast, which might have still been glowing – I didn't look. Instead, I swore into the wind, and it pushed air down my throat as if it didn't want to hear it.

I needed to get to Mikkel; because I knew that if I could get him to run to the lower deck, everyone else would follow without thinking twice. I left the mainmast, rushed to some rigging, waited for a moment, and then scurried to the foremast. I touched Mikkel on the shoulder and opened my mouth to yell, but no words had the chance to come out.

In one single instant, the ship's bow plunged into the ocean, and a massive wave curled in on us. All of us who were standing there – Onni, Mikkel, and myself – were easily knocked free of the mast and fell onto the deck, sliding away, eyes fighting to stay open, arms swinging wildly. The water clung to my body, dragging me past rigging and equipment, until I smashed into the rail, where I was pinned against the metal as the water sieved around my body, and drained off the deck.

And it seemed that just as quickly as the ordeal began, it was over. I thought I was safe, thought I was lucky. I looked around for a second and noticed that I was alone, and wondered if Mikkel and Onni had caught hold of something on the way, or had simply been washed away. I didn't know, and nor, at that moment, did I really care. The only thing to do was to grab onto the rail and pull myself to my feet as quickly as I could while there was a chance to do so. What I didn't know was that I was choosing the absolute worst moment to do it – because as soon as I got to my feet, the ship thrust upward, and I was flung effortlessly into the air, and over the rail. But I was still holding onto it with one of my hands, and I gripped it as tightly as was humanly possible, falling against the outside of the boat like a broken hinge, where I latched my other hand onto the tubing as soon as I could.

I knew at that moment, in a strange sort of way, that if I let go or was knocked off by the next wave, I would be dead in a minute or two, which is the kind of understanding that makes one tighten one's grip substantially more than one already had. It also made me try to quickly pull myself up, pressing my feet against the side of the ship to get my weight up higher. But they only slipped away. I tried again, and then again, but it was proving impossible; it took everything that I had to just stay clenched to the metal tubing as the ship was being flung around in the waves. My body probably looked like a tattered flag in the wind, flapping pathetic and helpless, almost tempting the elements to mercifully blow it away forever. After swearing at the top of my lungs, I looked down at the dark water again, and resolved to give one last concentrated effort to pull myself over the rail. Which is when I felt Mikkel's fingers wrapping around my forearms.

I looked at him for only a second before starting to heave myself up, both of us pulling as hard as we could. And with one fierce lunge, I was suddenly teetering on salvation, my chest hanging on the highest rail, where we struggled against the heel of the ship to get my weight over the top. I squirmed, tried with everything I had, even bowed my head down as if that would provide the needed load to drop my body onto the safe side of the railing. But in the end, it was the same sea that seemed so bent on taking our lives, which saved me. As the boat dug into the water, another wave crashed into me from behind and pitched me back over the rail. I slammed onto the deck and, again,

Mikkel and I were sliding along the painted surface, eventually being washed up against the cabin wall, our heads clunking against it with empty sounds.

I shook the water from my face, my eyes stinging with salt, my throat paradoxically dry. How perfectly frustrating this all was! We were grains of pollen rushing inside a jet stream. We had no control over the boat, over the situation, over our survival. Over anything.

Mikkel was nearby, wiping water from his eyes as well, and as soon as he could see, he turned over and started crawling toward the hatch. Finally, some sense. I followed, and when we were getting close to it, I remember thinking about the crew, hoping that they'd already made it below deck, hoping that we were about to find every one of them there, safe and sound. But unfortunately, they weren't there. No. They were still on the upper deck, where, instead of worrying about saving their own lives, they were busy creating the most effective way to kill us all.

We were almost at the hatch when the air ripped open with the deepest, most terrifying sound I have ever heard. "WHOOMP!" Both Mikkel and I flinched, covering our heads for a second before looking up in the direction of the sound. I'm sure that once we saw it, both of our mouths must have dropped wide open. The crew had raised the main sail.

The small group that I'd seen below the mainmast must have laboured fanatically between the pauses of the waves to hoist it up. And they'd succeeded; because there it was, full, bulging, the cloth trembling at its edges. Anyone, even the most ill-trained sailor that has ever lived, could have seen that the wind was much, much too strong to have such a massive surface area propelling the ship. The mainmast bent and shuddered as the boat picked up ridiculous speed, and all of the flattened bodies lying on the floor began to slide toward the stern with the strength of the acceleration. We looked at the bow to see what the ship was flinging us toward, and could see, in a brief flash of light, that we would be crashing into a mammoth swell in the matter of seconds.

There was no communication, no altruism, and certainly no bravery. None of us thought, for even a split second, about approaching the wildly swinging boom to try and take down the sail, nor did anyone think to go to the helm to try and steer us into a better direction. No. There was only one thing left to do, and only an instant to do it.

Using both hands and feet, everyone scampered as fast as they could toward the hatch, which someone had already managed to fling open and dive into – all of us, like rodents fighting to leap into a burrow, sliding bumpily down the stairs headfirst, our bodies piling on top of themselves inside the water of the lower deck. I was somewhere in the middle of that heap of limbs and torsos, and was busy trying to squirm my way out, so I have no idea who had the presence of mind to close the hatch. It wasn't me.

And we were still in the process of getting off of each other, still trying to breathe, trying to figure out which way was up, when the ship crashed into the first swell. None of us had time to brace ourselves, and least of all Onni, who almost drowned with that first impact. There was a deafening crash, and the mass of water in the gangway, with all of us in it, rushed toward the stairs, where Onni, who was one of the first people to have jumped through the hole, still hadn't even managed to get his head above the surface of the water. I remember first feeling the water sift around me, and then submerged bodies pushing against me on every side, and then I remember being pressed against the stairs for a moment, then jostled free again, back in the direction that we'd just come from as the water subsided, carrying our limp and tired bodies with it, strewing us randomly throughout the gangway.

When I shot my head above the surface, I could hear Onni gasping and coughing, choking out bouts of seawater. Mikkel, who must have been closest, was trying to steady himself enough to pat him on the back, doing nothing for the water in his lungs of course, but showing, at least, that he was concerned.

We could hear a strange thundering, which was probably a wave breaking over the deck again, and we all braced ourselves for the next impact, which didn't seem to come. And in that pause, some of us looked at each other with blank expressions and then looked away, as if we were all waiting for something without knowing what that something was.

It's interesting to think that we might have all drowned in the gangway during the night, had cowardly Niels not opened the door of his quarters to vomit on us. When he flung it open, some of the water from the gangway drained into his room, seeming to lead us there in some bizarre way. He puked, his hands gripping the doorframe, and we all watched him without an inkling of sympathy. When he was finished, Knut was the first to crawl through the disgusting debris that was bobbing on the surface near Niels' legs, and had soon disappeared into the relative safety of the room. We all followed; Niels, recovering quietly, wiping his mouth and blinking at us as we passed.

The next swell that we struck closed the door, the water swishing from one side of the room to the other, and our bodies bounced off of the berths and against the tight walls that seemed to be everywhere. The lantern in the room had gone out, and our world was suddenly completely void of perspective and shape.

We felt our way from wherever we'd landed, and crawled onto the bunks, huddling in heaps of bodies, finding what corners we could. And just as we all seemed to have found a place, there was another impact, which caused one or two people to fumble to the slippery floor again. We could hear them floundering desperately to get back onto the beds, but all of us, being blind, and raking the darkness with our searching hands to try and help them, couldn't.

I heard someone else vomit, though maybe it was only Niels again.

Finally, the last person crawled into place, and we all reached out to hold him there, a collection of limbs netting him in. There was a strange stickiness to his skin, which made me assume that it was Aimil.

Another impact. The ship groaned loudly, crackled. No one fell back onto the ground again, and this meant that we'd all found a stable hold or stance, which seemed to be the most important thing at the time, though I'm not sure why.

From what I could tell, everyone was touching someone else – someone's hand on my arm, someone curled against my back – and I don't think that all of the contact was just for the purpose of collectively bracing ourselves, either; there was something else in it. Maybe we wanted to be reassured, or maybe we just didn't want to die alone. It's hard to say.

Another impact, only this one was more forceful than the last. I heard someone gasping for air, probably because he'd had his back against the wall and had the wind knocked out of him.

Judging by the sounds and sensations, the storm was right above us; the movements of the ship were becoming more sporadic, more violent, and the noises that it was making were louder, sounded more painful, damaging, and below these noises we could hear the water in the gangway rushing from one end to the other faster than it ever had before.

I felt our bodies flex. We held our breath. I think that we were all waiting for some kind of sign that would signify the end, something that would let us know that the structure of the ship had finally reached its limit, that it was finally splitting apart and about to spill us out into the sea. And those of us who were waiting for that moment thought it had finally come, when, suddenly, it felt like the room jumped, then twisted, and we could hear an ear-splitting noise even above the thunder and surf, and the growling of the ship; and it was a very different kind of noise, one of bending metal and cables twisting undone, shrieking, screaming before they snapped. And then, it felt like another ship smashed into our side and was scraping along the gunwales. All of us must have been looking around, waiting for the room to collapse, waiting for the sound of rushing water to break through the darkness. But nothing came.

After a few minutes of waiting, I started to notice that the movements of the boat had become very different, slower, almost sluggish. I breathed a sigh. It occurred to me what had made the horrible sounds; it was the mainmast breaking.

Of course, we weren't safe by any means, but at least we wouldn't be crashing into the swells anymore, damaging the ship more severely with every blow. And this meant that if the storm didn't get any worse – and as luck would have it, it wouldn't –

198

then we just might make it through the night after all. I wasn't relieved; it was just that I allowed myself to become distantly hopeful for the very first time.

I could hear someone whimpering in front of me, and this soon turned into muffled crying. I didn't know who it was, but I could certainly understand them. The person who was touching my arm spoke. "Hey, it's okay… it's okay. The sail's gone. We might make it through now." It was Mikkel, always gracefully filling in the gaps that I left open.

I wanted to thank him; thank him for being everything that I wasn't, or at the very least, thank him for saving my life. And knowing then that it was his hand touching my arm, I reached over to his shoulder and squeezed it tightly, then patted it gently, twice. But Mikkel didn't react. He didn't shift or turn his head, he didn't mutter a word or a sound, nor did he even squeeze my arm in return, which would have been the subtlest reply. Nothing. And I didn't understand this at first, though felt sure that he was trying to communicate something.

I remembered once asking Dana why we didn't have money on the island, as was the case in all of the historical cultures. He said that, mostly, it was part of our collectivism, and then, which was very strange, he smiled this dry smile and told me that, regardless of our not having money, human beings would always find some form of reciprocation, and that the island had simply found other currencies in place of coloured paper and precious metals. Of course, he didn't mention what these currencies were, but that was the least important part. The important part was about reciprocation.

And while we braced ourselves for hours in the jarring blackness that night, I considered Mikkel's reaction – or lack thereof. Until eventually, I came to understand what he was trying to say. This was his way of letting me know that he had absolved his debt, that from that moment on, we were even.

21

I had always imagined that if a person narrowly escaped death, they would be stronger afterwards, more complete; I thought that such an event would empower them in a way that no other experience could. But I was wrong. And maybe this was only due to the fact that we hadn't survived because of anything we did, or as the result of any special skill we had – we were alive because of pure dumb luck. I remember there once being a storm on the island where most of the tallest trees on the northern shore were blown down and only a few straggling survivors were left. Of course, there was no reason for the remaining trees to have been spared; they weren't special in any way, weren't stronger or more robust, and they certainly hadn't been 'picked' by some higher force, they were only fortunate to have grown in the right spot, that as chance would have it, would be sheltered from the squall's random and powerful winds. And standing on the deck the next morning, we must have looked just like those trees; battered, swaying timidly above the wreckage of the night, numbingly blessed.

We didn't say much. In fact, the only sound that I remember hearing was the sea smacking up against the hull, and the water still sloshing around in the dark gangway where we'd come from. We fanned out across the deck, our legs delicately stepping over irreparable debris, as if the tangle of cables and splintered wood might be damaged even more by the sound of our footsteps. And after inspecting everything at our feet and in our periphery, one by one, we raised our heads, some of us mouthing silent curses to ourselves.

The mainmast had given way at its lower third, and some of its rigging still drooped sadly from its remains. Of that rigging, we could see that most of the stays and cables had stretched, frayed, or completely snapped, while the bolts and clamps that had once strengthened them, had been stripped, bent, and sheared. The damage was stunning. Eventually, as if with a serious weight, our heads sunk back down to the deck, and we continued walking through the rest of the spoils. Yet, after we'd toured the whole ship and seen the long list of destruction first hand, I was amazed to see that there wasn't an all-out panic spreading throughout the crew, and I was incredibly thankful for this, as I wouldn't really have known what to do with it if there was.

I remember Toivo picking up a piece of cable that wasn't attached to anything and throwing it overboard. We all looked at him, awakening from our stricken trance. I was happy he started it; it was time to begin cleaning up whatever we could. Dana and I had talked a lot about what to do in complex situations that involved several problems. He'd repetitively taught me that the best thing to do was to take one problem at a time, systematically, from the most urgent to the least; so as was natural enough, we started with the water in the hull.

It was an enormous job, and we took shifts manning the only pump that we had while everyone else gathered every bucket we could find and formed a human chain up the stairs to bail the water out manually. Some of the crew, like Toivo, and Aimil, whose blood-caked face had been cleaned and bandaged, worked much harder than the others, so I called on Onni, who had done very little, to clean the galley and reorganize it, and also to prepare us some food in it once he'd finished.

The grain must have been one of the last things that he checked and reorganized, because we'd almost finished with the water, chasing it into corners and scraping the buckets along the floor, when Onni stepped into the gangway with the news. "The grain is ruined," he stated flatly. We stopped to look at him as he held out some of the starchy seeds as evidence. It was wet, and seeing as it was obviously out of the question to spread it out and dry it under the grey and drizzly skies, and knowing that it was extremely susceptible to going off in the first place, it seemed that he was right: we'd have to throw it away. "But that's not all," he continued, once we'd absorbed the first blow, "There's lots of other stuff that the water's gotten into as well." Then he turned away from us and walked up the stairs, stepping to the rail and dropping the handful of grain into the sea, brushing his palms clean afterward.

The panic, that had until that moment been absent, or was at least being kept at bay, began to surface in the form of people swearing to themselves under their breath. Mikkel smoothly interjected before it could escalate much further though, and as he spoke, I couldn't believe how buoyant his tone was, almost as if he were having fun with the news. "It shouldn't be too much of a problem. We can live for ages on fish alone. Besides," he nudged Aimil to get his attention and nodded jokingly toward Onni, who was coming back down the stairs, "it saves us from having to eat that grainy slop he makes." He smiled and winked at Onni, who gave an embarrassed simper, while the rest of us broke into forced snickering. The grain, which made up about two-thirds of our diet, was gone, which, all things considered, wasn't really much to laugh about. I searched through the expressions of the crew for signs of genuine worry, and noticed that they were there. I also noticed a strange look on Toivo's face, and hoped it wasn't because he'd thrown away some of the fish we'd caught.

"Aimil, we still have the two fish that you and Niels caught yesterday, right?" I asked.

"Mm-hmm" he affirmed, looking even sillier than usual with the massive white bandage slashed across his face.

"And that's what I cooked," said Onni, "But besides those fish and a few spices, there isn't much we can use."

"I see. Well... let's check everything again just to make sure. Knut and Niels, go with Onni and help him out with that, and Toivo, Aimil, and Solmund, you go and rig some fishing lines. I imagine we'll have to keep them rigged from now on to feed eight people without the grain. Meanwhile, Mikkel and I will finish up with the water here. We'll meet in the galley once we're all finished, okay?"

I noticed that they all dispersed a little reluctantly, which I didn't like. I wondered if I was going to have to remind them that I was still the captain, even though Mikkel had taken over for a bit during the storm. I thought about mentioning this to Mikkel while we were alone, but he'd quickly leaned in and started whispering about things that were much more pressing than the wavering line between captain and first mate, which only made me feel stupid, again.

"How far will the engine take us?" he asked. I could barely hear him his voice was so low.

"What do you...? Mikkel, we can't use the engine. It's only for getting us into port, and who knows what other kind of manoeuvring we'll have to do once we reach land. Remember: the bay we're heading to is supposed to be incredibly sheltered – meaning no wind well out to sea. And it's not like we can expect to use it now, and then again later; it isn't exactly the most reliable machine. Mitra warned me that we'd probably only be able to start it once. I mean – the fuel inside the tanks is ancient, stale, and we've had to add a lot of distilled alcohol just to improve the chances of it working. And besides all of that, and the fact that we'll be running on what is most likely the only refined fuel we'll ever come across in our lives, the tank is only an eighth full."

"And...?" he persisted, becoming impatient, "How far exactly will that amount take us?" I gave him a look that illustrated how ridiculous I thought he was being. He continued, "Look, you're the only person on this ship that has a working knowledge of the engine. So... answer me, please. Do you know how far we can get with it, or not?"

"I have no idea." I too, was becoming impatient. "Maybe half a day... a day. I don't really know. Why?"

"Because...' he shook his head at me, amazed, "because, as you saw with your own eyes, the only thing left to propel the ship is a foremast with no rigging. If we can't figure out a way to raise a sail, we'll have to dash to land in whatever way we can. That seems clear, no?"

I sighed. "Well... yeah. Look, let's just talk about this later, okay?" I turned and walked away from him. What I wanted was hours of time to think things through. Everything was happening so fast, and it's always been the same for me: absorbing events is one thing, but knowing how to react to them is quite another. I decided to go check on the grain with everyone else – as if that were needed.

The galley door had burst open during the night, which wasn't really much of a surprise, as the entire structure of the ship had been heaving like the rib cage of a monstrous animal, only with the added dynamic of having water inside the ship as well, pounding against the already flexing doors. I could see that once the water had broken into the room, it quickly found the worst things to get into, and almost anything of any kind of importance was sodden, spilled, diluted, or displaced. It was a mess, but I was happy to see that Onni was actually doing a fairly good job with cleaning it up and reordering it. After I'd looked around a bit, Knut and Niels called me over to show me that the grain was, in fact, genuinely ruined, both of them reaching into the bin and squishing fistfuls of the creamy mass until it oozed through their fingers. So Onni was right; we would have to depend exclusively on fish for the rest of our time at sea, which, all things considered, wasn't all that bad, it only meant that we'd have to spend more time fishing. And lucky for us, time was something we had.

Onni had finally finished cooking and called everyone in to eat. He'd used the grain for the last time, and had managed to concoct some kind of rank, slimy, fish smelling mush with it. After looking into the pot, I wished he'd just been wasteful and spared us the resourceful notion. Toivo, Aimil, and Solmund were the last to come into the galley to eat, and I noticed as soon as they entered that the strange expression Toivo had flashed before seemed to have spread to the other two as well, and I was watching them closely, suspiciously. They all stood in front of the table, waiting for someone to ask them what was wrong, which no one seemed very eager to do, so they were forced to begin on their own.

"Mikkel," Toivo spoke slowly, looking for elegant words for cumbersome news. I felt a pang of irritation that he chose to speak to Mikkel instead of myself, "uh…"

"What is it, guys?" Mikkel asked, "Come on. Let's have it."

"Uh…" he looked at me for a moment, and then at someone else, and then at the floor, "the fishing box is gone."

The room inhaled, waiting for more information. None came.

Veracity

"Hmmm," Mikkel droned. He acted as if this statement were a poisonous dart that had struck him, and he leaned back slowly, his posture rigid, until he was resting against the wall, thinking toward the ceiling.

I, however, was not quite as calm. "What do you mean exactly by 'gone'? I... I don't really understand that sentence. Do you mean 'not on the ship', or 'not where it should be on the ship'? You must mean 'not where it should be on the ship', because I can't imagine the fishing box unlatching the door to the storage room, hiking up the stairs during the night, and pitching itself over the rail in a fit of desperation. Can you? Can any of you imagine that?" My eyes examined each of their faces for answers. Toivo cowered, busy with the task of surveying his feet. At least I knew who hadn't put the fishing box away when he'd been asked.

Aimil spoke softy, his words unarticulated, probably because of the pain smarting across his face, which he still hadn't complained about in the least. "I don't think it was put in the storage room before the storm. I'm pretty sure I remember seeing it on deck."

The room exhaled. My arms were crossed on the table, which made a perfect place for my forehead to land in total frustration. There was silence for quite some time, interrupted by people sighing loudly, the boat creaking. Finally, Mikkel broke the spell. "Well... let's eat," he said, bouncily, "And while we do that, why don't we throw around a few ideas of what to do." His tone was light, as if asking us to join him in thinking about what might be a suitable garnish for our next meal. I looked up at him from my arms, completely appalled; how dare he be so calm.

Mikkel dished some slop onto his plate and began to curiously pick through it with his spoon, his gestures delicate. The crew followed his lead, albeit nervously, as if they were sitting in the company of a madman who might lash out at any given moment. But we weren't sitting with a madman, and for my part, I wasn't nearly as intimidated by Mikkel's actions as I was fascinated by them. I actually couldn't wait to see how he planned on pulling this off. Did he really think he could retain

205

this collected air of his, all while fumbling to compensate for the ever-increasing weight on the other side of our scale? I didn't think so.

Of course the food was vile, but no one could say a word to that effect. Instead, we fought to swallow it down, sometimes leaning forward over the table as we did so, gulping mouthfuls of water to wash it down. Onni was the only one who had a quiet smile on his face, as if, with the worst possible sense of timing and humour, he'd purposefully made the food disgusting, and was relishing in our having to eat it without complaint. But I doubt that was the case.

When we'd finished eating, Mikkel leaned back and put his utensil down carefully beside his plate to speak. We all stopped what we were doing and listened like leaves. "Solmund, I bet you have something figured out for us – or at least a couple ideas?" Knut, who was sitting opposite me, snickered and shook his head. Solmund tried to ignore him.

"Well," he began hesitantly, leaning in and casting one more look in Knut's direction before speaking, "I don't think that Toivo ever actually said that everything was gone, but it is. It's all gone. We have no rods, reels, hooks, lures or line." He leaned back, put his hands on the table, and looked into them as he spoke. "But as far as I can see, our biggest problem is the line. We can bend the safety pins in the first aid kit into hooks, though they won't be barbed so won't be nearly as reliable. And we can us this," he fingered some fish that he'd managed to pick out of the slop, and which he'd gathered into a neat little pile on his plate, "as bait, and we shouldn't need rods if we only jig off the side of the boat. But the line... the line, I don't really know."

This was good; in fact this was very good. With all of the nodding and murmurs of praise, I thought that Solmund might have redeemed himself in some way. Niels even patted him on the knee, smiling. These were great ideas; but as it was, we needed more than that, and we all sat looking around the room, trying to think of what we could use in place of a fishing line.

Toivo, who had spent the brainstorm narrowing his eyes and wearing his customary expression of total confusion, began slowly, "Couldn't we use strands from the torn sail."

Our eyebrows lifted, and we all turned to look at Solmund, who seemed a bit doubtful. He shrugged. "Maybe. But I already thought of that. Because one thread wouldn't be strong enough, we'd have to braid a few of the threads together, and as they're thick and white, it would make for a pretty visible line, which would probably stop the fish from biting in the first place. But who knows, it might work. And it might also be the only option."

Knut sighed a deep sigh, apparently not very satisfied with Solmund's first stint of usefulness. I shook my head at him, glared. Yet, there was nothing surprising about this; after all, the scope of pettiness, its astonishing reach, is unbounded inside the social setting of our kind. It can pry its niggling tentacles into every facet of our lives, even the most important, most crucial moments aren't sacred; nothing that we do can ever be completely exempt from its careful attention, its dissecting instruments, poking, prodding, hunting for some insignificant tissue to attach significance to. I honestly believe that pettiness is the greatest social crime, which we all, unfortunately, have the tendency to commit; and how maddening it is that this complete attention that we give to trivialities, which should be below everyone, is really above no one.

Knut was beginning to squirm under my disapproving stare, and leaned forward to speak. I thought he was going to say something about Solmund, to support his long sigh that I'd so painfully noticed, but he didn't. "Well, nobody seems to be thinking about the weight. Like always, we'll need some kind of a weight on the line to keep the bait in the water, right? Well, maybe the weight will pull the strands tight enough, and they won't be so visible." Everyone nodded, though Solmund only shrugged, and then started to pick the dirt from under one of his nails.

"Hey – this is really great stuff," said Mikkel, encouragingly, "and we'll get to work on it right away. But... while we're all brainstorming and easily coming up with solutions, I think we should do a quick walk around the ship and address a few other problems. What do you guys think?"

There was more nodding; after all, this sounded reasonable. We all stood and followed Mikkel as he walked out of the galley and headed straight to the upper deck. He was, of course, alluding to the mainmast when he spoke about 'a few other problems', and I was already getting nervous as to how the crew was going to react. I was the last to leave the room, and we all walked in single file through the ship, myself straggling at the very end of the line. There was no real question as to who was leading things.

We crowded around the mainmast with sceptical looks. The elements had been ruthless. We could see that, at first, the massive metal pole hadn't broken; instead it had buckled at one third of its height and collapsed, hinging the upper two-thirds of the mainmast into the water. When it fell, it smashed into the side of the ship, doing quite a bit of damage, and then had scraped back and forth along the gunwale for another little while, scarcely being held by thin strands of lacerated metal that were holding the two pieces together like stubborn ligaments. But at some point throughout the storm, after being pounded relentlessly, the twisting strands and fibres finally gave way, and the top two-thirds of the mast slipped into the water, dragging with it the main sail, and all of the rigging, stays, cables and yards attached to it. The lower third of the mast that was left was nothing but a frayed end, which pointed its clawing fingers accusatively at the water, as if trying to indicate exactly who was responsible for stealing away its counterpart.

Mikkel stood with his hands on his hips, looking up at what had once been a towering citadel, but was now only a pathetic post that ended in a bit of twisted shrapnel. When he spoke, there wasn't a lot of expectation in his voice. "Any ideas?" he said, turning to look at Solmund. We followed his eyes and Solmund looked on either side of himself, as if Mikkel was speaking to someone else, and when he realized that it was him that was being asked, he began to shrivel up under hunched shoulders.

"Are you serious?" he asked, and then paused long enough to realize that, yes, in fact, Mikkel was serious. "Then: no. Of course I don't have any ideas. Do you know what we would need to do anything with this mast? We would need a mountain of manpower; we would need enormous machining tools, moulds, kilns, raw metals, alloys. I mean – just forget about the mainmast; and while you're at it, forget about the rigging on the foremast as well. Anything on this ship that was metal and happened to break, stays broken. Period. Are you guys too stupid to understand that? I mean – we should really stop wasting time talking to me about the masts when we should be talking to Joshua about the engine."

"I already talked to Joshua about the engine," Mikkel retorted, without missing a beat, "It'll only take us one day out of a several day journey. It's not enough. We'll all need to pull together to find a way of using these masts. That's all there is to it. So let's just stop here for a second… and think about it again."

But we weren't thinking about it. We were watching Solmund, who didn't look too happy about this news of the engine. In fact, he looked terrified. "If the… oh, man… if the engine will only… oh shit…" He was sputtering his words, escalating into alarm.

Mikkel tried to stop him before it spread, but it was too late. "Solmund. Please…"

"No! If the engine… oh man…" He scuttled gawkily to the rail and squatted to the ground, facing us, apparently at his wits end. He blurted out one final, ill-advised remark, "Well then… then we might as well just face it: we're finished. Can't you see that? Oh man… oh man, we're dead… Dead." As soon as he fell silent, you could almost see the frenzy rippling through the crew.

Mikkel bowed his head to his hand and cleaned the sleep from his eyes in annoyance; he'd wrongly judged our engineer to be levelheaded enough to take the news. And Solmund hadn't only failed, he'd reacted to it in the worst possible way anyone could. Eyes were darting everywhere, looking for reassurance. Surely someone would have a plan, even a far-fetched idea would do now – anything. Some people looked at the masts again, someone scurried to get a few charts, maybe wondering if we could use the engine to get us into a current that was heading toward land, but Niels, curse him, decided to grasp at some distant hope in the story that the Elders had fed everyone.

He stepped forward, looking at me, and spoke in a voice as desperate as I'm sure we all felt. "The island," he said, and my stomach dropped. I already knew where he was going with this, but what I didn't know was how to stop him. I could only think to shake my head, which didn't deter him in the least. "We can call the island. We can ask the Elders to come and help... with that thing you brought – that machine in the big grey cases in your room. I mean – we can use it now, can't we? This is an emergency, an exception to the rules. At least we could... we could talk to them and tell them what happened. And if they can't come and help us, then, maybe they'll have an idea of what we could do."

I stood there, squinting, thinking about the best way to answer. Should I have gone into my room, made some strange mechanical sound effects, and then told them that the device didn't work, that it had also been ruined by the water? How likely would they have believed that? And even if they did, wouldn't they have wanted to see this strange, broken instrument before I threw it overboard; and, more importantly, wouldn't that have rendered the entire expedition useless in their minds? I swallowed. I was at a complete loss for words.

But as it turned out, Mikkel would answer for me, and he would do so without saying a single thing. Suddenly, after watching Niels and I stare at each other for what must have been a little too long for him, he gave a callous, satirical snicker and looked out at the sea, shaking his head, and drawing everyone's attention to himself as he did so. My stomach sunk even lower, and I twisted to glare at the back of his head. I'm sure he knew I was looking at him – that we were all looking at him – but he just kept staring at the water, answering a million questions with his silence, or at least inducing people to ask them.

Long seconds passed. And before we could find our way back to the more pressing issue at hand, Knut had something to add, seemingly under the guise of 'reassuring' Niels, who was standing in the middle of everyone, trying to understand what had just happened. Knut's voice sounded tired when he spoke,

"That's right. Those cases are only filled with chemicals and lab equipment," he said to Niels, then turned to aim his words at me, "which are probably a cure of some kind, I'm sure," he said, and turned back to Niels, "So… I'm afraid: no. There's no special instrument. No one can hear us. And no one is ever coming to help."

Everyone turned to look me over apprehensively. And all I could do was stand there, dumbstruck, until eventually, I had to drop my eyes to the ground.

So. Here it was. They finally knew that they'd been lied to, deceived. I could almost hear the questions swirling through their heads: For what reason would they have been told an untrue story? Was it because they would have been reluctant to come if they'd known the truth? And if so, what exactly was this truth that was so precarious that their whole world, and everyone they trusted in it, would conspire to hide it from them? What exactly were they doing on this unlucky ship, if not to help save the world? Were there other things around them that weren't quite what they seemed? And if so, what – who?

I had no idea how Knut had known about what was in the cases. I was sure they were secure, that no one in the crew had access to them. Though, I'd fancied myself sure of a lot of things until that moment. Knut had implied that he was aware, or at least suspected that we didn't have a cure, which was almost the biggest slap in the face for me, as it revealed that I wasn't the only one who spent time trying to probe deeper into the world around me. Who knew? Maybe it was natural for everyone to do, and I'd only imagined myself to be the clever exception, which, of course, would make me the greatest fool of all.

22

The drab sky began to drizzle, and I watched the floor around my feet as it speckled with tiny drops of rain.

Eventually, I decided to look up to see if everyone was still staring at me, and when I did, I looked straight to Knut. He was fuming. It wasn't exactly clear where this rage was coming from or whom it would be directed at when it finally emerged, but it seemed likely that it would be at me, the liar, the mysterious conspirator. I took a step back, looking around to see if I was the only one who had noticed him. I wasn't. And I must admit that, when he started to speak, and I realized that, in fact, it wasn't me who was going to get the brunt of his anger, but Solmund, there was an ignoble part of me that was quite relieved.

"So... why," he began, giving Solmund a sidelong glance, "I mean – can you tell me – why did we bring you along then? Weren't you supposed to be this genius that could make anything, fix anything, figure out anything? Isn't that the reason we've been putting up with your shit every day, all day long – because we thought you'd come in useful at some point? And now that we finally need you to fix something, what do you tell us, what great enlightenment do you give us? That we're finished. We're dead." He shook his head, his voice quickly heightening in tone and volume, "Is that all you're here for – you little snivelling shit! To tell us when we're dead! Like we couldn't handle that on our own?" He started to hop on his toes as if he were about to run, and squared his shoulders to Solmund who was still cowering near the rail; and shrinking more by the second. Then, seeming to know better than anyone else what was going to come next, Solmund let out a sorry whimpering sound and covered his head. "Do you know what I should do to you!" Knut pressed his lips together, shaking his head madly now, "I should just..." Finally, he snapped, and broke into a dash toward Solmund, who had managed to instantly shrivel himself into a tiny ball of flesh.

Veracity

A few of us threw half-hearted hands out and took a step forward, as if we were going to intervene, but no one did. Knut stopped just before him and let the built-up momentum of his body follow into a vicious kick, and Solmund shuddered against the rail. But Knut didn't stop there, he continued kicking him as hard as he could, three, four, five times, producing strange hollow sounds, the rail ringing with each blow. I remember that my heart was racing, but as much as I wanted to do something, I wouldn't have moved closer to Knut for anything. His arms were swinging wildly through the air to help him kick, his hair flapping around on top of his head. And I wasn't alone, the rest of the crew were just standing there as well, ogling at the scene with stupid expressions on their faces, some of them looking around, searching for the person who would be brave enough to stop him, waiting, waiting for that elusive 'someone' that would finally step forward and do something.

When Mikkel screamed, there was something in it that we'd never heard before, something that was threatening, dangerous; his voice was deep, breaking, and I'm confident that it would have stopped anyone doing anything. "KNUT!"

Knut stopped and turned toward Mikkel, blinking at him idiotically, his arms slowly sinking to his sides; his expression was somewhat puzzled, as if he were wondering what was actually wrong with repeatedly kicking Solmund as hard as he could. We all watched the wild expression on Mikkel's face slowly melt into something calm and composed again. And when he finally spoke, his words were incredibly quiet, almost sad. "Come here."

Knut walked obediently, if not shamefully over to him, where he stopped and stood, waiting like a child to be reprimanded. It's interesting that all of our attention was devoted to Mikkel and Knut, and that Solmund, whose safety we'd supposedly been so concerned about only seconds before, sat forgotten in a sorry heap of bruised flesh. I noticed him enough to see that he'd already grabbed onto the rail to steady himself with one hand, while his other hand had dropped from its protective position on his head, his face poking out from behind

213

it; it seemed he was also interested to see what would happen to Knut.

But Mikkel's words would baffle everyone. "You're a good sailor, Knut," he said, and then paused for a moment, turning his head to eye the horizon and nodding at it to reaffirm what he'd just said. Then he looked back at him, "So let me ask you a serious question: What would you do with only one mast and no rigging?"

"Me?" Knut pointed to himself.

"Of course you. You're on this ship with the rest of us. And I happen to think it's every much a responsibility of yours as it is Solmund's. Wouldn't you agree?"

"Yeah, but... I'm not supposed to be the..."

"I don't give a shit what you're supposed to be. I asked you a question, and I want you to think about it. Do you understand that? I want you to stop and really think about it: How would you use a mast with no rigging?"

At first Knut only shrugged his shoulders. But then he looked up at the mast for a few seconds, pondering the actual problem for the very first time. He answered more readily than any of us expected. "Well, to be honest, I would just fix the sail to the mast with rope."

"How?"

"I don't know. I guess – I don't know – I would... maybe I'd cut holes in it, and then wind the rope up the mast, threading the sail through the holes. I mean – we wouldn't be able to raise or lower it... and it would be hard to tack with, but... it would probably be enough to make it to land."

Some of the crew began to nod and mumble in encouragement, and a modest smirk spread across Knut's face. Even I began to nod. It was a great idea, and I wondered why he hadn't spoken up before, though it was probably just the lazy fact that criticizing is infinitely easier than offering solutions.

Mikkel hardly blinked before jumping into action. He took a few steps away from Knut and addressed everyone. "Okay then, we need two groups of four; one group working on the fishing line and tackle and the other on the sail. Let's see hands for who's interested in working on the sail. Perfect. So... Knut,

Toivo, Niels and myself will work on fixing the sail in place, while Aimil, Solmund, Joshua, and Onni work on trying to braid a fishing line, making hooks, and hopefully even catching some fish."

Bodies moved to their respective places and soon there were three of us huddled around Solmund, and we bent down to help him get to his feet. He didn't seem to be any worse for wear; or at least nothing was bleeding or broken.

"You okay, Solmund?" asked Aimil, his bandages flexing with his words.

"What does it look like? I'm standing aren't I?" he spat.

"He was only asking," said Onni, with his sleepy voice.

"Look," I jumped in, hoping to move to another topic before things escalated, "if you're really okay, we'll need you to walk us through how you envisioned doing this." I chose these words to try and reassure him of his worth as well, as Mikkel might do in the same situation, but it didn't work. Solmund only rolled his eyes and limped off toward the place where we'd stowed the damaged sails. I think that he was limping more for the spectacle than for anything else, that he felt a need to demonstrate that there had been some kind of damage done to him. Because there had been: how we viewed him, and how we viewed his potential had suddenly changed. And how frustrating this must have been for him! To have finally been recognized as a valuable member of the crew, to have been accepted, appreciated, for only a few brief minutes before slipping back into his difficult role as the clumsy eccentric. And I think he knew, as did we all, that he'd missed his chance in the unforgiving world of group dynamics, to rise from that role; that he would have to stay there.

The truth is I felt sorrier for him than I ever had before, because he really was brilliant, he really could take things apart in his mind and put them back together again in a better way, as those of us who worked with him that day saw. He would show us – though always impatiently, snatching whatever it was from our hands and holding it up close to his face to inspect – the most efficient way to go about everything. In fact, after working with him that afternoon, I felt sure that if he hadn't panicked when finding out about the engine, he could easily have figured out a better way to raise a sail than Knut had, because in the end, he'd succeeded in directing the three of us through every step of every invented process; and in only a few hours, we'd created functional fishing equipment from almost nothing. And by the time the sun had set, and after losing several would-be meals to the barbless hooks, we actually caught a fish. Not a favoured fish, or even a substantially sized fish, but a fish nonetheless. (It's amazing the kind of sudden and remarkable gratitude misfortune can endow us with. Whereas before the storm, we would have scoffed at such a sorry specimen, tossing it back into the quick shutting lips of the sea without even thinking twice, suddenly, it had become a blessing, a prize, and we held it up with long, proud arms as it tried to breathe our alien air, shouting screams of joy into its face while its yawning mouth became slower, its silhouette dripping against the dull sky as we carried it away from the water, lest it find a way to slither back into its element.)

We weren't the only ones to succeed, either. The other group had figured out a way to climb the foremast and fix a sail to it using one of the ropes, exactly as Knut had suggested. And to add to our luck, we had a light tailwind, which gave us the advantage of testing its strength a bit before having to use it in harsher conditions; and it seemed to be working well, plump with air and moving us closer to land with every minute. This accomplishment had also produced a fit of hollering joy, everyone jumping up and down, patting each other on the back. Each group then congratulated the other in turn, and I remember this giving way to a wonderful ambience that lasted a few hours afterwards. People smiling and joking with one another, laughing louder than usual.

We eventually found ourselves in the galley with the same elevated spirits, gathered around the table to eat. No one had mentioned Knut's attacking Solmund, and I didn't think that anyone ever would, but nevertheless, Knut's elevation in status was noticeable, his air self-satisfied, noble, people watching him forgivingly. Whereas poor Solmund was noticeably more withdrawn than usual, more subdued. But I tried not to think about him, and to just enjoy the general feeling of accomplishment that we all deservedly felt, for it is a wonderful thing to have succeeded in the face of desperation, to have attained something hard won. I can still remember every detail of that night perfectly: the smiles, the warm fluttering light of the lantern, Onni picking up his string instrument and plucking away at some contented little tune before our meal was set on the table, the enormous ceremony in which it was placed between us all, our trying not to acknowledge its blatant inadequacy, the reaching in and licking of fingers wet with the slimy oil of sea creatures, the jokes after we were finished eating, people asking if anyone had room for seconds, for thirds, the laughter that accompanied them and its tinge of solemnity buried beneath, the short pause before someone picked up a few bones and spines and started sucking them clean, and then everyone following suit, moving onto the skin afterwards, then the fins, until nothing was left but the head, which we needed to salvage for bait, our smiles trying to linger on, past the uncomfortable facts, beyond our hunger and the gravity of our troubles, but finding it difficult and feeling it slipping away, deciding to disperse to other parts of the ship to leave the sensation of success untainted, the few doubtful glances brushing over me as everyone rose from the table and filed out of the room. I remember it all, but I especially remember Mikkel, avoiding my eyes as he stood to take the helm. He had never done that before.

I didn't leave the galley for a long while. Instead, I sat there alone at the table, worrying. We'd had two enormous challenges to get through, but in both, we'd managed to succeed; and now they were, almost unfortunately, over, as was the celebration for having accomplished them. There were no distractions left. They would have time to think about the events of the day, about what had been said, about what hadn't. I heard some of them gathering into one of the rooms to chat. They closed the door, moved onto the bunks, and the indistinguishable murmuring began. I sighed. The Elders had always known about the peril that lurked in quiet conversations, that place where mysteries willingly unravel themselves to imaginative minds, where new information is haphazardly folded into an old story,

217

and the swirling truth revises itself, is turned over, and then revises itself again. It is a precarious place where inaccuracies and discrepancies can be overlooked, ignored, ironed out with a few linking bonds of inventive rationale. Yes, they'd been lied to, that much was now clear to them, but the danger was in their theorizing exactly 'why' they'd been lied to; and to what extent the story that had been fed to them was factual, if at all. Yet, what facts did they have? From what certainties would they be building their story? They knew that we were all tired and hungry, that we were helpless, completely alone on the ocean without any possibility of assistance, support, or intervention, that we were on a broken vessel, limping to an unknown place for, what had become, an unknown reason. That was all they knew for certain; and with this kind of foundation, what could I really expect them to come up with?

I blew out the lantern and sat in the dark, listening to the ship creak, to the humming of voices, the liquid of whispers behind wooden walls. I must have sat there for an hour or two, trying to think of a solution, or even a vague plan of action. At some point, I looked through the tiny window of the galley and noticed a few stars pulsing between the thinning clouds, and decided to go up to the deck to check on the weather and our course. I thought that I might even take over Mikkel's shift, as I doubted I was going to be able to fall asleep.

I left the galley and crept into the gangway as quietly as I could, hoping to catch bits of the conversations that were going on behind the walls. I passed the room with several of the gathered crew, and pressed my head against the door to see if I could make anything out. The whispers were rising and falling, interrupting each other, overlapping one another. It was clearly a fervent discussion, which only made me feel worse. But after listening for a few minutes without being able to make out a single word, I thought about continuing down the gangway again, and I would have, had something not stopped me just before I lifted my head from the door. The hisses were becoming louder, many of them talking at the same time, someone hitting someone else to shut them up so that another could speak. Then it happened. One of the whispers became loud enough that it was almost on the verge of being comprehensible. I held my breath, listening. I managed to make out one word, but only because it was being spoken as a means of emphasizing a point. Of course, I had no idea who'd uttered it (why is it that a person's voice is so distinct from individual to individual, yet a whisper can belong to anyone?) but the speaker wasn't nearly as important as the one word I'd managed to catch. "…Asah… nn… es Peik sah…"

They had found it – the key to unlocking everything they shouldn't know. And as much as I'd always known that Peik's words might someday be recalled, rehearsed, or reinvented, that there might come a point in time when his last fumbling sentences would suddenly make sense, I'd always assumed that I wouldn't be there if it happened. But I was; I was in that very place where everything would be pointed at me when it came time for staking the blame. And what was I supposed to do? How could I have stopped it, how could I have put an end to their destructive mumbling? Give them the real truth? Walk into the room, sit down in the centre of it, and let them in on the cute little secret that they were on this ship to unknowingly assist in putting out the destructive flame of our kind? No. Just like there was no intricate lie that would ever be swallowed again, there was also no degree of honesty that would appease them. There was nothing I could do. Nothing. Except run – if there were only a place to run to. Even if I wanted to escape, to disappear from the ship in the middle of the night and never be seen again, I didn't even have the option to do it until we were in sight of land.

And how far was that? How long would it take us to get there with only the sorry foremast functioning as our main? I didn't know, but I could find out. Knut had already taken a reading from the blurry sun as it pierced through the clouds at one point throughout the day, and I could take a second reading, which, with a few calculations, would indicate our speed and progress, and with this, I could estimate how long it might be before we arrived at the coast.

I gently crept up the stairs to the deck and walked to the navigation table where Knut kept his sextant. Mikkel was at the helm in the cabin, a lantern swaying back and forth over his shoulder like a pendulum, creating a cavern of light around him with his swaying shadow in the middle. He gave me a quick glance as I approached, and then looked away. I paused for a moment behind him, feeling strangely guilty for wanting to know exactly where we were, and then continued to the sextant and picked it up as casually as I could.

He began with his back to me, "Okay – look, I'm sorry. I know I wasn't thinking when I laughed at Niels' suggestion, okay? It was just that – I don't know – things seemed a little too serious to be wasting time chatting about imaginary gadgets." He sounded sincere, yet also a bit impatient, as if he were being forced to answer some thorny question that I hadn't asked.

I looked at the table as I spoke. "Yeah... well, we sure didn't waste any time on it."

I stepped out of the cleft of light and walked into the centre of the deck. After finding the star that I was looking for and taking a measurement from it, I returned to the charts and pinpointed where we were on the map. I then compared our position with where we had been a few hours before, scribbled a few numbers on a slate, and then erased them with the side of my hand when I was finished. I left the room for the last time. Mikkel didn't say a word, but was watching me carefully.

Out on the deck, I leaned against one of the dented rails, eyeing the makeshift sail, which was shivering and tight. I could only hope that it would carry on functioning as well as it was, because we were making better time than I would have guessed. If the calculations that I'd done were right, then we'd sight land in about three days time. It wouldn't be the best land, and nowhere even close to our destination, but I didn't need a place to land the ship, in fact it would be best if we couldn't land the ship. All I needed was to get close enough to a shore to escape and continue on my own. Three days. I nodded encouragingly at the sail, honestly believing that I would find some way to slither through the hours, the minutes, the seconds between where we were and the peninsula we were creeping toward.

And while I was standing there on the deck, Solmund was somewhere below me. He was in a room by himself so no one can know what he did, but I like to think that he was having a hard time finding sleep, and that he might have pressed his face against his quarter's window to see the first pulsing stars that had exposed themselves in a couple of days, framing the clouds in sweeping arcs of speckled light. I like to think that beyond all of the contempt and disappointment that he must have felt about the events of the day, that he'd experienced something beautiful that night.

It would be his last.

23

We woke to a perfect day. There wasn't a cloud in the sky, and the blue of it was vibrant, glaring. The rain of the previous days had washed the air of its dust and haze, so we could see far into the horizon, which seemed to sprawl out around us, becoming more distant, sharper.

When I'd first greeted the crew in the morning, I'd expected to see strange expressions on their faces, maybe even catch them exchanging a few secretive glances out of the corner of my eye, yet surprisingly, everything seemed to be normal. Despite having discussed some of the mysteries surrounding the expedition, and maybe even of the island, they were as willing as myself to pretend that everything was still the same – at least for the moment. The only thing different about them was that they were a little quiet; but so were Mikkel and I; and I think this was owing to everyone's hunger more than anything else. I saw a few people holding their stomachs, and I wouldn't be surprised if every one of us was thinking about food; splashing images of fruit-laden trees taking over our thoughts, or pictures of past community feasts, fish and vegetables sprawling out across wooden tables. In fact, Niels and Aimil were so preoccupied with the thought of food that they dragged the bin of grain up to the deck, hoping to salvage the tiniest bit of it by drying it in the sun before it was ruined. But as soon as they lifted the lid, and everyone caught the wafting smell of how rank it had become, we all knew it had to be dumped overboard.

So it was natural enough that the crew wanted to untie the bottom of the sail and try to catch some fish, and they had asked me first thing in the morning if they could do this, albeit with voices that were a little more polite than usual. And maybe it was because of this politeness that I felt I could postpone it for a while. I was bent on getting to land as fast as possible, and I saw every minute that wasn't spent moving in that direction, as increasing my risk of not making it there at all. So, initially, though with the understanding that we would have to fish at some point, I succeeded in putting it off for a few hours.

As the sun climbed higher, their polite requests decayed into a gentle demand. They were quick to point out, with clear voices, that we also hadn't washed ourselves for days, and they certainly had a point with this; every one of us reeked of sweat, vomit, and Aimil's blood. And when somebody sighted a few fish rising to starboard, there was nothing I could have said or done that would have impelled them to continue. Indeed, I didn't even get the chance to try. Mikkel suddenly jumped into command as if I were invisible, and called for the sail to be untied and reefed, and for people to start getting the fishing tackle ready. I was half frustrated at this, but also half glad – my stomach was stinging just as much as everyone else's.

I was standing at the helm when the decision was made, and noticed that, at once, there was a light, playful mood in the air, excited smiles spreading from face to face, people clapping once, then rubbing their hands together. And, admittedly, there was a lot to be excited about: soon we were going to be clean, but more importantly, full. The only thing we had to do was catch some easy food and cook it. We were happy. It was still a perfect day.

In truth, there was nothing strange or out of the ordinary about anything, and thinking back through all the specifics, I don't remember seeing any peculiar looks or worried sighs, no hesitation; none of us, as far as I know, had the slightest inkling that we were teetering on the edge of tragedy.

I watched a fish breach the surface to port, and slip back into its liquid world with a soundless splash. I thought to myself that it was a good sign that they were on either side of the ship, and that we would probably catch enough fish to feed us all within an hour or two, and then move on. I nodded to myself. I could afford an hour or two. Then I scratched the back of my right leg.

This is the insatiable detail of disaster. Everything that occurred in the minutes that followed were so scorched into my mind that I've retained even the most insignificant information, and, though I couldn't count how many times I've recalled these seconds, I believe that I've always done so without alternating or mutating their trueness.

The air was warm, yet still preserved the crispness of morning. As Mikkel had asked, Aimil and Niels were walking to the stern where they would set up our newly improvised fishing gear. Mikkel had descended to the lower deck to get the head of the fish that we'd kept, and would be in the galley for the next few minutes, cutting it up to use for bait. Onni, as usual, wasn't really doing anything; he was tapping his hips excitedly at the idea of jumping into the water, and was standing near the gunwale, staring down along the side of the ship, watching the water pass by. His right foot, with toenails still dirty with the sand of the island, began tapping in time with his hands.

Meanwhile, I watched from the helm as Solmund, Toivo, and Knut tried to figure out how to release the sail. When the group had attached it to the boom the day before, they were more concerned with its strength than they were with how easily it could be released, and the obvious drawbacks to this were just being discovered. The sun caught Solmund's back as he gripped one of the ugly knots. He shrivelled up his nose and put his face up close to the tangle of rope, probably analyzing how best to begin the process of taking it apart. But there was something in the way that he did this that seemed to bother Knut. He clicked his tongue. "What are you doing?"

Solmund took his face from the knot and squinted at him in his disdainful way. The tone he used matched his expression perfectly. "Gee. I guess I'm trying to figure out how you tied this stupid knot." Then he shook his head, "Wish a bowline wasn't too complicated for you," he muttered, bending over to continue his inspection. I remember that there was something in his posture that suggested he was satisfied with the wit of this remark. But I wasn't; and only rolled my eyes at him. He'd grabbed hold of the ball of rope and was beginning to work at it, apparently thinking that there wouldn't be any reaction or ramification to his snide remark.

But of course there would be, and I was expecting Knut to reach over and give him a quick punch in the arm, as he sometimes did with Solmund, but this wasn't the case. Instead, he looked over his shoulder at Toivo, who was also struggling with one of the knots, and he must have winked at him because he smiled impishly, dropped the rope in his hands, and began walking in a large circle around both of them, closing in on Solmund from behind. I was watching this, thinking that Toivo was going to hold him steady for the quick punch in the arm. I didn't say anything.

As Toivo neared, Knut leaned in toward Solmund, who was completely unaware of what was transpiring around him, and sniffed the air in front of his face, wincing. "Do you know what, Solmund? You stink like shit. Come to think of it, I don't think you've washed yourself once since we left." Toivo's posture perked up, suddenly understanding what the wink had signified. "Tell you what, because you need some extra time to soak, why don't you let us untie the knots while you wait for us..." his voice was taunting and condescending. Toivo suddenly grabbed him from under the shoulders and Knut bent over to seize him from his feet. Solmund was rigid, silent, bewildered. "...In the water!" finished Knut, laughing.

I opened up my mouth to tell them to put him down, but again, didn't. I really doubted they were going to throw him overboard; I thought they were just scaring him, giving him something that was deservedly a little worse than a quick punch in the arm. And even if I had said something, I think they still would've thrown him in. After all, none of us knew.

Onni turned his head to watch as Solmund's tiny body arced over the rail. He stopped tapping.

But there was something disturbing about Solmund's silence; he was gasping, inflexible, petrified. And when his body turned in the air to face the water as a natural course of the throw, he held his knees and palms out at the surface defensively, as if it were solid ground and he were dropping from a hopelessly high tree. No one who had ever jumped into water before in his life would have done that.

I saw the soft shadows of every contracted muscle on his neck as he descended out of sight.

We heard the expected splash, and Toivo and Knut leaned over the rail in hysterics. Onni was watching the circle of foam

225

Mark Lavorato

that Solmund had made pass by him as it ran alongside the ship, and with his look fixed on the tiny bubbles, I could gauge our speed for the first time; and saw that there could be a problem.

"We're moving pretty fast, Joshua," Onni said, still watching the water. Then he looked up at me to see if what he'd said had registered.

I dropped my shoulders in annoyance. Why couldn't they have waited until they were finished to throw him off? What were we supposed to do now? Stop the wind? The only way we had of slowing down the ship was to release the sail, which appeared to be a fairly complicated process. It looked like Solmund was going to be in the water for quite a while, and I thought that this, at most, would turn into a bit of a humiliating experience for him. He would have to swim a good deal to catch up, and the whole time the idiots would be watching him, pointing, laughing. But there was no alarm, no reason to fear for his life – until he surfaced.

Knut, who was still giggling and watching to see where he would come up, was the first to panic. When Solmund finally shot out of the water, we could see that he was well in our wake, and it became painfully obvious in the first second of his being above the surface, with his arms thrashing the air, his head shaking the water from his face, that he had no idea how to swim. Knut's smile disappeared. "Oh shit," he mumbled.

And then there was one slow instant where no one moved. We all just stood there, still as rocks.

Knut was also the first to act. He suddenly spun toward the boom with his hands in front of him and began attacking one of the main knots attaching the sail. And I think the urgency in which he did this is what sparked the rest of us into action as well.

Flustered and unthinking, I left the helm. "Onni! Throw the rope!" I yelled at the top of my lungs as I rounded the corner to grab the ring buoy. The ring buoy had always been perched on the wall, its silky rope that had never touched water, drooping from it in colourful sweeps. It was such a permanent part of the ship that I'd stopped noticing it – or its absence. It wasn't there. Like so many other things that had gone missing

226

from the ship during the storm, the probing fingers of the sea must have found it and snatched it away, claiming it as another one of its ragged treasures.

I turned my back on the empty bracket, swearing, and saw Aimil and Niels standing wide-eyed and eager to help. "Find something that floats and throw it!!" I yelled at them, and turned to look for Onni who should have had the rope by then. "Onni – the rope!"

But he reeled around the corner and held out empty hands. "It's tying the sail." As soon as he said this, everyone muttered a curse and shot another look out at Solmund. He was becoming more desperate. He'd started coughing.

"Fuck!!" Knut screamed. He had been trying as hard as he could to untie the knot, but it hadn't budged. He also stopped for a second to look back at Solmund, who was only getting further away, his fists punching at the sky, the darkness of his mouth swallowing gulps of air whenever he managed to get his head above the water. Knut turned back to the knot and grabbed onto it for another second, "FUCK!!" he screamed at it. Then he let go, paused to think for a moment, ripped off his shirt and pants and broke into a run toward the stern of the ship, diving into the water with a clumsy splash. A few seconds later, after struggling to get his pants over his ankles, Toivo followed. Meanwhile, the rest of us scoured the deck for buoyant objects, Onni running below deck to look there, and the rest of us bumping into each other on the upper deck, searching in the same fruitless places.

Finally, after either hearing all of the commotion or being summoned by Onni, Mikkel ran up the stairs. He sized up the situation quicker than any of us, and ran to the helm to spin the wheel to starboard. We braced ourselves, and those who didn't, tumbled onto the floor as the ship leaned heavily to port. I gripped the rail, shaking my head at my lack of clear thinking. Why hadn't I done exactly what Mikkel was doing? I pounded a fist against the metal so hard it hummed.

The ship circled around, our bodies pivoting to watch as the two boys neared Solmund. His energy was draining; we could hear the distant sounds of his coughing beginning to fade, and his flailing arms, like a bird flying into the blurry distance, were appearing less energetic, random. By the time Knut was close enough to almost touch him, we saw a final arm flounder in the air, exhaustedly trying to grip at an invisible apparatus that might hoist him out of the water and into safety. But his fingers found nothing, and the white of his arm fell to the surface, limp.

Knut reached him right after this, grabbed hold of his clothing, turned, and started pulling him toward us. Toivo met him within a few seconds and both of them gripped Solmund at his armpits, his pale face bobbing out of the water with each heave toward safety.

Mikkel had turned the ship entirely around in a gigantic sweep, and had commanded Aimil and Onni to manipulate the boom so that the sail wouldn't catch any wind. Meanwhile, Niels and I prepared to get Solmund on board, tying some clothes together into a loop to hoist him from his underarms.

No one spoke while we watched them get closer. Because the truth was that Solmund's body already looked lifeless; his mouth was open, his eyes closed.

When they arrived at the ship, both Toivo and Knut were spent, and they clung to the rope ladder, which we used to get out of the water when we were swimming, and caught their breath. Meanwhile, Aimil and I jumped in and began trying to wrestle the loop of clothing over Solmund's arms. It was difficult. His limbs had become flaccid and heavy, and only after Knut and Toivo had recovered enough, and had joined us in the battle, did we manage to lift his arms enough to get the loop over his head and under his armpits.

When we were ready, hands came from everywhere, and we all heaved, pushed, and pulled to get him onto the deck, slowly inching his weight up the rope ladder. And as we did this, Aimil brought the gravity of the situation to another level by mumbling an eerie encouragement. "Come on Solmund, you're almost there," came muffled words spoken through bandages, which were soaking and had flopped in front of his mouth. A few of us exchanged a doubtful expression. Solmund couldn't hear us – and we knew it.

Mikkel had left the helm to help lift him onto the deck as well, and with all of us grabbing hold at every angle, we finally managed to heave him up with one determined effort, and those of us in the water watched as his legs disappeared over the gunwale.

The first thing they did once he was on board was to drag him toward the centre of the deck, as if the water were an exploitative and devious creature that might try to claim him again if we weren't careful. The rest of us climbed the ladder as quickly as we could, and gathered around him, Mikkel already kneeling at his side. "Solmund? Solmund." He leaned in close to his face and pulled his eyelids up. They stayed open, staring unblinking and unfocused at the bright sky. There was no reaction. He slapped him across the face. Still nothing. He slapped him again. "Solmund!" he screamed at his forehead. The rest of us cluttered in a circle and stared down at them both. Finally, Mikkel formed a fist in the air above his chest, as if threatening to punch him if he didn't react in some way. Solmund was perfectly still. "Come on!" hollered Mikkel, bringing his fist down against his chest with solid force. But the sound that was produced was not the hollow sound of childhood play fighting; it was a thin, dense noise, as if striking a piece of wet wood. A bubble of murky water oozed out of his mouth, streaming down the side of his head and over one of his ears. His expression was still placid, unmoved, unconcerned.

He was dead; and we all seemed to realize it at the same time.

Everyone reacted in their own way. Some of us raised our heads to look at one another before taking a few slow steps away from him; others put a hand on their forehead and paced around the deck; Mikkel stood up and looked down at the body for a few minutes before walking over to the rail and slumping onto it with all of his weight; while Onni was the only one to stay there, standing over him, looking down with his hands cupped over his nose and mouth, shaking his head every once in a while. The only thing consistent between our reactions was the silence.

It was shocking, to say the least. How many minutes ago had Solmund been alive and well, provoking people with his squeamish dignity? How was it that one tiny second of bad judgment, or of mistaken caution, or even of completely normal behaviour could be exchanged for a life?

And so I stood there, dizzy with a sudden appreciation of consequence; knowing that from every one of our actions was born some unknowable effect, which, in turn, would give birth to another of equal unpredictability – and then another. It was somehow daunting. Solmund had been walking around unaware of his approaching disaster for weeks of his life, days, minutes, seconds, all without ever coming to understand how very thin the thread was that he was dangling from. In the same way that I was oblivious of all the things that were just about to be snipped from me.

24

After a long, long while, Mikkel interrupted everyone's self-consoling quiet to ask the obvious question, which had to come at some point, but which, unfortunately, no one was really prepared to answer. When he asked it, his tone was sorry, unsuspecting, "What happened?"

Toivo exchanged a quick glance with Knut, who looked at the ground.

Onni slid his hands from his mouth to the sides of his face, continuing to look at Solmund's body. "He couldn't swim."

I shook my head. A drop of seawater trickled down my arm and curled into my fingers.

"Yup," sighed Mikkel, turning around to face us, "we now know that Solmund couldn't swim. But I guess I was asking: what was a person who couldn't swim doing in the water? Did he fall? Was he setting up the fishing gear? What happened?"

Toivo suddenly seemed to jar awake. "Yeah," he professed, "he fell."

Mikkel turned to look at him, blinking.

Then, Knut, also seeming to snap out of the state he was in, stepped forward. "Toivo's right. Solmund fell in by accident."

Onni looked carefully in my direction, wondering whether this was the safest story to endorse. But I could only squint at all three of them in complete amazement. I simply could not understand why they were saying this! Knut and Toivo didn't mean to kill Solmund. Not a single one of us knew he couldn't swim. So what was the incentive to lie? What would we serve by it?

But I knew. We would serve our cowardice, our incurable cowardice – the very thing that the Elders had endlessly preached about. Perversely, the damage to Solmund's life seemed less somehow, than the damage we would cause to ourselves by admitting we took it. Yet we had. We'd all made a horrible mistake, myself included, and we had to see it as such – we absolutely had to see it as such. Did they think they were going to absolve themselves by ignoring their mistake? And even if this worked for them, absolving ourselves of something doesn't wipe away the culpability. We didn't murder Solmund, but nothing was ever going to take away the fact that we'd killed him.

I looked at Knut, measuring his words. I was furious. He narrowed his eyes at me and crossed his arms over his chest, probably knowing full well what was coming. "What in the fuck are you guys talking about? You know perfectly well what happened. You and Toivo…"

"NO!!" he screamed, interrupting. He took his arms from his chest and pointed a finger at me, "No! No, I don't think I know a lot of things, Joshua," he took a step forward, and, after seeing my reaction, judged it safe enough to start walking toward me as well. I swallowed, looked behind myself nervously. "I don't know why we're on this ship, for starters. And I don't know what your chemicals are for, either; or what our Incision is all about, or what you learned in secret inside the Great Hall. But most of all, I don't know why you lied to us – or why you keep lying to us."

What had I done? Why hadn't I just kept my big mouth shut? Looking back, I find it almost poetic that I would demand unconditional truth from someone, all while standing behind a quickly thinning lie. I began to step backwards. I tried to say something, but couldn't. (There are times in our lives when silence is the wisest alternative, and then there are times when it isn't, yet it is somehow the only thing left to say.)

"But I can tell you some things I hear; some things we've figured out." Though it probably wasn't the case, it seemed as if the others began to step in my direction as well, their heads twisting to abandon their guilt and pity. There was suddenly something more interesting to pay attention to. Something easier. After all, why confront yourself with things you've done when you can pounce on someone else for something they have?

"There are people on this ship that think there's still a big secret, that when we Came of Age, we weren't told anything close to the truth – which is why the Elders had to be there whenever we were rehearsing the bullshit they fed us." Knut

232

stopped walking as my back pressed against the rail. He seemed to be angry, but still able to contain himself, making his accusations without losing control. It couldn't have been worse. Somewhere in the back of my mind, I understood that this would be the end of the story that the Elders had so carefully constructed, that the crew's version of the truth was about to stride out into the open and make a stand there. And after hearing Peik's name the night before, I had known that this moment, whether I was there to witness it or not, was on its way, but I couldn't help but feel that its timing was completely tactless. There we were, squabbling over a dead body, and one of our companions no less; someone we'd grown up with, someone who'd always been in our lives – no matter how much we didn't like him. It seemed vulgar, degrading, and I glimpsed at Solmund for a moment, and then back at Knut, almost wishing that he would lower his voice.

"Would you believe me if I told you there're even people who think this 'big secret' is exactly what Peik said it was, that the Elders are the ones that somehow killed everyone in the world, and that this voyage is really meant to wipe out the only people left – not to save them?" I looked at the floor, wondering how far Mikkel would let this go before he intervened. "And that maybe," Knut continued, "like the Elders, you want everyone in the world to be like Solmund is: dead. And that once you've used us for your sick plan, you're going to kill us with those poisons you brought along." He moved his face close to mine, the reek of his empty stomach fogging my face. "And maybe," he shot a glance over his shoulder at the purple lipped body, "Solmund is only the beginning.

"Because everything matches up, doesn't it? The Elders' constant criticisms of everything that people do, the things Peik said before his 'suicide', the expedition being announced – just as he said it would – your secretive training, the strange vials in your room, your lying about the communication device, even your objecting to the knife game." Both Niels and Toivo had joined the confrontation by coming to stand at Knut's sides, and he seemed to be encouraged by this, shoving his finger into my face and lowering his voice, "Because you hated the idea of us

233

having the skills to stand up to you; because you were afraid we'd rebel if we ever figured it out – like Peik did. What you want is for us to just stand by and obey, to be easily manipulated." He paused, seeming to understand something for the first time, and when he spoke again, he completely surprised me by trying to involve me in the conversation, "Don't you have anything to say to all of this?"

"What? No. I… don't know what you're talking about," I uttered pathetically, quickly worsening my position.

"Oh!!" he yelled, turning his head to the crew, who seemed to be gathering closer after hearing the lack of conviction in my voice. Some were eyeing me with a kind of shock, others with disgust. "You don't know what we're talking about!" he called out. "Of course you don't! And we can see that. Of course. Can't we guys?"

There were some concerned mumblings, a few shaking heads. Knut could see that his well-chosen words had had an effect; the crew were nervous, afraid. Because whispering wild theories behind closed doors was one thing, but actually having them loosely confirmed was another. And I think now of how frightening it must have been for them. They had no idea where they stood, where their questions would lead them. What was true? What was a lie? What were they going to do with me, now that I wasn't who they thought I was? And whom could they trust to make that decision? They were looking around frenetically, in need of something definite, explicit. Knut, seeing this, decided to give them what he could.

"So… let's think about what we know for sure." He walked into the centre of the crew, counting the 'facts' on his fingers. "We know we can't trust anything Joshua says. And we know that he's working with the Elders to do… something – we don't really know – but we can assume it's something we wouldn't really agree with, or they would have told us about it. We know… let's see…" he paused for a second, his eyes lighting up, "we know that he was the last person, besides the Elders, to see Peik alive! Yes! That's true isn't it! And that he hid the knives from us so that we wouldn't be able to defend ourselves." He gave me a suspicious glance, as if he were half expecting me to suddenly yank out weapons from under my clothes and massacre everyone in sight. I rolled my eyes at him, but he moved on as if he hadn't seen it. "Do you know what we know? We know that we're in danger. That's what we know. And maybe that's enough."

Knut hadn't gone out and actually said it, but the implication was pretty clear, and the crew looked me up and down, shifting nervously. It's an intimidating responsibility, weighing someone's life. But, all things considered, they seemed to be doing a fairly good job at it, busily scanning me while they mulled everything over, maybe picturing me creeping into their rooms at night, dripping poison onto their lips. Onni was the only one that looked at the ground.

Mikkel, who was standing furthest out of the circle, scratched his forehead. Perhaps, like myself, he was having a hard time grasping exactly how it was possible for the atmosphere of grieving over someone's death to crumble into a deliberation over killing someone else. Yet it had; and it felt like the air was becoming hostile, explosive, and if Mikkel wasn't going to interject with some sense, then it seemed like it was up to me. "Okay, look…"

"Shut up!!" Knut screamed, whirling around to face me. He had opened up his hand as if to slap someone and was pointing all of his fingers at my face. When he spoke again, his voice was struggling to be calm. "You just shut up. It's not your time to speak. Do you hear me? It's ours."

He took a step toward me. "Do you know what I think we should do with you?" I could feel the blood pulsing in my neck. Could he say it? And if so, could he be the one to do it? Though, thinking about it now, it might have been a lot easier than I'd like to imagine. I mean – throwing a person overboard wasn't the same as killing him. No. They knew that I was a strong swimmer; which meant that they would only see me bobbing healthily on the surface as they sailed out of sight. No gruesome corpse, no violent battle, no gushing blood; there would be nothing to deal with after the fact. It would be clean, simple. The only thing they needed was the nerve to push – and the consensus.

235

For some reason, my eyes wandered over to Solmund again. He was still dead.

Finally, Mikkel spoke up, interrupting both the judgment, and the flow of everything that was slowly setting itself in motion. His voice sounded drained of energy, "Knut. Step away from Joshua."

Knut turned around, and we watched as his expression transformed from a state of surprise to a state of defiance. The fact was that he had the support of the crew, and it must have crossed his mind to see just how far he could get with it. He thought very carefully of what he was going to say before saying it, that one word that none of us believed he had in him to say. "No."

But that was the wrong word. Mikkel straightened instantly and broke into a powerful stride toward Knut, stopping directly in front of him with a stamp of his foot, their faces only inches apart. Knut, understandably, had already begun to squinch. "Let us understand something right now Knut. You have no rank on this ship, no authority. And if you think that you can manoeuvre your way into power with a little childish intimidation, you are sorely mistaken. I will happily show everyone here exactly what you are. And if you want that, then please, deny my request again and face the consequences. If not, then step away from Joshua. Now."

Knut slowly shuffled to the rail. Mikkel was watching him closely, probably to see if he would display the slightest mark of insolence. He didn't.

There were a few disapproving mumbles at Mikkel's back, though he didn't seem to mind; because he wasn't finished yet. And once he'd watched Knut settle himself against the rail, he turned to look at me along with everyone else, a cheerless smirk – which I think was meant to be sympathetic or comforting – creasing his face. It was obvious that he had to do something with me. Things had been said which could never be taken back. And because I hadn't provided anything to defend myself against the accusations, they would be taken as truth, and things would quickly spiral out of control. The only way to maintain order would be to completely change the leadership and intentions of the expedition, and this would have to be done immediately. I couldn't blame him, even though I knew he'd always secretly looked forward to this day.

"Joshua. In light of what's been said – some of it being bullshit, but some of it, as you and I both know, being true – I'm taking over control of the ship and the expedition from here. You will be locked in your quarters, treated respectfully, and given food and water until we reach land, but from there, I'm afraid you're on your own. Do you think that's reasonable?"

I nodded quickly. Putting my life in Mikkel's hands was worlds better than putting it in Knut's, or anyone else's for that matter. As soon as I'd nodded, there were a few curses; most of the crew had brought a hand up to their head as they strained to keep up with it all. Their world was changing faster than they could possibly learn the rules.

"So... I'll take you to your room," Mikkel said, turning from me and walking toward the stairs. He looked at Solmund as we passed by, whereas I looked at the floor in front of my feet, avoiding the scowls and shaking heads, the appalled expressions.

We walked through the gangway and into my room, where Mikkel took the key from inside my door and put it on the outside. Before he closed it, he addressed me, looking around the room uncomfortably. "I hope you see that I'm locking you in here to keep you safe, not us. Okay?" I nodded. "We'll bring you some fish whenever we catch some, and in a little while I'll give you a bucket of water, and you can use the one that's already in here to piss in." He began to shut the door.

"Mikkel..."

"Sorry," he said, closing and locking it, and speaking from the other side, "I don't really want to talk."

But I pressed my face against the door to say something anyway. It was urgent. "Listen: I want you to know that it was Knut and Toivo who threw him in. I mean – I don't think they knew, because... well, none of us knew. But I also think... I think you should make them admit it."

There was a thoughtful pause. "Why? I mean – what's the point? Whatever they say, he's still dead." He removed the key from the door and turned, his footsteps receding quickly, leaving me alone with the quiet of my room.

I sighed and walked to the bed, laying down on it and staring up at the ceiling. It's interesting, because a million thoughts should have been going through my head at that point, things about The Goal or the Elders, or what I'd done to allow things to deteriorate so quickly, maybe even how I might gain control of the ship again, but nothing of that nature entered my mind. I could only think of Solmund, of his arms outstretched against the water as he fell, of his desperate struggle. I was imagining the things he must have heard, the fear he must have felt. But what I thought about most was the bubble of water that had swelled from his open mouth when Mikkel had struck him, and that, at that moment, his eyes had become so calm and definite, so peaceful, that – and for the first time ever – he could have easily held someone's gaze. But we'd all looked away instead.

25

When our senses are deprived of what they unconsciously and incessantly gorge themselves on, they seek sustenance elsewhere. They begin to scavenge, to crawl along the ground, meticulously sifting through the grass with their fingers in hopes of coming across some kind of nourishment; and when they find it, they shovel it into their pockets and hoard it, dwell on it, take it out more than they need to afterwards, greedily turning it over in the light. My hearing had replaced all of my other senses. In fact, sometimes I even closed my eyes as I listened, as if the sight of the few inanimate shapes in my room would blur and distort the sounds that made it to my ears. And sometimes it worked. Every hour it felt like I was catching more detail in the muffled noises, hearing different tones in the voices, coming to understand the different creaks the ship made when people were weighting specific parts of the deck, or the floorboards in the gangway, or each individual stair.

There was a story being told through the cracks around my door, behind every one of my walls, and through my ceiling. A story that, strangely enough, I was removed from, yet was also the centre of. It was about me; what I was, and what the crew were going to do with me (and with themselves) once they knew the bigger story that they had all unwittingly been a part of. And the only thing I really had to do with my time was piece this story together. And think.

There was no movement for a long while on the upper deck, only a thick, drawn out silence. Which, I was sure, was because of some kind of impromptu ceremony that Mikkel was giving, in order to throw Solmund overboard in the most respectful way possible. I tried to imagine how and what he was saying, which wasn't too difficult really. He was probably just following the Elders' example of what was said after Peik's death, offering a few vibrant words about what Solmund 'was', which, of course, would have had little to do with what he was, and more to do with what we wished he was; a few sentences that would help lead the crew toward that age old and venerable process of inventing memories.

Though, as opposed to what the Elders would have done, I couldn't really imagine Mikkel saying anything ideological before throwing Solmund into the sea; and not because it wasn't in him, but because he probably considered it as redundant as the rest of us. Since, in terms of the design of the universe, we all understood perfectly well what was happening to Solmund, just as we understood it when it was happening to Peik. After all, the workings of God had been relentlessly drilled into us throughout the span of our lives, having to meet with different Elders on a regular basis, who would then point out specific natural processes and break down exactly what God was doing in every one of them. This was the pedantic nature of our religion, which we would later learn, was not usually the case with belief systems involving God.

One of the first things that you did after Coming of Age was begin studying geography for the first time, along with learning the bare essentials of a few cultures, whose ruins you would be walking through if you happened to be chosen for the expedition. Whereas Mikkel and I – and as I'm sure Peik would have done as well – got to learn about these cultures in a bit more depth, focusing on their historical problems, political and social strife, and the amount of damage that they'd caused to themselves, neighbouring cultures, and the world around them. But one of my favourite parts in learning about these civilizations was talking about their religions; and not because they were interesting or novel, but because the Elders held such an animated contempt for them.

They would begin their lessons by rolling their eyes and thumping a finger onto a picture, which usually depicted the same kind of scene: a white-bearded man, his hair falling in lazy curls over muscular shoulders, sitting in the clouds with a melodramatic pose, looking down on the people of the world and dwelling on their every minuscule action. Though He wouldn't just think about those actions, He would also control things according to what He saw or what people asked for – provided they were moral people, of course; and if they weren't moral, then provided that they'd at least told other people, who happened to wear special black costumes (and were often just as corrupt themselves), that they had, in fact, been immoral like everyone else. And so long as these steps were followed, why then, He would happily manipulate the universe to suit those 'exceptional' people inside it. (Though, interestingly enough, if it didn't suit them, then it suddenly became obvious that He was trying to teach them some unseen lesson that they were apparently in need of learning, and of which they would have to spend a considerable amount of time interpreting in order to divulge its 'true' meaning.) Harek, but many of the other Elders as well, would get incredibly worked up at these notions, pacing around the room, mockingly holding his hands up to the ceiling and speaking in a raised voice, as if he were addressing someone walking on the roof above us. And when he was finished with all of his satirical theatrics, his hands would finally drape back down to his sides, and he would turn to me, shaking his head, and say something like: "Believe me, Joshua – religion is nothing but a direct product of our arrogance or fear; or both."

Then he would go on to talk about the birth of all belief systems; how they usually began with our insatiable need to categorize things, to put them in their 'right' place for our later reference. "Everything that we see around us and learn in books and from our lives, every question that we ask ourselves and to the learned men and women around us, and every answer we receive, we quickly place alongside the rest of the world's learning, tidily in its corresponding spot. And after we've done this, it's natural enough to find ourselves sweeping our eyes across the breadth of our knowledge base, though not really to learn or refresh our memories, but to make sure that there is nothing missing, that there are no gaps or holes in what or how we understand things. But the fact remains that there are holes. There are things that are completely beyond our capacity to understand, enormous questions, which, due to their very nature, are completely unanswerable. And so, if we were ever to lean in and look closely at this neat and tidy foundation of knowledge, we would see that there aren't tiny gaps in it at all, but rather mammoth voids that stretch from one subject area and span wildly across the next three or four! And those few brave minds in every culture that come to this realization, take a quick step back, stunned, afraid. They watch, horrified, as the voids become more obvious, begin to swell and bulge, and then they take another step back. These holes in our understanding somehow demean them, insult them, taunt them with their blaring unknowability. So what are they to do? They can't just leave them there!

"And alas! The solution lights up in front of them. Yes. There is only one thing to do with unanswerable questions: give them unquestionable answers. We need only look to the heavens, creating gods that supposedly created us, along with havoc, and the universe, and good, and evil, and, conveniently, every other inexplicable thing that remained blank in our knowledge base. And suddenly, the sounds echoing from those throbbing voids are completely pacified, smothered into silence, and as the inexplicable becomes increasingly easy to explain, we reassure ourselves that we have indeed discovered the glorious missing piece to our puzzle, and that, finally, we can rest assured in our conviction, safe and content, wherever we are, and whatever we do. We find ourselves leaning casually in the corner again, a modest smirk on our faces, and the entire universe and everything in it, neatly ordered at our feet — just the way it should be. There are no slippery questions anymore, we have found a way to supersede them, to ignore them, but most importantly, to feel as if we've confronted them, and won."

Then Harek would shake his head, scoff with a sad laugh, and slam the book with the painting of God in it shut, both of us watching the streams of dust spewing out of the pages and billowing into the room, curling in the shafts of light from the windows.

But sometimes I would think to myself that, if he were right, and religion was merely a means of answering the unanswerable, and knowing where and how each individual fits into it all, then, I'm not sure we all should have been rolling our eyes so dramatically; because our culture was no exception. We too had a religion, just like every group of people before us. And, like every other culture, we also believed in it with blind confidence, convinced that our belief system was superior, or at least more accurate than the rest of them. We didn't have any questions that couldn't be answered; we 'knew', without a doubt, where we were coming from, and what would happen to us after we died.

And we knew it all so automatically, so verbatim, that I honestly don't think Mikkel would have felt the need to reiterate it before throwing Solmund overboard. It was enough to just talk about him – him and some of his 'wonderful' attributes (which we would all dearly miss, of course). We already understood that he wasn't passing into heaven, nor was he patiently lingering in an invisible place, waiting for his soul to find another body. What Solmund was doing, in the grand scheme of things, was simply sinking to the bottom of the ocean to be consumed by fish. And to our minds, this unquestionable fact wasn't offensive or demeaning, but rather beautiful, regardless of its unimaginative nature.

The island's belief system was – I think – both mundane and magical at the same time. It went like this: The universe is naturally chaotic, disordered, faltering. There is only one thing that consistently brings, or attempts to bring, some kind of order to the things in it, which is energy. Energy has multiple forms: the nuclear forces, gravity, and electro-magnetism, and through these forms, it organizes, arranges, regulates, and reorganizes everything. From atoms into molecules; molecules into minerals; minerals into cells; cells into beings; and scattered matter into stars, planets, and galaxies. And as all life had the commonality of being organized by, and containing energy, and as energy couldn't be created nor destroyed, then, it fell that nothing really dies; and that all things, as they innately have some form of energy inside of them, are 'alive', so to speak. What we think of as death for a cell, or a plant, animal, volcano, or star is really only a phase, a rearrangement of sorts; the inevitable passing from one organized form of matter, to another organized form of matter. It is a necessary part of the ebb and flow of energy.

And energy, or God, opposed to the belief system of countless peoples, was not a righteous, vehement being. It was indifferent and indiscriminate. God did not belong to us; He

243

belonged to every religion before us as well. Though the name had changed countless times, as had 'His' supposed attributes and attitudes, shape, and language, in reality, God, being energy, was constant, immutable, even quantifiable. Because we could give energy numbers, measure gravity and assign symbols to depict the poles of magnetism, even calculate the heat of the sun, but never could we really, really grasp it. Giving a number to something's gravitational pull according to its mass was one thing, but understanding gravity in any kind of absolute sense, was quite another. Yet, regardless of its inexplicable nature, we knew for certain that energy had created everything, and in learning as much as we could about it, yes, we could even manipulate it on a very modest scale. Though, just because we could find a way to make God run through the tiny coloured wires in the shelter, didn't make the things He was responsible for any less magical for us. Regardless of whether we figured out how to use it or not, energy was still mysteriously in everything, shaping everything, organizing it, and transforming it. It always had been, and it always would be.

And so we knew accurately what would happen to Solmund. He was simply going to slip into the water; the rest, the energy in different organisms would do by undoing. He would be dismembered, eaten by fish, bacteria, and microbes, and through these creatures, he would be directly introduced into the active ecosystem to sustain other beings; and those beings, would, in turn, be eaten by others. He was going to live forever. He already had.

I could hear a few creaks above me, then something sliding along the deck for a moment – Solmund was being lifted and carried to the rail. There was a quick splash, followed by a deafening quiet. I sat up on the bed and looked down at the floor.

I thought of Solmund then – really thought of him. I thought about what it might have been like in his skin, always having to be around people like Knut, like me, people who had no qualms of passing their cold judgments onto him, people who alienated him with their words or actions, or with their careful pauses after he spoke. I tried to imagine how much he had suffered, and how dispiriting it must have been to have so much

244

to contribute inside of his head and no one around that would acknowledge it. In fact, thinking of him now, I find myself wishing – even if it was once, at some point in my life – that I had said sorry to him. Just once. Those might have been the kind of words that rolled around in his head afterwards, words he would repeat to himself when he was alone, maybe even finding that they fuelled him in some way. But, of course, I didn't. And there isn't much point in wishing it now.

There was movement again on the deck, along with someone coming down the stairs. I heard the person who had descended walk past my room and go to the water tank, open the valve, and fill a bucket with the fresh water we'd taken from the island.

I looked out of my tiny window. It was hard to tell, but it seemed like we weren't moving very quickly, if at all, and because of this, I assumed they'd finally found a way to untie the sail and were about to fish. I let myself hope for the taste of something besides the saliva in my mouth (which, naturally, only succeeded in introducing more saliva into my mouth to taste). Then I heard the person who had fetched the water walking back through the gangway toward my room. I had assumed that it would be Mikkel bringing me water, but couldn't remember him walking so light-footed before, and so listened for clues of who it could be in the way he was fidgeting to get the key inside the lock, but couldn't really figure it out.

The door opened, and, of all people, it was Onni who poked his head inside. He stood still for a moment, probably wondering whether or not it was safe to come into the room unarmed. Then, after seeming to have decided it was, he quickly stepped inside, and stood in front of me with the bucket of water. He was shifting uneasily on his feet, as if trying to find an acceptably way to act, which, I guess, was understandable, with all of our roles having changed so suddenly. But it bothered me; we'd always gotten along so well; had even sought out each other's company. And now, he wasn't even sure how to stand near me.

I decided to speak my mind. "You know, this is – uh… weird for me, too," I offered, giving him a crooked grin.

245

It seemed these were exactly the words he'd wanted to hear; and he smiled a gloomy smile before taking a couple steps forward to put the water at my feet. As he did this, I noted, with my newfound appreciation for sound, how quietly he moved through the room. And after thinking about it, I realized he'd always had this grace about him, it was just that I'd never had a reason to notice it before. He even placed the container on the floor as gently as he could, and the bottom of the bucket settled onto the wood almost without a sound.

He looked up at me, "We're fishing. But in a couple minutes Mikkel's going to tell us all about 'what we were never allowed to know'."

I drew in a long breath, "Yeah... well... I kind of guessed that would happen at some point."

Onni seemed to be searching for something in my words. Then, after a short silence, "Right. But – uh... I mean – what he's going to tell us... should we believe it?"

I cocked my head with the greatest of interest. I'd already assumed that I was completely on my own. Yet, here was our esteemed musician, wondering who to side with before even hearing a single word from another viewpoint. A viewpoint, mind you, told from someone who was sure to be more honest with him than I'd ever been. "Well, I obviously won't be able to hear what he's saying, but... I could imagine him telling you something... fairly close to the truth. I guess."

Onni looked at the floor, thinking. "Right."

And then he lifted his head, stood up straight, and cleared his throat. "Look. I want you to know something: No matter what he tells us, I'll never think of you as an evil person. You aren't. I know that much."

I could only smile at first, understanding that these words were a kind of offer to help in whatever way he could. And in the few seconds it took him to say them, I must admit, my admiration for Onni had grown tenfold. Because helping somebody is one thing, but helping somebody when there is an inherent risk involved – a risk to one's social standing or maybe even well-being – is nothing short of remarkable as far as I'm concerned. And it's certainly something I couldn't picture doing myself.

But as much as I valued the gesture, I was also pretty sure that I didn't need help. What I needed was to make it to land alive, and from there, I would have to figure out everything on my own anyway, regardless of any devoted companion I might leave behind, who would then have to face the consequences of assisting me on his own. Though, I must admit that it was comforting to know I had a friend on board if I ever needed one, and I imagined just knowing that much would be enough. "I appreciate that, Onni. But – uh… things might be different after you hear what Mikkel has to say. Because Knut was right about one thing: things weren't what they seemed on the island; and nor was the expedition; or the Elders." It was on the tip of my tongue to tell him that my role also wasn't what it had seemed to be; or my beliefs; or my intentions. But I didn't.

He nodded slowly, absorbing what I'd said for a few seconds. Then he stood and walked to the door, opening it again and slipping his body onto the other side, but leaving his head in the room with me. "Mikkel has trusted me with your key. I'll be the one bringing you food and water and washing out your waste bucket. That okay?"

"Of course," I said, smiling.

He grinned before closing the door, locking it, and removing the key. I listened to him tiptoe down the hall, and then weight each individual step as he climbed the stairs to the truth.

I really had no idea how this was going to turn out, and I lay back down on the bed again with the sensation of having become heavy. Though, I'm not sure if I was feeling concerned for my safety as much as I was feeling sorry for the Elders again. Knowing that everything was finally going to come out, I could only think about all the effort and fanatic attention to detail that had been dedicated to first building, and then holding together, an entirely separate reality. It almost seemed absurd that in only a few minutes, the value of decades of dedication could be rendered worthless. And really, after the fact, would the crew be 'better' in knowing what had happened behind closed doors, finally hearing all the things that had been planned without their consent? Because to me, it didn't seem like they had it so bad living in the dark; at least they were never forced to acknowledge what we really are. Yet, once they were told the truth, a very small part of them would have to question the basis of The Goal, to stop and wonder if there was actually any substance to these strange beliefs that the most respected people in their lives had held – at least for a second or two. And it was hard to say how they were going to react to such dangerous implications. I could only wait and see. And worry.

After maybe an hour and a half, I felt the boat begin to pick up speed, which could only mean that the improvised fishing gear had worked again, and that they'd caught enough fish to feed everyone. Some of them scuffled around on the deck, adjusting the knots on the sail and steering the ship back on course, while I heard a few others coming down the stairs, presumably on their way to the galley to prepare the fish. They were passing through the gangway without so much as mumbling a word, which was quite unlike them; and as they passed by my door, and without any warning or pause before doing it, someone kicked it with the greatest of violence. For a split second, the wood flexed like a lung coughing out sickened air, but by the time I'd straightened up, it was over, and they all filed into the galley, their silence suddenly sounding stiff to me, furious.

I remember sitting motionless on the bed, tingling. I'd guessed that their reaction was going to be something like sadness, and not, for some reason, rage. Though, the more I sat thinking about it, the more it was plain to see: it would almost be instinctive for them to want to lash out, to want to throw rocks at the Elders for having been so deceitful, for having raised them on rations of dishonesty. Isn't that exactly what I'd been taught, that for a human being, the urge to carry out some ugly retaliation after the fact, comes as natural to us as breathing? Yet the Elders, who had been so careful to teach me this, were now out of harm's way. Whereas I, on the other hand, was only a slender locked door away from it.

Veracity

I stood up and scooped a bit of water into the plastic cup that was floating in the bucket, and listened to the room fill with the sounds of my swallowing. I was tense, jittery. But I was also trying hard to reassure myself with the fact that Onni was in charge of my key, and not anyone else. (It occurred to me that Mikkel had thought very seriously about who he was going to give the key to before handing it over, and had decided on Onni because, out of all of us, he had the greatest capacity to forgive.)

I could smell the fish they were cooking in the galley, along with the strange fuel that we'd concocted in the lab, the sour smelling fumes seeping through the cracks around the room. I grabbed my stomach, drank another glass of water. I only hoped they wouldn't be thinking of retribution when it came time to giving me food; I hoped that some kind of sustenance, a morsel of fish, the skin of it, the head, even the slimy bones, might pass through my doorway after they were finished eating. And it would. But certainly not in the way I would have liked it to.

26

Several hours later, after they'd all congregated in the galley to eat and had finished, and after the people whose shift it was to sail had returned to the deck, I heard the remaining crew disperse into one of the rooms. Mikkel must have been at the helm when Onni, who had probably been waiting in the galley, thought it safe enough to bring me my portion of fish. But it wasn't. His gentle steps, creeping along the gangway toward my door, were being listened for, anticipated; and when the key turned in my lock, I heard another door quickly open, then a few muted curses, a hollow blow to someone's chest, a body slamming against the dampening sound of wood, and then, after a slow pause, I could hear that body's defeated steps limping away in a stymied silence. The steps were Onni's.

Several people gathered on the other side of my door, whispering, readying themselves, the floor creaking with their weight. But as scared as I was, there wasn't much I could do but sit on my bed, almost obediently, feet placed squarely on the floor, hands folded on my lap, waiting for them to come in. I watched the handle rotate and the door edge open.

Toivo's large frame slipped in first, his posture, which was ready for an attack of some kind, relaxed when he saw me sitting on the bed. He had one of the sharpened diving knives in his fist, the handle, a playful neon yellow, was almost glowing it was so bright. Knut came in next, carrying my plate of fish; and then Niels, slinking guiltily behind them both.

We all stared at each other stupidly until Knut spoke. It seemed he'd rehearsed what to say again; "Stand up and turn around," he commanded. But for some reason I didn't; I only looked at him, blinking. He snickered, as if he'd expected me to be defiant in some way. No matter – he'd rehearsed what to do in this case as well. "To be honest, if I were you, I'd do exactly what we say," his head didn't move, nor did his expression change, but his eyes skirted to his right and focused on the knife in Toivo's hand.

Veracity

Message received, I nodded, stood up, and turned around.

I heard someone step forward and then felt Toivo's strong fingers clutch both of my wrists and hold them in one of his hands. Then he passed his other arm like a rigid bar through the loop made by my elbows behind my back. I remember that I wasn't thinking about what they were going to do, I was only thinking about Toivo's knife, and wondered where it had gone. He tightened his grip, immobilizing me, straining my shoulders; then, shuffling his feet, he began to steer my body so that I would be facing the other two. While Toivo was doing this, I hadn't heard Knut even take a step, but he had, because just as I'd pivoted enough to see the other side of the room, he was already right in front of me, and I had no time to react, even to flinch; by the time I saw him, his body was already twisting, his fist driving through the air. I closed my eyes.

He put every bit of his weight into the first punch, which sunk deep into my stomach, forcing the air from my abdomen. My body curled over, straining for breath, but Toivo pulled me back, straightening me so that my torso could be exposed again. Knut leaned into another blow. And another.

Then, all of a sudden, they dropped me; and I collapsed onto the floor, wheezing for air and holding my stomach. It took me quite a while to recuperate, my face pressed against the floor, breathing as hard as I could, waiting for the pain at the centre of my stomach to recede. And as it did, and I started to take in my surroundings again, I could hear them chuckling at me, giggling. I waited to recover a bit more before I turned my head to look up at them, my eyes focusing slower than I'd expected them to. All three of them were huddled together, smiling away, and stuffing what was left of my fish into their mouths. Niels, who must have been holding the knife for Toivo when he was restraining me, as he now held it in his hands, noticed me looking at them and nodded his head worriedly at the floor.

Knut turned and smiled, bringing the fish that was in his mouth forward and displaying it for me on the end of his tongue. And as this didn't seem to provoke the reaction he was looking for, he plucked one of the last pieces of the flesh from the bones on the plate and leaned toward me, holding it out in front of him

251

as he crouched down to the ground. "Would you like some? Just a bit?" he asked, his words muffled by the fullness of his mouth. He jiggled the piece of fish in the air, "Here, you can have some," his voice was highly pitched, as if he were coaxing a timid animal. I didn't think to reach for it. It was clear I wasn't going to get any; and I certainly didn't want to give him the satisfaction of doing whatever he planned on doing when I tried to take it from his hand. But once he realized that I wasn't reacting a second time, his face grew serious, and suddenly, unexpectedly, he spat, smattering pieces of chewed and salivated food all over my face. I recoiled and buried my head in the darkness of my arms, facing the floor again, wiping the debris from my cheeks and eyes. The three of them chuckled.

I could hear Knut smacking his lips dramatically, cleaning his mouth to speak. He remained crouched beside me, unafraid. "Thing is, we know everything now, Joshua." Some more arrogant smacking and subtle licking sounds as his tongue wiped across the shining skin of his teeth. "See... we know who the Elders really were, and what the expedition was really for," his voice was composed, factual, "I think Mikkel called it 'the third phase'? No? And..." he said conclusively, as he stood up, as if he were coming to an important point, "we know all about what you were going to do. Don't we, gentlemen?" I could hear him wiping a hand across his mouth. He seemed calm, so I wasn't expecting it in the least; I even heard him lift one of his feet off the floor, but still didn't cringe. With a sudden ferocity, he brought his heel down on the back of my head as hard as he could. My face, or more specifically, my nose, slammed into the floorboards, sending a blinding pain through my head. My nose began to bleed right away; warm liquid streaming out of my nostrils, through the fingers cupping my face, dripping off my knuckles, and collecting in the cracks of the wood. I was moaning.

I didn't hear them leave the room, but I heard Knut poke his head back in after I'd recovered a bit. He spoke in a quiet, secretive voice. "You know – I hope Mikkel doesn't find out about this. Because that would make us mad. No?" He asked this almost kind-heartedly, as if expecting me to turn and give him a tender response. Then he closed the door, locked it, and left the key inside, probably for Onni to get it back without having to hand it to him, and risk Mikkel seeing the exchange. The three of them returned to the same room they'd come from, and closed the door, undetected.

I lay there for a long time, not even attempting to get up. I felt the blood in my nose and on my hands gradually cool and coagulate, and because I couldn't seem to fully catch my breath, I continued to take in deep gulps of air. I wasn't crying, but tears were uncontrollably streaming from my eyes and through my nasal cavity, mixing with the general medley of liquids collecting at my mouth: saliva, tears, blood, Knut's spit, particles of fish. I felt pathetic, and must have looked it; but I didn't care. I didn't care about anything. I just felt tired. So tired that I could have sunk into the wood, seeped into the grains like the disgusting mass of fluids dribbling from my lips. I had lost. I had lost everything; control of the ship, the tremendous faith that the Elders had placed in me, my purpose, my companions. I had lost it all. But most importantly, I had done this to myself. I was there on the floor, bleeding and sore with tears, because of my inadequacies as a leader – nothing else. Though, that certainly wasn't the only thing that I was falling short on. I understood that I was just as flawed as them, and knew that if I'd had the chance, if I'd had weapons and people standing behind me, I would have evened the score with Knut, Toivo, and Niels without a second's thought; and I would have done it with the same degree of callousness, or more.

I had once sat with Dana, talking about something that I don't recall, when Anu, that terror of a child, ran screaming into our view. He was running toward Siri and yelling at the top of his lungs, his fists poised at the ends of his straightened arms like a battering ram. I remember that when she saw him, she only threw her arms over her head and braced herself, letting out a desperate little squeaking sound just before he crashed into her. She fell on the ground and started to cry. Anu, knowing that her crying was only going to bring the Elders, and with them some kind of scolding, tried to get her to stop by slapping her lightly on the head. But this obviously didn't work. And just as the first Elders were scurrying into view, he scowled and, picking up a fistful of dirt, pitched it at her, which, of course, only produced louder crying. The Elders, who had previously only been scuttling through the trees, found themselves breaking into a full out run, hollering and waving their arms. Finally, Anu turned and raced off into the forest, with several people in pursuit.

As the whole scene galloped out of our view, I shook my head and muttered that children were cruel; and not because of Anu, but because he'd reminded me of the things that we all do as children. However, Dana was quick to object. He had said that it had nothing to do with children at all, but that people were cruel, and the only difference between children's cruelty and adults', was that adults had the duty to perform theirs within societal parameters. They had only replaced the pummelling and face slapping with snide remarks and critical glares; the damaging ridicule that resulted was the same, the only difference was that a child's was more candid and obvious. Though, of course, when it became socially acceptable, adults were also allowed to lash out with open violence, strip themselves of their polite barbarism and get down to something more raw, more satisfying. If conditions were right, they could act like children again, only with the added advantage of having no grown-ups to keep them at bay, and more than sand to throw. (Come to think of it, maybe that's what a war was.)

And suddenly, it seemed like everything Dana had said was right. Maybe cruelty was simply one of those archaic weapons that we wield every day of our lives, a tool whose weight we grow so used to having in our hands that we stop to even notice it. And maybe, likewise, we had also grown accustomed to the daily ducking, dodging, and deceiving that we do to make sure we're on the least dangerous side of that weapon; all without ever really coming to appreciate the destructive power it has. Until, that is, the moment we happen to find ourselves backed into a corner, covering our faces from that swinging blade, the merciless metal finally sinking into our skin.

I sniffled some blood into my throat. Swallowed. I was being dismal, and I knew that. In the same way that I knew I could be more, that there was a way for me to shrug this all off and move on. And finally, after a long while, I put my palms to the floor and lifted my chest off the ground. Once I was standing, I touched my nose. It hurt. I touched it again; then shook my head at myself for doing it. I found my way to the bucket of water and washed my face until the liquid that dribbled to the floorboards no longer had a reddish tinge to it, and, patting my face dry with the bottom of my shirt and leaving some faint pink lines along the hem, I sat back on the bed and nodded at the door. I was okay. I was going to be okay.

Eventually, the light from my little circular window began to fade, then darken, then blacken, and I listened as most of the crew went into their quarters and settled into their berths before sleep. But not everyone disappeared into their rooms; Onni sat somewhere on the deck for quite some time, playing his flute. I don't know where the music came from – if he'd learned it before, or if he was composing it on the spot – but whatever it was, it was incredibly sad, a slow melody swaying back and forth through some obscure minor key. And I'm sure that a few people cursed him for playing it. They already had enough on their minds without Onni stirring things, pressing everyone further into their thoughts.

One thing was certain: I didn't envy the crew, or what they probably found themselves thinking about while they stared into the darkness in front of their faces. Because it wasn't just that every one of us, whether directly or indirectly, had been responsible for the death of one of our companions that day, there was also the uncomfortable fact of knowing where we were really coming from, and where we were supposed to have gone, which they would have to grapple with as well. Though, it might have been that with such heavy thoughts bearing down on them, they simply chose to push them away, squishing their hands against the sides of their heads to block out the music, curling into embryonic balls, and straining to find sleep before any of the implications could filter through their skulls. But whether they acknowledged it or not, some serious responsibilities had just fumbled into their hands. After all, the Elders, the very people who had cared for them, raised them, and sent them on this inauspicious errand in the first place, and who had always known considerably more than them, suddenly, perversely, knew something less; which was that everything about the expedition had changed, and would never be the same again. The power to manipulate and change the future of the world had, unbeknownst to them, been whisked out of their hands and shoved into the fingers of a few simple young men.

I wondered if any of the crew were going to have nightmares of reaching for something that they couldn't touch, or of trying to give away something that they could touch, but didn't want to; their bodies flexing in their sleep, arms straightening into the space at the ends of their bunks, hands opening wide in the dark.

I have to admit, there was a part of me that hoped they had nightmares. And, considering the way I was woken the next morning, they probably did.

27

I didn't even hear them unlock the door; nor had I heard the creaking of the floorboards when they gathered in the gangway before bursting in. I was just suddenly awake, the doorknob crashing against the wall as it flung open. I shot bolt upright, my arms raised defensively in the air, looking around, trying to understand what was going on, how, who, why. The entire crew was streaming through the doorway, scattering throughout the cramped space with loud footsteps, filling every corner with their urgency. Before I had time to say anything, Knut and Toivo came rushing toward me with knives in hand, and, stopping at the edge of my bed, pushed their blades into my face, ever closer, until I was cowering on top of the sheets, covering my head with my arms, leaning away from them and against the wall.

I was waiting for hands to grab onto my shirt and wrestle me to the floor, or for the tip of one of their knives to be poked into my back followed by a stern command, but nothing came. And as the seconds passed without anyone even brushing against me, the thought crossed my mind that they might have come into my room for something other than me. I turned my head just enough to peek under my arm and saw Onni wobble past me, obviously carrying something heavy; and that was all I needed to understand. They had come for the cases.

There were four cases in all, three of them containing verified mixtures, and the fourth, lab equipment and instruments. They were made of a thick plastic and were waterproofed with a gasket and a hefty levering mechanism that sealed them shut. I could hear people unfastening them from where they were fixed, dragging them off the shelves, and taking them out of the room, one person per case. Mikkel was one of those people, and I watched him through the space under my arm as he disappeared around the doorframe, the load stretching his arm straight. They were carrying them to the upper deck. And once all of the cases were out of my room, Knut and Toivo backed away from my bed, closed and locked my door, and followed the others up the stairs.

I took my hands slowly from my head, as if someone might still be there, standing over me, ready to pounce; and then got off the bed and stepped into the centre of the room, gauche on my early morning feet. I noticed a scattered soreness in my chest for the first time, which wasn't the only reminder of the beating I'd received the day before; I still couldn't breathe very well through the swelling in my nose, and if I touched it, the sting crawled up to the bottom of my eyes. Though, all things considered, the pain in both areas was dull, tolerable.

I had only been standing there for about a minute before I heard the volley of splashes to port. The cases. I squinted up at the ceiling. Because I have to admit, at first, the crew's logic didn't really make a lot of sense to me. Considering that we were a limping vessel in the middle of nowhere, and were heading to a place that we knew nothing about in terms of its available resources, why would they throw anything away? I'm sure they could have found a few uses for the things inside: the small amount of fuel that we'd made for the burners, the vials, even the cases themselves; and their uses could have been essential: the making of medicines, the boiling of water to purify it, or even, if need be, the boiling of water to trap the steam of seawater and channel it into a cup to get freshwater. They could have been throwing away their survival, or at the very least, some of their comfort; and this must have crossed some of their minds. Yet they had still felt the need to throw them overboard. Why?

I started to circle the room, thinking. For some reason, it wasn't enough that I was locked in my quarters, defenceless and beaten. No, they wanted more. They wanted a guarantee, some kind of assurance that I would never be able to carry out what I had been trained to do. Which could only mean that Mikkel had done some talking.

I had always known that Mikkel wasn't 'ideologically fit', as he had called it, but I was never really sure as to what degree he was 'unfit'. But now I knew. He had been biting his tongue, biding his time, privately holding onto his ridiculous notions of sparing our foul race from the only thing we had rightfully earned. He probably told the crew about Anu and Siri, and about the possibility of there being other people in the world like them, who, provided they were found before the members of the expedition grew too old to search for them, could be educated and protected from other third phase expeditions; could be saved. Which, of course, was an idea that the crew would have bought into without a moment's hesitation. In fact, they already had (and, ironically, it was the Elders who had sold them on it).

Which would explain their wanting to throw the mixtures overboard; it would be the first definitive step they could take to safeguarding people from The Goal. Even if, in reality, sinking the cases to the bottom of the ocean wasn't really doing much, seeing as the knowledge of how to make the mixtures was still safely guarded in my head. And I wondered if this had already occurred to them – because if it had, it had undoubtedly raised a few questions. Like: Could they really release me out into the world, wave a hearty farewell as I disappeared into the shadows of the trees, the whole time believing that I was heading out to do exactly what they wanted to prevent? Could they just cross their fingers and hope that they would be the ones who might be blunderingly lucky enough to come across a tiny group of people during their lives, and not me?

I started to think about how they'd been acting that morning: Mikkel's involvement in taking the cases from my room, the crew's pursed lips as they pulled them from the shelves, and the fact that Knut and Toivo were given the charge of holding me at knifepoint in the first place. Something was weighing heavily on their minds, and it wasn't the vials of murky liquid in the cases. And the more I thought about it, the more I could almost feel it in the air around me, could hear it in the footsteps throughout the ship, in the way that people were opening cupboards and closing doors – the argument for allowing me to live was growing thinner.

For the next little while, I could hear a lot of movement on the deck, along with some loud but indecipherable words being exchanged, which were followed by a long silence. And once, at the end of that long silence, I felt the ship veer abruptly to port, which wasn't done for reasons of tacking, because, judging by the ripples on the sea's surface, the wind was still directly at our backs. The only reason for the quick change of direction that I could think of was that, perhaps, whoever was supposed to be manning the helm at the time, had been involved in the intense discussion, and felt the need to abandon it to make a point, or to listen to one, and then had to correct the course later on. The loud voices, the silences, the neglecting of important duties, to me, they all pointed to the same thing: they were discussing whether to kill me or not. Though, thankfully, it also seemed like they were having a hard time coming up with a consensus.

One thing was certain: Mikkel had quite the balancing act to perform. After all, one of the only things the crew had learned since we left the island was that a mutiny was easier to accomplish than they'd ever imagined; and Mikkel wasn't standing on very solid ground himself, after having known about The Goal since he'd Come of Age, and only divulging it for the very first time the day before. The crew might have been a little suspicious of him, or at least would be for a few days. Emotions would be running high in the debate, and there was the danger of alliances forming, of canyons being carved between those who were in favour of my death, and those who weren't.

After the conversation was finished, I could hear people going back to their chores and duties, moving throughout the ship. No one was saying a word. I pressed my ear against the walls as people passed, trying to catch a phrase or two that might explain a bit about what had been said, but there was nothing to hear.

Then, at one point during the morning, a few people gathered into the room next to mine, their mumbled voices and sneering laughter humming through the veneer as soon as they closed the door. This continued for a little while, until there was a sharp thud against the wall, a few quick steps, and then the grainy sounds of a knife being worked out of the paneling. A muffled voice came from the other side, accompanied with cold giggles beneath it. "Hey – is that bothering you?" Knut pounded a quick fist against the wall, "Hey! Can you hear me in there? ...Because – uh... if it's upsetting at all, just let us know, okay? I mean – we want you to be comfortable in there. We want you to be having a nice time." The last part of this sentence didn't have much volume to it, as his back was turned while he was walking to the other side of the room to throw the knife again. It clunked against the wall. There were more giggles. "So if you need anything, don't be afraid to ask. Because we'll get right on it. Promise."

The throwing of knives against my wall continued until its novelty must have begun to wane, and eventually, they settled down on the bunks to talk. Knut must have sat with his back to my wall, because someone continued to stab at the wood with constant prods. But they were mechanical and lacked in violence or intent, and I think were just done in an attempt to annoy me. Soon enough though, even the jabs slowed, and then finally stopped.

For the first time, I could press my ear against the wall without being deafened by the knocks on the wood, but when I did; I found that I couldn't really pick any words out of the steady murmuring. Then, at one point, the tones became more subdued, more secretive, and Knut suddenly moved away from the wall and to the centre of the room, where their voices gave way to concentrated whispering; which was almost impossible to distinguish as whispering, let alone understand.

I took a few quiet steps away from the wall and looked around for something that would help me hear. I remembered the plastic cup that Onni had placed in my water bucket and tried pressing it up against the wall to listen. I found, to my surprise that I could almost make out words; but it wasn't enough. I stepped back again and inspected the wall. I noticed a black knot in the wood, which was close to the floor and had a tiny section missing near its centre, and I lay down on my stomach to try it there. I covered the knot with the cup, and, after listening for a long time and not understanding a thing, someone raised his voice above a whisper, getting caught up in what seemed to be a counterargument of some kind. "...ya... tha... bah ... No. No. Not if the life raft is gone too." There was the sound of someone being slapped – maybe on the leg, maybe across the face – it was hard to say. Then there was a stiff silence, after which the whispers died down into nothing more than breath that must have formed words. Every now and then I could make out the broken shape of the letter S, but that was all. Though, I continued to listen anyway; until, after an incredibly long pause where there were no sounds whatsoever, I heard everyone stand and leave the room, dispersing to other parts of the ship. It sounded like there were three of them walking away, but I couldn't be certain.

When I was sure they were gone, I let myself fall onto my back and stared up at the ceiling, letting the cup roll out of my hand and onto the floor, where it arced in small circles at my side, being dragged in different directions by the flux of the ship. True, for all my eavesdropping, I hadn't heard much, but it was enough to know what they were talking about. Knut, along with one or two others, was busy planning my murder. And what was more, I understood both the plan, and the fact that it would probably work. A few of them would come into my quarters in the middle of the night, take me by knifepoint in complete silence to the upper deck, and then throw me overboard, maybe stabbing me first so that I couldn't wake anyone by yelling once I was in the water, and afterwards, toss the life raft in with my body. Then they would break open my door first thing in the morning, where the sounds of the splintering doorframe would be masked by their screams of alarm as they 'discovered' that I had cunningly escaped during the night.

It's interesting that after realizing this, while lying on the floor and staring up at the ceiling, the cup still drawing plastic circles beside me, I didn't really feel afraid – it was more a kind of pragmatic detachment. I was just taken over with the need to come up with a plan of my own. That was all.

The first thing I thought to do was slam a fist against my door and demand to speak to Mikkel. But I knew that he would only shake his head and speak to me in a soothing voice from the gangway, using the word 'paranoid' as many times as he could in one sentence; if, indeed, he would see me at all. I'm sure, as he was probably one of the few people who wanted to spare my life, that he had tensions of his own to deal with, and that he would be incredibly wary of appearing to back me any more than he already had.

The next thing I thought about was Onni; wondering if I could use his vague offer to help in some way, but couldn't think of anything. Onni didn't have an aggressive bone in his body, which, I imagined – in this case anyway – made him of little use to me.

Then I thought about what I could do on my own. I knew that my murder, if they had wanted it to be covert, would have to be done at night; and, as I doubted they would risk being so obvious as to kill me only hours after they'd had a group discussion where the overall decision was against it, I assumed that they would try the following night, or the night after that. If we were still making progress as I'd calculated, then we should have been in sight of land within a day or two, where perhaps Mikkel planned on finding an island to leave me behind on (where I would be alive, but also in a place where I couldn't do any harm). Which meant that, when they finally tried to kill me, we would probably be in sight of the spiny peninsula. And so long as I was ready for them, and could catch them by surprise when the door edged open – and then scream, punch, yell, scratch, break bones, and maybe even rip a knife from one of their hands and cut some skin – I could cause such a scene that everyone would wake and come running, only to realize that some of their fellow shipmates had taken it upon themselves to remake a decision that had already been made. And, provided I was still breathing after all was said and done, they would almost certainly find themselves looking over their shoulders at the land in the distance, and have no choice but to feel some kind of twisted obligation to let me go.

That was my plan. And I was convinced it was a good one, even in the case that I didn't survive; because, I rationalized, this way, I would have won to some degree. I would have at least tried to save myself. And it just happened that, in the process, I would also hold them more accountable for their actions. I would take the power out of their hands, and no longer would it be as easy as turning their heads away from my bobbing shape in the water to appease themselves. No, they would be forced to deal with the blood that they had spilled, to clean it up, to see the ugliness of what they'd caused; and I was sure that the bright red of it would be burned into their minds for the rest of their lives.

I grinned at the ceiling, then stood up, and began pacing around the room, clenching my jaw, my fingers wrapped tight. For some reason, it all seemed rather clever to me at the time, this idea of leaving them with a lasting imprint, with a voice that would echo through the years. I was certain that, provided I screamed loud enough, the sound of their wrongs would surface again, maybe come back to them in the form of some blurry whisper, a scratching message through chattering branches on a cloudy afternoon, a distant hum sticking to the walls of their conscience that would become louder once they were alone.

That's what I would leave them with.

28

A few hours later, I heard people go into the galley to cook the midday meal, and within minutes the same familiar smells that had seeped into my room before were again slipping through the cracks. My stomach stung anew, and I listened obsessively to the sounds they were making, everyone gathering beside the stove to serve themselves, the thick clay plates being set onto the table, the utensils clanking together before they ate. While everyone sat forking food into their mouths, I noticed that the usual conversation between the crew was restrained, quiet, which, to me, only served to illustrate how divergent their opinions had become. After they had finished, and plates were being scraped and cleaned, I listened for the footsteps that might remember me, hoping, wishing that if something was actually sent to my room, that it wouldn't be stolen again and eaten greedily outside my door.

And those footsteps came; two people were walking down the gangway toward my room. I backed away from the door, swallowing. While I was waiting for them, I recalled an odd tradition that I'd once read about in an unassigned section of a book that Mitra gave me (a sea epic that I was supposed to be studying for its technical details). In this tradition, the very people who were about to put a man to death would give him one final and extravagant meal, supply him with a bounty of nutrients that his body would never use. At the time, I'd wondered if the custom had sprung out of a need to try and console the dying man. But now I'm pretty sure that it was just to console the part of the executioners that would die with him, the part of their conscience that needed some mollifying nourishment; a little act of charity to help convince themselves that they were acting out of necessity and nothing else. Though, whether this same perverse concept was at play that afternoon or not, I didn't really care. I just wanted food.

The key clattered to get into the hole, and the door opened quickly. It was Onni, and he had a plate of cooked fish in one of

265

his hands, of which, I'm sorry to say, I couldn't help but focus on with what must have been a completely crazed expression. He had a small pail of water in his other hand as well, and walked into the room watching it, careful not to splash any on the floor. Meanwhile, Toivo stayed in the gangway, looking around uneasily. He was obviously there for 'security' purposes.

My eyes followed the plate of fish moving through the room until Onni bent over to put it on the floor beside my water bucket, which struck me as an odd thing to do. (I wondered if I was expected to eat on all fours now; and if he had been specifically instructed to give it to me in this way.) But there was something in the reverence in which he did it that stopped me from saying anything. And, as I wasn't about to crouch down and shovel the food into my mouth as they might have expected me to, I could only stand there, pretending to be patient, waiting to see what would happen next.

Onni picked up the small pail of water and took a few steps over to the large bucket that he'd brought in the day before, apparently intending to fill it to the brim, even though I hadn't really used much of it. This was already strange enough, but then he moved around the bucket until he was at an entirely unnatural angle to it, so that the pouring water was facing the gangway as it came out. He seemed to be pointlessly shaking the water as well, as if it were solid and needed help to spill out of the pail. And it wasn't until I saw the piece of cooked fish slither out of his sleeve and land on the floor, the sound of which was timed perfectly with a quick clearing of his throat, that I realized what the spectacle was all about. The fish had crumbled into a couple of pieces, but still lay behind the bucket he was filling, hidden from Toivo's view.

"Hey – uh… thanks for the water, Onni," I said, sounding suspicious. I looked up at Toivo with a stupid wooden grin on my face to see if he'd noticed, but he wasn't looking, and nor did he seem to care. He was busy watching his feet, lifting his toes off the floor, lowering them. He didn't even raise his eyes from them as he spoke.

"Come on, Onni. Let's go."

Onni had finished topping off my water, and so walked out of the room, closed the door, and locked it. But neither of them walked away, and when I heard that they were exchanging a few hushed words, I crept as fast as I could to the door to listen.

"…Yeah but it stays in the door from now on."

"What? Says who?"

There was no reply, only a quick silence followed by the sounds of Onni being pushed to the ground, his hands squeaking along the wall, trying to catch hold of something, and a dull bump signifying that he hadn't. Finally, after the sound of Onni getting to his feet again and another tense pause, their footsteps departed in opposite directions. Neither of them had removed the key.

But at that moment, I had other things to think about. The second that I'd heard their footsteps recede enough to know that nothing else was going to happen, I scurried to the food on the ground, crouched beside it, and shoved both the fish on the floor and the other on the plate, into my mouth, bones scratching along my throat as I swallowed. Once I'd finished, I scooped the plate from the ground and began to lick it, wiping it up and down across my face until it was spotless, and then moved onto the ends of my fingers. Only when there was nothing left anywhere did I begin to slow down. I drank some water and sat on the floor with my back against the bed, a hand on my stomach, which I could feel contentedly working away.

Finally, I could think.

So, it seemed obvious enough that the key was left in the door to help my assassins, taking out the factor of getting it from Onni in the middle of the night, but what I didn't understand was whether this could signify what day they planned on doing it. I was sure that Mikkel would see the little ring of silver sticking out of the keyhole when he walked by it in the gangway, but it seemed they were confident he wouldn't do anything about it, that he would avoid the touchy subject as much as he could. Though, it also occurred to me that he had made the suggestion to leave it there. Maybe it wasn't only a few members of the crew that wanted me dead, but the majority of them, and Mikkel's insistence on keeping me alive was only proving to undermine his authority more by the hour; and, for the sake of maintaining order, maybe he felt that he had no choice but to let them kill me and stage my escape. Maybe it was the only way to keep everyone happy. Yet, even if this were the case, once again, I doubted my murderers would be so obvious as to take advantage of the key being left in the door after only a few hours. It would be in their interest to wait at least a day or two, when people would begin to see it as commonplace; even if everyone knew what it was for, including Mikkel.

That afternoon stretched out into long hours of worrying; worrying about what would happen, how many people I would have to fight off, what time of night it would take place; wondering if I would have a day to prepare before the door inched open, or two; questioning if my plan would really work, if they would really feel a warped obligation to let me go if I survived the attack. I spent my hours being eaten away by guesswork.

And then, just as the light from the window started to grow weak, I heard what seemed like the entire crew, except for whoever was at the helm, gather in the galley. They ate the rest of what had been cooked at the midday meal, and began to play a game of some kind. The laughter that accompanied this game sounded strained at first, but soon gave way to something a bit more genuine, and became louder, and then louder; until eventually, the room was heaving with it. I imagine that it was a competition of some kind. At one point there was a thick pounding sound, as if someone had fallen onto the floor – which the room bellowed in a raucous response to – so it had to be something quite physical. Whatever it was, I'm sure a few of them were trying fairly hard to enjoy themselves, hoping to distract their minds from what they were constantly and secretly thinking about.

I was looking out of my window, listening to them, watching the grey of the sky darken, the swells on the sea's surface reflecting less and less, the blue of it becoming more metallic, black, when I started to become aware of something subtle and indistinct that could be heard under the din of their laughter. I looked at the door, listening intently, trying to filter out the loudest noises. And then I heard it, a creak in the floorboards, someone walking as gently as they could through the gangway.

Everything seemed to fall into place in one flaring second. I had been wrong about their plan. It wasn't in the middle of the night, when they would have to risk waking people. No. Instead, it was when everyone was still awake. Knut had simply given a few people the charge of creating the noisiest distraction they could in the galley, while, surprisingly, they had expected only one of them to march me up to the deck by knifepoint, stab me, and push me over.

I smiled. They had seriously miscalculated.

I walked to the door on the edges of my feet, listening to him get closer, trembling with aggressive energy. He stopped directly on the other side of the door, which only meant that I was right. This was it.

I watched the one shining dot on the door latch, the reflection of the tiny bit of light leaking in from the window, waiting for it to move, listening for the lock to unbolt. My mind was empty. Red.

There was a strange sound on the other side, like that of a scratching sigh, then a muffled crinkle, then an irregular hiss. He hadn't even touched the key, and the door latch hadn't budged. I noticed movement near my feet, and my eyes shot down, alive with attention, focusing on an unlikely shape slipping into view; it was lighter grey, angular, and passing along the piece of wood that you had to step over to get into the gangway. Paper.

I bent over and grabbed hold of it, holding a hand out to the door lest it be shoved open while I was in a vulnerable position, and pulled the sheet into the room. Immediately, the person on the other side stood and began walking back to the upper deck with the same gentle steps that had brought him, his sounds quickly fading into the clamour of the galley.

Interesting. I looked down at the piece of paper, squinting, the darkness of the floor bleeding into its hazy edges. The paper was fairly thick, its texture course, and I recognized it as being a ripped corner of one of the maps. Obviously, there was something written on it, but it was impossible to make anything

269

out. (The fact that I didn't have a lantern in my room seemed to be a bit of an oversight on the sender's part.) I brought it to the window to see if the first bit of starlight would be enough to read by, varying the angle of the paper to catch the most light. I could barely see the thin grey lines at first, but after focusing on them for several minutes, I started to be able to distinguish letters, and then words. Slowly, I pieced them together. And once I did, I had to read it over and over again to make sure that I wasn't making it up.

Sighted land at sunset. Others don't know. Will get as close as I can to let you off with the raft. Wind in your favour. Will come later tonight. Eat this note. Onni.

I leaned against the wall, looking out the window, and the muscles in my body relaxed to a point that I felt I was floating off the ground. The air in the room was stagnant, stale, yet every breath I drew in seemed to fill me. Suddenly, there was a very real chance that I would walk on land again, that I would smell the stickiness of budding plants, that I would feel soil pressing beneath my feet, or the warmth of a rock in the sun.

It turned out that I'd completely underestimated Onni. Smuggling in the fish alone was enough of a risk; but the risk that he was taking in helping me get off the ship was a very serious one. And though neither of us knew what would happen if he were caught, he seemed to know enough to avoid it at all cost. Which was why he had slid a note under the door instead of crouching down and mumbling the same lines through the wood; because, considering the racket they were making, the galley door could have burst open at any moment, a few people toppling over each other and spilling into the hall; and then they would have looked down the gangway and noticed him there, his face pressed up against my door; or worse, they could have seen him quickly shutting it, their smiles melting into grave comprehension. And the fact that he knew enough to avoid even the possibility of that happening meant that he understood the dangers involved, that he must have weighed them out carefully – yet had still decided to help me. With that thought, and

270

knowing that I couldn't do much for him in return besides what he'd asked of me, I shoved the note into my mouth and started chewing, its taste bitter, the fabric of the paper stubborn, until I could swallow it down in one gummy mass.

I paced around the room, thinking about drifting on the dark open ocean, and trying to come up with useful things to do. I thought of a few; like locating every spot on the floor that creaked when weighted, even prioritizing them from the loudest to the most quiet. And after doing this, I mapped a path between my bed and the door that was absolutely soundless, and another one to the window. Then – thinking that the lantern in the gangway would probably be out when he came to get me, and that fumbling on the stairs, or even running a hissing hand along the wall to help guide myself, could mean disaster for us both – I took to closing my eyes tightly for long periods of time, and then opening them, suddenly awake to a few more details that I wouldn't have seen before.

But there was something about Onni's plan – that had also been a part of Knut's plan for staging a realistic escape for me – which I couldn't help but think of as a little intimidating. And that was the life raft. Because, really, it was a contraption that none of us knew the slightest thing about. Mitra had 'trained' us on the use of the raft, but really only told us what we could have figured out from the clearly labelled procedure list on the side of it. She confessed to never having deployed a raft of this kind in her life, shrugging her shoulders to begin the explanation. "I don't really know what it looks like, but it's supposed to hold 10 people and it inflates itself in an instant. The only thing you have to do is unfasten it from the ship, and then pull this red cord and – poof – you have a raft." A few of us raised our eyebrows sceptically; it wasn't an explanation that evoked a lot of confidence. But, like Mitra, we all thought the chances of having to use it were so slim that it wasn't worth the energy to think about. Yet, after having shaken my head at how dubious it all sounded, I would have to go on the faith that whoever had created it, and from whatever time, knew what they were doing. Which was a bit scary, to say the least.

271

I continued to mull over the other details as well, and the more I thought of them, the more critical they seemed. Like the sound that the raft might make as it inflated itself, which made me think to swim with the bulky red bag in my hand and deploy it as far as I could from the ship. I even thought of how I would get into the water. If I jumped, the splash might be enough to stir someone from their sleep; so I decided I would lower the rope ladder and climb down it, easing into the water in complete silence.

I also thought once more about what the land looked like on the map. I knew that the very first thing we would come to was the same spiny peninsula that I'd chosen as an ideal means of escape only a few nights before. It was both scratching the edge, and marking the beginning of the wide gulf that we would be passing through. It happened that the deeper inside this gulf that one went, the safer the points of disembarking became. So for the ship and the crew, the peninsula was useless, not even viable, but for me it was perfect. It had access to the mainland, which would give me the opportunity to continue on if I wanted to, it was so small that the ship would pass by it in the matter of hours – the shoreline probably being lost in the haze of distance by the time the morning came – and I could be sure that they wouldn't turn around to try and find me, as it was a spit of land that they wouldn't be able to access anyway. So, I imagined, it was only a matter of making it there alive. Everything else would work out wonderfully.

The fact that Onni was the only one to have sighted the land, or even to have known about it, didn't really surprise me. Our course hadn't exactly been foremost on their minds over the days prior to that, and I'm not even sure Knut had taken any readings. Instead they were busy worrying about whether they should kill me or not, which, oddly enough, stood to be the one thing that might save me. I'm sure they had no idea that Onni had veered toward the peninsula, because they didn't really have a reason to look at the charts or worry about distances anymore; the sail worked, as did the fishing gear – we were out of danger. But as it stood, as soon as we reached land, I would be released, dropped onto some random island, free to walk away, which was something that, perhaps most of them, didn't want to see happen. No. Instead they needed time to carry out their plan, and maybe even time to convince a few others of its necessity. If anything, they wanted to stall a bit, because, as I'd already ascertained, it would have been far too obvious to do it that night. They wouldn't dare be so bold. I was sure of it.

I listened to the noises in the galley slowly diminish, and then came the sounds of a few people wandering into their quarters to go to sleep – all of them perfectly quiet as they passed by my room – then a few more, and finally, the last of them. Doors closed, latches shut, and bunks squeaked as people found the most comfortable position to fall asleep. Then, finally, it was quiet, except for the predictable to and fro creaking of the ship, which was accompanied once in a while by Onni's movements on the upper deck, and someone, somewhere, snoring contently.

I lay on my bed, wide awake, thinking about the brand new life I would be given before the night was through; amazed that it was all going to come to me without costing anyone a single thing.

29

As the time passed, my mood faded, and the darkness seemed to press up closer against my face, smothering me with restlessness. The muted black had no end, no beginning, it was just empty, which, somehow, as if time needed a reference of space before it could advance, seemed to make the hours slow to a crawl.

Finally, at one point, I noticed the circular rim of my window giving off a point of light. I walked over and saw that a sliver of moon was rising out of the ocean. Perfect, I thought to myself. Let alone was it a respite from the oppressive darkness, it would also give me the light I would need in the ideal scenario that I was still holding in my mind; the one that had me drifting away undetected, uninjured, and no one on the ship having inflicted an inkling of harm to one another. I grinned through the glass.

After following the path of soundlessness back to my bed, I lay there for what felt like a few more hours, though might have only been a few minutes. I spent that time wondering how I could thank Onni, what I could say before slipping into the water, what momentous phrase I could whisper that would stay with him for the rest of his life. I wanted to find the right words that would let him know both how completely indebted I was to him, and the fact that I would always remember what he'd done for me, what he'd risked. And I was turning over different phrases in my head, even thinking about the intonation I would use, when it happened.

There was a creak in the floorboards along the gangway. Just one. Then nothing. It had come from the end of the gangway that Onni wouldn't be using. I lay there, not breathing, my body stiff.

Silence. Absolutely nothing. Just the gentle rocking of the boat, the wooden groans accompanying the oscillation of the ship's weight as it shifted on the sea. There was nothing else, no sounds haphazardly shoved between the predictable ones,

274

nothing breaking the endless rhythm. I had imagined it. I was being foolish. Paranoid.

I ventured a guarded breath.

Another creak. But this time, it was much closer and just off from the rhythm of the ocean. Whoever it was, was advancing with the sounds of the ship to go undetected. I bent all of my attention at the door to listen.

Another. Only this time, I distinctly heard two separate pieces of wood being weighted, two complaints from the aged joints in the floor as someone passed over them.

These were my murderers, there were two of them, and they were already nearing my door.

The truth is, I don't remember thinking much. Everything I did, the strategy that I formed, the set of tasks that slotted into my head – which I knew I would have to move through as quickly and quietly as possible – were all automatic, instinctive.

I stepped on one of the memorized locations on the floor in front of my bed and arranged the sheets to appear something like a sleeping body – at least at a glance. And as I did this, I worked in the same noisy time intervals that my rivals were working in, with the same precision, all of us fluttering into movement with the creaking of the ship; a clatter of noises one moment, silence the next.

I turned to look behind me and saw the latch twitch slightly. Someone had his hand on it, probably to help find the key sticking out of the lock in the dark.

I crept through the room, stepping in all of the right places, and crouched to sit in the darkness, away from the dull light of the window, and beside one of the shelves near the door that had kept the cases. I had time enough to notice my heart thumping, and to flinch at the sound of one of my toes cracking.

They were doing a perfect job at unlocking the door. Slowly, the mechanical parts rotated, and didn't so much click out of place, but settled there, with only miniscule dripping sounds like sprinkled water on grass. There was only one definitive click near the end, timed well with the creaks of the boat. They obviously intended on taking me by surprise. I would have been stirred out of sleep with the sensation of cold metal against my throat and a finger over my lips.

The latch began to rotate, then stopped. The door opened in one quick swing, also timed with the creaking of the ship. A knife entered the room, followed by a body. Then the second person, hunched forward and moving in the same way. I recognized their profiles. Toivo turned to close the door as quietly as he'd opened it, while Knut continued toward the bed. They were both easing into flat-footed steps, distributing their weight evenly on the floor.

Knut was in reaching distance of my sheets and about to touch them and discover the illusion; Toivo was lagging behind, a little apprehensively, his arm extended out to the side. It was my side; the knife was almost right in front of me.

I stood, aware that I was in Toivo's periphery, and moved toward him. I only had to step on two of the silent spots before I reached his hand with my face. I grabbed onto the knife with one hand and onto his wrist with the other. He flinched, jerking his grip toward himself, so I had to follow his arm with my head before I could sink my teeth into his hand. I felt a joint of one of his fingers dislocate in my mouth, could taste the sharp metallic flavour of blood.

Suddenly, the knife was in my hand. He'd let out a stifled whimpering sound when I bit him, and was now covering his mouth – which had momentarily betrayed his code of silence – with both of his hands, his good one massaging the injured. He looked at me, baffled, seeming to need time to take in what was happening. He was awestruck, useless. I grabbed him by the hair, and instead of pulling him toward me, only really succeeded in pulling myself toward him. But I adapted quickly, circling around him from behind and putting the knife to his neck, exposing it more by pulling back on his hair. He didn't resist. He was petrified.

Knut, of course, had realized what was happening, and was waiting for an opportunity to do something about it. I didn't give him one. I turned Toivo to better face Knut and pressed the knife up tightly against his throat (a little too tightly actually, as I felt a warm liquid creep down the blade and over the handle of the knife, oozing into my fingers).

I spoke to Knut in a whisper, though my words were quick, commanding. "Put your knife on the bed. Now."

He didn't think about it for a second. He twisted around and tossed it onto the sheets, probably knowing that I would have ended Toivo's life without the slightest hesitation – I had nothing to lose. He turned back to look at me again, waiting for the next order. I gave it to him. "Kneel down facing the wall. Don't make a sound." I took the knife from Toivo's neck and jabbed it lightly into the back of his head, "You too." Both of them knelt as they had been told.

I moved onto the next task, my mind still numb, still blank. Stepping forward onto one of the silent spots on the floor, I grabbed Toivo by the hair, and waited for the ship to creak. Just before it did, I brought my fist down, with the blunt handle of the knife protruding from the bottom of it, and struck him on the top of the head with a furious blow. His body went limp. I lowered it to the ground as gently as I could, wads of his hair coming out in clumps as he settled to the floor. I let go, throwing the sticky tangles to the ground beside him.

I stepped over to Knut, who was mumbling something under his breath, and clenched his hair in my fist, raising the handle of the knife above my head. The moment the ship groaned, I brought it down on the top of his skull. But he wasn't unconscious. And suddenly, he spoke with a completely normal volume; his words, which were mumbled drunkenly, sounded like hollers in the quiet of the room. "Ow. Thah... tha hurtz." I hit him again, hard; but still, he was awake. He was beginning to moan, trying to turn his head, maybe even trying to get up, his fingernails scratching against the grain of the wood on the floor. I brought the knife down again, as hard as my body would allow. Finally, he was quiet. He had become a heavy weight in my hand, and I lowered him to the ground by his fine blonde hair, which was quickly being blackened with a runny darkness.

I stepped back from them with a kind of cold satisfaction, looking down at the shapes that they made heaped together on the floor, their limbs sprawling out from under them at unnatural angles, like the fallen boughs of trees.

I turned and walked to the bed, stepping carefully in the memorized places. I put the knife that was in my hand beside the other one, a blotch of darkness from my fingers smearing onto the white sheets. But before I turned to leave, I hesitated, thinking of the noises that Knut had made. They might have woken someone. And more importantly, if that someone was awake, they could be listening carefully for movement, waiting for just one other unfamiliar sound before they roused cautiously from bed and gathered some others to investigate. And with that thought, my hand hovered above the handle of the knife for a moment more. Yes. I scooped it back into my hand and turned from the bed. Just in case.

Across the room again, to the door. I turned the latch as quietly as Knut had, and slipped into the gangway. Closing it, I made a louder click than I would have liked. Then I waited for the ship to moan in its rhythm before I moved, doing exactly as Knut and Toivo had done: a few fast steps, then stopping, waiting, then a few more. As I passed by one of the doors, I could hear movement on the other side. I swallowed, dug my fingernails into the handle of the knife. Someone was urinating against the side of a bucket. This wasn't good.

I crept on until I gained the stairs, easing onto them two at a time, still in keeping with the predictable flux of noise. Then I was through the hatch, on the upper deck, and in the cool breeze and brightly shadowed night.

I looked around for Onni, but couldn't see him nor did I have time to find him; he could have been anywhere. I imagined that he was nestled in one of the dark corners, stealing a half hour of sleep – like every one of us did on night watches. It looked like my well-chosen words would have to go unsaid, which, I must admit, didn't really bother me at the time. The only thing I really cared about was getting into the water before anyone came up the stairs behind me.

I followed the direction of the wind to the horizon and could see some low-lying cloud crawling toward us, which, if Onni was correct, was actually land. I hoped he was right.

Veracity

I tiptoed over to the container that held the life raft, which was mounted near the gunwale, and carefully unlatched it. I'd almost succeeded in taking it out in perfect silence when I knocked one of the buckles of the plastic container, causing it to rattle a bit. I cringed at the sound; then stood and skulked to the rope ladder, cradling the heavy bundle protectively in my arms, as if someone were going to steal it from me. I had to put it down on the deck while I fed the ladder into the water, which I lowered with painful slowness, my body moving automatically, hand over hand, a few fingerprints of blood marking the rungs, the knife making subtle clicking sounds with every contact that it had with the wood, until finally, it was all in, stretching out into the wake, cutting frothing lines in the black water. I was almost there. I was almost free. I only had to climb down the ladder and let go. It was that simple.

But I stopped. Or, rather, everything in my body stopped. I was immobile. It wasn't that I had heard something behind me, it was that the air at my back had become still, maybe even slightly warmed. Someone was there. Someone was about to stop me from escaping, after I had gotten so close to it that I'd almost tasted it. The ladder was in the water, the life raft out of its container and beside me, the land in the distance, the wind blowing in the perfect direction; every last thing was aligned in my favour. I knew that this window of opportunity would never come up again. Never. And if I missed it, I would die. The back of my eyes warmed. I tightened my grip on the knife. I would not miss it.

In one quick motion, I stood up, spun around, and swiped the knife through the air as hard as I could.

He was so close to me, that I thought my wrist would strike him before the blade would. He flung his hands high and forward, sucking his stomach in, trying to get as far from the metal as possible. As soon as I had followed through with the swing, his hands shot to his lower stomach, covering it. Neither of us really moved after that.

"Shit!" I heard my voice whisper, "Shit!" It was Onni.

Thinking about it now, I imagine he had simply heard the buckle of the container chatter, stood up from wherever he was sitting, saw me, and had walked over to bid me farewell, stepping as quietly as usual – nothing out of the ordinary.

He didn't look up at me. He was far too busy looking down at his hands covering his stomach, as if he were watching for something – maybe blood to start streaming through his fingers, drawing long, dark lines down the front of his pants. But nothing came. And, for a moment, I let myself think that I had missed, that I hadn't even touched him, that he was fine, that he was just imagining things. But in the back of my mind, I knew what the resistance when the knife passed closest to his waist had meant. The blade had met with his skin. He would be injured in some way. It was only a question of the degree.

Finally, after seconds passed without anything happening, his curiosity won over, and he withdrew his hands to inspect the wound. But when he did, there never seemed to be a space between his fingers and his stomach for us to see it. He turned to better face the grey light of the moon, and the brightness suddenly explained everything, hid nothing. He was holding something that we'd only seen in anatomy books and while cleaning fish: intestines. They were poking out from the deep gash across the lower part of his stomach.

I will never forget the way he looked up at me at that point. He was calm as always, but also stunned, scared. He lowered his eyebrows, taking in my expression, taking in exactly what I was, and turning his head a bit, as if he wanted to sadly shake it, but didn't. He looked as if he were questioning himself, as if he were wondering whether or not he had set out to help the wrong person – maybe even someone who didn't deserve to be helped. Someone who was more base, more sordid than he'd ever suspected.

"They'll kill you for sure now," he said, deadpan. "Better go while you can." He eyed the helm before continuing, his voice a perfect monotone, "I'll steer us away from the peninsula. You should be safe. Go." He turned and started shuffling away like an old man, his footsteps treading tender on the deck, one of his hands on the rail, the other on his stomach.

I didn't move at first. I only stayed there, watching him trundle along the rail, wishing that there were something right

280

that I could do or say. But I couldn't even remember my well-chosen words; and, even if I had, they would have been wrong. Everything was wrong.

I thought I heard someone clearing his throat below deck, which seemed to wake me up. Onni was right. There was no use in standing around. I had to go.

I bent down and picked up the bundle with the life raft in it, and noticed the knife still in my hand. I held it in front of my face, looked at it disgustedly for a moment, and threw it into the ocean. I crawled onto the rope ladder and climbed down, the bundle tucked awkwardly under one of my arms, and was fully submerged in the black water within seconds. I let go.

Everything was black, boundless, desolate. I came up for air, eyes wide at the naked cold, and started treading water, my legs whirling in panicky circles. I gripped onto the life raft bundle with a grip that increased by the minute, watching the boat become smaller. While I waited, the expanse of ocean that surrounded me began to seem like a dizzying display of space in comparison to my cramped quarters, which only led me to the bleak realization of where I was and what I was doing. I was in the middle of the ocean with nothing but a red sack in my hand and a bit of empty faith that it would magically turn into something that would save me, while the only reliably buoyant object within days of travel was irrevocably drifting away. I had spent so much time imagining that the second I entered the water, I would be safe; but that couldn't have been further from the truth. I'd only traded in one form of critical danger for another.

I waited until I thought the boat was well out of earshot, treading water, shivering. When I finally thought it was, I grabbed hold of the largest chord dangling out of the bag and yanked on it. Nothing happened. I pulled harder. Still nothing. I closed my eyes to stop myself from swearing at the very top of my lungs. I grabbed hold of another plastic strand that was sticking out and gave it a stout tug. There was a furious hissing noise and the bag leapt out of my hands. I dove below the surface to get away from it, afraid that whatever strange mechanism was responsible for instantly creating a ten-person raft from a small bag would kill me. When I surfaced, to my amazement, and exactly as Mitra had promised, there was a plastic raft bobbing on the surface. I swam over to it, grabbed hold of the side, and hoisted myself over its edge, foundering against one of its inflated walls.

It took quite a while to catch my breath, and once I'd recovered a bit, I looked up at the vertical smile of the moon. I didn't smile back. Yes, I was finally safe; I had escaped; but I didn't feel free. I don't remember any sense of relief or joy. It was a coldness more than anything else, a detachedness.

Already, I found myself busy pushing images out of my mind; the thin, black fingers of blood spreading through the lightness of Knut's hair; Toivo's arm sticking out from under his chest, his palm opening toward the ceiling; the moonlight glistening on what was in Onni's hands when he moved them away from his stomach, the expression on his face for that one, slow moment of recognition when he looked up at me. Yes. It was all I could do to push these images away, far away, shoving them back into some remote recess of my mind, where they would stay. Waiting. Patiently.

30

I was cold, huddled with my back against the bulging plastic, my arms crossed over my chest, knees drawn up close to my body. The little pool of seawater that was inside the raft – either from the moment of its being inflated, or by my entering it soaking wet – gathered into my corner, sucking away any warmth my body could make.

Every once in awhile I would stretch my neck over the rim of the raft to see if the ship had glided out of sight, its triangular sail like the needle of a compass, pointing at me, shrinking and dimming with every fathom travelled, gauging how small I was – how much smaller I was becoming. Until finally, I lost sight of it altogether, and the enormity of the sea swallowed everything.

I gathered my limbs into another crook of the raft, and the water that had been making me cold in the first corner, crawled over the glossy coating to collect around me again, lapping against my lower back, sifting my warmth through its fingers, giggling.

The night seemed endless. I fell in and out of a shallow, fitful sleep; and when I woke, it was with stiff muscles and anxious movements. Though, once I realized where I was, along with the fact that the only thing I could do was wait, I would gradually crunch myself up into a ball again and attempt to doze off for another short while. At one point, I happened to stir awake in that brief period during the dawn of every clear day, when the light is a drab, featureless grey, and it's impossible to tell whether the sky is overcast, or perfectly clear. I squinted up at the zenith, felt a little uneasy at the fact that a stratum of cloud had somehow sheeted over since the last time I'd looked up and saw stars, and then slowly shut my eyes, my chin sinking back onto my chest, and nodded off once more.

When I finally woke to the day, it was to a sky that was surprisingly cloudless. And, realizing that with the light of morning I would finally be able to tell whether or not the low-lying clouds I had seen were land, I shot up from where I was and looked around. Then I relaxed, smiled. The horizon was filled with the peninsula I had seen on the map. A coast emerged out of the haze on my right, while ahead of me, and exactly the spot I was drifting toward, was the end of the cape, where the coastline sunk back into the water. I was close – or at least closer than I thought I would be. The land looked green and inviting, and I imagined that it was high enough to have accumulated a bit of fresh water. I could also see that where the steep terrain met the ocean, there was a broad band of vegetation missing, a swath of wrinkled and exposed rock. Though, at the time, I didn't really make the connection of how important this was.

The morning stretched on into afternoon, and the sun beat down on me with a sticky, relentless heat, despite the raising of the flimsy canopy I found tucked into one of the sides. (I remember there being only a few short minutes on the raft when the temperature was agreeable – the rest of the time I was either uncomfortably cold, or uncomfortably hot.) And while I sat there, grimacing against the glare of the water and sun, I realized that if I had been a little more clear headed, I would've almost drowned myself with freshwater before leaving my room the night before; guzzling cupfuls out of my bucket until streams spilled over my face and soaked my shirt. After the first hour of sunlight, I was already thirsty; which I could do nothing about, other than watch the land inch closer by the hour, looking for natural low spots and drainages that I could seek out once I was there. As I did this, I consciously tried to keep my mind away from how dry my throat was becoming, which, I must admit, is a difficult thing to do when the only thing you look for, see, hear, and feel, is water.

Eventually, I tried to think of other things to busy myself with, which led me to bailing all of the seawater out of the raft; my hands cupped into a broad scoop, flinging arcs of it over the rim, watching the orange plastic through the streams of liquid as it distorted for a fraction of a second before the stringy lens disappeared over the side. Then I lay down on my back and watched the blank sky, sitting up to check the land every few minutes to gauge my progress.

As the hours passed, and I was getting closer, I noticed that the winds had changed somewhat. And, after holding a wet hand in the air for several minutes, found that I was no longer heading toward the very tip of the peninsula, but just to the left of it. I would miss the cape. And if I didn't try to swim to it, the next land I would come to, or, more accurately, the shore that my shrivelled and decaying carcass would wash up upon in a week or two, would be wherever the massive gulf ended. Obviously my only option was to stay in the raft until I came as close to land as I could, and then jump out and try and swim the rest of the way. But from what it looked like, without knowing anything about the currents underneath of me, nor what they would be like near the tip of the peninsula, the distance would be a long one; something that could either be just close enough to feasibly swim, or just far enough not to.

I waited, growing nervous, watching the land slope closer by the hour, its bulk in my periphery broadening. I began to be able to make out individual trees, even the features of some of the larger ones. I also started to become aware of a kind of low sigh, something that sounded like a damp wind humming through thick leaves. It was faint, but insistent, and getting louder. I honestly didn't know what it was until I stood up in the raft to look, wobbling precariously in the waves. The entire coastline was white; waves churning in on themselves, growling, clawing the shore, scraping the rocks, ripping any vegetation that had tried to grow there out and into the water, and gnashing it with their salty teeth.

There is, of course, a leeward side and a windward side to everything at sea. And what I was looking at was the windward side; the side that the air and ocean currents, after having accumulated speed and strength over the breadth of an entire ocean, were pummelling against. It was interesting that we had thought of this land, of any land, as a kind of salvation when we were hit by the storm. But now it was plain to see that if we had managed to get there, we would only have succeeded in dashing our ship against the cliffs and killing ourselves.

I grew more nervous, watched the tip of the peninsula sidle closer, watched the waves pound the steep rocks and bounce back through the air in towering curls, looking like twisting arms, falling fists, sprawling fingers.

It was only when the sun was almost setting that I started to think of the peninsula as being within swimming distance. I was right about the raft missing the cape, as well as the distance that I would have to swim to reach it. But, after watching the waves for as many hours as I had, I could also appreciate that the change in wind direction was a lucky one. If I had any chance of surviving, it would be in accessing the leeward side of the promontory – the side that I could not see, but soon would, as I floated past the tip of the cape.

I neared the apex, watching the rest of the coastline become obscured by its rocky point, until it was the only thing I could see. I was close enough for the waves to sound as deep as thunder, and to be tossed up and down in the surf by their after effects. The water had become creamy with tiny air bubbles, and it hissed as they rose to the surface in the millions and burst around the raft.

Seeing the dividing line between the part of the ocean current that collided with the peninsula, and the part that continued on, I could get a feeling as to the strength of the undercurrents and eddies that I would have to swim through. It didn't look all that promising. But I also didn't have much of a choice.

I studied the other side of the peninsula as it slowly opened up. It was just as steep – maybe even a bit steeper – though at least the water there was relatively calm. I looked for some kind of target to swim toward along the cliff, but didn't really find one.

Then the moment came; the second that I could tell I was getting further away from land instead of closer to it. The sun was sinking into the sea behind me, the light almost inviting, gentle. I thought about taking my clothes off before diving in, but remembered how cold I was during the night. I would need them when I got to shore. If I got to shore.

Finally, I shook my head, swore aloud, focused on the closest point of land, and jumped into the water. I started swimming as frantically as I could, and after only a few minutes, was already reasonably spent. I paused to look behind me and see where the raft was, as if I might be able to hold onto it for a few minutes and catch my breath. It had already become small, remote, jauntily springing up and down in the surf, being swept away with the light wind, out into the bay that looked the same as any endless ocean.

I knew that if I could get into the leeward shadow, where the current was being blocked by the land, there might be an eddy that would pull me back toward the cape, so I swam parallel with the cliff, though still watching its features closely, trying to judge where the unseen currents were dragging me. The new side of the peninsula was opening up like a broad-shouldered body turning toward me, which meant (and not very surprisingly) that I was being carried out to sea. And within a few minutes, the land that had only seemed like a long swim away had come to appear impossibly far, almost intangible.

I had to think of ways to stop myself from panicking. I began counting my strokes, slow methodical arcs with my arms, smooth kicks with my feet, whispering numbers out to the fading light.

Then, finally, I passed through a few strange waves that were twisting the surface with tiny whirlpools, and felt a rush of current tug at my clothing in one direction, and then in another. This was the eddy line. I had crossed over from the main current that was pushing me into the bay, and was in the eddy that would draw me closer to the peninsula. After only a few more minutes of swimming, now toward the cliff, I noticed it rising for the first time. Which was lucky, because I was getting incredibly tired. At one point, I rolled onto my back to take a rest, heaving air into my lungs that never seemed to fill them. My strokes were becoming ineffective, my limbs sloppily sifting through the water, probably holding me back more than they were propelling me. It was up to the currents now.

The sky was growing pasty, its colour fading. Soon it would be dark, and it occurred to me that I might meet my end while scraping along the rocks, looking for a way onto land during the night, which almost seemed worse than being crushed by the waves during the day. I could picture myself struggling to climb out of the swells and onto the cliff, the inky sea pulling me in after each failed attempt, wrapping around my face, shoving its fingers up my nose and down my throat, smothering me, putting its palms on my shoulders and pushing me under the surface. Understandably, I allowed this image to enter my mind only once.

When I was finished resting, and turned around to face the peninsula again, I was amazed to see how much closer the currents had brought me. And even more amazed to see a recess in the cliff, something like a cave, which, in what little light there was left, looked like a yawning mouth with a tongue of rounded boulders, like giant taste buds, licking the very edge of the water with its tip. It wasn't a beach by any stretch of the imagination, but at least there seemed to be a possibility of getting onto land in the dark.

I settled into an exhausted pace, steering myself in the cave's general direction while the current carried me along. I stopped counting my strokes, my movements becoming reflexive and constant. I lost track of minutes, of time. The sky darkened; everything became colourless, and then black. The fuzzy silhouette of the cliff neared, looming over my head, splashes resonating off of its walls in different directions. I continued until the rounded boulders at the mouth of the cave were taller than I was, their globular heads shimmering with night, looking down at me, feeling nothing.

I could sense land everywhere; the crispness of the echoes, the loamy breath of rock, the pockets of warm water. My legs, overtired and heavy, sunk under my waist. My arms, still trying to make circles, but quickly fading into useless flaps instead, lifted out into the water at my sides. I seemed to be waiting for my body to bump up against something, a blade of coral, the spines of sea urchins, rock. Which happened. My knee finally struck one of the slimy boulders, and this is what initiated my flustered and pathetic scramble to find a way out. I seemed to wake up. I was there. I had made it. I just had to get out of the water.

I felt around until my hand ran over another slick surface. I moved closer to it, pawing the stone until I found a divot on one of its sides. Then I started to pull myself through the water with one hand, and searching for the next hold with the other, moving toward the loudest sounds.

Swells were bouncing off of rocks, capping, tossing me from side to side. One struck me from behind and pushed me forward. I felt things sliding along my legs, and ended up being jostled between two boulders, where I stopped, a hand on either of them, teetering on a notch that was made where they met under the water. I tried to steady myself, but couldn't, and fell forward into a channel that was filled with large rocks, my chest crashing against one of them.

The sea rushed over me again, and I took in some water, my hands fumbling blindly in all directions. Finding nothing, I put my feet flat on the rocks and pushed off of them, shooting above the surface, and succeeded in hitting the side of my face against one of the boulders. I bounced off of it and fell once more to the side, somehow managing to land on my hands and knees in a pool of small stones. My head was above the water for the first time. Land.

As much as I wanted to stand while I had the chance, I had to cough the water out of my chest before I could do anything else. I might have even been on my way to recovering when I heard another surge of water tumbling through the channel behind me. I hung my head in frustration, braced myself, and was hit from behind in mid-cough, and carried along with the rush of the swell. The water dumped me further up the channel, my hands and knees settling onto smaller stones where the pool was shallower.

As soon as the wave subsided I tried to stand, still coughing, the earth swaying uncontrollably under my feet. I stumbled and fell backwards, but got up quickly and tried again, managing to walk two, three steps before falling. Only this time, when my hands hit the ground, they were holding onto a fistful of dry stones. But this wasn't enough; I needed to be higher; I needed to be sure that the sea couldn't find me in the middle of the night and drag me out again. I stood one last time, every muscle in my legs shaking with fatigue, and walked forward, feeling around, until my hands scuffled across a ledge of some

289

sort. I pulled myself toward it, and, with all the energy I had left, lopped myself on top of it.

The moment I'd settled there, and was sure I was secure enough and wouldn't fall off during the night, I let myself relax, coughing until I recovered. After that I just lay there, taking syrupy air into my lungs, breathing, breathing very deeply, my head resting against the cold stone, staring out into the noisy darkness, until my eyes closed of their own volition. The very last thing I remember about that night was the sensation of my tingling body, drained of everything, melting into the rock.

31

I woke up coughing, a hand reaching out to steady myself on the ledge, the other in a fist at my mouth. When I recovered, I rubbed my eyes at the grey morning light, jumped off the ledge, and stood on one of the boulders, clearing my throat. The muscles in my legs and arms were stiff, and my nose, ribs, and the left side of my face were sore, but, really, considering all that could have happened to my body, there wasn't much to complain about.

As I turned in a slow circle to take everything in, the first thing I noticed was that I'd somehow managed to stumble upon the ideal place to get out of the water. The channel that I'd accidentally fallen into, and was then pushed further along, seemed to be the only access to land that wouldn't have involved climbing. Steep boulders, which probably would have been impossible to scale during the day, let alone in the dark, rose out of the water everywhere else.

I kept turning until I was looking up at the cave, where birds' nests clung to its roof, and stone protuberances of every imaginable shape dangled around them like petrified drips of water. The mouth of the cave seemed to be exhaling; a cool, stagnant air, which had a vague smell of urine and bird droppings, cascading over the boulders as slow and constant as breath.

Then I looked to the right of the cave and noticed a weakness along the wall. There was a point where the cliff sloped to a more modest angle, and the limbs of bushes and stunted trees sprung out of a vertical crack that ran from the bottom of the cliff to the top, essentially creating a ladder of vegetation that disappeared above me, where the steepness of the wall tapered off even more.

Seeing as there wasn't a shore to walk along, I really only had two options of finding a way out: I could either take my chances with the ocean again, swimming along the peninsula to look for a better way to access the top, or I could try to climb

291

this weakness beside the cave. I looked at the swells just once before making my decision; then cleared my throat again, turned, and started making my way over the rocks toward the crack in the wall.

It turned out that the ladder of vegetation was easier to ascend than it had looked, and only became more so the higher I climbed. Though, as the slope of the cliff tapered off, the crack also became more vegetated, which meant that I had to fight my way through denser foliage, branches scratching at my face, and pink lines streaking down my forearms where twigs had scraped them. Eventually, the rock on either side of me was replaced by sloping earth, and I clambered up on my hands and knees, grabbing onto grass and shrubs, pulling myself up the forested hill until I could finally stand. Once on my feet, I continued up the rise, this seeming like a natural thing to do. The forest that I climbed through was thick, and it was gruelling work hopping over and ducking under branches, breaking through the netting of underbrush, all while having to fight against the angle of the hill as well. After quite a while, the slope of the rise continuously lessening, I came to the rounded ridge at the top of the peninsula.

I had imagined, for some reason, that once I found myself at the highest point there would be a grassy clearing; however, if anything, the forest had become thicker. I leaned against a tree whose texture I'd never seen before and caught my breath. And the more I was struck by this strange bark, the more I looked around and realized that everything was foreign to me; the insects crawling along the branches, the vegetation at my feet, the smells, the sounds of the birds, the calls of the animals in the distance, everything. And now that I was out of immediate danger for the first time in days, there was a part of me that just wanted to sit down and take it all in; to stare up at the sky and acknowledge that I was finally free, that I'd made it.

But being out of immediate danger didn't mean I was safe. I had no water, no food, and no shelter. Which meant that, realistically, I couldn't afford to waste a minute of daylight. I had to keep moving; at least until I found water.

Luckily, like every ridge I have ever seen in my life, there was an animal trail that followed its crest, which made the going quite easy. While I walked through the forest toward the mainland, my bare feet getting used to the new ground, roots, and leaves, I could hear animals in front of me, fleeing from my smell and the sounds that I was making in what must have been their normally quiet world. Birds sprung out of trees and into the air, explosions of flapping sounds that quickly faded into silence, flashes of wings between the leaves that would vanish the moment they appeared. Once, I even caught a glimpse of a four-legged animal as it thrashed through the undergrowth, running down one of the sides of the ridge. I was happy to have come across it, as it meant that there was fresh water within a reasonable distance from where I was.

After walking for an hour or two, I saw a break in the trees up ahead, a light that was brighter, filtering through branches that stood at the edge of a clearing. The trail became wider as it drew closer, and I walked along it as quietly as I could, thinking that I might come across some exotic animals grazing in it. But as I stepped out of the trees, I found something much more interesting than that.

There was a tower sticking out of the shrubs of the clearing. It was incredibly thin and high, constructed of metal bars (that had since helplessly rusted), which were joined in a row of triangles that climbed toward the sky, getting narrower right at its peak. It probably would have crumbled to the ground years before were it not for the cables that were securing it from every side; some of which were taut, while others were drooping ineffectually with their own weight.

As much as the Elders had educated me about the ruins I would come across in this land, there are some things that I couldn't exactly be prepared for. For some reason, I'd expected the relics to be quiet, had already pictured the tattered buildings, the glassless windows that would gape open like deadened eyes, woodless doorways creating awestruck mouths; I'd imagined the stillness in the settlements as the buildings slowly buckled at their joints and collapsed to the ground. Yet I could see that there was going to be nothing silent about these things. Unlike

293

coming across a dead animal, which might give a few clues as to its death, things that were structural or inorganic had the capacity to relay a record of how they lived. I wasn't going to find a world of decayed flesh and liquefied remains which could no longer be recognized, but skeletons of an existence that were still poised in movement; things that not only asked questions, but responded to them. This tower was demanding me to contemplate what a massive finger of metal sticking up into the sky could possibly serve. I had no idea, of course – and still don't – but I know that the answer was there, somewhere. And though I didn't have time to try and find it, it was enough to recognize that this new land was going to be telling stories, that it would relate how my ancestors had seen the world around them, give an account of their accomplishments, their defeats, and where they went wrong. I watched the tip of the tower move steadily through the sky as I crossed the clearing, amazed, trying to imagine how they had built it, what they had done around it, and how often they had come to this place to use it.

When I arrived at the other side of the clearing, to my surprise, I found a massive track along the ground that cut through the trees ahead of me. I'm sure that at one point, like the walls of the shelter, the entire lane was cemented over – a road, as I had seen in books – which must have been built to access the tower. Grass sprouted from the cracks in it and snaked along the surface in blotchy patterns, and there were a few trees that had fallen across the width of it, which would be nothing to hop over. I would be able to cover a lot of ground quickly and easily.

I walked down the road for several hours as it meandered more or less along the ridge, watching the sea below through the few gaps in the trees, hoping to judge my progress, waiting to see a coast in the distance that would indicate how close I was to the end of the peninsula. At one point, the track dropped below the ridgeline, and I was glad to get a bit lower, thinking that I might come across a tiny stream of water collecting on a hillside. And though this wasn't the case, I did find something that was just as good.

The road continued to descend until it passed through a kind of basin where water would naturally collect. There was no sign of a stream or pond, but the lush vegetation that grew at the lowest points was a sign that there was a lot of moisture underground. I noticed a different kind of tree that I hadn't seen anywhere else on the ridge, and as I got closer to them, I realized, excitedly, that there were long melons dangling from just below their tops.

I quickly found the shortest tree and climbed it from a sloping side, my feet pressed flat against the bark, inching my way up until I was within reaching distance of the melons, and then, balancing delicately with one hand around the tree and the other on the fruit, I twisted them until they fell to the ground. After seeing one of them split open, and that it was dripping with yellow juice, I tried to toss a few others into bushes where they wouldn't break, hoping to take a couple with me.

I climbed down and shoved my face into one of the broken halves. It was sweet, had an orange, fleshy texture, black seeds, and was saturated with water. The rind was bitter, and only after I'd tasted it did I notice that other animals had left them scattered around on the ground to rot. I ate faster than I should have, finishing a full three melons before stopping, when all I could do was lean against a tree, feeling bloated and sick to my stomach.

After the waves of nausea subsided, I stood and wandered through the grove, poking around for other foods that I could take besides the melons. I didn't find much, but, looking up at these fruit trees, I did notice something that was a bit strange. It seemed that the steeper the tree, the more melons there were, which was something that was never the case on the island. And for some reason, I felt like I had to spend a few minutes trying to figure this out.

The first thing I did was look at the bark of the trees to see if I could find any claw marks, as something like a sloth or a tree shrew might leave behind, but there weren't any. And as the animal that was feeding on these melons was so poorly adapted for climbing that it could only access the fruit from a sloping tree, it couldn't be a monkey, either. No, this was something quite different. Then I noticed that there were woody strands that stuck out from where the fruits had been twisted off of their

stems, which meant they were removing them in the same way I
had. I picked up the freshest looking rind to look at the teeth
marks that were left in it, and saw that they were made from
fairly uniform, small teeth, and that both the upper set and lower
set met in a perfectly straight line; and, as there weren't any
imperfections on either extremity of the marks, I imagined that
they didn't have a pronounced set of canines, and so ate mostly
fruits and vegetables. I compared the marks to those left in the
rinds that I had eaten from, but found that they were nothing
like a human's. Yet there was something similar enough (and
maybe this was only in the way that we had picked the fruit) that
made me resolve to learn as much as I possibly could about
them. That day I would create a category in my mind for these
creatures – which I would unimaginatively call 'The Creatures' –
where I would sort out every piece of information I could gather
about them. I'd already learned that they weren't very good
climbers, the size of their teeth, the likely dimensions of their
head to fit such teeth, their lack of claws, even more or less what
they ate. And I would be keeping an eye out for anything else
that I could learn about them along the way, tallying it onto my
list whenever I did. There was, of course, something dangerous
in all of this; but at the time, I was completely oblivious to it.

I continued down the meandering road, carrying a melon
in each hand, until the sun drew close to the horizon. At one
point, it was perfectly aligned with the road, trailing behind me,
making my shadow stretch out into a gangly man with
enormously swollen stumps at the end of thin arms, his feet
rising high with each step.

I had planned on walking for another half hour or so
before looking for a good tree to sleep under, when I came across
the first building I would see on the mainland. It was a house on
the side of the road, which was set at the end of a short track. It
wasn't built like anything we had on the island, its walls being
made of some kind of white plaster, which had since yellowed
and cracked, vines netting its sides like arteries. Most of the
windows were broken, but the door was still on its hinges,
hanging ajar, leaves and plants creeping into the dark interior.

Veracity

I put the fruit on the ground and walked up to the entrance, pressing my face into the open space between the door and its frame. The air was musty and still. I pushed on the wood and felt a soft resistance on the other side, which finally gave when I put more force into it, and I could hear something sliding across the floor, being shoved out of the way as the door swung open. When there was enough room for me to squeeze through, I poked my head inside and could see that a thick cloth, which had since been devoured by mice and was gathered in giant folds behind the door after I'd forced it open, had once covered most of the floor. I stepped inside.

The interior of the building had been ripped to shreds, the furniture turned over, drawers flung out of cupboards, sheets and blankets strewn throughout the rooms. Pictures, which could only have been cut out of books, and, for some reason, were encased with wood and glass, were sprawled all over the ground, the long shards still held by their wooden borders, pointing at the places where the glass was impacted; plain-looking people behind the spider web fractures, lined up shoulder to shoulder on closely cut grass, clasping each other with arms that seemed stiff. There were light-brown water stains that spread out along the walls like lobes of lichen, scat on the floor from the different animals that had scavenged or nested there, along with broken plates, utensils, pots, clay shards, and shredded decorations with bright colours.

I rummaged around for useful things, stepping carefully between the pieces of broken glass with my bare feet. I shook out a thin blanket, which I could wrap in a certain way and use to carry things as we had done on the island. I was also lucky enough to find a dull knife with a sheath, a very thin and transparent plastic bottle with a cap – in hopes that I would soon come across water – which was so aged that it was more opaque than transparent, and a pair of sandals that, like the sheath, seemed to be made from a type of animal hide. I wrapped everything into the blanket and slung it around my chest, walking out the door while there was still enough light to spot the broken glass on the floor.

Seeing as there wasn't much time left in the day, and that my feet and legs were tired with the unaccustomed exercise, I decided to sleep under the relative shelter of the building's entrance. I leaned against the wall, cut up one of the melons and ate it, watching the sky until the first stars appeared, and listening to that cacophony of sounds that takes place as the diurnal creatures of the world settle in for the night, and the nocturnal ones wake and stir into movement. The sounds were different from any I'd ever heard, strange chatters, screams, squeaks, and moans, along with a haunting call of three notes being repeated over and over again in the muffled distance, which almost sounded like a wood flute; though a bit harsher, deeper.

There was one fleeting moment after dark, when the forest had quieted down and I picked up the knife to put it back into its sheath before going to sleep, that I was suddenly struck with a flashing image of Onni, covering his stomach, looking down at his hands. I rejected it as fast as I could, thinking of something else, concentrating on a few new sounds that were rising in the trees, bending all of my attention at them as if they were the most imperative thing in the world. But I wouldn't be able to do this for long. The fact remained that already most of my basic needs had been met, that my situation was becoming less urgent by the hour, and that soon, my mind would find itself wandering outside the confined spaces of immediate necessity. Soon, I would have no choice but to acknowledge what I'd done to Onni.

I wrapped myself in the blanket and slept on wooden boards in front of the door, waking only once during the night, after an animal, probably a large rodent of some kind, overturned a few stones as it scurried across the road in front of the house. I remember hearing it stop to look at me, but I think I might have drifted off to sleep again even before it moved on.

32

I woke to a cloudy day of soft light and flat shadows.

After I packed everything into the blanket and tied it around myself, I walked around the perimeter of the building trying to figure out how it had been supplied with water. I couldn't find anything, and so could only assume that it was an underground system of some kind.

When I left, I followed a black wire that sagged low to the ground and strung from the roof of the house to the road. Once at the road, it turned and continued down the entire stretch of it, as far as the eye could see, never seeming to stop. This was the beginning of the cable, or rather system of cables, that was attached to the top of huge steel poles lining up in an endless procession of rotting shafts, all of them bleeding dry puddles of orange onto the ground. The wires had a plastic sheathing that had decayed and blistered open in places like the flesh of a carcass gnawed away by scavengers, only with a twined mass of metal strings instead of bones. I imagined that this was for the transportation of electricity, and found myself wishing that Harek had told me more about the way past cultures had depended on it. We had talked about it once, but he was dismissive; pointing out that the systems for producing and handling it, apart from being ruined, were also complicated; and, he had added, as there was no way that they could be fixed, they certainly weren't worth wasting our time on. When he had said this, I'd thought about the elaborate scheme around the few electrical lights in the shelter, the coloured wires writhing along the ceilings, through holes, over doors, slinking along the upper corners of rooms, and finally into black sheets of glass that were lying on the roofs, then back out again, continuing on their twisting journey. I could see that he was right; it was complicated. Which, if anything, after seeing how extensive the network of wires on this mainland was, only made me wonder why these people had gone through all the trouble in the first place.

In the middle of the day, after losing sight of the ocean for an hour or so, the road I was walking on ended, intersecting with a wider one. I had to choose between right and left, the stringy poles stretching off into either direction. I chose left, only because it was descending, as water would, hoping that I would come across a stream or river at some point in the near future.

And as a main trail usually has branches that veer off from it, so was there with this road. I began to see a few, and then many smaller tracks that broke away and disappeared, curving out of sight or being overgrown and hidden by the foliage; the strange rusted shafts, hanging with both vines and cables, following them into the trees. Until eventually, the side roads were everywhere, and the number of wires had multiplied until they looked like a loose fishing net that draped over the landscape. Which was when I caught sight of the town.

I had seen a few cities in books, but their scale had always seemed a little abstract to me. Enormous towers poking into the air, concrete streets sprawling beneath them, dots of buildings filling the land to the horizon. It was either that or a picture of a corrupt palace with statues perched in front of it, where the city was in motion around it, eerie streaks of red in the blurry foreground and background. But the town that I came across was neither one of these expanses of infrastructure, nor of palaces and fountains. In fact, the closest thing I had seen to it was in paintings from the art book; the ones with a little cluster of buildings crowning a hill in the distance, fortified walls wrapping around it.

To be honest, from what I could see of this town while I descended into it, it wasn't all that impressive. And though its size was about the same as the ones in some of the paintings, it wasn't even surrounded by a defensive barrier (which, Dana had pointed out, were used to protect the townspeople inside from their neighbouring townspeople, in the likely event that they were as violent and opportunistic as themselves). But regardless of the fact that it wasn't anything close to what I thought it would be, I was glad to have the chance to walk through it. I imagined that if anything could offer insight as to how my ancestors thought, it was the place where they had lived their everyday lives.

I stopped just before entering the grid of streets, spotting a stream at the lowest part of land on the other side of the town. This stream had also been a flooding river in the not so distant past, as the banks were terraced and bare, except for new vegetation that was interspersed throughout silt-coated rocks. Just above the stony terraces that the flood had made were several different kinds of fruit trees, and I could see further upstream that there was a crop-type plant that grew in clumps in the same way that the grain did on the island. I had found plenty of food and water, and would gather whatever I could after I had inspected the town.

However, before even walking into it, I was already getting a feeling as to this culture's odd way of thinking. There were remains of a massive cemented wall lining the banks of the river, which must have channelized the stream toward some designed end. Though, the flooding water had since gouged through and around it, reclaiming what had been its natural path.

Where I entered the town, the wires amassed into a fantastic jumble of poles and lines, stretching along every road and on every side of every building; and as I ducked under the ones that were sagging close to the ground, and looked down one of the streets, I suddenly realized why these people had gone through all the trouble to produce and transport electricity. For some reason, they were afraid of the dark.

There were electric lights everywhere – or at least the inverted bowl that had held lights at one point, their remnants dangling at the end of tall, arcing poles (which were different from the ones on the road, but just as rusted and vine laden). They dotted every imaginable street, side road, corner, intersection, and were in front of every dwelling. At night, they must have flooded the entire town in light, drawing a clear line at its outskirts between the place that was inhabited by people, and whatever lay beyond. And when I thought of it that way – that they had felt a need to distinguish between what was swallowed by the night and what wasn't – I realized that it was

301

probably something much more than the dark that they were afraid of, it was wilderness itself.

The hints were everywhere; in the barricade along the stream, the grid of streets, lines abrupt and even, the careful angles of the roofs edging down, troughs to collect the water lest it spew out wildly from the shingles and onto the soil, the faces of walls squared with the roads, the windows parallel with the ground beneath them. These were a people who felt a need to apply strict rules to their environment. And I could see that, when the earth shifted outside of the parameters they had placed on it, when the cemented walkways lining the streets bulged and skewed, they had repaired them as quickly as they could, pounding down the soil, reshaping it, subjugating it. When the natural world fluxed, they reacted in ways that must have made them feel like they were still in command.

And it seemed like the closer the nature was to them, the stricter the rules became. There were corners of their rectangular lots with trees and bushes that still had scars from being endlessly pruned, truncated, and sculpted. There were containers of soil that hung from windows, which must have had carefully trimmed flowers, plants, or herbs inside them, where there was no room for them to grow out of control. There was a square plot in the centre of the town that probably served as a kind of public garden, a paved lane winding through the centre of it, and a pond lined with transported boulders and filled with redirected water, where domesticated birds most likely paddled around waiting to be fed.

I imagined that these people saw the wilderness as a kind of adversary in a continuous battle, something that was devious and cunning. Because regardless of their calculations and inventions, it would have still found a way to poke its fingers into every facet of their lives. I could picture them, frustrated, watching as it crept across the fields that they'd cleared and squared, growing back in oblong shapes, slithering toward their houses; stubborn leaves bursting out of branches that they'd cut, vines crawling over their newly constructed walls, spiders finding the corners of their rooms as the ideal site for a web, mice vigilantly checking the doors and foundations for imperfections, and finding them. Its fortitude was inexhaustible. And as they seemed to be pitting themselves against it, no wonder they had drawn a line with light at the edges of their towns. It illuminated the one space where they would be able to convince themselves that they had won, a place where they could believe that their constant manipulation was actually necessary, where they were important. And at the same time, it would allow them to put their backs to the wilderness that was stirring in the dark behind them, which could effortlessly point out how insignificant they really were.

Then it struck me that people had probably lived whole lives in these places, 'safe' inside one of the grids of wire-ridden buildings, that they spent their years without ever feeling the wind on their faces, or the rain run over their scalp, without even once being completely enveloped by the dark or by a true silence. And whoever these people were, I'm sure they were secretly haunted with a feeling that something was missing from their lives. Because they would have been living in a lost place, forever drifting between two worlds – one that they wished they hadn't come from, and another where they would never really belong.

I walked out of the town and descended into the flood plains without ever entering any of the houses. What I didn't know was that this town would be the biggest settlement I would ever come across, and I regret now not spending a little more time there, poking my head through windows, snooping around through looted kitchens, because I'm sure I could have learned a lot more about that culture. But the truth was that the few things I'd gathered about it were already enough to push me away, out from their streets and their paved walkways, and into the fields that surrounded the town. I felt uneasy there, for obvious reasons.

After drinking from the stream and filling the water bottle that I'd taken from the house the day before (which, to my surprise, didn't leak at all), I headed toward the trees and plants I'd sighted above the floodplains. While I picked through them, I began to get a good feeling about how much time I would have to spend searching for food in this land. The soil was fertile, and things seemed to grow easily. I gathered a few different varieties of fruits and vegetables, some that looked plump and ripe, and others that were a bit thin and dry but still seemed like they might have some sustenance to them. (I would later learn – after carrying it for two full days – that one of the largest, heaviest, and most succulent looking of these was completely inedible, and I would throw it to the ground after putting some in my mouth, spitting it out, wiping my lips with my sleeve, and shaking my head at myself for not having tasted it earlier.)

I wrapped everything in the blanket, tied it around my chest and stood on the edge of one of the banks, looking out at the ocean in the distance, the river squiggling through the landscape toward it. It was an interesting moment. Because now that I had food, water, and could see that shelter wasn't going to be much of a problem, I seemed to be at a loss for what to do next. Where exactly should I go, and what was the point of going there? Though, mostly, I wondered what I was going to do about The Goal. Was I going to start collecting the plants that I'd been trained to find, pillage equipment to make the sterilization mixtures, and then search the land for people on my own? And was that something that I wanted to do, or was obliged to do? Or neither? Or both?

I didn't know, which meant there were a few things that I had to figure out. But to do that, I would need to find a place where I could rest and think for a while – preferably somewhere far from the sad lattice of streets and wires that was still in front of me. And knowing that freshwater was going to be harder to come by than food, it was clear that I would have to stay along the river; I just wasn't sure if I should follow it down to the sea or venture deeper into the mainland. Of course, providing for myself would have been easier on the coast; I knew how to fish, swim, catch crabs, dig for shellfish, and gather seaweeds. Though, I knew there would be enough resources inland as well, which seemed to be the decision I was leaning toward. Maybe it was simple curiosity. Or maybe it was in thinking that the river could have come from giant hills of some kind, and maybe even from melted snow and ice – from mountains. Whatever it was, my legs seemed to make the choice for me, and I turned and started walking upstream, hiking until the land steepened, and the water was roaring down a thick chute beside me. When this rise tapered off, I lost sight of the town, and soon after that, the ocean; which, it turns out, I would never see again in my life.

I stopped after a few hours, and spent the night under a tree beside the river, the rushing water seeming to fade in and out of urgent whispers in a language I couldn't understand.

33

I felt like the land was growing, as if the contours were rolling away from me, the horizon crawling ever further into the distance. Its size was on a greater scale than anything I'd imagined, than any guess at enormity I'd ever made. I travelled for three days up the river, a tiny dot of movement being swallowed into the folds of the terrain, and though it felt like I was making some real distance, I'm sure that in relation to the entire landmass, I'd barely even scratched an edge.

While I walked I would switch between being barefoot and wearing the sandals I'd taken from the house. It was good to have something between the pads of my feet and the ground, and I could certainly move faster with them on. But after only a few hours, I would start to get blisters from the straps, and so would have to revert back to the waddling pace of hiking barefoot.

As it turned out, finding food along the way was a little more difficult than I'd guessed. While there were straggling patches of crop plants and fruit trees in some areas, there were also long stretches of woody vegetation that didn't seem to yield anything. Though, between what I'd already collected and what I was picking from the trees whenever I could, I had at least two days of provisions in the blanket with me at all times, which was enough.

The only time I stopped during those three days – besides to eat, drink, and sleep – was to examine a few interesting things that caught my eye; strange animal tracks that crossed the blotches of dirt along the riverbed, colourful insects scurrying away from my feet and into the cracks between the rocks, curious shorebirds that fed along the banks, which would flutter a safe distance away and perch on rocks to watch me pass. Once I found a deposit of clay-like mud that had countless prints imbedded inside it, one of which looked like the distorted palm of a human hand. I crouched down and compared them with the size and markings of my hand until I was confident they were different – though it was definitely a primate of some kind. I also stopped every time I came across a stray building that was perched on the edge of the river, peering my head through the door for a few seconds, eyeing the tools on the walls and the debris on the floor, speculating that most of them were temporary housing, maybe belonging to farmers and herders that stayed in them according to the harvest or seasons. However, none of these buildings ever struck me as a place that I could picture myself staying in for a longer period of time, or even, for that matter, to sit beside for more than a brief and needed rest. And so I would press on – on and up.

As the land steadily rose, the vegetation changed to better suit the differences in the air, moisture, and temperature of the rising altitude. The flora was becoming more lush and dense with every hour of travel, until finally, near the end of the third day, I came to some woody shrubs that were so thick that they seemed to create an almost impenetrable barrier. I had been watching this line of bushes get nearer all day, along with the clouds, which were sinking ever lower, growing darker, their bellies fat with rain.

The slope that I was climbing became steeper, more pronounced, and it seemed to end at a massive plateau where the dense and woody bushes began, visibly marking the beginning of another ecosystem. These bushes, I would later learn, were a tangled mass of branches that stood well over a person's head, and required something of a battle – usually involving at least some loss of blood – to move only a short distance through. Just below the plateau, under the lip of the dense bushes, was a fairly large terrace that had some surviving crop plants and fruit trees interspersed throughout. And at the edge of the terrace, close to the white and tumbling stream, was a small hut, which, like the other buildings I'd come across, had probably served as a kind of temporary housing for whoever kept the crop that had once grown beside it.

Everything was pointing me toward this tiny building: the wall of high bushes, my tired legs, my blistered feet, the rare crop food beside it, the darkening sky that was threatening to break open any minute – everything. It seemed like I'd found my spot to rest and think for a while.

I first walked around the terrace, breaking open and tasting one of the crop fruits to see if they were as edible as they looked. Then I circled the hut, pushing against the walls to make sure it wasn't going to fall down any time soon. Once I had done this, I went to see what kind of access I had to the river to get water. I even walked up to the barrier of tall bushes to see if there were any breaks or trails leading into it that I couldn't make out from a distance. (There weren't; which meant that the straightforward travelling would definitely stop there.) By the time I opened the rickety door, rain was speckling my clothes for the first time since the drizzling days after the storm. The timing couldn't have been better.

The hut was small, there being only enough room for a bed and a little table adjoined to a cupboard in the corner. There were also two windows on opposite sides of the room, but only one of them was intact, the long shards of glass from the other still scattered across the wooden planks of the floor. There were buckets, metal tools for crop growing that were hanging on the walls, strands of frayed rope, a few broken plates and bowls, utensils, two stools with wide cracks in the wood and wire reinforcing their legs, and a small frame on the floor that must have held a picture of some kind, but now only gripped a piece of paper that was bleached and curled with exposure to the elements.

I nodded my head. It was going to take some time, a little cleaning and mending, but that was all. I bent over to start the job, placing the slender shards of glass into a bucket first. Then I dragged the mattress outside, which had been shredded by mice and still had quite a few living inside, all of them scattering out of the mesh of springs and frayed cloth while I propped it up against the side of the building. By the time it was dark, I had everything fairly organized inside; and things that were broken, decayed beyond recognition, or simply of no use to me, were outside in front of the mattress.

I sat down at the table on the only stool that was salvageable – which complained of my every movement with the loudest of creaks – and ate some fruit in the dark. The rain pattered on the roof, and I looked up every once in a while, surprised that it still seemed to be waterproof (except for a drip that fell in one of the corners every few seconds, which was easy enough to remedy with a bucket on the floor).

When I had finished eating I felt my way to the open doorway, and, sitting down on the ground and resting my back against its frame, I looked out into the dripping night. This was ideal, I thought to myself, this place, the tranquility, the respite from travelling, the fact that I wouldn't have other people to muddle my thoughts, it would all be exactly what I would need to sort things out in my mind, and to make a plan for what I was going to do next. Yes, I reaffirmed, there certainly wouldn't be people to muddle my thoughts. In fact, there wouldn't be people in my life ever again. Ever.

For some reason, this seemed to strike me for the very first time. True, I could have made the connection long before, but I guess I'd been so worried about making it to land and then surviving that I hadn't really bothered to think of anything beyond that. Yet, whether I'd considered it or not, I had already begun a solitary existence that would continue on for the rest of my life – which was a sobering thought.

As a way to try and comfort myself, I thought back to a conversation that Kara and I once had about aloneness. She had begun it by saying to me, stolidly, that we are born alone, live our lives alone, and then die alone. She went on to explain how we have no choice but to see the world through the constraints of our own perception – through our individual experience, awareness, knowledge, and the personal limitations of our senses, of which the exact combination of, no one else who has ever lived throughout the span of our history could possibly share. We are alone in the world that we experience, prisoners to the way we see it.

Which, she had said, is why there are things inside us that we never share: because part of us recognizes that, even if they were spoken, we would be the only ones who could understand them. The quiet memories of our childhood, the kindnesses that we never had the courage to carry out, the wild dreams and aspirations, the sordid sexual fantasies, the doubt, the hate, the jealousy, the nightmares. We hold these things in places no one else can see, and not necessarily because they are secrets, but because they're facets of our being that, outside the air of our prisons, are unfathomable, indecipherable, meaningless to anyone else. The silences we choose are the echoes of our solitude.

At the time, I had argued that, if this were all true, then why weren't we impelled to live on our own. Why did it feel like we needed people, were drawn to them, wanted to be around them? But at that point in the conversation we heard someone coming, and she had to jump to her feet and leave. However, before she turned away, she had enough time to retort to my line of questioning by cocking her head to the side and raising her eyebrows with a bit of pity. After she left, I sat there in the shade feeling stupid, knowing why she had looked at me that way. It was simple: we are naturally drawn to people for two reasons; one, because having others around us is the easiest way to evade the intimidating fact that she was pointing out, that we are, in reality, completely and absolutely alone; and two, because we are simply wired that way. We are group animals, and have evolved to be so over hundreds of thousands of years. And the reason she had given me such a look was because it was obvious that the act of depending on the people that we flock toward, and understanding them, are worlds apart; and also happen to be completely unrelated.

So then, if she were right, I was just as alone as Mikkel was with the entire crew around him, or Dana surrounded by everyone eating in the dining hall. I tried to feel reassured by this, but didn't really.

The hiss of rain intensified outside. I held my hand out into the dark and caught a few drops.

How was I supposed to appease the cells in my brain that were linked in a way that made me a herd animal, a social being, something that would need to have interaction of some kind? I was sure I wasn't the first person in the world to be physically isolated, so what did other people do when this happened? Who knew? Maybe they found some kind of outlet, something to talk to; an animal, a plant, some invented friendship, some voice that seemed to answer back, or maybe just appeared to listen. And if

310

so, was that what it would come to: my scurrying around on all fours trying to catch mice or lizards so I could while away my days jabbering at their terrified faces, waiting for them to give me a meaningful blink in response? Was that what I would become, a withered man walking through the trees, babbling to a stick in his hand about the importance of maintaining a healthy state of mind through the use of imaginary social interaction?

The sudden call of an animal pierced through the noise of the rain, and I sat up, listening for it to be repeated, knowing that it would have to be quite close. I didn't hear it again, and, eventually, I stood up to go to bed, taking a few minutes to try and close the door, the wood having warped so far out of shape that it didn't match the dimensions of the frame anymore. I lifted and pushed until it fit as well as it was going to, and then felt my way to the bed, which was a kind of box that was raised slightly higher than the floor. It turned out to be infinitely more uncomfortable than sleeping on the soil under a tree, which is where I had been sleeping every night until that point, and I shifted around under the blanket, resolving to gather small branches and leaves to make it more comfortable the next day.

I fell asleep wondering how creative I'd have to get to fill the void of being alone in this land. And as I did this, drops of water fell from the ceiling, drumming the pool in the bucket with rhythmic precision – like Onni tapping on a rail.

34

It wasn't raining the next day, and I spent most of the misty morning exploring the area around the hut. The river, which seemed to be the only weakness I might be able to use to travel further into the plateau, had thin trails of fog stringing above it, as the air was still sodden with humidity from the night before. Though, I would soon find out that the river didn't represent much of a weakness at all. Very near the hut, only a few minutes walk up along it, the banks began to narrow, and soon led into the entrance of a small gorge. The gorge's walls were smooth and steep, with incredible scooping shapes carved into them, and marbled veins of lighter rock that streaked through the bulges and curves. Once inside the gorge, I tried continuing upstream, but it quickly became impassable; places where you either had to get into the rushing water and fight against the current, or try traversing along the slick rock walls, which, when they weren't vertical, were filmed with a slick algae or moss. Either way would probably have ended in drowning while breaking most of your bones in the process, your body plunging downstream from one rocky pool to the next. It seemed that if I wanted to go further into the plateau, it would have to be through the high bushes.

On my way back to the hut, I took a better look at some reinforcements that had been made to the bank, just before the entrance of the canyon, which I think had served to slow the erosion of the loose slope. They were essentially cages of wire that were holding back boulders; though the metal had almost entirely decayed, and the rocks would soon be breaking loose and rolling down the long bank.

I returned to the hut and walked through the terrace of land that had once been covered in crop plants, but had since been taken over by native grasses for the most part, leaving only a few straggling vegetables behind. It occurred to me that I could save the seeds from these, and try to cultivate the terrace again. It would make life a little more secure for me, in terms of having most of my food in one place. It would also involve quite a bit of work; but if I sharpened some of the tools that I'd thrown out of the hut, I knew that it was more than feasible. I walked to the edge of the terrace, thinking over some of the details of this re-planting idea.

Having arrived just as it began to rain, I hadn't really taken in the view. But as I was standing there, looking down at the land that gently sloped away until it met with a few hills at the horizon, the river creasing the terrain and penciling in a line of white, I noticed that it was an impressive one. Which is when it hit me.

Maybe it had something to do with the fact that I felt calm for the first time in what seemed like months, or that, finally, I was letting the very last bit of my guard down; whatever it was, it was then that Onni's image entered my mind – and this time, it refused to leave. With it, something sunk into the pit of my stomach and seemed to physically pull me down, until I found myself sitting on top of a boulder, my shoulders heavy, blankly staring ahead, thinking about what had happened the night I escaped.

At first, I have to admit that I was almost frustrated with Onni. Why in the hell couldn't he have said something, whispered something, found some way of making his presence known before standing in complete silence behind an armed and desperate man who was on the tentative verge of escape? I could think of a few brighter things to do. But, of course, he had come up behind me, and he had done this naturally, walking in the same way he'd always walked. Just like I had naturally spun around and slashed his stomach open.

Slashed his stomach open. I slouched even lower, put a cold hand on my forehead, understanding, for the very first time, the full implications of the wound I'd inflicted. Because the truth was that even if the crew had the sum total of all the surgical knowledge of the island in their heads, still, such a cut would need a sterile environment and complicated medicines to heal. The ship had neither. Which meant, simply enough, that Onni would die. Maybe later than sooner, but he would definitely die. I had killed someone. No, more than that. I had killed the one person on the boat who was trying to save my life. And even more than that, I had killed the one person who, out of all the people I knew, seemed to embody our innate ugliness the very least. What did that mean exactly? Where did that put me? And was there a single thing I could do about it?

These, unfortunately, were questions that only became more complicated the deeper I probed. First of all, the only reason Onni was trying to save me was that he believed the others had judged incorrectly, that this notion that I was conspiring to help remove our species from the world was absurd. Instead, he thought that the entire situation was being misjudged, and that, whatever lies might have been told around me, I still had a sense of kindness and morality that was being deliberately ignored. Which, in a way, meant that it wasn't really me, but rather the traits that he had believed were inside me, that he was trying to save. Only, as it turned out, he was wrong. I didn't have those traits; I was a conspirator; I was involved in something very close to the plot that the crew believed they had uncovered; I had been raised and educated for the sole purpose of carrying out the final stages of The Goal, and I had always planned on doing exactly that. And as much as he couldn't imagine my being capable of it, I did believe that it was the right thing to do. (And, really, that belief hadn't exactly been challenged along the way. Everything I'd learned about my 'fellow man' on the ship, about our fear and lust for power, about our cruelty and mercilessness, in addition to the things that I'd gathered about our ancestors while travelling through the mainland, had done nothing but confirm how valid The Goal was to me.)

As this jumble of barbed thoughts continued to fold in on itself, there seemed to be only one thing I was sure of, and it kept rising to the surface over and over again: I felt some kind of strange obligation to Onni. In exchange for his life, I felt like I at least owed him something, some attempt at atonement, some meagre act of redress. Yet, what was in my power to do that could possibly rectify anything?

But I realized there was something, as strange as the idea might have been. The one way I could offer a degree of compensation to him would be to set out to become more like the person he thought he was saving. If I could find a way to contort my being around the lies that he'd believed I was, and do this until they became closer to the truth, then this would take away from the futility of his dying, would add meaning to his intentions. However, the lie that Onni had believed was that I had nothing to do with The Goal, which meant that the only way to bring his belief closer to the truth would be to abandon it in every way inside my head. I slumped even lower.

For days afterwards, I walked around the terrace with a gnawing sensation in my chest. I spent a lot of time picturing Dana, burying his head in his hands at the prospect of my throwing away everything they'd been working toward, breathing a slow, heavy sigh, swallowing hard. I could picture Harek, furious, slamming a fist onto one of the wooden tables, his eyes wide, sharpening with something like violence; or Chalmon, sliding his fingers over his face, rolling his shoulders a bit, curling his fingers around his thumb and clenching down until he heard it crack.

But as much as these images weighed me down, my rationalization seemed increasingly capable of lightening the load. I reasoned that, all things considered, I wasn't even supposed to be alive, that the crew had intended on killing me, or at best, were going to drop me off on an island where I'd have been as little use to The Goal as I was abandoning it on the mainland. So if I should've been dead, what would be the harm in living like I was? I knew the Elders well enough to know that they would have planned for a contingency like this. There would be other expeditions of the third phase searching for fertile survivors, and we'd probably all been given overlapping routes in the case that some of us shipwrecked or were killed by other unforeseeable events. I could rest assured that there'd be other people to pick up where I left off. Meaning that, if I decided to shirk my responsibilities, there wouldn't really be much of an effect, much consequence. In fact, considering how often I'd blundered, The Goal was probably even better off without my fumbling hands juggling its leaden weight in the air. Wasn't it better for everyone if I just lay it down on the ground and quietly walk away? Of course it was.

And the more I thought about my decision as the days passed, the easier it sat with me. I would often nod my head at the river while I sat beside it, almost relieved with the idea that I could do whatever I wanted with the remainder of my life. Until eventually, the anxiety of disappointing the Elders began to feel more like a kind of refreshing independence from them. I started to feel lighter, less burdened. I began to grin when I was standing in the sun. And in time, it sometimes even crossed my mind that, if Onni could see me, he would actually be happy he'd steered the boat off course that night, that he would be content in the fact that he'd risked everything – even if he had ended up losing it – to save me. I felt my world slowly becoming smaller, simpler. I felt like it was becoming a place where it was easier to breathe. And I felt this all willingly. Willingly.

35

I soon settled into a pattern of working hard during the day and sleeping sound through the night. I cleared a few strips of land, planted the seeds from the straggling crop plants that remained, and began to collect others that I found while foraging around the hut.

It occurred to me that if I grew as many different kinds of fruits and vegetables as possible, it would guard against a single disease or a plant-specific insect wiping out everything I had. So I decided to head out on a bit of a gathering journey to collect as many seeds as I could find. I had been living in the hut for almost a moon before I set off, wrapping a few things in the grey blanket and descending into the land, walking away from the river for the first time since I'd arrived.

I had grown used to the plants and animals that lived along the water and on the edge of the shrub plateau, so most of the flora and fauna that I came across was quite new to me. However, at the end of my first day of hiking, I also came across something that was somewhat familiar: a patch of trees with the same yellow melons I knew the Creatures fed on, which I was more than happy to get the seeds from. I also found a few peels that had almost entirely decayed, which had the markings of the Creature's teeth scraping along a few of their dry surfaces.

I learned some new information about them. It appeared, as there were already new fruits forming on the sloping trees where they'd foraged, that they hadn't been there in a long while, and from this, I speculated that they had to be roaming animals, and that the only way I would ever see one would either be by accident, or by waiting for a long period of time in one place. I scoured the area for other clues, but couldn't really find much more than that.

I spent the evening under those same trees, watching the light on the swollen fruit fade until they became dark globs against the night sky, goggling down at me like the extended eyes of a hermit crab. I slept well, dreaming of the pounding surf

317

and the chatter of crustaceans as they scuttled across shining slabs of rock.

I began hiking early the next morning, and before the sun had even fully risen, I'd already climbed to the top of a massive rise that began not far from the grove. Once I reached the crest and looked around, I was surprised to see a group of buildings scattered below with an overgrown road leading out of them. I would be hesitant to call it a settlement, but it was a complex that was definitely big enough to have farmed from, which meant there might be a chance of finding some remnant crop plants nearby. And I was right; as I descended toward the houses, I stopped to remove the seeds from three different varieties of vegetables that I'd never seen before, and decided, after counting how many kernels and pips I'd gathered, that I now had more than enough for the terrace, and that this would be the end of my journey.

But before turning back, I thought I might walk through the buildings, which were overgrown and strangled by vines and creeping plants, just for curiosity sake. I passed between two buildings and walked toward what must have once been a kind of courtyard at the centre of them all. I had put my sandals on, knowing that there were often shards of glass hidden in the vegetation around ruins, and so didn't know that there was a stick under my foot until I stepped on it. It broke with a loud crack, and I flinched at the sound, as if sorry for disturbing someone's peace. Though, hearing the noises that came as an instant reaction to it, it seemed like I actually had. Something was moving inside one of the buildings.

I froze, like a statue in the centre of the courtyard, my hands still suspended in the air. The noises were almost like cloth flapping in the wind, or someone shaking the dust from a shirt before putting it on. I looked up at the sky for signs of a breeze that might be responsible for this; there were none. The sun had just poked its eye over the horizon, and was drawing long shadows across the walls, while casting slats of light on the grass in the courtyard as it filtered through the spaces between the buildings. After listening more intently, I realized that the sounds were coming from one of these spaces instead of from inside. I watched the light on the ground, half expecting to see a long shadow pass across it, but there was nothing, and the noises soon stopped.

Part of me wanted to just turn and run, while another part – a curious and more stubborn part – held my feet in place. I tried to calm myself with logic, listing off every reason I shouldn't be afraid: I hadn't seen any evidence of living people since I'd set foot on the mainland, nor had I seen anything that was organized or cleaned in the buildings as I'd approached them, or even a trail that a person would use to come to and from the houses. I should have had nothing to worry about. In fact, come to think of it, I told myself, I wasn't worried. No, I was confident. I nodded at the grass, paused, then reached behind my back and dug through the folds of the blanket until I found my knife. It would have been impossible to walk away without investigating.

I walked toward the thin space between the two buildings where I'd heard the sounds, and as I got closer, they started up again, in sync with a flickering movement in the slat of sun on the ground in front of me; and then suddenly stopped. I continued to the edge of the building and spent a full minute or two in the quiet – reassuring myself that I was really not in any way afraid – before finally peeking around the corner.

The first thing my eyes were drawn to was a spool of yellow rope that the elements had frayed into bristles of tiny threads scratching at the air, and then I noticed the large black bird that had become tangled inside it, a strand of rope wrapped around one of its legs. It must have accidentally stepped into a loop, maybe while hopping through the tangled mess in search of twines for its nest, and this loop had then cinched around its foot when it tried to fly off. It had been there ever since, uselessly struggling to get away. And as soon as I stepped out from around the corner, it tried again, but only succeeded in bouncing from wall to wall at the end of its tether, until, after a frantic effort, it recoiled back to the ground with a graceless crash.

The bird itself looked terrible. Judging by the plumage that was scattered around and its scraggly, emaciated body, it must have been trapped there for days, maybe even weeks. There were blotches of white skin that could be seen under its thinning layer of feathers, and the base of some of them were bare, appearing almost like rows of bones, as if its frame were trying to push through to the outside, eager to become a skeleton. I didn't move for a long while, waiting until it settled to the ground, exhausted. It hadn't even bothered tucking its wings close to its body; they lay draped open, scarcely covering its sides.

It's interesting, because my first reaction, the first thing I felt inclined to do, was kill it. I wanted to pick up a heavy rock and hurl it between the buildings, ending its suffering with a conscientious act of mercy. But something stopped me, and, for some reason, I paused to think about it before looking for a stone to throw.

I imagined myself, or any person really, trapped under a fallen tree in a forest, and, though this person calls out until their voice is hoarse and breaking, no one comes to their aid. Eventually, after days pass, and it becomes clear that nobody will ever come, somewhere, deep in their minds, they come to understand that they're going to die. And as this knowledge surfaces, slowly transforming from a guarded thought to a certainty, I think it would be natural for them to begin a process of preparing for it, in whatever way they personally saw fit. They might even manage to find a kind of peace, to embrace the warmth – that is really a coldness – which they feel spreading throughout their bodies. And perhaps it is even with a feeling of ease that they begin to drift off into sleep for the last time.

Then I imagined that, suddenly, a giant monster with a club in his hand appears out of nowhere. Reflexively, the person writhes into panic once more – the same panic that they'd felt when they first recognized their lives were in danger. And, unable to prevent their bodies from reacting, they twist and struggle, yet again, to try and squirm out from under the tree, but obviously still find it impossible. Panicked, they turn toward the monster, which is now looming over them and raising the club above his head. The person does not see the monster's greater intentions, what they see is the club, and they hold their arms up to shield their face from it as it swings down through the air. It strikes them, their ears ringing with the effects of adrenaline and terror, and, instinctively, as a last ditch effort, they turn and dig at the earth with their fingernails, labouring frantically to free themselves, to run, to hide, to defend their bodies from the blow that finally strikes them in the back of the head and ruptures their skull into fragments that pierce into their brain and end their life.

I wonder: how is that so much better than dying on your own terms? The truth is, only a human being would see the monster's thought process as sound. Only a human being would see a simple act of violence as the solution to a complex process. And regardless of how self-aware the Elders thought they were, this is how we were taught to treat animals that had unluckily fallen from trees: bludgeon them to death. But what I now understand is that we weren't taking those rocks into our hands and smashing their tiny skulls in because we felt sorry for them, but rather because we felt sorry for ourselves for having come across them, powerless and incapable. We did it as a means of answering our helplessness, not their suffering.

So. It was decided. Contrary to what I would have done on the island, I wasn't going to kill this scrawny, dying bird. Instead, I was just going to leave it be, let it die on its own.

I turned to walk away, but stopped after only a couple of steps, staring at the ground, tapping a hand against my leg. This second idea didn't sit well with me, either. And regardless of the fact that chaos dictated this path for the bird, and that I had renounced the idea of interjecting to kill it, I could not, no matter how hard I tried, renounce the idea of interjecting to save it. I was well aware that this was because of our uncontrollable urge to poke and prod into natural processes with our arrogant fingers; I was well aware that I was just as guilty as the monster in my imagined scenario, but I could not, no matter how hard I strained to move my feet forward, keep myself from turning around.

The bird seemed sorry that I'd returned. Almost reluctantly, it cocked its head up to the sky and, collecting what little energy it had left, jumped from the ground and tried climbing through the stubborn air once more. After it was yanked back to the ground with a thump, it turned to face me, its beak opening as I neared it with the knife in my hand. I bent over and cut the strand of rope that was tying it to the spool without getting my hands within pecking distance. Then, fluttering and reeling more like a ragged ball of cloth than a bird, it ricocheted out from between the two buildings and into the tall grass beyond. And it was there that it toppled to the ground and stayed, a miserable heap of breathing feathers, buried in the meadow that surrounded the buildings.

Did I think it was just going leap into the sky and go on its merry way, that I would be patting myself on the back while I watched it disappear into the horizon? I hadn't 'saved' its life. In fact, I'd probably even placed it in more jeopardy than it already was, as it was now out in the open where predators and scavengers, which might have been reluctant to go into the unnatural and confined spaces of the buildings, were free to pluck it from an open field.

I walked out from between the buildings and folded my arms across my chest. "So," I said, aloud. The bird turned to look at me with a kind of renewed shock; which wasn't very surprising – I hadn't heard my own voice for what felt like a few weeks. "What do you think we should do with you?"

The bird blinked.

I scratched my head, "I mean – I think we should finish what we started here, don't you?" Then I paused for a moment, "Actually... I have no idea why I used the word 'we' there, but I think the saving part is clear enough, no?"

When I snickered, the bird shrunk even lower, evidently terrified by the sound of this as well.

"That 'we' reminds me actually; I've been joking to myself about finding some animal to talk to. You know, a 'keep me from going crazy' kind of thing. But, as I'm chatting away to a half-dead bird that doesn't understand a single word I'm saying, along with referring to myself in the plural... I should really just shut up and find you some food – no? Insects, I imagine?"

The bird blinked again.

Insects are everywhere. We see them scurrying in front of us, running through the grass, across the walls of buildings, flying through the air, dropping from leaves, and committing suicide into our ears and eyes at the most inopportune moments, but I can't remember ever trying to catch them before. Instantly, they seemed to have disappeared from the world. I was crawling on my hands and knees, sifting through the grass, looking in every imaginable place that it would have been logical to find them, but they seemed to have anticipated this, melting away into mysterious and unseen corners of the landscape. When I did manage to find one, I was met with the second challenge of capturing it, and, after pilfering a couple of jars from one of the houses, I managed to develop a method that had at least some degree of success. This method relied heavily on the finding of beetles; which were slow, big enough to detect, and rarely flew when you tried to catch them. Though, after about an hour of concerted effort, I'd only caught five.

I walked up to the bird with a rock in my hand, and after catching it again when it tried to flutter away from me, I tied the strand that was still hanging from its leg to the rock. Then I cleared a circle in the tall grass around it, the bird eyeing me suspiciously as I did so. It was beyond exhaustion, terrified, and now completely confused. And whenever it managed to regain a bit of strength, it would try and fly away again, only to be wrenched back down to the ground by its tether. (I was hoping that the stress I was putting it through while trying to save it wouldn't end up being the cause of its death.)

I sat as close as I could for quite a while, waiting for it to calm down enough to notice the beetles crawling inside the jar in my hands. When it finally did, I removed the lid with slow, fluid movements, and poured the beetles out into the grass between us. One flew away, while another, which was much faster than I remembered it being, scurried deep into the grass and escaped. But once the bird seemed to recognize that its window of opportunity was closing, it tentatively hopped toward me and pecked the other three from the ground in rapid succession. It was over in seconds.

"I see. This might be harder than I thought," I said, with as soothing a voice as I could muster. "Do you eat fruit?"

I picked through some of the fruit that I'd been carrying in the blanket and sliced open one of the sweeter ones, cutting it into tiny cubes and placing them in the same jar as I had the insects. When I returned, the bird tried to fly away again, and I decided to scatter the pieces of fruit beside the rock and walk back toward the houses until it calmed down. When it did, it noticed the bright colours and began to snatch the pieces of fruit from the grass and swallow them down.

The rest of the day was spent gathering insects and experimenting with different kinds of fruit, trying to find out which ones it preferred. I stayed as close to it as possible, hoping that it would become accustomed to me – even though this never really happened. No matter how slowly I moved, when I approached, it would try and fly away, and subsequently batter itself against the rock or the ground. It had lost so much plumage that, even if it were to have several days of food and rest, I doubted it would be able to fly. It would have to grow new feathers, which could take weeks, maybe even a month. And seeing as I wasn't prepared to stay beside this useless set of buildings for more than a night, if I really wanted to save this bird, I would have to bring it back to the hut with me.

That evening, I lay in the grass, watching the subtle colours of the sky shift and fade into darkness, 'conversing' with my newfound companion in a mild voice. "So I've been thinking about the name of your species. I tried to remember it the first time I saw a flock of birds like you crossing the sky. I remember there being a reference, and I'm not sure if it was in the art book, or medieval history; one of the war books, belief systems – but there was definitely a reference to you somewhere along the way."

The bird made an odd gurgling noise, and in this respect, it was something like conversation, as it often murmured sounds between my pauses, as if it were reacting to what I was saying.

"I'm pretty sure you're either a crow or a raven – though they might be different names for the same thing. I don't really know. But I do know that you sparked people's imagination enough to be mentioned in books, which, Dana would say, meant you either represented something people saw in themselves and hated, or saw in themselves and wished they had more of; or both. I'll have to think about that.

"Anyway, tomorrow, we'll travel all day and see if we can make it to the hut. You've eaten a lot of food, and I'm thinking that, after resting for the night, you should have the energy to survive being carried for a long day of hiking. What do you think?" I put my hands behind my head and crossed one leg over the other. The bird crouched low to the ground in reaction to these movements, ready to flap its wings, but didn't.

"And as far as tonight goes, you certainly won't have to worry about predators. I'm sure my smell alone is enough to keep anything from coming within eyeshot; because, well, everything alive is afraid of humans – which I guess only makes sense. For tens of thousands of years we've sent mixed messages, either holding out gentle hands to lure animals closer with food, hoping to catch them and change them from what they are, to mould them into a form that we could see more of our domesticated selves in; or simply luring them with those same gentle hands until they were close enough to kill."

I slowly turned my head to look at the bird, "You should know that I'll release you when you're well again. Promise. Really."

That night, I slept in the grass beside the bird, and woke the next morning to a grating call that I hadn't heard it make before, and which, at close range, almost hurt my ears with its volume. "TOC!" It was abrupt and assertive, and seemed to signal that it was feeling better, regardless of how mangy and pathetic it still looked. It was more active than the day before as well, and was hopping around at the very end of its tether, furthest away from me, taking in the world as only birds do, jerking its head gracelessly in all directions, tilting its neck to eye things with furtive, sidelong glances.

I had gone to sleep forming a plan of how to carry the crow, or raven – or whatever kind of bird it was. (Eventually, I settled on calling it a raven; but only because I had to pick one of them, and, out of the two possibilities, I liked the sound of this one a little better.) This plan of mine was largely based on the appealing image of the raven perched on my shoulder, patiently balancing itself as I walked. It was also, as I would find out, completely unrealistic. After preparing to leave, I untied the rope from the rock and walked up to the bird, which was watching me nervously, as if well aware of the ordeal that was about to take place. When it tried to fly away, I grabbed hold of the rope, quickly looped it around my arm, and yanked down on the tether so that the bird would be drawn up to my shoulder while it was still flailing around. At which point, the back of my skull was beaten with the thudding of its wings, and I tried to lean away from it; but I wasn't far enough, because it managed to jab the side of my head with its beak. I swore, flinging both the rope and the bird up into the air, proving, if nothing else, that it really was unable to fly. Despite flapping as hard as it could, it crashed into the grass, and then began hopping away with the greatest of urgency.

I touched the side of my head, sucking air between my teeth, inspecting the blood on my fingers. "I'm trying to save you! Do you get that?" As if in reply to this, the bird plunged behind a thick bunch of grass and continued to flee through the meadow, apparently not caring to 'get' anything – it just wanted to escape. I wasn't worried about losing it, knowing how weak it was; I imagined it would stop as soon as it thought it was out of sight.

I went into one of the buildings to get cloth of some kind, hoping that if I covered its eyes, or beak, or maybe its entire body, it would make the journey more bearable for both of us. While I was inside the cluster of buildings, I also decided to cut off a large section of the rope that I found the raven tangled in. It would be useful, as I only had frayed cord that I was constantly braiding into longer pieces back at the hut. I uncoiled the spool until I came to a spot where it wasn't as damaged by the sun, and cut a long piece from there.

When I returned, I found the raven not very far from where it had disappeared, squatting in the grass, trying to lay hidden, a ragged black shape against the green-yellow strands. "Okay. Let's try this again," I said, holding out the piece of cloth that I'd taken from one of the houses. The bird, seeming to understand that there was going to be another attempt at picking it up, turned and began scurrying away through the meadow again. "Look," I shouted after it, "you can come with me and be fed, grow your feathers back, and be released when you're strong enough; or you can stay here, starve to death and get eaten. The choice is yours." But it wasn't really, and I walked up behind it, tossed the cloth over the whole of its body, and wrapped it into a kind of bundle.

We travelled the entire day, stopping to rest and eat some fruit now and then. I found that as long as the bird was completely covered, with only its beak sticking out of the cloth in order to breathe, it wouldn't try to flap or escape, or even worse, gouge my skin. Unfortunately, it took me a while to learn that I couldn't let my guard down for a second when it came to its opportunistic pecking, and my arms looked like a map of welts; red islands splaying across a skin ocean.

When we arrived at the hut, just after the sun had gone down, I tried to bring the bird inside for the night to keep it safe from predators. But it didn't think much of that idea, stubbornly flapping and squawking until I brought it back outside. In the end, I decided to take the boughs and leaves that were padding my bed and move them outside, having to sleep a second time under the open sky for the raven's sake.

The next day I built a cage out of sticks and some of the tattered strands of rope from the hut, which worked quite well. While I tended the terrace during the day, I would keep the bird tied to a rock, where it would flap and exercise its wings, pluck beetles and other insects that happened to wander its way along the ground, and eat fruit that I cubed and placed in front of it every few hours; then, overnight, I would put it inside the cage to keep it safe from other animals. But one day I spotted a long and thin scavenger ambling along the rim of bushes, which looked similar to a cunning little mustelid that we had on the island. I hadn't been taking an animal like this – which could easily fit between the bars and kill the raven anytime it wanted to – into consideration when I'd built the cage, or when I'd been placing it on the ground outside my door overnight. As a solution, I decided to hang it in my open doorway, thinking that if my smell wasn't enough to keep the tiny predator at bay, then the raven making noise as it approached would be; as I would wake and probably scare it away before it did any damage.

It had only been dangling in the doorway for five nights before that very thing happened, the raven flapping wildly and clawing at the sticks of the cage until I roused from sleep. Only, it didn't turn out to be the tiny scavenger that woke me.

36

I rolled over, suddenly awake, my eyes darting around the darkness of the hut. There was a deep, sickening feeling in my chest that something was wrong, but that I'd become aware of it too late; as if I'd been thrown into a race without having any idea which direction to run. The raven was restless, rattling the wooden cage, wishing that it could break out and fly away, vanish into a jagged silhouette in the night sky where it could watch things unfold from the safety of the air. The fact that it wasn't making any vocal sounds only added to the urgency, as if it somehow understood that in this kind of situation – whatever this kind of situation was – silence was a far better tool than alarm; that the time for giving signals of warning had long since passed. It clacked its beak together when it noticed I was up, seeming to chide me for taking so long to wake.

"Shit," I whispered, rubbing my eyes, "What is it?"

The bird crouched down and jerked its head to look out into the night.

I crept out of bed and ducked under the cage, stepping into the cool air outside. I stood in front of the door and listened for what must have been a few minutes, until I heard a sound above the rush of the stream; just one, coming from behind the hut, far into the terrace.

Believing that there were only animals left on the mainland, and knowing that animals would run as I approached, it didn't cross my mind to bring a knife; I just rounded the building and walked toward the fruit trees, stepping as noisily as I could to give fair warning that a human was on its way. A gentle breeze drew up the long slope to the terrace, pressing my clothes against my skin, and I could hear some of the leaves in the fruit trees rustling, one of them tapping a distracted rhythm against a branch. There was no moon in the sky, yet there was enough starlight that I could make out specific trees, and I kept walking until I was roughly in the centre of them all. Which is where I stood, looking around, listening, wondering why I hadn't heard anything scurry away as I'd approached.

I must have been there for a few minutes before a disturbing thought crossed my mind: the small scavenging animal, which I was so intent on protecting the raven from, would have had ample opportunity to climb the doorframe and crawl into the cage in the minutes I'd been away from the hut. While I was investigating what was probably only a piece of fruit falling to the ground, I might have been giving the sly predator a golden opportunity. In fact, I thought to myself, it might even have been the mustelid skulking closer to the building that had agitated the bird in the first place. I turned to walk back, shaking my head, feeling stupid, careless.

But then I stalled, and was suddenly standing stiff, holding my breath. There was something in the stillness, something hidden beneath the lazy flutter of leaves. And the more I concentrated on it, the more I was sure it was there. It wasn't anything specific, or, for that matter, even audible; it was more like a tenseness that didn't belong to me, the weight of another's anticipation. And it seemed to be in every direction, as if I was surrounded, as if my movements were being watched from all sides with fanatical concentration.

I don't know why I chose to speak, but, for some reason, this is what made sense to do. My voice was hesitant, doubtful. "Hello?" I called out.

At the exact moment the word left my mouth, the trees and vegetation around me came to life. There was motion everywhere. From right behind me, to far below the terrace, near the rim of the bushes, close to the hut, high in the trees, immediately to my left, directly in front of me. Everywhere. I didn't look around to try and see what was happening, or stand firm in a defensive stance, nor even try to run; instead, my knees weakened, and then buckled, and I crumpled to the ground, covering my head, waiting for a spear to pierce my skin, or plunge through my rib cage, pin one of my limbs to the ground.

Between the spaces of my arms, and against the backdrop of a star spotted sky, I saw a figure run in front of me. I would have described it as looking like a man, but its silhouette was smaller, more petite, its waist crouched low, the legs gawky and awkward, the knees having to bend with acute angles. However, almost contradictory to these gangly limbs, it ran with an incisive posture, a grace, an extraordinary speed. I could hear the thudding of their feet on the soil, could feel the thumping reverberations on the ground as a few of them jumped out of the trees. While the frantic scattering whirled around me, one of them must have stepped quite close, because a bit of dirt bounced onto the skin of my hand, making me cower even more. And with my head buried deep into my arms I couldn't see anything anymore; I could only hear hectic sounds that could have signified any number of things: their fleeing, regrouping, encircling me, or maybe preparing for something unknown, an attack – anything was possible. I could predict nothing. I had no idea how this was going to end.

After a few seconds, the sounds began to recede. They were running over the lip of the terrace and down the hill, and I listened to the pounding of their footsteps until they faded into the whisper of rustling branches and the hiss of the river. And just as suddenly as it had begun, it was over.

I didn't take my head from my arms for quite a while; and when I finally did, I only ogled around at the dark, still afraid to move. It had crossed my mind that some of them might be lingering in the trees – perhaps a few scouts that would be watching for what I was going to do next, and who would then slip away to inform the others so that they could react accordingly; maybe readying themselves for a battle, which, as was plain to see, they would effortlessly win.

Before I'd even gotten to my feet, I heard a set of long, haunting calls coming from the slope below. I recognized them as the same sounds I'd heard when I slept on the doorstep after finding my knife; the same three melancholic notes repeated over and over again. Only this time, I also heard what must have been a kind of answering call, echoing in the distance. And after that, I could have sworn I heard another, even further off. But while I listened to them, I realized that it hadn't only sounded like a flute that I'd heard that second night on the mainland, but that it really was one. Which, I think, was the most intimidating realization I could have come to.

Because it meant that, not only were they advanced enough to communicate with other groups of the same species, but that they had the intelligence to make musical instruments (or at least warning horns with variable notes). And as all of these haunting calls had sounded exactly the same, it also meant they could construct flutes that were in a consistent key from one to the next, which would require their cutting tools to be incredibly precise. And if they were producing and using cutting tools of that calibre, one could only guess at the type of weapons they were capable of making.

Which made me wonder what this group of Creatures was so urgently communicating to the other groups, after having seen me. (I'd already made the link that these animals were the Creatures, which, as I would find out when there was enough light to look at the bite marks in some of the fruit they left behind, was an assumption I was right to make.) Were these flute calls only a warning, something urging every Creature to be extremely careful because a human had been spotted? Was it perhaps a signal to take flight? Or was it a command to gather for an assault, to come together and protect their territory as a united group?

I knew the Elders would have told me about an intelligent hominid living on the mainland if they'd known about it, which obviously meant that they didn't. No, this had to be a new animal, probably one of the strange mutations Dana had warned me about, a product of the horrible weapons we'd used at one point in our history. This was something that no one, anywhere, knew anything about. I was blind. I didn't even know enough to begin helping myself. All I really understood was that if they decided to come in large numbers with weapons, there was no way I could defend myself against them. I understood that if I wanted to survive, I had to think of another strategy. And soon.

I got to my feet, brushing the dirt from my clothes, shaking soil out of my hair, constantly looking over my shoulder as I did so, still half doubting I was really alone. I went back to the hut, ducking under the cage in the doorway, and sat on the edge of my bed for quite a while, as if trying to find the right words to break all of this news to the raven. "So – uh… I think we're in a bit of trouble," I finally said. The bird opened its wings, flapped once, and then tucked them back in, the sound of settling feathers scratching at the quiet.

I didn't sleep for the rest of the night, worrying about the Creatures returning, and with what I was going to do in preparation for it. But by the time the sky began to blanch with the light of morning, I had at least formulated some kind of plan; and though I understood it would take a lot of work, and more than a few days to complete, I imagined it would be a fairly effective one. I couldn't wait to get started, and I was out of bed at the earliest hour possible.

But before I could begin, I had to satisfy my curiosity, and walked out into the terrace to study the tracks that the Creatures had left behind. I realized that I'd seen them once before, in the mud along the river while I was looking for the hut. They resembled a human hand in many ways, though the fingers looked shorter and contorted. I carefully picked through the peels and fruit that they'd eaten as well, trying to learn something new about their habits, but didn't really come up with anything further.

Then I returned, hung the raven's cage from the ceiling in the middle of the hut, left it some fruit, and closed the door as best I could. I picked up the length of rope that I'd taken from the cluster of houses, and the sharpest cutting tool I had, and set out to complete the first part of my plan.

Because it was clear that between running and fighting, running was my only option, I didn't bother wasting time carving spears or trying to make bows and arrows. Though, I did go for a few minutes to carefully inspect the wire cage of boulders that was reinforcing the bank before the entrance to the canyon. It had occurred to me, when I first looked at it, that this cage would break open once the rusted wire had corroded enough, sending the heavy rocks tumbling down the slope to the river. Which meant that if I weakened the wire at strategic points, and could invent a kind of release mechanism, I could let the boulders loose as a trap, or at the very least, as an imposing display. (It was doubtful I could kill more than one or two of them with a barrage of slow moving rocks, but I could probably inspire some caution, making them reluctant to pursue very close at my heels; which was enough.) That's where the second part of my plan came in.

Thinking about how the Creatures had run away the night before, I realized that they had completely avoided the shrubs, despite the fact that they could have crawled into them and disappeared by slithering only a body length inside. This only made me assume that they were as unfit to travel through them as I was, and sparked an idea to use the bushes to my advantage. I thought that, if I could fight my way through the shrubs for a day, and find a spot to drop a rope into the canyon, I could then use it as an escape route. If they came, I could run up the canyon from the hut, climb the rope, and pull it up after me, thus having already gained an entire day on them, as they would have to struggle through a day's worth of bushes before they could get to the place I'd tied the rope.

That first day was spent with this aim, battling my way along the top of the canyon. I thought I would weave through the shrubs where they were thinnest, following the lip of the gorge as closely as I could. But the branches hung over the canyon's rim like mud oozing over an edge, and if I wanted ground under my feet, I had to pass through vegetation that was just as dense as everywhere else. I also discovered that the shrubs weren't only dense, but were also littered with thorns and spines that relentlessly scored your skin. But I still wrestled my way through them, lifting the heavy limbs and crawling beneath; at some points, I had to climb up and traverse small sections by squirming through the prickly forks of higher boughs, and then scuffle back down to the ground again, my skin grated and raw. I avoided cutting as much as possible, especially at the point where I first began making my way through. I didn't want to leave any clues that it was possible to pass through there, which meant when I had to cut branches, I did it strategically, scarring the wood in places that wouldn't easily be seen.

At the very end of the day, with blisters of blood lining some of the deeper scratches on my arms and legs, I made my way to the steep edge of the canyon, and looked down into the river from some of the overhanging limbs. I tied the rope to one of the trees at a point where it would be easy to climb my way to safety, and then lowered down, a little nervous that the rope might not be strong enough to hold my weight; but, thankfully, it turned out to be fine.

This was great. Now that the rope was in place, I could use the cutting tools from the hut to construct a trail, which would begin from the point where the rope was tied. This trail would hopefully circumvent the impassable section of the gorge, following the edge of the canyon, and would access the river further upstream, where I could then travel along its banks and continue my escape, deep into the plateau.

I returned to the hut at nightfall, and brought the cage outside to feed the raven there. It complained as much as usual when I moved it, but, happily, if uncharacteristically, it didn't peck at my hands when I placed pieces of fruit between the bars. It was looking healthier by the day, and was certainly becoming more animated, more vocal, watching my every movement with more of an interest than with intimidation. I brainstormed aloud in the dark, leaning on an elbow, talking through different possibilities for the release mechanism of the boulders, the raven almost managing to sound interested with its well-timed gurgling noises.

I didn't sleep well that night, waking to every movement the bird made in its cage, thinking that it was another warning, that it might be the signal to make a mad dash for the rope, which, I was at least comforted to know, was dangling in the gorge, bright yellow against the marbled green rock, ready to save me.

37

I had imagined that I was going to clear a clean path that tunnelled through the limbs of the bushes, a tube of slashed branches that would allow me to run through the plateau and arrive on the other side of it within minutes. But if there was one thing that I learned on my first day of clearing, it was that this plan would need some serious rethinking. After tying my cutting tools to the end of the rope and climbing it, and then hoisting them up behind me, I began chopping and thrashing the bushes with the greatest of determination. But at the end of the day, I hadn't really made any progress — maybe five to ten metres — which only brought me to the conclusion that I wasn't going to be cutting a trail through the shrub plateau at all. Instead, it would have to be a kind of chaotic line that followed the path of least resistance, a meandering route that I would set out to weaken, define, and memorize.

While I did this, every night after returning to the hut raw-skinned and exhausted, I would carry the raven's cage out into the grove of fruit trees and sit down to eat something. And as I put pieces of fruit in my mouth or tossed them in front of the bird, I couldn't stop myself from giving the land below slow, worried glances; my senses alert, waiting for signs of the Creatures.

However, as stressed as I was about them, there was one thought that would sometimes calm me, which was that if they hadn't returned yet, it almost seemed likely that they never would. True, they might have been using the days to gather and organize as a single force, but they might also have simply chosen to run away and steer clear of me. Maybe I was safe. Maybe I was overreacting and didn't have anything to worry about except growing enough food for myself. I couldn't know. The only thing I knew for certain was that I had to continue working as hard and as fast as possible on the route through the bushes. Just in case.

Veracity

On the fifth day of weaving back and forth, chopping certain limbs, shaving off the spines of others so I could pass over them, or cutting away the vines and thorny underbrush so I could pass underneath, I made my way toward the river to check the depth of the gorge for the last time. As I'd hoped, the canyon walls had become low enough to jump inside, and the ravine of the rushing stream was wider. I was also happy to find that the vegetation right beside the water had been cleared away (as had been done further downstream) from the frequent flooding of the river. I imagined I would be able to continue into the plateau with relative ease from that point on, following the shore of the river. I now had a functional escape route.

I devoted the next couple of days to weakening the rusted wires that held back the boulders, and building a release mechanism that I hoped would free the massive rocks when pulled. I had placed a thin log into a kind of makeshift bracket that I'd made, and then tied the meshing of wire to it. Once this was done, and I was sure that it would hold, I unfastened all the joints of the wire until the entire weight of the boulders was on the log, so that if I could bring it above the shallow brackets, everything inside would come toppling down the hill. (Though, I obviously couldn't test this. It would have to remain in the abstract world of theory, until the moment came that I would need that theory to be absolutely surefire.)

Yet, despite all of these precautions, I still didn't really feel safe, and I managed to think of one last thing I could do to prepare for a potential ambush. It occurred to me that I knew nothing about the land beyond the plateau, the terrain I would actually be fleeing through – were it to come to that. So, in order to prevent getting cornered or lost while being chased, I decided to do some exploring. At first, I planned to venture further upstream for a few days, but this would mean leaving the raven behind to fend for itself; and as it had been spending so much time suspended in the hut, which it absolutely hated, I thought it would be best to spare the poor bird the added stress. Instead, I decided to explore as much as I could for only half a day. That way, I could be back by the evening, as usual.

337

I travelled light, only bringing some fruit and a knife and set off at daybreak. I quickly threaded through the bushes and jumped into the far end of the canyon, where I began hiking along the wide riverbed, deeper into the plateau. After a few hours, the river began to wind and curve, snaking back and forth through the bushes. I followed the endless twists, moving fast, trying to cover as much ground as possible before midday, hoping to sight the end of the plateau or the beginning of a transitional zone that would lead into another ecological region. And after a few hours of hiking, that's exactly what I found.

The shrubs were beginning to thin, the spaces between them spreading and making way for different flora, usually taller trees with waist high plants at their base, until eventually, just as it was nearing midday, the land started to open up. As I followed the river around a slow bend, I caught sight of some hills in the distance, their hunched backs speckled with thinly interspersed trees. I was ecstatic. Finally, I knew what came after the shrub plateau. It wasn't another barrier of dense vegetation that was barring my way, but something completely manageable. Without even touching it or walking through it, I could already see it was a landscape that would lend itself to easy travel, a place that I could traverse quickly through, yet remain relatively concealed.

I was done; I had a trap that would buy me the needed minutes to get to the rope well in front of them, the rope itself, the route memorized through the bushes, and now the knowledge of what lay beyond the plateau. At last, after all of the work and preparation that had been carried out since the night the Creatures had come to the terrace, I was beginning to feel ready for them, to feel safe.

I looked up at the sun and figured I might, at most, have an hour to spare; and, seeing as I'd been trudging the entire morning, I was more interested in resting for that hour than exploring, and I started looking for a place to sit or lie down. Around the next curve of the river, I found an enormous rock in the centre of the stream, which had been sculpted and smoothed by the high water until it almost managed to look soft. There was also a series of boulders that poked their heads above the

338

surface, which I could hop across to get to this huge rock. In fact, it looked as if I could cross the entire channel using them, and had I not been so tired, it probably would have occurred to me that this was one of the few places along the river that an animal could safely access the other side, and that there was even a vague trail that led into the trees at both ends of the natural bridge that pointed that very fact out. But I didn't take any of this in. Instead, I just jumped across the boulders and ambled onto the giant stone, where I quickly found a spot to lie down. I curled up into one of the carved scoops, closed my eyes against the sun, and, lulled by the sound of rushing water, managed to drift off for a few minutes' sleep.

When I opened my eyes, it was with the pressing thought that I should get moving in order to make it back to the hut before dark. I quickly yawned, stretched out in the little nook that I was lying in, and stood up, poking my head above a shoulder of rock that I'd been unwittingly hidden behind. And there he was.

The Creature was squatted beside a small pool where the trail – which I was noticing for the first time – disappeared into the trees, scooping water into his mouth with his fingers, drops streaming through the hair on the back of his hand. And though I'd studied their prints and the markings of their teeth, and had even seen one of their silhouettes, the first thing I realized – almost with a bit of disappointment – was that they didn't look anything close to what I'd imagined they would. His limbs were slender, and his entire body was covered in fairly long, dense fur that was light brown. He had a petite nose and dark-rimmed eyes that were wide open and framed with darker fur, which grew in a pattern that made a serious, if anxious expression. It was somehow important to me that it was a male; probably because I'd always imagined that, in a man-like species, it would have been this gender that advanced in droves over the hills, wielding spears and armour. However, as it turned out, he hardly looked threatening enough to flick a drop of water in my direction.

Our frozen moment didn't last long. After a second or two, the Creature began to stand up, his motions incredibly slow and careful, his eyes fixated on mine, watching, waiting for the slightest hint of aggression, or maybe even of movement. And then, as soon as he'd postured enough to be able to use his legs, and without warning, he suddenly spun on his heals, planted his hands on the ground to shove off into a desperate run, and in one fluid leap, disappeared behind the leaves that overhung the trail, and was gone.

I waited for a few minutes, trying to see into the shade of the undergrowth, looking for a sign of him, knowing perfectly well that I wasn't going to find one, that he was still sprinting away through the trees. Eventually, I hopped along the boulders and inspected his tracks, confirming that he was, in fact, a real Creature. And while I was kneeling down, running a finger along his imprint in the soil, I heard his sad, three-note call above the rumble of the water. I obviously couldn't hear any responses echoing it in the distance, but I know that if I had, I wouldn't have been afraid – or even, for that matter, mildly intimidated. Not anymore.

I smiled; then I threw my head back and laughed, louder, hysterically, until I tipped over on the ground and had to lean on an arm. I felt like a complete idiot. And I felt like this because, well, I had been an idiot. I had just spent a full week of my life meticulously constructing an enemy out of thin air. And then, as if that weren't enough, I'd wasted my time and energy (even losing a little blood) building a series of cunning devices and escape routes that would combat this imaginary threat of mine.

But now, finally, I had seen the Creatures for what they were. They didn't have clothes, sculpt gourds to drink from, organize armies, have a trading system, fashion weapons, and they certainly didn't carve out precise instruments to communicate with – they were just tooting to one another with their mouths in a whistling sound that I'd never heard before, which also happened to be somewhat flute-like. And the fact that they belted out a series of distress calls while running away from me wasn't really anything strange or surprising – almost every animal does it in some way – I had just chosen to see it as mysterious. No, the Creatures were nothing more than some kind of large monkey, and if I'd had research material with me, I

340

could have simply flipped through the pages until I found them and read all about their habits and habitat, maybe even learning the name of the sugary melon they liked to feed on.

And the more I thought about them without some degree of anxiety clouding the images, the more things seemed to fall into place, making sudden and perfect sense. I imagined that, being both primates and ground foragers, they were simply filling in a niche that had opened up when people disappeared. There were probably countless orchards and groves on the mainland that had gradually become abandoned, but, as they were fairly interspersed and wouldn't produce fruit all year round, the only kind of animal that could take full advantage of them would be one that had evolved to travel long distances, and climb trees. The Creatures (which could have been transported to or from any one of the continents by humans long ago) had merely slotted into an opportune role, in which they were happily flourishing.

Yet I had chosen to see them as something else, something dangerous and menacing; and I had done this despite all my education, despite how 'conscious' and 'aware' I'd been trained to be. In exactly the same way that every culture had done before me, from primitive tribes to the most advanced civilizations, I had fabricated a myth that I could patiently feed the crumbs of my fear to. And, like them, I'd created something that could be touched, could be deterred by traps, could be tricked and lured into the wrong direction and washed away – something that could be controlled. For all my access to wisdom, I wasn't any better off. In fact, had the crew been with me, I'm sure we would have collectively convinced ourselves that we should set out to trap the Creatures, hunt them down, maybe even exterminate them completely, all while being thankful that the greatest peril in our world happened to be one that we could rid ourselves of. And we would do this, unknowingly, as the only way to appease the same phobia that exists in every human being: the fear that there might be something skulking in the shadows that has the potential to do to us, the things that we do to each other every single day.

It's interesting that I wasn't really frustrated at myself for not becoming aware of this earlier, that I wasn't annoyed at having displayed such predictable, conventional stupidity. I think I felt buoyant more than anything else, as if a weight had been lifted from my shoulders. I stood up, light, contented, and hiked back along the streambed, arriving at the hut with the last bit of usable light. For some reason, I was compelled to take the raven out of its cage and sleep beside it on the ground outside. It absolutely relished in this little bit of freedom, hopping around and flapping to exercise its wings, making continual clicking and murmuring sounds, pecking at unseen things in the grass. It never really seemed to settle down that night, continuing to flit around for hours, a fidgety dark shape invisible in the dark beside me. But its restlessness didn't bother me; I was busy watching the pulsing sheet of stars until I could make out their insistent, sluggish rotation, the sky slowly pivoting on its axis. I felt completely free, in the way we do after stumbling upon a morsel of real truth.

38

I had neglected my work on the terrace for almost a week, and it took me a while to catch up, watering the sorry-looking seedlings with buckets from the river, harvesting fruit that was overripe, and weeding around the vegetables.

Once this was under control and I had a bit more time, I started experimenting with different methods of drying fruit in the sun, as it proved impossible to eat an entire tree's worth of produce that all became ripe at the same time. After quite a few trials, I did figure out a way to dry thin strips of certain fruits until they became rubbery slices that wouldn't spoil for about a month.

All of these projects kept me busy for most of the day, and the days themselves began to pass by more easily, the raven and I settling into a kind of comfortable routine. We would wake up, eat some food, and go out to the terrace to begin working. Then, I would take a break at midday, eat something more and rest, usually sitting in the shade and talking things over with the bird – sometimes dithering my way through weighty deliberations, but most of the time just nattering on about trivial nonsense; the bird appearing to listen distractedly to it all. In the afternoon, I would work for a shorter period of time, and then go for a walk below the terrace, sometimes collecting other foods as I looked for beetles. When I returned, we would eat again, the bird gurgling enthusiastically at the sight of the plump insects in the jar before I spilled them out in front of it. We would relax after that, watching the slow day turn into night, and would retire into the hut after we'd seen the first few stars open their eyes.

As the weeks melted away, the bird continued to improve and look healthier. It had grown back most of the feathers it had lost while bouncing between the walls of the buildings, and when it was outside of its cage and tied to the rock, I noticed that it was flapping its wings with more force, beating stronger surges of air down at the ground, the grass rippling out in waves that were deeper, more defined. And, to be honest with myself, I think I'd been pushing most of these facts away for quite some time, convinced that it needed only 'a few more days' before it could be considered fully recovered. However, it was becoming increasingly difficult to do so. It was ready. And we both knew it.

It was during a midday rest when I finally ventured to say this aloud. "So…" I sighed.

The raven cocked its head and looked at me for a moment, and then quickly darted its attention elsewhere. (This was completely normal for us. I spent most of my time talking to the back of its head.)

"I've been thinking about letting you go."

It looked in my direction for another second and then looked away, as if dismissing what I'd just said, as if sure that I didn't really have the backbone to follow through with such words. I craned my neck up at the sky, like I was trying to gauge whether or not the conditions were suitable for flying. "Okay. Yeah, I might have kept you a bit longer than I should have. But… you know, it's…"

The raven crouched down, looking at me just long enough to blink its sharp eyes, and then cocked its head up at the trees exactly as I had done, only with a great deal more authenticity.

I picked up the knife and leaned in toward it. The bird suddenly stiffened, posturing as if to make itself look taller, attentively watching me. And while I struggled to cut the mess of frayed rope around its foot (which I'd never felt the need to replace) I had to duck under the shade of its body to see what I was doing. It was amazing, this level of trust that I'd somehow gained, the bird standing rigid and patient as I ran a blade back and forth within a hair's-breadth of its leg. In fact, it didn't even take advantage of the tempting proximity of my head or hands to peck at them.

I spoke as I was cutting the last strand, "You can come back for insects or fruit anytime, you know." And without even waiting for the bird to seem like it had acknowledged this offer, I sliced through the final thread and pulled the rope out from under its shadow. "Okay?"

Veracity

The raven, probably feeling the sensation of something missing from its leg, hopped forward into the grass, its head cocking in quick directions at the tops of the trees. It jumped forward again, and, realizing that it was further from the rock than it had ever been, it squatted to the ground for a fraction of a second, and then leapt into the air with an explosion of flapping wings. I thought it might hesitate once it reached the height where it was usually snapped back to the ground, but it didn't waver in the least. It understood it was free.

I watched my friend rise into the air, healed and healthy, spiralling upwards in long graceful arcs, its dark fingers pointing rigid and proud at the horizon on either side of it. The stubborn earth was finally passing under its body, the terrain broadening like an ocean with every circle as it climbed higher. Dana had once told me that the majority of cultures that had existed believed that animals (excluding our important selves, of course) weren't capable of emotion. I would have liked to have one of those ignorant people beside me then, watching that bird flap and glide in slow, beautiful rings that expanded with every new line it traced. True, I can't pretend to know what it was feeling, but anyone, regardless of how imperceptive they were, could see that it was some form of elation, a kind of euphoria, a type of celebration that we would never be able to partake in, but could at least witness, admire. Soaring high overhead, its serrated black shape finally began to drift out of view, and after giving out one last giggling murmur, was gone; leaving me with a smile that drew a long line across my face for the rest of the day.

It seemed reasonable to think I would never see the bird again, but this wasn't the case. Several days later, while resting in the midday heat, I heard it flutter noisily into one of the fruit trees. I walked out into the open until I could see it perched on one of the boughs, studying me with quick twitches of its head, as per usual.

"Well hello! Have you come for some food, my friend?" I called out. To which it promptly jumped into the air and flew away without ceremony.

But it returned a couple of days later, and this time, instead of speaking to it, I quickly found one of its favourite

345

fruits, cut it into tiny cubes, sprawled them on the grass in the centre of the trees, and walked back to where I'd been when it first arrived. After a long while the bird swept down and plucked one of the pieces from the ground, flying away immediately afterwards. It was wary, suspicious of me; which was only understandable.

However, that suspicion slowly faded, and it returned again, and again, sometimes staying for a few minutes, making its gurgling noises, or calling out from one of the trees with its grating, metallic 'toks'. More often than not, it would fly away right after it finished eating, though other times it would return to one of the trees and clean its beak before flying off. It even happened a few times that it didn't eat at all, but only slouched over on a branch, watching me for minutes at a time with a serious, brooding silence. I was glad when this happened, as it seemed to verify that I wasn't alone in feeling a kind of connection or friendship between us.

So I was always half-prepared for the raven to drop out of the sky for a visit, and spent a lot of my day looking over my shoulder. And I found that this constant anticipation of the sound of wings, along with looking up at every shape that flew across the sky between the branches, heightened my awareness to other birds as well. The shrill peeps and tiny songs, the ruffle of their miniature bodies coming from the dark spaces under the leaves, their beady eyes scrutinizing the world between the flashing of eyelids, the cluttered flocks of them, falling like leaves, twisting in the wind until it almost became a visible entity. They had always been in my world, but before my experience on the mainland, I don't think I'd ever stopped to appreciate how remarkable they were, how quietly extraordinary. There was something inside them – especially in the raven – that humbled me, that somehow turned my critical views inward. Until, one day, just as this inspired reflection seemed to be cumulating, something happened that would bring me to one of the strangest conclusions I've ever come to.

That day, the raven, which had been eating on the ground in the centre of the trees, sprung into the air and flew away as unannounced as it usually did; only this time, it lost one of its tail

Veracity

feathers as it took flight. As it disappeared over the plateau of bushes, I watched the feather spin to the ground in a slow, fluid spiral, and started walking toward it to pick it up. The early-afternoon sun was casting a hard shadow on the grass at my feet, and when I crouched down to the feather, and brought it out from my shade and into the direct sunlight, it came alive with every colour imaginable, dancing between luminescent shades of purple, blue, and green. Of course, I'd marvelled at the raven's colours before, but there was something very different about holding onto one of its feathers that particular afternoon. I continued to move it between the direct sunlight and the dark of my shadow, the plume shifting from brilliant colours, to a muted black. And then it struck me: this was exactly how a human perceived truth – or, for that matter, how we perceived everything.

I had been thinking about the Creatures a lot before that day; about how I had so easily contorted them into something they weren't, and how I couldn't really explain when or how I'd let that happen. Until it occurred to me that, though I might have begun thinking about them with some degree of objectivity, as time passed, my thoughts had shifted into patterns that were quite different, patterns that could effortlessly sculpt and reshape things that had already been established.

So even before that day, I think I was on my way to the source of the problem, which is that, as intelligent as we are supposed to be, seeing something as a fragment of a much larger and intricate network of relationships, or even just as being multifaceted, is almost impossible for us. Our brains are in love with easy-to-follow timelines, two-dimensional graphs, one-dimensional stories. In fact, so much so that, even if we try to consume things in their initially complex form, our bodies can find a way to override us, can amend the information without our knowing it, crudely breaking it down, splitting it up again and again – always rejecting the more difficult halves – until they deem it a simple enough form to digest. I think things that might be grey in our world are never really taken in as grey according to our mind's eye, that they are transformed into either black or white, that they are turned into a stark enough

347

shade as to be easily-referenced in the future, adjusted until their tone is bold, time-efficient, plain. In other words, if I hadn't seen the Creatures as a dangerous enemy, I would have almost certainly seen them as a docile, harmless animal – but nothing in between. And though the Elders had essentially said the same thing, the more I thought about it that day, the more I realized that it went much, much further than just this natural act of oversimplifying things; in that the act was perpetuated every time we mulled something over, or even just recalled it.

Nothing in our heads is stagnant; not even memories. True, they might seem like the frozen ashes of things that have burned, but what I'd learned through my experience with the Creatures was that, each time we blew on those ashes (in order to get the picture we wanted to see in the smoke), each time we consciously recalled a fact, a suspicion, opinion, or emotion, we also altered the shape that it was in when we'd first haphazardly stored it – the act of bringing something to mind was also the act of displacing our already tentative reference points. If I thought, for example, about a simple piece of cloth that I had found inside the hut and thrown away, and tried to remember the exact size, texture, pattern, and colour of it, I knew that the more I rolled these 'facts' over in my mind, the more imprecise they became. (This, I'd already proven to myself through countless examples in my life where I was positive I was right about some stupid, confirmable fact, and turned out to be shockingly wrong.) And, as if this weren't disturbing enough, I realized that, while the accuracy of the things in our minds are diminished by revisiting them, our conviction in their accuracy actually increases each time it's revisited. Meaning: the further we drift away from the truth, the more convinced we are that we have cleverly sailed right to it, and have been there all along.

I knew that it could only be evolution that was responsible for this, and so tried to think of ways that it might be advantageous to see the things that our complex species did – while living in a complex world, and wading through complex situations – as simple, as reasonable. And the answer I came up with was that oversimplification was the very thing that allowed us to make definitive judgments, to draw rigid lines through things, divide them, dominate them; whereas without it, we could only waver, hesitant and unsure, lost in a precarious pattern of inaction, always waiting for more information to decide, growing hungry, letting possible dangers loom closer. Evolutionarily, it doesn't really matter that none of our ridiculous categories or divisions exist – good people, bad people, right, wrong – because in nature, actions speak louder than truth.

So it wasn't that we were 'innately horrible' as much as it was that we were perfectly wired to deceive ourselves, constructed to fumble around in a blurry existence, certain that that blurriness was translucent, even illuminated. We were designed to whole-heartedly believe in the individual worlds that we constructed and then reconstructed, to believe in our opinions, our interpretations, our philosophies, even when others' ideas (or, often enough, our own) glaringly contradicted them. We were made to carefully quarantine our beliefs from reason, and then live for them, die for them, kill for them.

Which all seemed to be leading me into an intimidating direction. Because if this were right, then that meant that everyone's beliefs, especially ones that had been held over a long period of time and had been constantly recalled, reinforced, and re-established, could only be, at best, fairly questionable. How much certainty could really be left in the Elders' doctrines, after having been rationalized and re-rationalized thousands of times over? Hadn't they said that veracity – that path that I was supposedly walking along – was the undying dedication to truth, a devotion to upholding the accuracy of our reality? Yet, how could anyone profess to be doing this, when the 'upholding' was the very thing that corroded the accuracy?

I was finally starting to understand. The one greatest lie that we can ever tell ourselves is that we're not lying to ourselves. Because we are. We do. Everyday. The Elders didn't have the truth about what we are; in the same way that none of us does. It was just that I had chosen to believe them, that I had searched high and low for things that would support what they said, and then revisited the contradictions in my mind until I had chiselled them down into something dismissible. And, now that I

349

was seeing that their 'far-sighted' and 'advanced' ideas were just as lazy as everyone else's, I was forced to think back to some of the contradictions that I'd so carefully dismissed.

And as I did this, I quickly found that the weakest parts of their arguments always stemmed from the same thing, which was that they insisted on blanketing every part of every person as fundamentally malevolent. I had personally witnessed enough on the ship to know otherwise, to know that there were other things woven into that malevolence as well. As much as it might be true that we all had the capacity to be vindictive and pitiless, what Onni had taught me was that, from time to time, we also had the ability to be somewhat kind.

And as soon as I could admit to this, I found that it was possible to imagine someone like Onni in every depraved situation throughout history. For every stoning, I was suddenly sure that there were the people who would push to get to within throwing distance, the swirling crowd that would close in behind them, the people in the back who wanted nothing to do with it, and someone else who might have snuck the 'target' a sip of water during the night. For every genocide, I'm sure there were the set of ruthless organizers, the executioners, the compliant mass, and a tiny group of people that hid the persecuted, or even helped them to escape. And I understood that the existence of these individuals would be hard to prove, as I'm sure that historians, like all people, had a tendency to string the past together through its wounds. I understood that if we pressed our ears up against the doors of our race, that only the bellowing echoes of destruction would be heard – but I also understood that this wasn't because the screams were alone in there, it was because the kindnesses were being whispered.

Which, I realized, was something that Kara had always known. I remembered what she had said when I showed her the paintings, that they were about how we are worse than we think we are, and better. (I still find it amazing that she figured this all out long before I'd recognized that there was something that needed figuring out. She'd even tried to pass her understanding down to me; but, unfortunately, I was incapable of holding onto it at the time. Which is the problem with wise words: they can only be as wise as the people taking them in. They are unable to teach us anything, endow us with anything, they merely outline things that we've always known in some distant and murky way – and if we don't know them, or aren't ready to see them, no matter how concise or poignant those words are, their insight simply slides over our skin and dissolves around us like fog.) And what Kara had understood was that there is nothing more naïve than cynicism, that the notion of our being 'all bad' is just as crude and one-dimensional as the notion that we are 'all good'. She had come to recognize that pessimism is the act of blinding ourselves from the beauty in everything, and optimism the act of blinding ourselves from the ugliness; but that, regardless, they are both rooted in laziness. And it's crazy to think that, in the end, if there was anyone on the island who was 'as close to the truth as we could get', it was her, one of the few people who would live their entire existence without ever knowing anything about the lies she was raised in.

A bird fluttered into one of the fruit trees and I looked up to see if it was the raven again; but it wasn't. I couldn't say how long I'd been there, mesmerized, staring at the feather in my hand, moving it in and out of the light, carving something in the air in front of me that seemed to make sudden and perfect sense.

Eventually, I tucked the feather into a tuft of grass, intending to leave it there. But after I walked a few steps, I stopped, went back, and picked it up, deciding, in the end, to bring it into the hut with me. I placed it on the table, where it would become a fixture in the still air of the room, curled up at the ends, balancing delicately.

39

The life that I led on the terrace wasn't an exciting one by any stretch of the imagination, but I think that contentment rarely is. The days seemed long, unhurried, though the weeks somehow short, the months shorter. I would wake with the sun, often to the sounds of the raven gliding in and landing on the ridge of the roof with a few deep flaps, its feet scratching at the wood as it settled itself to perch. When I stepped outside it would fly away, only to return again at some point during the day, usually while I was within reaching distance of some fruit that could be cut up and thrown onto the grass. In the afternoon, when I sat down to rest and looked out over the land below, I would sometimes think about the conclusion that I'd come to with the feather, even managing to feel strangely enlightened by it at times, this understanding that we don't have it in us to be enlightened. Though, more often I would think about how I was living on time that was stolen, how I was alive and well because I had stood on the backs of others, had pushed them down, or had at least made the most of their bad luck. Yet, if anything, I think that this drove me to appreciate the time that I had even more, to hold it in my hands as assiduously as a thief should. I had become swollen with gratitude, and, for the first time in my life, I felt peaceful.

And it occurs to me now that this is where my story could have ended, that those months might have turned into years, then decades, and, slowly, like some of the Elders, I would have begun to move more languidly, to struggle a bit with getting out of bed, to squint at the details in the landscape, and, in due course, curl up and die. I might even have been expecting this to happen, might have been resolved to it in some quiet way. But that would change.

On the night that everything shifted in my life, it happened that the sky was clearer than usual, and so I'd decided to spend a little more time out on the terrace after dark. For months prior to that, I hadn't heard or seen the slightest trace of the Creatures, and had I not been standing on a section of the terrace furthest from the river, I probably wouldn't have heard them that night, either. But, suddenly, there it was, their distinctive call, the same haunting three notes that they'd always used as a warning after sighting me. Only this time they were coming from so far away that it couldn't possibly be me they were warning against. It had to be something else – another person. Other people.

It's interesting to think of my reaction, how automatic it was, how flustered. I ran back to the hut, swung the door open, ripped the blanket from my bed, threw some things inside it that I would need to sustain myself for a few days (including some of my precious dried fruit), and ran back outside. I headed upstream and had even passed the boulders before I started to admit that I was being a bit melodramatic. Finally, I slowed down enough to actually think about what I was doing.

I understand why I'd overreacted; I knew that if there were human eyes in the land below, they would be able to tell that the terrace was being cultivated, and so could assume that the hut – which was the very first thing a person's eyes were drawn to when looking up at the skyline from downstream – was inhabited. However, it was also impossible to guess at these people's (or this person's) intentions. They could have been anyone; members of another expedition that had strayed off course, or maybe only a solitary man or woman who was looking for a few different seeds to cultivate, as I had done. What if they meant no harm? Or better yet, what if they were afraid of me, and were making a point to steer clear of the hut?

Then it occurred to me that, even if it was a group of ruthless scavengers, if I chose to run, I would leave myself unarmed with vital information, like how many there were, whether or not they had weapons, or if it looked like they were going to pursue. It didn't make much sense to leave my secure life without even knowing what it was I was abandoning it for. Besides, I rationalized, I already had a system of escape ready, which meant that whatever they turned out to be, I could afford to wait until they were quite close – probably even close enough to gauge how dangerous they were.

Eventually, I returned to the hut. Though, wanting to be on the safe side, I didn't spend the night there, knowing that the building would be the very first place a person would inspect when they arrived. Instead, I decided to sleep on the bare and relatively soft soil under the shrubs, choosing a place that was close to the river, and therefore my escape route. I told myself that, with the first light, I would crawl out of my hiding spot and watch from the edge of the terrace throughout the day, looking for movement, waiting. I had to repeat to myself, over and over again, that I had nothing to worry about, that I had planned for this, that I was prepared.

40

"I'm sure he's long gone," Mikkel called out. His voice, which had sounded deliberately loud, came from just below the edge of the terrace, and was cut short by some quick and indiscernible retort. Then, as if it had never happened at all, there was nothing, only the crisp quiet of the morning.

I don't know what I dreamt. I don't remember anything about that night. I only remember opening my eyes to the sound of Mikkel's voice, and seeing a soft light on the knot of shrubs in front of my eyes, an ant crawling slowly and determined on the underside of one of the branches.

I shot up, my chest thumping, my breathing shallow, fast, uncontrollable, the dry taste of panic in my mouth. I swallowed to try and calm myself. I had to think. I couldn't panic. I had to be present.

I looked up at the sky. It was incredibly early.

My mind replayed Mikkel's words. I thought of how loud they'd been, how tersely they were shushed. He was trying to warn me, give me a window of time to get out of the hut and run. And that was all I had, a window of time, a sliver of it – which was only lessening with each second I thought about its length. I had to move. Quickly.

I stood up to run, but then looked down at everything that was sprawled on the ground beneath me. I couldn't afford to leave any of it. So I crouched to throw it all in the blanket: the bag of dried fruit, the knife, the plastic bottle. Then, after twirling the cloth – thorns catching on it as it spun, everything seeming to slow me down, to hinder me – I flung it around my chest and ducked under the space where I'd crawled into the shrubs the night before. Finally, I was out in the bright air of the terrace, squinting, looking around for a solution. But instead of finding one, my eyes were drawn to the hut, to the shadows cast on the grass behind it. They were moving. I looked upstream where I hoped the rope was still dangling, and did the math. If I ran, the crew would see me, and follow as fast as they could.

There was no way I would make it. In fact, the chase would probably only last a minute. Maybe less.

I turned around and scurried back into the cover of the bushes, realizing that the dirt I was uncovering by doing so would be another colour, would be evidence that I was there. I mouthed a curse and squatted down to watch their bobbing shadows lengthen along the grass.

Toivo was just coming into view. I eyed him, mortified, waiting for an indication that he'd seen me. But he hadn't. He was holding a spear out in front of him – a long stick with a knife that had been tightly bound to the end of it. I noticed that a pink line now divided his throat into two halves, which, apparently, was my doing. Knut was next, also holding a spear; though his was raised over his shoulder, ready to plunge. He was a little distance behind Toivo, trying to balance himself between avoiding the brunt of my potential counter-assault, and being close enough to the violence to make the calls. Niels was next, walking as guiltily as always; and then Aimil, whose wounds had healed badly and had formed a jagged scar across his face. Mikkel was the last to come into view, and, though all of them carried the same type of makeshift spear, he was the only one treating it more like a walking stick than a weapon.

They crept to the front of the hut, grouping together, waiting for everyone to gather before they rushed through the door. While they did this, I watched the grass behind the building for signs of Onni's shadow stretching along the ground, lagging behind like I could picture him doing. But the crew didn't seem to be waiting for anyone else after Mikkel had joined them, and for the first time I knew, conclusively, that Onni was dead.

A few of them nodded at each other, and Toivo's head suddenly jerked into the air as he kicked in the door, which yielded easier than he was anticipating. As it swung open, they all took a step back, crouching slightly, gripping their spears, ready for the onslaught. When nothing stirred inside, some of their shoulders slumped with disappointment. This wasn't what they'd expected. After they exchanged a few looks, Toivo took the initiative and poked his spear into the building, entering reluctantly after it, his head darting to either side of the door as he crossed the threshold, maybe fearing that he'd be bitten a second time. Knut followed closely at his back.

At the same moment, both Niels and Aimil looked over their shoulders, seeming to suspect that I was nearby, and maybe even still within eyeshot. I concentrated on keeping my chest from visibly heaving, knowing that the slightest movement or sound would give me away. And though everything in me wanted to just break out of the bushes and run, I understood that the only chance I had was to outwait them – as unbearable as that might prove to be.

The crew, seeming more than a little confused by my absence, started to mumble and spread out, beginning to either look for me, or for clues of which direction I'd fled. I was amazed with the manner in which they did this. It was unflustered, logical, and completely systematic. They knew exactly what they were doing, moving out in small circles, carefully watching where they stepped, pressing their feet into the soil beside my footprints to compare how fresh my tracks were, crouching to inspect the divots left by some of the tools that I'd been using the previous day. And this all seemed to be second nature to them, routine, which meant that they had been hunting me for a while, that they'd grown used to scouring the land for clues.

They had probably guessed that I would be along a watercourse, and had used the maps on the ship to locate all of the drainages in the area. And, after searching the closest one to where they'd landed and not finding any sign of me, they'd probably just patiently moved onto the next – and then the next. Considering the resources they had, the manpower, the information of where I'd most likely landed, along with the fact that there were no other people to muddle the clues and tracks that I left behind, finding me would be relatively easy, regardless of our being on a massive continent. And because I'd never imagined them coming to look for me, I'd even helped them out; I'd chosen to use a building in a painfully conspicuous place, and then had proceeded to loaf around there for months. And now that I was watching how delicately they picked through the clues, I could bring to mind a long list of careless evidence that

I'd left behind. The squatting to rest in the soft soil beneath the trees that were just off the road, the stepping into the mud in order to better inspect some tracks that I'd seen, the walking across sheltered dirt in the settlement; all of it, slowly leading the way to the hut, a trail of my footprints – my perfectly unique and distinguishable footprints! How easy I'd made it for them! They had only to link one scattered sign of me to the next, until they eventually spotted the hut on the skyline. Then they'd moved through the deep ravine beside the river to stay hidden, sleeping as close as they could to the terrace in hopes of catching me off guard in the early morning. I'd made myself the perfect sitting duck.

Except for Knut, who stayed in front of the door, they all continued to fan out in search of fresh clues, Mikkel doing a noticeably worse job than everyone else, staying in the same spot and staring down at one of my tracks, leaning heavily on his spear, almost managing to look disinterested. Eventually, some of them came to the trees in the grove, and quickly plucked a few pieces of fruit from the branches, tossing them to others who weren't as close. They had obviously become used to pillaging, and it was then that I noticed some of the shining trinkets adorning their spears, which they must have stolen from houses and settlements along the way. None of them were wearing the clothes we'd left the island with, either; instead, they had shirts that were slightly over or undersized, along with some form of footwear, and pants that had been roughly cut to match their height. Physically, they looked exhausted, thinner, their cheekbones sharper than I remembered them being. It occurred to me that they might have had a few ordeals of their own since I'd seen them last.

I heard the shushing of the raven's wings in the air above me, and its black shape soon came into view, coasting toward the crest of the roof where it usually landed. But, when it realized it wasn't me standing in front of the building, it flinched (for lack of a better word), quickly flapping in the opposite direction, climbing higher into the air, its neck darting around to take in the rest of the crew, which it also hadn't seemed to notice until then. I was sure it was going to just turn and fly away as fast as it had come, never to return; but instead, it surprised me, and began to circle, cawing out as if to reproach these visitors that seemed to have mysteriously replaced me. When I considered that the crew were most likely the only other people it had ever seen, I could imagine how confusing it must have been for the poor bird. One human had proven to be strange enough; now there were another five.

Aimil was the first to understand what the racket was all about. He smiled up at the raven and held out his hand, as if there was something inside it.

Niels, noticing this, walked over to him, carefully watching the ground as he stepped, as not to ruin any of my tracks. "What are you doing?" he asked. His voice, which had sounded a touch impatient, could just be heard above the water.

Aimil continued smiling up at the bird, holding his hand out hopefully. "It's Joshua's," he said, matter-of-factly, and took his eyes off the bird for only a moment to point at the remnants of the cage that were leaning against the back of the hut.

With this new information, Knut, who had circled the hut watching the raven, looked down at the ground for a moment, remembering something. Then his face lit up, and he dashed back inside the building. His quick movements caused the others to begin walking back from the trees, and when he burst out through the door again, they could all see him holding the raven's feather high in the air with the greatest of conviction. Though, no one really seemed to understand what this signified – myself included. Nor, I think, did Knut. True, he had linked the feather on the table with the bird in the sky, but from that connection, he could only be making a haphazard guess. It just happened that his guess was right. He waited until everyone was looking at him before he exaggeratedly mouthed the words 'he's still here'.

With this, the crew clutched their spears again, looking over their shoulders and bending their knees, readying themselves for battle, as if I'd raised a massive army in the few minutes that they'd lowered their guard, and was about to ambush them. They began to spread out once more, only searching more intently this time, a growing circle of busy heads scanning the ground.

My limbs drew in closer to my torso, my body trying to make itself smaller, more discreet.

I watched Knut, as he seemed to be the most frenzied of them all, the most consumed, his lips pursed into a tiny line, wide eyes raking across the grass and dirt, getting ever closer to the place I was hidden.

I started to move my arm, very slowly, reaching back, my hand weaving through the folds of the blanket to get the knife. I didn't know what I intended to do with it. I had no plan, no strategy.

I watched as Knut's eyes fell across the set of footprints that would lead directly to me, saw him follow the tracks until he reached the dirt that had just been disturbed, the soil that had drawn in the moisture of the evening, unnaturally spilling its darkness over the dry. His gaze rose slightly higher, and he squinted directly at me, trying to make out movement, trying to decipher my shape.

I could do nothing but stare at him, stock-still and breathless, feeling the sting of regret that I hadn't slit his throat when I had the chance.

The raven cawed somewhere above us.

Finally, his expression softened into recognition, and he took a hand off his spear and pointed a rigid finger at my face, "He's there!" he screamed. "He's right there!"

My ears rang. It was over.

Instinctively, I stood up. Then I jumped out into the light with the knife in my hand, and twisted my body to throw it as hard as I could in Knut's direction. I remember seeing him fall to the ground to duck from it, covering his head with his arms. Unfortunately the knife widely missed its mark, and I heard it clang and bounce twice off of rocks as I turned upstream. I started to run, huge steps pulling me forward.

They were shouting directions and encouragements to each other as they filed into line behind me, running as fast as I was, or faster. To the raven, we must have looked like a furious procession of swinging arms and plunging legs, a queue of

360

gangly animals with inconsistent coats, who chose to impede their natural gait by holding onto long sticks for no apparent reason. But there was a reason, of course, which became evident when one of those sticks was hurled into the air, landing in the soil just to my left. Another flew over my shoulder, rattling between the rocks on the bank in front of me.

So I wasn't thinking about the trap I'd constructed when I veered to my right and started up the hill; it was simply the only option I had to make myself less vulnerable to the spears. But when I saw the mesh of boulders right in front of me, and getting closer, I remembered, and I had the distant feeling that things were beginning to fall into place.

I ran up to it and grabbed onto the release mechanism, squatting down and pushing the thin log upwards as hard as I could. Nothing budged. There wasn't a creak or a splinter, nor the least bit of movement. I leaned against the corroded wires and took in a few breaths of air, shooting a look down the hill. Toivo was closest, doing his utmost to get to me while I was stopped. The others were close behind, Knut among them, trying to get ahead, hoping to be close to me when it happened, when someone finally drove the knife-end of their spear into my flesh. Mikkel, however, was still at the bottom, and I could hear him barking commands for everyone to stop, to come back; he'd even screamed the word 'trap'. But it was no use, they were caught up in the chase, they had become deaf and blind to everything but blood. Which was fine by me.

I grabbed the thin log again and pushed up with every bit of desperate energy I had, my muscles trembling under the weight, until I heard a snap. I continued to push until I heard another snap, followed quickly by another. The sounds were being made as the reinforcements, which tied the log to the wire mesh, ruptured. The massive rocks began to shift in their dainty cage, and then to crawl forward, rumbling as they ground against each other, until finally, the rusted structure burst open in several places at the same time, and released the boulders onto the slope.

Toivo, who had almost reached me, was the first to recognize the jeopardy they were in. He stopped dead in his tracks, and after pausing for only an instant, spun on his heels and began running back down the hill. He leapt past the others, and there was something so desperate in his movements that caused them to stop and look up. One by one, they focused on the rolling boulders for the same petrified instant, came to the same conclusion, and whirled around to retreat in a wave of flinging hands and bouncing heads, which rode above a cloud of dust and dirt that they were turning up, spears arcing through the air as they were cast aside. The boulders tumbled close in their wake, gaining sluggish speed and digging deep holes into the hillside as they collided with the soil. It was patently understood that if they didn't win the race to the bottom of the slope and scuttle to one of the sides, they would be killed.

I watched the mayhem unfold, stupidly remaining there, feeling somewhat satisfied with the panic I'd caused. I could see Knut's blonde hair through all the chaos, and concentrated only on him, wishing that he would fall, that he would lose his balance and miss the thinning window of time to get out of the way. I pictured him holding up his arms as one of the boulders sunk into his body, and could imagine the dull clatter of his bones cracking beneath his skin. I bent my every will toward this, wishing for it to happen, watching the spinning surfaces of the rocks and hoping, with every ounce of my being, that they would quash the life from him. But, in the end, he would live. They would all live.

I watched them round the corner, shoving and fighting to get in front of one another, the boulders passing just behind them and crashing into the river with watery clunks and wide-fanning splashes.

And all at once, I seemed to wake from the idiotic daze that was keeping me there. I started scurrying along the slope until I met up with the river again, and continued running upstream. When I got to the rope, I didn't turn around to see how far they were behind me; I only jumped onto it and started hoisting myself up. As soon as I'd climbed into the shrubs, I turned and quickly yanked on the line, hoping they wouldn't already be ascending it, as I no longer had a knife to cut it. But it was free of weight, and I hauled it up, hand over hand, as fast as I could. When the entire length of it was tangled in the branches around me, I felt safe enough to look down into the canyon. I saw Niels there, looking up at me, his spear in hand. His expression was neutral, calculating, wondering how I'd accessed the top to tie the rope in the first place, and probably already thinking over ways he could do the same, knowing that they would have to get to that same place in order to pick up my trail. Then he looked past me for a moment, up into the morning sky at my back. I didn't have to hear the raven to know what he was looking at, but it called out nonetheless.

I untied the rope and stuffed it inside the blanket, thinking that at least this way, they would all have to fight through the tangled barrier of shrubs to get there. Then I slung the blanket over my chest, turned into the bushes, and started running for my life.

41

The bushes had grown back quite a bit, and the spines, having healed and replaced themselves, caught and ripped both the blanket and my skin as I passed through them, beads of blood seeping from the scratches on my arms and under my shirt. As I didn't have a knife, I had no choice but to twist and yank out some of the new branches that were netting the spaces I'd cleared, ripping telltale scars along the bark and leaving an incredibly easy trail to follow.

After a long battle, I jumped into the other end of the canyon and began heading up the river. I kept up a good pace, only slowing down every now and then to throw a piece of dried fruit in my mouth and drink from the stream, water still dripping from my chin as I hurried on. When I made it past the giant rock where I'd seen the Creature, I could tell, judging by the sun in the sky, that I was moving faster than I had that day. Which was crucial, knowing that the ground I gained while they fought through the bushes to access the trail was the only thing I had in my favour.

There were times during that first day – while rushing over the rocks, my arms out to the sides to help me balance – that I would catch a glimpse of the raven watching me from a branch that hung over the bank. It would fly away as I approached, but would always reappear later on, a flashing set of eyes over my shoulder, a kind of obscure, recurring presence.

I travelled until after dark, until it had become too dangerous to continue (as twisting an ankle or cutting one of my feet would have slowed me to a crawl, making the chase that much shorter for them). I felt my way to the soil under a tree and wrapped myself in the blanket, staring out into the dark, wild, fidgety. And, afraid of sleeping through even a few minutes of the morning's usable light, I chose to stay awake, to watch the grey rocks beside the river until they had enough shape and definition to step on again.

Veracity

On the second day, the river began to cut into that other zone of vegetation that I'd sighted when I encountered the Creature. It was just as sparse as I'd thought it would be, and would have made for easy travel were I not so reluctant to move away from the stream. The reason I was hesitant was that, not only was it difficult to find water on the mainland, but the fact that I didn't have sandals meant I wouldn't be able to move nearly as fast as I could on the rounded rocks and stretches of loose pebbles beside the river. I imagined myself heading into the sparse trees, swerving in every direction to try and mislead them, hobbling over the thorns and sharp rocks as they fanned out behind me with their sturdy footwear and well-honed tracking eyes, effortlessly gaining ground. No, I was sure that moving away from the river would put me at a disadvantage in every way; so I decided to continue along it, gambling on the hope that I would come across a better option somewhere along the way. And until I found or thought of that option, I would just have to move as fast as, or faster than they were.

And I have to admit that, on the second night, after finding a tree to wait under in the dark again, I thought that was exactly what I'd done. I was exhausted, having run at a decent speed for most of the day, but was also somewhat smug, leaning back, convinced that I'd managed to widen the gap between us, that the number of frenzied miles I'd travelled would be impossible for the worn-down crew to match. I settled between the roots of the tree, staring in the same obsessive way at the rocks in front of me, waiting for enough light to keep running. As it happened, there was a light breeze against my face, which, after a few hours, would carry with it an unmistakable message. It was incredibly weak and fleeting when it came, but the smell could not be mistaken. Smoke. I couldn't stop myself from swearing aloud when I was sure of it, pounding a fist on the hollow-sounding earth beside me. They had made torches, and were continuing to cover ground through the night.

Yet, I also knew that tracking me – by distinguishing overturned pebbles from the ones that weren't, or finding a barely-missing footprint in the fine silt covering of a rock – would be impossible to do by torchlight. Which meant that the

365

only thing the crew were really concerned with was covering ground, that they had no reason to track me, that somehow they were confident in predicting where I was going. Maybe this was because they had maps and knew that this was the only watercourse nearby, and that if I ventured away from it I would eventually die of thirst. Or maybe, as they could see from my tracks that I didn't have footwear, they had figured out that the smooth rocks beside the water were the only part of the terrain I could run on, and so would be forced to stay there to move as fast as them. Maybe the only challenge they saw in catching me was in simply closing the distance between us, which, it seemed, they had already found a way to do.

But then it crossed my mind that I could use this certainty of theirs against them, that this might be the golden opportunity I'd been waiting for. Because while the crew were travelling through the dark, it would be impossible to verify whether or not I was still moving along the river; and if, with the first light of day, they realized that there was no sign of me in front of them, they would have to turn around and backtrack to the point where they had last seen evidence of me, having to search over their own tracks for the spot where I'd entered the trees. Which meant that if I could time my leaving the river to coincide with a stretch of it that they would be travelling along at night, it would buy me hours of time, maybe an entire day, and maybe it would even cause them to lose my trail altogether.

I tried to speculate how much ground they might have gained in total, estimating how long it would have taken them to cut their way along the rim of the canyon to the trail, how far smoke could travel in the wind and still be detected, and how much faster they would be moving with footwear. In the end, I guessed that they were a bit over half a day behind me. From this, I planned to continue upstream until about mid-afternoon, where I would hopefully find a long stretch of rocky shore – or some other land feature that would yield as little evidence of my passing as possible – and then carefully slip into the trees there. It was the best chance I had.

As with the day before, I began moving with the first usable light, running whenever I could. By midday, the land was opening up, the trees thinning ever more, exposing long sweeping hills that rose on either side of the river; hills that were covered with a coat of short, dry grass, and that ended with jagged ridges that notched the skyline. However, when the time that I'd planned to leave the river came, I was never more hesitant to do it. Nothing was the way that I'd pictured it. Firstly, I wouldn't be able to move under the cover of vegetation, and if I'd underestimated them, and they arrived earlier, they would be able to see me from a long way off, scampering over the naked ground between the trees. Also, in this new, grassy terrain, the shores of the river had become muddy for the very first time, and I imagined that regardless of how careful I was, I would still leave behind some kind of obvious indication that I had stepped over the bank.

I kept walking to look for a better place, and ended up searching for much longer than I'd wanted to before coming across something suitable, which was a small, dried up tributary to the river. I filled up my water bottle before I started tiptoeing into it, disturbing as few rocks and vegetation as possible. Then, after walking along this streambed for almost an hour, I found a place where I could climb out of it without leaving a trace, and was finally standing on the grassy slope among the thinly scattered trees.

Once there, I tried to look for the shortest possible route up the valley side, where I would be able to disappear over the ridge. I decided to head for a rocky saddle that seemed quite close, knowing that, though it was exposed and in plain view from the river, once I reached it, there would also be places that I could hide, places where I could watch and see whether or not I'd managed to outmanoeuvre the crew.

The long climb to the saddle was incredibly tiring, and I had to stop to catch my breath in the shade of every low-lying tree, crouching beside it and looking out at the land behind me, hoping that I wouldn't see anything moving beside the water. Once, while I was turned around, I caught sight of a black bird gliding high across the valley, which flew almost directly above me and disappeared over the ridge. It hadn't come close or showed any interest, so I assumed that it wasn't the raven.

I moved on, and as the afternoon turned into evening, I grew increasingly nervous, aware that every step I ascended I was becoming more visible from the river, and that the timeframe of the crew possibly coming into view was getting uncomfortably close. Until, after stopping to rest at one of the last trees on the slope, I decided that the risk of being seen had become too much, and that I would have to wait beneath the shade of the leaves until nightfall, when I could climb the rest of the way under the cover of darkness. I must have sat there for a few hours, drinking most of my water and eating the last of the dried fruit, watching the shadows in the valley swell into a pool of murky dark.

When I felt it was safe enough, I climbed the rest of the way to the ridge, blindly groping along the ground, feeling less grass on my feet and more exposed rock and sharp edges the higher I climbed. And because I had to step so carefully onto things that were impossible to see, it took much longer than I thought it would, and by the time I poked my head above the crest and felt a cool wind drifting up the slope from the other side, I was beyond exhaustion. With the little starlight there was, I could just make out the valley on the other side, which was quite narrow and had a ridge that ran parallel to the one I was standing on. It seemed like the perfect place to vanish.

I felt my way over to a few boulders, tucking myself into a protected corner that looked out onto the valley that I'd come from. I intended on spending the rest of the night there, watching for the crew's torches bobbing alongside the river, and after spotting them, watching them pass by the tributary that I'd used to leave the water, oblivious to the fact that they were losing my trail. And I can't say how long I actually spent like that, alert and waiting; nor can I really remember when it was that I dozed off, or if I'd fought for any length of time to keep my eyes open as the weight of my eyelids became heavier. Though, maybe, considering how tired I was and how little rest I'd had, falling asleep at some point that night might have been inevitable. In the same way that, maybe, what happened the next day might have been inevitable as well.

42

I opened my eyes to the sound of the raven's feathers pulsing air into the ground as it landed, and found myself squinting at a dull, overcast sky. Which is how I stayed for a few seconds, blinking hard, letting my eyes adjust to the light. Then the memory of the crew seemed to wash over me like cold water, and I shot bolt upright, wide-awake, addled. "Shit!" I whispered, quickly scrambling forward to search the valley for movement. But the only motion to be seen was the flickering white of rapids in the distant river, which held to the rocks in the centre of the channel like flame to its fuel.

Having fallen asleep during the night was a serious problem. I had no clue of what I was dealing with anymore: Were they upstream or downstream from the dry tributary? Was I fleeing from people who were hours behind me, or days, or weeks? Could I begin planning ways of eluding them long-term, or was it still just about making a mad dash out of throwing range? I felt like I needed to know these things before I could continue – or at least needed to know something, something that would allow me to make a reasonable guess, something more than the empty speculation that I'd been running on. Anything.

I heard the raven scatter a few pebbles as it hopped forward on the ground to my left. I turned toward it, stunned, remembering that the sound of it landing had woken me; but more importantly, realizing that it had been there for some unknown period of time, probably circling above me, an obvious dark shape against the overcast sky, its thick fingers pointing out the exact place that I was hidden in the rocks. I whispered another curse and started clambering toward it, hoping that, once I'd scared it into the air, it would fly away from the ridge as discreetly as possible – pass unnoticed into another part of the world.

"Go!" I hissed, throwing a hand into the air as I came closer to it. The raven crouched down, threatening to fly away, but didn't, its head confusedly darting in every direction as it tried to understand the sudden and complete change in my disposition. "Go!" I repeated once I'd come much closer to it, though being careful with the volume of my voice. After seeing that this wasn't working, I called out a third time while pretending to throw something at it, which was what finally caused it to take flight. It jumped into the air, climbed high above the ridge, circled once, twice, and then, on the third time, readied itself to land on a prominent rock a good distance from where I was.

I shot a guilty look out at the valley as it landed, sure that the crew's eyes were on me, that they were all pointing at the ridge, focusing at the rocks that lined it, looking for the slightest indication that this was more than just a random black bird loitering on the top of a hill.

I crawled along the ground, as low as I could, until I had dropped just below the ridgeline, where I began again to hobble toward the raven. But before I'd come close enough to make any threatening gestures, it took flight again, circling a few more times while cawing out. It landed a bit further off from where I'd sighted it at first, and began to hop playfully among the rocks as it waited for me to come after it again. It seemed to like this game.

"No, no, no! Please, please... just... GO!!" I finally hollered. The raven, with the safety of distance between us, made one of its gurgling sounds and sprung onto a boulder with what appeared to be nothing short of elated mischief, curiously cocking its head in my direction.

I sighed, defeated, and yet again, started walking toward it, stepping cautiously on the sharp stones, hoping to get close enough this time to throw something, to finally deliver an unmistakable message. "Please go. I really... I just need you to go. Can you do that for me? Just leave me alone? Because it's this simple: if they see you, they'll catch me, and if they catch me, they'll kill me." Just then, I stepped on a painfully sharp stone, having to suck in a burst of air through my teeth. But I didn't stop limping toward my obstinate friend; my pace was unbroken, and becoming more frustrated with every step.

"You just... you don't get what's going on here, okay? I mean – it doesn't matter that you're only some sorry bird that I happened to find, or that I've come to understand a few things and regret a few more, or even that I've abandoned The Goal. None of these things matter to them. Alright?" I bent over and picked up some small stones, but let them spill from my fingers, looking for something better. I chose a fist-sized rock instead, testing its weight in my hand as I straightened up, still cautious to keep my head below the skyline.

I took a few more steps and then stopped. I was close enough. "No, you have no idea what's happening here. Not the running, not me, not the crew. Because you can't. Because it's below you, it's beneath anything you are. Which is all the more reason for you to stay away. I mean – don't you get that much at least? That you don't belong here? That you don't belong anywhere near us... us vile... fetid..." I broke off, biting my lip.

"So just go, will you!" I was trying to hold myself back, trying to contain myself, but couldn't. So I turned and threw the rock with all of the force I had. "I said GO!!"

The bird jumped into the air to get out of the way, but found itself more in the rock's path than it had been on the ground. In mid-flight, it had to twist its body around to narrowly avoid it, maybe even feeling the rock brush against a few of its feathers as it whirled by. But once the danger had passed, the raven recovered quickly, gracefully turning toward the valley that the crew were in, and sweeping low inside of it, its head pointed forward, flying in exactly the opposite direction of where I was standing. There was no hesitation, no doubt. And there never would be. It had finally recognized me for what I was.

I stood there for quite some time, watching its black shape grow smaller, watching the flapping of its wings become more indistinct, until it was only a dark speck against the vegetation, and until that speck seemed to meld into the green and completely disappear.

When I was sure that I'd lost sight of it, I covered my face with my hands, felt the muscles in my arms flex, my fingernails digging into the skin on my forehead. I let out a scream into the flesh of my palms, then screamed again, and began stumbling forward, blindly, moving away from something, or toward it – I don't really know. I took a few steps and then tripped on a rock, crashing to the ground with my hands still pressed against my face. There was pain on my right side, which seemed to be exactly what my body needed to finally let itself cry. And it did.

I don't know how long I lay there, shouting out those long, muffled sobs into my hands, I only know that I didn't have any control over their coming or going, that I wasn't myself – or maybe that I was just too much of myself all at once. Too much frustration. Too much shame. Too much understanding. And it all seemed to come in waves that crashed against the walls of my rib cage, filling my chest until it felt like I would burst, only to subside again, to suddenly sink away, leaving me empty except for a dark trickling at the back of my throat.

When I finally regained some sense of composure, it happened quickly. I stopped and took my hands from my face, looking around as if someone else had moved me to a new spot on the ridge. I was in plain view, making up part of the silhouette against the sky. Not, I thought, that it mattered all that much. If I had caught the crew's attention, it wouldn't have been my sitting in a conspicuous place on the ridge that would have done it, instead it would have been my yelling, or my hurtling fist-sized rocks into the valley they were in, or my pathetic staggering around through the boulders and screaming into my hands. I sniffled, wiped my eyes, felt ridiculous. And with the air of someone trying to shake off a moment in time he wished had never happened by determinedly moving onto the next, I started to busy myself with looking for the crew again, stepping down out of the skyline and squatting against a boulder, blinking to clear my eyes so that I could make out more detail.

I remember that I was adjusting a few uncomfortable rocks beneath me, my head still raised, searching throughout the valley, getting ready for a long wait, when my eyes ran across a few specks in the landscape that I hadn't noticed before. I stopped, focused, the top of my head going numb. It was the crew. And they were climbing the long slope between the river and myself, tiny figures sifting through the few trees, pressing toward me as fast and constant as clouds.

"Oh no," I whispered, regardless of the fact that it was much too late for whispering. I didn't have the time to guess what had gone wrong with my plan, or whether it was the raven or myself that had given me away. But none of these things really needed thinking about, the only thing that mattered was that they'd found me, and were coming as fast as their legs could bring them.

I scrambled to my feet with the same rattled panic that I'd felt the days before, and turned to face the opposite valley, thinking about the blanket for only a second before abandoning it. I ran through the boulders of the crest, and then down the other side of the ridge, where the slope soon turned into runnels of loose stones and soil, which slid and gave as I jumped onto them. I was moving fast, and for a few brief seconds, could even ignore the fact that my feet were bare. I started taking larger strides, sinking deep into the soft scree as I landed, getting closer to the valley floor with each plunge. But somewhere in the middle of the slope, larger rocks started to be mixed in with the loose soil and pebbles of the scree, and before I could slow myself enough, I felt the skin of my left foot rip open against a sharp edge. I slid to a standstill, and had to sit for a few seconds before continuing on, rocking back and forth like a child, holding my foot in my hands, inspecting the blood on my fingers. But before the initial pain had even subsided, I forced myself to get up again, to continue downhill, to run, to keep running. I stole quick glances of the new valley between steps, looking for ideas of where to go, of what to do.

From what I could make out, there were three distinctive zones in the valley: a grassy meadow directly below the saddle – which, like a meniscus, crawled a little way up the ridges on either side of it, an area of scrubby trees that started at the edge of the meadow, and eventually a thicker forest further down. All of these zones were threaded together with a thin and meandering streambed, which appeared to be dry.

My first instinct was to cross the meadow and climb over the next ridge, thinking that the crew might not predict such a strange tactic, but the exposed rock would mean slow and painful travel, and judging by how quickly they were moving, I doubted I would be able to climb over it before they could spot me. Instead, I decided to descend to the meadow and head down the valley, into the trees, hoping to find some way of losing them in the thick forest.

I soon arrived at the meadow and started limping through the grass at a furious pace, heading toward the first trees. My mind was blank, thinking in tasks again. And because I was only concerned with moving from one to the next, I don't find it absurd that, after seeing something so significant right in front of me, I would have simply swerved around it and passed by, as if never having seen it at all. However, I'd only continued for a few steps before the image of what I'd passed began to worm its way into my mind, calling my attention to it, slowing me down. Until, eventually, when I realized the degree of which it changed absolutely everything, I stopped and turned around, almost surprised to see that it was still there, nestled in the green of the meadow as if wanting to hide. It was a firepit.

I limped back to it, watching it carefully, suspiciously. As I came closer, I could see that grass of a brighter green hung over its edges, and that there were a few charred sticks piled inside, rows of black squares running along the spent wood. I knelt down to inspect it, pulling back some of the vegetation to expose its base. It was exactly what it looked like: fresh shoots had replaced the ones that had previously lined the pit – the scorched and yellowed remnants of which were still visible – and the musty smell of wet smoke hung above the wood. It couldn't have been more than two weeks old.

People. There were people living nearby.

To be honest, I'm not really sure what was more shocking for me: the fact that there were other human beings on the mainland, or the fact that every one of us had been wrong when we'd guessed about their existence in the first place. Because all of us – the Elders, myself, Mikkel, even the crew – while hoping for different things, had still independently held the same belief; namely that finding anyone alive was a far-flung likelihood, that it was among the remotest of possibilities. Yet here was the evidence, stooping in the grass right in front of me, which definitively proved every one of us wrong.

And as it was obvious that the crew's sole focus was on catching me, I could be sure that they hadn't also come across proof like this, that I was the first (because if they had realized that there were other people alive besides ourselves, then they would have had enough idealistic work cut out for them to last lifetimes, making the task of hunting me down one of the lowest of their priorities). I stared at the coals, trying to think this through as quickly as I could.

It was interesting that everything in my education had focused on preparing me for that exact moment, but when I found myself crouching in front of it, my mind was free of voices, free of the cumbersome ethical questions that had always haunted me. But this was only because, even if those distant obligations had found a way to squirm into mind, I was in no position to act on them – whether I'd left The Goal behind or not, this was obviously not the time or place to 'discreetly infiltrate and sterilize' a surviving community. No, the only question that needed answering was in the context of immediacy: What would this group of people do when they saw us? And this was almost a redundant question. What would we have done on the island if an angry mob of men came sprinting through our forest, all but one of them armed with spears? Their reaction would be a conventional one. They were going to kill us all. And if a few of us managed to scatter and escape when they tried, they wouldn't be able to sleep a wink until they had hunted every last one of us down, cutting each of our throats in turn. (And, needless to say, these men – who would run the ends of their spears under our chins after we'd thrown down our weapons and held bare arms over our heads – would do so convinced that they were acting in the most valiant form of self-defence.)

Having thought this through, I looked over at the opposite ridge again, reviewing the first plan that had come to mind while I was running down the slope, ready to grasp at anything. But I found that it was still a bad idea. Choosing to hobble through the awkward rocks with one of my feet wounded and both of them bare was choosing to be dead within hours.

There was really only one choice. I would have to continue as I'd planned, running toward the thick forest of the new valley, away from the people behind me, who were, of course, bent on killing me, and toward another group of people who would most likely kill us all. And the only way I could make this decision was by rationalizing that the crew, who would pose much more of a threat bearing weapons, would probably be killed before me, as a matter of instinctive priority. I even allowed myself to entertain the idea that if I could find these people's community or gathering place before the crew had caught up with me, and lead them to its border, and if I hid as the community's soldiers poured out of the walls and the fighting ensued, then there might be a possibility that I, after the dust had cleared, could sneak away alive – and then, afterwards, somehow manage to outrun, outwit, or outmanoeuvre a new set of trackers, who would probably pursue me just as relentlessly as the crew had.

I flung a hand behind my head to furiously scratch my neck in a place that hadn't bothered me in the first place. Then I looked around the meadow, feeling as if the world were closing in, becoming suffocatingly close, the circle of the firepit rising beneath me, the sides of the valley swelling, the thick sheet of clouds pressing down. Everything had spiralled completely out of my control. And it seemed like the only thing left to do was to hobble toward the one shard of hope I had – or that I'd been desperate enough to invent. So I stood, gave the firepit one last glance, and started jogging toward the trees, my pace half-hearted.

As I made my way through the end of the meadow, I was busy reviewing my list of improbable tactics, but not, I'm sure, because it was useful, but because I wanted to keep myself from the quiet understanding that was just beneath the surface; which was that, inevitably, and very soon, my life would be coming to an end. And I wish now that I had forced that thought out into the open, that I'd admitted it and used it to move toward wiser things. Like thinking about how I should die. Like thinking about dignity and integrity, and what I could still do to honour them. Like thinking about what I had stupidly pushed away, and what I was foolishly, foolishly leaving behind.

43

I threaded my way through the trees, which became higher and denser with every minute I ran, until the leaves began to block out the light and the ground lost its soft covering of grass, giving way to exposed soil. Dirt and debris crammed into the wound on my foot, making it increasingly sore, inhibiting. I had to favour my right leg more and more, my stride becoming jerky, awkward, my arms swinging out to compensate. I clenched my jaw, concentrated on clearing my mind of the pain, in the same way I concentrated on clearing it of my closing future. Everything rested on luck, and luck requires no thought, no acknowledgement – it doesn't even require belief.

I watched the mounting evidence of humans as it passed. At first it was slight: a faded trail, the twigs that had hung over it cleared away, a fallen tree that was stripped of its dead branches to be used for firewood. But soon, the trails and snapped branches seemed to be culminating toward one central spot, and I walked toward it, often stopping to listen for movement, though never hearing even a breath of sound. Not that I was expecting to; the most recent evidence that I'd come across was still weeks old.

Finally, I came over a small rise and could see something horizontal through the trees, something clearly manmade. I stopped to listen to the stillness again, making absolute sure that no one was around, and then walked toward it, knowing that I had to learn as much as I could about these people, as fast as possible.

When I came closer I could see that they'd cleared a patch of the forest, and that the horizontal beam that I'd spotted, which was a simple log running between two trees, was one of several that were in the area. There was another firepit in the centre of the clearing, and a spot where the soil had been cleaned of leaves and underbrush, which they must have used to sleep on or raise temporary shelters. There was a horrible smell in the air, which along with the droning sound of flies, became stronger as I approached, until it was so strong that I had to pinch my nostrils to continue. I imagined it was an animal they'd killed and had left to rot at the far edge of their camp. But once I'd followed the smell to its source, a few tiny scavengers scurrying out of the way as I came into view, I realized that it was much more than that.

The carnage of numerous animals was placed neatly inside a shallow pit that they'd dug, and I stood at its edge, looking through the pile of unwanted tissue and bones. There were hoofed legs, a few heads, and the recurring arcs of rib cages splattered with flecks of remaining flesh. (I'm sure that such a gruesome sight would have seriously affected me at any other moment in my life, but as it was, I could look at it with rational eyes, my need for useful information pervading everything else. I was only searching for something that could help me, and if I couldn't find it, I would simply carry on, unmoved, indifferent.)

With the rotting waste so close to the camp, I could assume this was only a temporary site, which probably served as a place to quickly kill, gut, skin, and butcher the animals they could find, taking with them the hides, and as there was still a lot of wasted flesh on the remaining bones, it looked like only the best of the meat. And because travelling fast and light seemed to be a priority, I guessed that their community was much further off than I'd first imagined.

But before the implications of this could register – which were that now, even my most fantastical and imaginative strategies were void, and every last bit of hope, even the most absurd of it, had finally ambled out of reach – my eyes fell across something recognizable in the pile of rotting limbs. It was on the opposite side of the pit, sticking out into the swirling cloud of insects, and it had caught my eye because, unlike the other limbs, this one was without a hoof or foot; it was only an appendage of dense fur that ended in a grisly stump, bulging with the darkness of clotted blood.

I circled around the pile to get closer to it, probably knowing that it was a Creature before I'd even seen its face. Half of its torso lay exposed near the outside of the pit, while the other half was still submerged inside, the rotting entrails of another animal lazily draping over its stomach. Its skin had been cut in countless places, and, judging from the amount of blood that drenched its wounds, the cuts had been made while it was still alive. I noticed a ring of thinned hair and exposed, chafed skin around its neck as well, as if it had been bound by a rope and yanked along for several days. The Creature's eyeballs were wrinkled and dull, covered with a dusty skin; and though they'd lost their moisture and life, I could see that they hadn't lost their expression. It was frozen there, and probably wouldn't fade until the tissue had collapsed and liquefied. The expression was one of terror.

I swallowed. I could feel my numbness slipping away, could feel myself becoming more awake, more present.

I looked again at the bloodied stump that had caught my attention. Its hand. They had cut off its hands – and this, while it was still alive. It had been tortured. It had been dragged away from some trap that they'd set for it, and made to die a slow and horrible death. It had been made to suffer.

And yes, I might have been able to understand why they had felt the need to capture it. I had also feared the Creatures, had invented an intimidating story around them. And before I'd actually seen them and consciously ripped apart my delusion, I probably would have condoned killing them as well, maybe even to chopping the hands off their corpses. But what I couldn't understand, no matter how hard I tried, was the act of doing it while they were still alive. What do we prove by making something suffer? Why had these people, who'd already captured the Creature, who'd already clearly subjugated it, who'd won their struggle for unquestionable domination, still felt a need to torture it? In what way was this gratifying, fulfilling?

The buzzing sound of the flies seemed to be getting louder, their monotonous song becoming more grating, maddening.

I knelt down to look at the Creature more closely, at the ring of gauzy fur around its neck, at the wrinkled film over its eyes, still staring at the indescribable last moment of its life. Then I reached a slow hand out to touch it. Its fur was grimy, sullied. By us.

I was disgusted, furious – so absolutely furious – at everything about us. At our cruelty, our destructiveness, our brutality, at the idiotic self-deceit that keeps us from seeing those exact traits for what they really are.

And then it struck me: the people who were responsible for this base, depraved act, were the same people that Mikkel wanted to save, the very beings that he believed should persevere throughout the ages. Even if he had no idea of what saving our kind would mean outside of the context of his petty little self, even if he didn't have the slightest clue about what we would do to the world if we were given another chance, he was still bent on it. Because he hadn't allowed himself to see what we really are. Because he couldn't afford to.

Which meant that, after he found out about these people's existence, he would figure out a way to make diplomatic contact with them. It meant that he would tell them about The Goal. Then he and the crew would probably settle into the community and spend the rest of their lives watching the horizon for other third phase expeditions like ours, ones that had been better structured, more organized, successful. Mikkel would prepare these people for their coming, tell them what to do, give them a strategy, give them direction. And perhaps, within only a few weeks, this community would be opening its arms to roaming strangers, making a meal for them, giving them shelter, and then slitting their throats during the night in case they were people like me – people who knew better. Mikkel would ensure that this culture lived on, populated, spread. And then nothing, nothing would ever be given the chance to heal from us.

I stood up and looked at the ground, at my footprints leading to this place, and realized where I was. I was at the beginning of yet another chapter in the long destructive cycle of our history. I was standing on another first page. I was even helping to write it. Because it was me who was leading the crew to them, showing them the way.

And then I understood. Looking back, it's hard to believe that I'd dismissed the immeasurable importance of the firepit. It was the catalyst. It was everything. If the crew caught sight of it, they would know, and that would be enough. From that point on, the string of events that I'd imagined would fall into place as predictably as the sun's path.

I shook my head, asking myself what I'd been doing ever since the crew had appeared – and the answer was that I'd been reaching. I'd been reaching for hope, and pushing away the ideas of pain and my inescapable death. I'd been busy concentrating on all of the things that didn't matter in the least; namely my capacity to suffer. That was how small my world had become, how easily I'd thrown away my beliefs, my ideals, my honour.

I was going to die – there was no way around it. So the very least I could do was die without sacrificing every one of my principles. Was that such a revelation? Was that such a difficult conclusion to come to? No.

It was time; and it should have been time much earlier. I turned from the carnage and started walking away from it, retracing my steps into the forest. I began to jog, my pace soon quickening to a run, and then to a wild sprint, the pain at the bottom of my foot fading from my mind. I would have to beat them to the firepit, I would have to draw them away from it, keep them from ever noticing that it was there – and then, I would lead them as far from this valley as was physically possible, running until I was too exhausted to continue. And when they finally caught up with me, I would lash out like the monster they believed I was – like the monster that we are. I would gnash my teeth, claw at their faces, gouge their skin, and I would do this until they severed the life from my body. That was my plan.

The forest began to thin, and then to thin even more. I sighted the meadow through the trees ahead of me, terrified energy jolting to my legs, and I ran into the wide-open space, searching for the crew, wishing that I wasn't too late. And I wasn't. I could see them moving down the slope from the ridge. They were pointing at me, screaming flustered commands to one another. I'd surprised them.

I felt the grass on my feet, saw the firepit out of the corner of my eye as I passed it, careful not to look in its direction, and headed toward the ridge that was opposite the crew. I started to run up the long slope, and had ascended half of it before looking back. When I did, I sighted their tracks, the darkened lines in the grass where they'd run across the meadow, and I could see that none of them had come close to the firepit. I smiled. I felt reckless, free. I felt like I'd won. I screamed out, goading them, laughing. But they weren't paying attention. They were concentrating on closing the gap between us.

As I climbed higher, the grass thinned, and the rocks became more exposed, sharper. I had to focus on where I was stepping, unable anymore to look back, to know how far they were. Though, I could hear them behind me, scrambling through the rocks as well.

I was almost on the ridge when I stumbled for a moment, and as I was getting back to my feet, I picked up a fat stone and flung it over my shoulder, listening to them holler as they scattered out of the way – their voices nearer, always nearer. They were gaining on me more rapidly than I would have given them credit for, and I bent myself on running faster, gouging my feet with each stride, determined to lead them deep into another valley before they could catch me.

I crossed over a saddle and started down the other side, moving fast. But the new slope was filled with giant boulders, and was surprisingly steep. I did my best, sliding along them, over them, between them, scraping my hands along the surfaces of the rocks to slow myself down.

The crew neared. Until it started to sound like they were right on my heels, like they were close enough to throw their spears. And I pushed myself to go even faster, to jump further, to teeter on the edge of losing control. I had no choice.

Then I leapt over a low, massive boulder, and when I tried to land, I faltered, holding onto my balance for just an instant, my hands clawing at the air for something that would keep me there, something that would stop me from falling. Nothing. I watched the slope spin around me, holding out my hands, trying desperately to stop myself from tumbling a second time. But I couldn't. My body kept falling, kept turning. Again. Again.

Time slowed. I remember plummeting down the slope, I remember the odd silences that hung in the air between impacts, but mostly – if this is even possible – I remember thinking nothing. My mind was void of all thought, of all cognizance, it was only my body, twirling uninhibited, almost peacefully, interrupted by instants of complete violence, of pounding against the rocky slope, the quick snapping of bones, and then back into the thick air again, hanging suspended inside of it, quietly, waiting, waiting for the final impact to come, and when it did, everything turned black, and I felt like I'd plunged into nighttime water, suddenly slow and alone in a liquid silence.

44

It wasn't like waking up. It was like coming to the surface at night through the same heavy water it seemed I'd plunged into. Everything was black except the sounds, which were slowly losing their muffled tones. The monotonous cricketing of insects moved toward me through the dark, gradually becoming crisper, clearer. The next sensation I remember was an unimaginable thirst. I opened my mouth and felt my lips parting as dry as fingers. Then I swallowed, felt my saliva wetting the walls of my throat, spreading life through it, sensation. I tried opening my eyes but had to shut them again, the brightness being unbearable, almost painful. When I'd instinctively tried to cover my face with my hands, I found that I couldn't move them. They were behind my back, and either damaged beyond belief, or simply tied there. So instead, I squinted as hard as I could, carefully letting flickers of light in, slowly adjusting to the intensity, blinking the water from my eyes, until eventually, I could see enough to begin taking a few things in.

I was in a forest, and there were a few boulders amid the trees, which probably meant that it was just below the slope where I'd fallen. The air felt crisp, fresh, and I guessed it was sometime in the morning. I was perched upright, and as best I could tell, bound to a tree. No one else was around.

Naturally, I tried to squirm free of the ropes, but was instantly countered with shots of pain from all over my body. It took me minutes to recover from this; breathing steadily, deeply, until the sharp sensations began to subside. I didn't try moving after that. And I'm sure that, even if I could have untied myself, could've miraculously broken free, there was no way I could walk. The jabs of pain I felt when I tried to move were almost certainly the results of splintered bones grinding against themselves, because even after the pain had gone, I could still feel a disturbing tingling sensation. I looked down at one of my ankles – slowly, my every movement measured – and could see that there was something about it that wasn't quite right, though

385

couldn't exactly tell what. I was surprised that I didn't feel anything strange with the shin of my other leg, as it was also slightly misshapen in some indistinguishable way. There might have been other broken bones as well – I think one of my shoulders, maybe a few of my ribs – but I couldn't be certain.

However, considering the amount of damage that was done, so long as I didn't move, I wasn't in a lot of pain. Of course, there were areas of my body that would sting for a few seconds, but other than that it was mostly all a soothing kind of numbness, a complete lack of sensation merging into patches of my skin that felt awake and intact. For instance, I couldn't feel the leg with the broken shin, nor move it, but I could feel a thread of liquid running down the inside of it, tracing a line through the hairs on my calf.

I began to think about what it must have been like when they first touched my body on the slope, and how unlike the monster, which they were convinced they were chasing, I must have looked. Limp, broken, almost lifeless – rather inadequate as far as monsters go. After having prepared themselves for gnashing teeth and claws, all they came upon was a meagre heap of dead weight. They'd been denied their furious battle, the promise of thrashing weapons, of spurting blood. Which, I realized, wasn't good. Because if they'd felt a lack of gratification, they would have to find a way to compensate for it.

Exactly. Compensation. I understood why I was still alive. It would have been far too anticlimactic to kill an unconscious man, to stick a knife into someone who doesn't react in the slightest way, who doesn't even feel it. Yes, that was the reason I was tied to the tree. It was in the hope that I might become conscious, in the hope that they would still be given an opportunity to play with my life, or with what little capacity I had left to feel pain. And once they'd realized that my body was mostly without sensation, that their blades running slowly across my skin didn't really affect me, they would probably move on to trying to injure my dignity – pissing into my face, shoving disgusting things down my throat. Maybe they even planned on feeding me the dismembered parts of my body. Whatever was going to happen, I could be sure I was going to suffer, that there wouldn't be any mercy. I was going to meet with the most degrading and agonizing end imaginable.

But, I told myself, I had to remember that I'd come to this end intentionally, that this was all part of the sacrifice I knew I was making. And most of all, I had to remember that in making that sacrifice, I'd actually succeeded in luring them away; albeit a much shorter distance than I'd intended.

Which meant that I might not have succeeded. Anything could happen. Maybe there were recent signs of people in this new valley as well. Or maybe they would climb back over the ridge – for reasons that could be as simple as wanting to find out why I'd been running toward them instead of away, or to return to the sea the same way they'd come, simply thinking it most efficient to retrace their steps – and accidentally stumble upon the firepit. And if not, who knew how long they might live, journeying in search of people.

But I also understood that it was over. This was the end – or at least my end. What happens after our death we have no control over. (Though, not that I had much control over things while I was alive, either – apart from my thoughts.)

My thoughts. I stopped to fully appreciate that for a moment. It was amazing that my brain was even functioning. The impacts against the boulders were enough to break bones, and I'd smashed my head hard enough to be knocked unconscious, yet, the damage wasn't so severe that I couldn't use my mind. In fact, I felt completely coherent. And the more I thought about this, the more I recognized it as a kind of salvation in itself. I wasn't at a total loss, I still had my mind and everything in it – my opinions, beliefs, feelings, attitudes, ideas, and memories – and these were all things that the crew could never degrade or lessen, no matter what they did, no matter how hard they tried.

Yes. I could use my mind. I could rummage through my thoughts, think of the conclusions I'd come to, the experiences I'd had. I looked around again, hoping to find some clue as to where the crew had gone or when they would return, to even get a vague estimate of how much time I would have to do so. I noticed their spears piled on the ground between some trees a little distance away from me, but couldn't figure out what this meant. However, before I even began to guess at it, I stopped myself. There was no real need to know when they would return. I would have as much time as I was given. And that was all.

So I thought. I thought about everything, the things that I'd learned, the people who'd taught me, even the particulars of the landscape that I'd travelled through – everything that was important, which had helped bring me, in one way or another, to this very tree. There were times during the day that I would become so frustrated, so exasperated that I would begin to fidget or squirm, but the pain that I met with when I moved always had an incredibly pacifying effect, and so I've come to make the mistake of shifting less and less.

And now, having recalled my story, I find myself thinking of the other people throughout history who died horrible deaths at the hands of their own kind. Because there were others like me – countless others. I wonder how they might have managed the pain that I'm about to experience. Maybe they'd found a way to completely separate themselves from their bodies, or even from their fear. Actually, come to think of it, I remember seeing a picture in a book where a few extremely disciplined religious men set themselves on fire to prove a point. As is usual, I forget what the point was, but I remember the gruesome picture perfectly. They are sitting cross-legged in the middle of a street, their posture serene, tranquil, and meanwhile, their bodies are burning, their flesh becoming charred as the flames lick their skin and crown their heads. It must have taken a while for them to die, and I imagine their bodies were capable of feeling pain for quite some time, yet they looked as if they were sitting in the middle of a field on a beautiful day, gently drawing air into their lungs. What kind of discipline is required for that? I can't even guess, but I can be sure that I don't have it. As much as I admire those people throughout history, which have attained such an exceptional level of peace that they could entrance themselves into nullity, I realize that, not only am I incapable of it now, I don't think I ever would be.

Yet why? Why is it that peace is something so difficult to achieve? I think of the few times I've experienced something close to it, and realize that it's never been a distinct feeling or insight. I don't really know what it was, but I know that it was there, beneath the surface. Which I think is an accurate description, because I've often had the suspicion that peace was an entity imbedded inside of things, that it was within the overwhelming complexities of nature; in the atoms of chemicals and the structures of plants, in the pulsing of creatures' organs, the interconnectedness of everything that has lived, in the relationship of time to those beings, and to geology, to the asteroids crashing into the earth's surface, and in the gravity that pulled those asteroids into our atmosphere, in the sun, in the wobbling orbits of the planets, the spinning galaxies, in the composition of the universe itself. I had the notion that one couldn't point their finger at peace, couldn't touch it, but that it also wasn't all that abstract. And I still hold to this. I'm convinced that it's something here, now, something that is both around me and inside of me, and not nearly as indistinct as I'm describing it. I think it's something palpable; and for some reason, I'm convinced of this.

I look down at a few of the plants growing under the shade of the trees, their leaves fanning out to catch the little bit of light that happens to make its way through the branches above, and these plants suddenly strike me as exceptional. I have the sensation that there's something here, something all around me, a kind of secret, which I might have been able to uncover had I had more time, or been more dedicated. Maybe I was on my way to uncovering it while I was living on the terrace, before people came back into my life. Though, maybe not.

I think of all that I'd learned from my experience with the raven, all the tranquility and simplicity that I felt. I was surrounded with beauty, and I think I was growing inside of it, flourishing even. But none of this can alter the fact that it only takes a few severe conditions for us to instantaneously regress back to our natural ugliness. Whereas the previous day I'd been walking quietly through the fruit trees, feeling that I somehow fit, that I'd become kind, even beneficent, the first few minutes of the following day would find me willing rocks to pummel the existence from people who had been my friends, hoping with all of my being that they would be injured, even wishing them to suffer – and probably with the same intensity as they are wishing me to suffer now.

Maybe, though I feel like I was so close to some kind of understanding of peace, I had always been far from it. And perhaps this is because so little of it exists inside us that we can never actually experience it. Perhaps what I experienced on the terrace and in my childhood was merely a heightened appreciation of its ideal, a romantic admiration of its possibility. And now I'm smiling, because even if it was, I'm glad to have at least felt that much.

I focus on the dull green of the plants again, and am suddenly filled with contentment to have had this day. I wouldn't have traded it for anything. And I should feel fortunate that I still have some time to look closer at my surroundings, to mull over the details of the trees and rocks that are…

The sound of a twig snapping in the distance stops me. I'm listening for something else. And there it is again. Only this time, it's a larger stick that breaks. It's not an animal. I can hear distinct footsteps.

45

Now I can hear leaves rustling as well, but it doesn't sound like the whole crew. I'm sure that all of them walking through the underbrush would make more noise than this. Yes, I think it's only one. But one is enough. And maybe they've planned it this way, for everyone to have their own turn.

I'm trembling, I'm so afraid. I am so completely afraid!

He's getting closer. He must be able to see me. He's approaching from the front, probably on purpose, hoping to savour every moment of my mental anguish. He'll probably sharpen his knife in front of me. Or dull it.

I want to scream.

No. I can't. I won't give them the satisfaction. I refuse. I just have to keep looking at the plants between the trees, and try to stay calm. I have to stay calm. I have to stay calm.

I can't stay calm. My breathing is already out of control.

Whoever it is has stopped walking. He's a little distance in front of me. I can feel his eyes on me. He seems to be waiting for me to look up at him. I'm trying not to. But I don't think I can stop myself. I have to look; I have to see who it is. I raise my head.

Our eyes meet right away, and I'm completely surprised to see him. I could have imagined any one of them coming first, but not Mikkel. I'd imagined him distancing himself from it all, whittling a stick out of earshot while they had their fun. But instead he's here, and this somehow reassures me. I breathe out an enormous amount of air from the top of my lungs, and feel drained once I've done this. I find it odd, but nevertheless appropriate that a grin should come to my face. He grins back, apparently also finding the moment odd. Our eyes stay fixed on each other as he comes a bit closer.

Because this is Mikkel, and I certainly couldn't picture him torturing me, I have no idea what's going to happen, and I'm even more curious when I recognize something like sympathy in his expression as he looks over my body. "Are you in pain?" he asks. His words are quiet, sincere.

I've forgotten the spell that Mikkel puts on people, the one that makes you want to win his respect. But it's important to remember that he's part of the crew, and that he's almost certainly come here on behalf of them. And so I open my mouth to lie, to give him some tale about the agony I don't really feel, even stopping to think about the tone of voice that would suit a suffering man. But I abandon this idea at the last second, only because nothing I could say would fool him anyway. "Well... well, to be honest, not really. I'm mostly numb; as much as that must disappoint you."

Mikkel snickers, shakes his head. "Shit, Joshua. Is that what you think – that I wanted this? That I'm finally, perfectly... happy seeing you like this?" He pauses, apparently thinking about what to say next, but I don't let him say it.

"Tell me, what should I think? My bones are broken; I can't do anything, any harm, yet you've still tied me to a tree. Do you understand what that implies? I'm tied to a tree, Mikkel. I mean – that's a pretty deliberate action. It's hard to accidentally tie people to trees. So, as the leader, if you didn't want this, I wouldn't be here. I'd be dead. And you know that."

His voice is quiet, and he speaks to the ground, "Yeah, well... that might be true. But... it's not that simple." He kicks at a rock that's imbedded in the soil. The rock doesn't move.

"It hasn't been easy, you know. None of it – nothing has been easy. And you, you haven't exactly been..." he waves his hand through the air at a loss for words and never completes the sentence. Instead, he shakes his head, turns around, and takes a few steps away from me. I know that he wants to tell me everything, stories about the crew's hardships, stories about his own, but Mikkel knows that words have a tendency to either magnify or belittle, and he's looking for the ones that do neither. I admire that, and wait for quite a while before he speaks.

"When we woke up that morning – after you'd escaped – none of us were really surprised at what happened to Knut and Toivo. In fact, I think most of us thought they deserved it. I mean – you did what you had to do, and I can respect that. But...

with Onni…" Mikkel pauses. My stomach churns at the mere mention of that name. I'd always been so removed from the reality of his dying, or at least the particulars of it. I want to interrupt him; I want to stop him from even beginning. I want him to listen to how ashamed and regretful I was, how sorry I am. And I want that to be enough, even though it wouldn't be. But I stop before I say anything. I am the perpetrator here, and I know that everything that comes out of my mouth will either sound insensitive or hypocritical. No. It isn't my turn to speak. It's my turn to listen. I owe Onni at least that; in fact, I owe everyone that.

I watch the back of Mikkel's head as he begins. "You should know, he told us over and over again that you didn't mean to cut him, that it was all an accident. But to be really honest with you, on a ship, with no chance of outside help, the questions of how, or why, or if it was intentional or not, don't really matter. What mattered was that his stomach was slashed open. That's all… and that we had to deal with it.

"For the first couple of days, I actually thought it might heal. We did everything we could think of for him, took shifts keeping the wound clean, propping him up, making him comfortable. You should have seen the crew. They were great; so concerned, so eager to help. And I think it was the fact that we were all so focused on it, so intent on bringing him back to health, that really pulled us together. We were dedicated to it; every one of us wanted it so badly. But… still, despite everything we did, despite how careful we were, and after boiling and disinfecting everything that ever touched him… the infection still came. Little by little, he got worse… and likewise for his pain."

Mikkel turns his head as if wanting to look at me but doesn't.

"So, we decided to head to the closest land. I'm not sure what we thought we were going to accomplish with that – maybe we thought we'd find the shore littered with medical supplies and somehow save Onni with a few clean bandages – I don't really know. But looking back, I think it was probably just something, we had to try and do something for him, and there was clearly nothing we could do for him on the ship." Mikkel finally turns to me. He has a painful smile on his face. "We just headed to a coast, to some random shore. Can you believe that? After all the trouble the Elders went through to find us the safest point to disembark, after everything they'd weighed out, what did we do? We ignored it. It was a stupid move.

"We didn't have detailed charts of the coastline we came to, only a few large scale maps that confirmed that there weren't any ports nearby, but also indicated a few beacons, which of course didn't function anymore, and were probably only there in the first place to hazard ships away from the area. Yet, when we sighted the coast, everyone was jumping up and down on the deck. We thought we'd made it, thought we were safe. I mean – we knew it wasn't going to be an ideal coastline in terms of landing, but we thought we'd at least be able to find some way of getting close enough to shore to access it. And who really knows, we might have, if we'd even made it through the first night. We got hung up on a shoal just after dark, and the ship started taking on water right away.

"One of the first things we did was start the engine to try and drag us off, which, I'm sure you can imagine, only caused more damage. We stayed there for days, hoping that maybe a swell or the tide would lift us off, hoping to at least get within swimming distance, but nothing happened. You have to remember that you took the only raft, and without it, it seemed hopeless.

"So… helping Onni wasn't exactly the most important thing anymore; we had to worry about surviving, and that was all we worried about. Besides, he was only going to get worse, and there wasn't anything we could do about it. And soon, he'd stopped sleeping, stopped talking, stopped listening, he just sat there and stared ahead, groaning to himself with these long, airy moans. It was unbearable.

"So… eventually…" Mikkel stops for a moment. He's staring into the trees, and keeps this glazed expression as he speaks, his voice distant. "Eventually we had a meeting. We decided that the only chance we had was to inflate every plastic bag on the ship and try to swim ashore, which obviously meant leaving Onni behind. We timed it so that we'd swim with the tide, and we put a few light essentials inside the inflated bags, like maps and some clothing, and tied the knives to our bodies. Everything was prepared, and one by one, we said goodbye to him, even though he didn't hear us. I'm sure he wasn't taking anything in at that point. He was just… blank, staring forward, groaning.

"The crew were getting ready on deck. They were quiet. Everything was quiet. I was the last one to say goodbye to him. But after I did, I found that I couldn't walk out of the room. I couldn't just leave him like that, Joshua. He was in so much pain, and who knows how many days he would've suffered; what he would've gone through – and alone?" Mikkel looks at the base of a tree, pursing his lips shut, trying to stop them from trembling. He doesn't cry, but his words are quavering. "He bled a lot."

Silence. There is nothing to say, nothing that could even start to fill in the hollow space that is inside us both; that unimaginable void that was created by taking the life from someone we loved. I understand how Mikkel had suffered, and for this, I want to utter the words 'I'm sorry', but find I can't; I choke on their appalling inadequacy. I can't think of anything appropriate to say, and realize that nothing is appropriate at this moment, that everything falls short, every feeling, every word, every certainty of remorse; even the silence seems tactless, clumsy, and I'm relieved when Mikkel finally breaks it.

"When I came on deck, the crew looked at the blood on my clothes, but they didn't say anything; nor have any of us mentioned it since. Instead, we all just jumped into the water and started swimming for our lives. It was all there was left to do.

"It took us most of the day, and for quite a while during the swim, I really thought we wouldn't make it. By halfway we were spent, and when we stopped, we became desperate and fought for the larger bags to rest on. Sometimes the fighting was so charged I thought they were going to draw their knives. Most of the bags burst during the struggles, and we lost almost all of the maps and clothing. We nearly lost Niels, too. We were almost there, but he couldn't swim anymore, and every one of us left him for dead, except Aimil, who somehow managed to help him through the last little bit.

"Once we reached land it took us quite a while to recover, and we were lucky to find a ruined community nearby, which had everything we needed in it, including some crop food growing on its borders. We stayed there on the coast for a couple weeks, fishing and gathering other foods.

"I spent a lot of my time thinking about Onni, and I'm sure that I seemed quite miserable. But I wasn't alone. Everyone was miserable. And I guess that's where it all started, out of a need for something to focus on, something to help sidetrack their minds. Because the more free time they had in this state, the angrier they became; and obviously, every bit of anger they had was directed at you. And within a month, everything imaginable had become your fault: their almost drowning, Onni's death, the reason they were on the ship in the first place, Solmund, even Peik – it was only a matter of naming the hardship, and instantly, you would turn into the cause.

"I knew how ugly it was, how adolescent and pitiful. And for a while, I really thought about putting a stop to it, but it had quickly grown into something that seemed essential to them, something they needed. I remembered poor Solmund, and I thought that, if there was always going to be a scapegoat anyway, then I should be happy it was someone who was removed and out of harm's way, someone who could never be injured, simply because he was already dead. And that's what you have to understand, Joshua, that I believed, without a doubt, that you were dead. I was positive of it.

"After you'd escaped, I studied the maps, the wind direction, the relief of the peninsula that you were supposedly drifting toward, and I could see that, even if every single factor was in your favour, you would still be killed. From what I could make out, the main current was pounding into a steep cliff. To me, the chances of your surviving were almost nil."

"You were right," I say, feeling like I'm interrupting. He turns to look at me, nodding, glad that I've verified this long held suspicion of his. "I only made it by the skin of my teeth. It was just blind luck."

"I knew it," he says, sounding frustrated that such blind luck should exist in the world, and looks back into the trees. He carries on speaking after my words seem to have sunk in.

"So, anyway... we started looking for you. And I thought of it as a blessing, as a simple way for the crew to use their frustrated energy on something productive. And in the meantime, we were getting to know a bit about the landscape, developing some useful skills, and even discovering a few things about our ancestors – all of them, beneficial things. And that wasn't all; because for some reason, all of this combing the ground for clues and spending the evenings looking over the few maps we'd managed to find or had salvaged from the swim, and having these ordered discussions about where you might be, really managed to pull them together again. They had a mutual goal they were working toward, and that was enough for me. So I stopped worrying about it and just let them have their imaginary chase, knowing that eventually their enthusiasm would dwindle. I was sure that, once they'd spent more energy than it was worth, they would have to let their ideas of revenge go. Then, about a week ago, we came across one of your footprints.

"And I just... I couldn't believe it. I couldn't believe my eyes! I was wrong the whole time. You were alive. You'd actually made it. And man! I wish I would've known that, because everything would have been different. I would have found something else, some way to point their energy in another direction.

"And do you know what's crazy? In the last weeks leading up to that day, the crew were even beginning to settle down a bit, slowly becoming disinterested, distracted by other things. But when we found your tracks, everything changed. They'd become unreasonable, fixated on catching you. At first, they were just screaming and yelling, running around, jumping up and down, praising themselves; but they soon became serious, making spears, analyzing the maps, planning. The only thing they could talk about was you. You, and what they were going to do when they caught you.

397

"I was quiet the night we found your footprint. In fact, I don't think I said anything. I could only think about what was going to happen, and if there was anything I could do to stop it. I went to sleep early and heard Knut begin one of his little whispering frenzies, and already by the morning, the group dynamics had changed. Everyone was watching me, just waiting for me to say something that would prove Knut's suspicions to be true. They were ready to pounce, Joshua. And only then did I realize that this 'harmless' thing that I'd let build and build, had grown into something completely explosive, something that could have been turned around on anyone, at anytime – even me.

"So the only thing left to do was to surprise them by snatching a map and suggesting a few things that would improve the chances of finding you. I knew that any influence I had was slippery. I mean – I was still their leader, but Knut had managed to seriously undermine me with only a night of talking, and any open confrontation with him would've ended with them justifying what they'd already begun to think: that I really wanted to protect you, to stick up for you, just as I had done before.

"No, there couldn't be a confrontation. So the only option left was to follow along and keep an eye on things from a distance. Which is what I've been doing for the past week, standing in the background, waiting for a chance to take control again. And obviously, with all of these new factors involved, and everything that we'd thought and planned changing into something new, today is the perfect opportunity to set things right.

"I mean – this is the turning point of everything! It must be the most unique opportunity that anyone has ever had throughout history. Imagine it! Imagine the possibility of having a fresh start, to begin every single thing on the right foot. It's here, now, right in front of us. The crew are combing the valley as we speak. They're spread out, travelling alone, and they should only meet up for the first time just before they arrive here, which was my intention – to give them as little time to whisper as possible. And while they're gathering as much information as they can, I've made sure that they're unarmed.

That way, if any of these people should see them, they won't appear to be much of a threat or a…"

"What people?" I interrupt. But I already know it's useless. Apparently, Mikkel and the crew had backtracked after I was knocked unconscious. Which only made sense. They were far too thorough to let my self-defeating tactic of running toward them go uninvestigated.

"The people in the next valley," he says, sounding a little confused, as if this was information that we'd already established earlier in the conversation, and he was wondering why I'd forgotten it. "The people who made the firepit that your tracks pass by and come back to – the ones who made the hunting camp you found." He raises his eyebrows waiting for a response. I don't give him one. "Well, the crew are gathering information about them." Mikkel stops, still watching me curiously. I feel like a child who's just been caught doing something he shouldn't, and when he begins to shake his head at me, in what seems like utter amazement, I look away.

"I can't believe you," he says, sounding as amazed as he looked.

"What can't you believe?" I mumble, defeated.

"I can't believe that you spent all that time alone, and that you're still exactly like them, that you're still indoctrinated, still brainwashed with all that shit. I can't believe that you haven't figured out a single thing on your own."

"As a matter of fact, you're wrong," I say, perking up a bit to defend myself. "You're completely wrong. I've learned a lot of things on my own. You'd be surprised."

"Like what – that the Elders were right after all? Wow. Some epiphany."

"No. And that's one of the things I've figured out; that the Elders weren't right. They were guilty of oversimplifying things – like we all do."

"So… you've figured out that the Elders were wrong, yet, for some reason, you were hoping that we wouldn't find out about the people in the next valley? In fact, judging by your reaction right now, I wonder if you were trying to keep us from finding out. Which would explain why you were running in the wrong direction to start with. You were trying to lure us from the firepit."

"I was."

"Why?"

"Because... well, first of all, you're putting words into my mouth. I don't think the Elders were wrong; actually, I think they were mostly right. They were wrong in the way that you and I are wrong, because they only saw one side of the story, and it was only that side we were shown. And that's the whole point: even the Elders – people who were dedicated to the truth – could still only see one side of it. Can you grasp how important that is? All of us as human beings, certainly myself included, are only capable of seeing one side of a story. It's like the crew with me, or you with the Elders, or one of the historical cultures with their 'enemies'. We don't see the world, Mikkel; we see a rendition of it that suits us.

"And you know, I think when we look at animals we consider them to be fairly simple creatures, maybe even shake our heads at how primal they seem. They eat, sleep, reproduce, and live according to their instincts. And because we build roads and towers, we're confident that we're superior to them, better somehow. But what I've realized is that we aren't; we are exactly like them. In fact, we are those animals. The only difference between us is that they are living according to their instincts, and we are living according to our own individual illusions, which happen to conveniently hold that our instincts are always right. No, stop smiling and really think about it: the only difference between the 'foolish' animal world and us, is that we have the capacity to fool ourselves."

"You know something? I was smiling because I don't think you heard what you just said. I mean – I couldn't have thrown away the Elders' argument better myself. You said that we were exactly like the other animals, and that, even though we think we're better, we're not. And I agree. But to me, the fact that we are the same makes us just as much a part of nature as they are. If what you say is true, then we have as much a right to live as any animal does. Nature, which we are a part of,

400

automatically finds a balance between the things living inside it. So we should just let it find that balance, no?"

"That sounds logical, but it isn't – only because we can't trust ourselves to see what is balanced. We will inevitably step recklessly outside of that 'natural harmony' that you speak of, and suddenly, miraculously, see it as balanced."

"Oh, come on, Joshua! It's still the same old shit that the Elders fed you, you're only putting a few twists of your own on it," Mikkel blurts out, throwing his hands into the air to help emphasize his words. He squares his shoulders with me before he continues.

"So, if I understand you correctly here... you think our instincts are simply wrong, and that we, the most intelligent beings that have ever lived on this planet, just don't have the mental capacity to see it that way. And... you wanted to keep us from finding out about the people in the next valley, only because their instincts and the illusions they hold of themselves, like every human being's, are just plain wrong?"

"Something like that, yes."

"Then let me ask you an obvious question: how do you know what's 'wrong'?"

"I don't really. But I find it impossible to think that causing something to suffer could ever be 'right'."

"What do you mean by 'causing something to suffer'? You mean the animals they killed?" Mikkel asks, his voice losing its aggressive tone.

"No. I mean the animals they tortured."

"Joshua, I happen to doubt very much that they tortured any of those animals. They killed them and took away the meat, and only because they needed to survive. They did what they did out of necessity, and that's all."

"No. Again, you're wrong. Though I honestly wish you weren't. But you don't have to take my word for it, you can see for yourself if you know where their camp is; which is something I would recommend doing before standing firm behind your 'necessity' theory. Take a good look at the carcass that has no hands – at the one animal in that disgusting carnage that would have walked upright."

It takes a moment for Mikkel to absorb something I've said. "What do you mean 'would have walked upright'? Like a monkey, or like us?"

"I guess a little more like us. And they're about our size, too, though maybe a bit smaller."

"Really?" Mikkel says, sounding concerned. "Are they dangerous? I mean… are they aggressive, or… or are there a lot of them?"

"No… hold on. Listen, it's important for you to understand that in no way are these creatures dangerous. They are simply an intelligent animal, which is easily capable of coexisting with us."

Mikkel twists his head to the side. He seems doubtful. "What do you mean by intelligent?"

I open my mouth to speak, but can't. And I know that as I'm pausing to carefully choose my words, every microsecond of silence is being counted against their credibility. "I said fairly intelligent."

"Really? I thought you said something else."

"Look, it doesn't matter! The point is: they're not dangerous, and there's no reason to fear them. It is that simple. Can you understand that?"

"Okay, okay… don't get excited." Mikkel shows me his palms and takes a few steps backward before he turns around. He pauses, thinking. I'm hoping with all of my being that he doesn't ask any more questions about the Creatures. I know that I haven't done them justice, and I certainly haven't protected them from any kind of cruelty. It wasn't as if Mikkel was going to be dissuading people in the next valley from hunting them any time soon, not after the description I've given of them. He probably thinks there was a good reason for those hunters to do what they did. I shake my head at myself.

"Alright," Mikkel says, turning around, "I don't know anything about the animals that you're talking about, and I didn't see anything like that in the pile. But if you're right, and the people in the next valley did torture an animal, then I would completely agree with you. It's wrong; in fact, it's horrible, inexcusable. But this only brings me to a very important point.

402

Why do you think it is that we have the exact same opinion on this? Are you surprised that I could have such a belief?

"Because I'm beginning to wonder if, inside your head, you've made me into this blind, idiotic fool that supports every conceivable human action. I hope you remember that you weren't alone in being educated about our history; you weren't the only one being shovelled the 'proof' of our wicked nature, who was forced to see all those appalling pictures. Do you really think it's possible to have gone through all that without being affected in some way? Do you think I could just dismiss everything we were shown – just like that?" Mikkel asks, snapping his fingers.

He waits for a moment before continuing. "No. No, I know what we've done. You and I both know what we've done. And we also know, firsthand, what we're capable of doing. But can't you see how important that makes us? We were specifically educated to see where and how humans went wrong, but as you said, the Elders were oversimplifying things, and they only told us that human kind would always go amiss.

"But – and just imagine this for a second – what if they were wrong? What if all your ideas about our 'inevitable self-deception' and 'defective instinct' were wrong? What if people could be taught... as we were taught? What if they could be shown how to be like Onni... or like Kara, or Siri, or Mitra? Do those people deserve to die? Do they have a 'defective instinct'? And if so, could you be the one to take away the 'evil life' running through their veins? I don't think so. And do you know why you couldn't? Because deep down you know it's not that simple. Those people were taught, Joshua. And if they could be taught, then so can the people in the next valley.

"Yet who could possibly teach them? Who would know enough about us – about our history, about our successes, our failures? Who would know the things that one should know before taking on such a responsibility? The answer's obvious: it's us.

"Please. You don't have to look so appalled... though, I can imagine what you're thinking. You're thinking this has all gone to my head, and that even the idea of this power is going to effortlessly corrupt me. But that's not the case. And do you know why? Because it can't afford to. Just stop and think about it for a second: If you had the onus to show the world the way, how vigilant and meticulous would you be, how extremely, extremely careful and deliberate would your actions be? I think you know the answer – I think you would be as cautious as I will be.

"The slate is clean, Joshua. This is the greatest chance that has ever existed. It is the perfect time to show people what it's like to live in the most conscientious manner we can. This is the beginning. It is a brand new era. Because this time, it will all have started off on the right foot. We're going to be better than we ever were. We're going to grow from our mistakes. Everything about humanity will be different from here."

"I wonder – do you really think you're the first person in history to have said that?" I ask. Mikkel looks at me with stern eyes. I don't look away.

"I might not be. But I honestly don't care. Because, maybe out of all of the people who've said it, I'll be the one who's finally right. And you know, even if I'm not, the very – the very least I can do, is try."

"Of course," I say, dryly.

We've come to an impasse, and we both stare at each other, knowing that no amount of talking will sway either one of us from our obstinate views. And as the silence becomes more rigid, Mikkel breaks eye contact to take a few steps to my left. I'm frustrated with the dead end of our conversation, and I'm sure that Mikkel is as well. I try to think of a way to open it up again, but everything that jumps into mind is either sarcastic or cynical, and I'm sure that neither would be productive. Yet, after several attempts of trying to put abrasive words into a tactful order, I give up and just let them out. "So – uh... do you plan on ushering in this age of a 'better humanity' before or after the crew tortures me? I'm just a little confused with the sequence of things."

Mikkel doesn't answer, he only turns to look at me with the greatest of disappointment in his face, and I immediately regret saying it. I feel cheap, and shake my head at myself to apologize. "Look... I'm sorry. But... obviously we don't agree on this, and we're not going to anytime soon. I just... I guess... I really just want to know what happens now."

Mikkel has become nervous, and for some reason, chooses to speak to the ground, answering without seeming to have understood my question. "Well, to start with, I'm going to take away any authority that Knut has managed to swindle out of the situation; and I don't think I really have a choice but to do it as soon as he comes through these trees – which should be in a few minutes."

I want to specifically ask what will happen with me, but decide to respect his evasiveness for a moment more. "And how do you plan on doing that?" I say, perhaps a little more acerbically than I'd intended.

"Joshua," he snaps his head toward me, his tone has also become curt. "I don't know. Okay? I can't know. But I'll do what I have to do. And really – let's be honest – in the end, after everyone's had their speech, after all of the longwinded philosophy is out, isn't that what all of this comes down to anyway? We do what we have to do. Period. I mean – how do you think you got off the ship? It wasn't exactly a symposium, was it?" Mikkel seems to be surprised by his own outburst, and shakes his head in the silence that follows, quickly regaining his composure.

I can understand his frustration, but the fact that my name has still not been mentioned in what will happen in the next, apparently 'few minutes', has let a chilling possibility enter my thoughts. And the more I think of it, the more I can see it as the obvious reason for his increasing agitation. I decide to confront him with it, and I really can't believe that I'm not nervous. The voice I choose is a compassionate one, gentle even, and the tone of our interaction changes instantly; it becomes something almost tender. "Mikkel, I think you're right about what you said earlier, that allowing the crew to be driven forward by fear and hate has turned this all into something irresolvable. Only blood will appease them now, and if they don't get it from me, they'll get it from someone else – probably you. So whatever you do to Knut, however dramatically you divert their attention or motivation, there is no possibility of my walking away from this.

Which… is why you've come here a few minutes ahead of them, isn't it? It wasn't just to have a stubborn conversation with me… was it, Mikkel?"

I watch him as he crouches down and picks up a pebble from the ground. He throws it into the forest and speaks toward the spot that it landed, sighing before any words come out. "And you were right when you said the only reason you were alive was to suffer. It's what they've planned on; it's what they're coming here to do." He shakes his head. "And there's no way to…" he opens his mouth, pauses, "I just can't – can you understand that? – I can't let that happen to you." He sighs again, and when he's let all the air out of his lungs, he doesn't seem to breathe again; he just stays there, hunched over, deflated. I watch his hand move to the bottom of his shirt and pull it up, exposing the skin of his belly. There is a knife tucked into his pants, and he draws it out with painful slowness, holding it in his hands, staring at it as he speaks. "I can't let that happen to you."

At the sight of the knife, my body goes limp. I feel instantly released of every tension that I had during our conversation. Amazingly, I'm not afraid. There is no fear inside me. The time has come. My time has come. Mikkel is going to spare me the horrible death that I'd imagined. And I guess I should feel thankful for this, but I don't. I don't feel anything. But, really, I don't want to feel. I just want to think.

I look at the same plants that had caught my attention before, and realize that, unfortunately, even my thoughts are slipping away from me, or at least from my control. They are becoming slow, random, and I don't really know why, but I share some of them with Mikkel. My voice is calm, already far away. "You know, just before you came I was thinking about peace. I was thinking about how it might be all around us, that it might be everywhere, in every single thing. Like in these plants in front of me. I mean – look at them. They are really amazing, really… beautiful. Like there's something there." I look up at Mikkel as if I've asked him a question.

"I am so sorry, Joshua." His words are shaking.

But I don't know what to say in return, so I just smile as quietly as I can, as forgivingly. Language has become senseless, even ridiculous, and I decide it's best to keep my thoughts to myself.

Mikkel is looking around at the trees on either side of him, as if he's waiting for a cue to move onto the next step; or maybe he's just trying to find something that will make the act a little easier. In the end, I don't think he finds either, but begins walking toward me anyway, his steps unsure, his eyes shifting in every direction, the knife in his hand pointing at the rocks on the ground.

I don't watch him approaching. He's so completely awkward and uncomfortable that I have to look away. I find the undergrowth between the trees again, and I keep looking at the plants there, focusing harder. And the beauty that I saw before is shifting in and out of different forms.

At first it was only their aesthetics. But now it is that indistinct and unknowable peace that still hangs between the leaves, and in the soft shadows beneath them.

And now, I find the beauty to be in their remarkable indifference, in the fact that these plants haven't changed all day, all century, nor through this entire epoch of life. They are a kind of dynamic constant, and I value the fact that they aren't concerned in the least that I'm about to die. My coming or going won't matter to them – our coming or going won't matter to them. They will wait; yet not even know that they're waiting.

And maybe, now that I think of it, this could be exactly where that mysterious peace lies. Maybe the peace that exists in all things is this same kind of timeless and unconscious tolerance… an extraordinary patience of sorts.

I smile. Yes. Maybe that's it.

Mikkel has reached me, and is whispering into the side of my face. "I'm so sorry," he repeats. He's speaking in a nasal voice, his breath warm with tears.

I can feel the point of his knife on my skin between two of my ribs, and I speak to him, still looking at the plants. "It's okay."

And it is. I understand. And I keep smiling as he pauses. He is gathering the courage to do it, and I close my eyes and wait until he finds it.

The knife sinks into me all at once, and I can't stop myself from groaning, because it hurts for a second – and then a second more. But that's all. The pain is gone, and instead, I feel a soothing warmth spreading across my skin, moving toward my feet, streaming over my body in an intricate web. It's nice.

I can hear Mikkel, feel his hands on my shoulders. He's crying. I want to reassure him. I want to tell him that it's okay. And I open my mouth to try, but nothing comes out.

I'll have to wait a moment. Yes. Yes, I just have to wait.

I can feel something spreading through me, and I wonder if it's that same peace that is between the leaves, that is everywhere. But I don't know. Whatever it is, it's dizzying. And it's spreading quickly.

I try to breathe and find that I can't. I hear a strange gurgling sound instead. But there's no panic. If I wasn't afraid before, I'm even less so now. There is no fear. There is only patience. That extraordinary, remarkable patience.

I feel a warm liquid stream out of the corner of my mouth, and then drip off of my jaw in slow, thick drops.

I remember my eyes, and try to move them. And I find that I can. So I open them, look around. Over Mikkel's shoulders. Into the forest. Into the shadows there.

The plants are losing their colour. They're blurring. And I notice, too, that the sounds... the sounds seem to be moving... underwater again... and I'm listening to them sink.

Now the shadows are spreading out. And that's okay. Because I'm growing tired. Exhausted. In fact... I think I need to... sleep... here... for a minute or two...

Or is it waiting? Yes... it's waiting... I'm just going to... close my eyes... and wait... here... for a few seconds...

Also by Mark Lavorato

Novels
Believing Cedric (2011)
Burning-In (2012)
Atavism (2013)

Poetry
Wayworn Wooden Floors (2012)
Blowing Grass Empire (2013)

.